BREAK THE SKY

NINA LANE

BREAK THE SKY

Cover Design & Interior Design by VMC Art & Design, LLC
Cover Photo Credit: © Michael Stokes, Michael Stokes Photography

Published by Snow Queen Publishing

ISBN: 978-0-9905324-0-8

You will hear thunder and remember me, and think,
"She wanted storms."

—Anna Akhmatova

BREAK THE SKY is a standalone, spin-off novel of the Spiral of Bliss series from *New York Times* and *USA Today* bestselling author Nina Lane.

Atmospheric scientist Kelsey March is under siege. Her tornado research project is on the skids and she's fighting conflict in her university department. So when irresistible bad boy Archer West suggests a hot, wild fling while he's in town, Kelsey is unable to resist his sexy offer.

Kelsey and Archer embark on a intense, exhilarating affair. But soon their differences and private battles encroach on their desire, and Kelsey discovers she is caught in a storm she can't control…

PROLOGUE

ARCHER

WE CALLED IT THE CASTLE. FIVE ROUGH, SPLINTERY BOARDS nailed to the tree branches and three sheets of plywood stuck to the sides. We hadn't put on a roof, though, because the leaves of the oak tree made a thick canopy. We both liked the way the sun fell through the branches. If it rained, we put up an old tarp that kept most of the water out.

We'd cut a rectangle in the plywood wall opposite the tree trunk and made a door out of a piece of crate siding and some hinges we'd found in the garage. The door didn't close all the way because of the heavy rope we used to climb the branches.

We pulled the rope up for security when we were both inside. "Raise the drawbridge," Dean would shout, though sometimes if I went to The Castle by myself, I'd pull the rope up after me so I could be alone.

Sometimes I just didn't want my brother around. Dean was bigger, older, smarter. I was the runt of the litter—the youngest and the stupidest. I always had trouble in school, couldn't keep up, was assigned to special ed. Dean did everything so easily, was so much better. It was the reason our parents always paid more attention to him.

But we were equals in The Castle. Sometimes the tree house was a pirate ship, a secret island, a spaceship, the peak of a mountain where the intrepid explorers, the West Brothers, would reach the top, plant a flag, and celebrate their victory by dining on messy sandwiches and chocolate milk.

I remember it all. Sometimes we were friends. Sometimes we were enemies. Then as Dean got older, he started to lose interest in The Castle. He had more homework, more sports, more friends. Girls teased him and liked him. He soon forgot about The Castle.

I didn't. I still climbed the old oak, pretending I was the lone survivor of a shipwreck, a lost mountaineer, the sole guardian of a fortress under attack. And even though I didn't always like being around Dean, it was different without him. Harder to battle pirates and fight monsters alone.

When Dean was thirteen, our parents let him buy a Sega Genesis with money he'd earned doing neighborhood yard work. He kept the video-game console in his room and only sometimes let me use it.

One Sunday afternoon, bored and restless with fears of a

spelling test the next day looming, I wanted to pretend to be Wolverine taking down Magneto.

"No." Dean grabbed a soda from the refrigerator and shut the door.

"Why not?" I argued. "You're not using it."

He shrugged and went into the family room. I followed.

"Come on, Dean."

"No." He threw me an annoyed look. "Leave me alone."

I knew he was irritated because of something our father had said to him about his grades, but that had nothing to do with me using the Sega.

"Please?" I begged. "Come on. Just for, like, an hour. I want to try and beat your high score."

He frowned. "No."

His voice was starting to sound deep, like our father's. I kicked the leg of a chair, my frustration rising.

"Come on," I persisted. "I'll tell Dad you're not sharing."

"Go ahead." He grabbed the remote and turned on the TV. "It's mine anyway."

"Why won't you let me use it?"

"Because."

"You're such a jerk, Dean!"

He shrugged, his gaze on the TV. My frustration exploded into a strangled noise. I kicked the chair again and ran upstairs. Dean's bedroom door was open.

His stupid soccer trophies lined the bookshelf. Science-fair ribbons hung on the walls under San Francisco Giants pennants and posters of Joe Montana. And there, sitting on his desk like the Holy Grail, was the Sega Genesis.

I didn't think. I just grabbed it with the intention of locking myself in the basement rec room. I hurried from the bedroom, passing the stair railing that overlooked the entryway.

I stopped. Stared down at the tiled floor. And dropped the game console over the railing to crash on the floor below.

The controllers cracked, the plastic broke. I looked down at the smashed game and wondered why that destructive act had felt so good.

"What the hell are you doing?" Dean ran in from the kitchen.

Startled, I looked at him. I didn't know if he'd seen what I'd done, but he was furious anyway. Fists clenched at his sides, face red.

I shrugged. "Accident. I tripped and it flew out of my hands."

"What were you doing with it in the first place?" Dean yelled, coming up the stairs. "I said you couldn't use it."

"It was just sitting on your desk," I snapped back. Even though I knew I was in for it, I was glad that I'd enraged my brother. "Stop being such an asshole."

Dean shoved me. I stumbled back, my hands flying up in defense. Rage pumped through my blood. I hated that he had a Sega and so many trophies. I hated that girls liked him, teachers favored him, and coaches wanted him on their teams. I hated that he didn't want to battle pirates with me anymore.

"You're paying for it," Dean shouted. "When Mom and Dad find out, they'll make you pay."

"I don't care." I didn't, either. It wasn't like I had the money to pay for anything.

Dean stalked toward me. He was so mad he was shaking. He shoved me again, and this time I let my fist fly in return. My punch caught Dean on the side of the head. In less than a second, Dean tackled me, bringing me down. Even as I hit the floor, I knew I didn't stand a chance.

I tried, though. I'd been in enough scrapes at school. I knew how to fight dirty. I kicked and hit and yelled, trying to get at my brother's weak spots, trying to land a punch through Dean's own flying fists.

"What the hell is going on?" our father's voice thundered. Dean was yanked off me and flung against the opposite wall. "What's the matter with you two?"

"It's his fault," Dean shouted, swiping at his bloody nose.

I pushed to my feet, feeling a grim satisfaction at the evidence showing I'd landed a direct hit.

"What's his fault?" our father asked.

"He broke my Sega!"

I felt the weight of my father's gaze. I tried not to squirm. Sweat ran down my back.

"How did that happen?" he asked.

"Archer threw it over the railing," Dean said, still glowering angrily at me. "Stupid idiot."

New rage filled me. I lunged at Dean, but my father grabbed my arm in an ironclad grip and pulled me to a halt. I tried to get away, but couldn't. My frustration exploded.

"You're an asshole," I yelled at Dean. "You think you're better than everyone, that you're so smart when you're really just a selfish bastard who—"

My father smacked me. Hard. Right across the face. Pain spread over my whole head.

"You're the bastard, Archer," Dean snapped. "And stupid too. You didn't even know that he's not your real dad."

He stabbed a finger at our father then turned and ran

down the stairs. My sister Paige stood in the kitchen doorway, white with shock. I knew she'd heard everything.

I couldn't move. The air seemed thick. It was hard to breathe. I was still sweating. My father didn't say anything at all.

Cold prickled my skin, along with a horrible, sinking feeling of having just been told something that I already knew. My father released my arm. I stared at the floor. I heard his heavy footsteps going down the stairs. The front door slammed.

It took me a long time to move. I went downstairs. The Sega still lay broken on the tiled floor. I walked to the garden and out to the woods. I climbed the rope ladder and crawled into the tree house, breathing in the familiar scents of rotting wood and oak. I pulled the rope up and closed the door. I didn't leave for a long time.

Everything changed after that. And everything stayed the same.

My mother, upset and weary, told me she'd made a mistake once and none of it was my fault but that I couldn't tell anyone. It was a secret. She said Richard West was the man raising me and that he *was* my father. My father… well, Richard West, treated me with the same detached attention. Paige pretended nothing had happened… like my world hadn't shattered.

Dean stopped talking to me. Or maybe I stopped talking to Dean. I couldn't remember. I just knew it had been the beginning of the end.

CHAPTER ONE

KELSEY

HE SAT ALONE AT THE BAR, FLIPPING A COIN. HIS FEATURES WERE shadowed in the light. First he balanced the coin on his index finger, then he tossed it into the air with a flick of his thumb. The coin flashed quicksilver as it spun and dropped into his palm. He flipped it again. It was a rhythmic movement, hypnotic, like the ticking of a clock.

I watched him catch the coin, then let my gaze travel up his muscular arm. An elaborate tattoo curled around his upper right forearm and biceps, but from a distance I couldn't make out the design.

His profile was sharply masculine, his jaw dark with stubble, his black hair thick and messy. He wore an old navy T-shirt and jeans that hugged his long legs. Though his shoulders were slumped, a tense, restless energy wound through his body, as if he were an eagle poised for flight.

As I watched him, something fluttered deep inside me. I knew men like him. He'd once been like the rough boys from my old Chicago neighborhood, the boys who radiated insolence and defiance. The ones who fought, cursed, and cut school to sneak behind buildings and smoke. The boys who dared each other to shoplift from the Russian shops on Devon Street. The boys who liked me because I was a tough girl who met their challenges without fear.

This guy was no longer a *boy*, though. Far from it. He was every inch a man, from the rugged planes of his face to his powerful torso and clear down to the scuffed, well-worn boots.

He flipped the coin again, closed his hand around it, and pushed it into his pocket. He grabbed the bottle resting on the counter and tilted his head back to drain the last of the beer. The column of his throat worked as he swallowed. I watched with mesmerized fascination, not missing a detail, from the curve of his hand around the bottle to the way his lips pressed against the top.

He set the bottle down and wiped his mouth with the back of his hand. He turned. And through the smoky light and shadows, our gazes met.

Oh.

My heart flipped just like the coin—a wild, seamless spin flashing silver. I felt my heart suspend in mid-air for an instant, poised to drop, and I had the sudden, irrational sense that it, too, could fall right into the palm of his hand.

I tore my gaze from his and looked at my drink. The scotch reminded me what the hell I was even doing in a dingy bar on the outskirts of Forest Grove. The crushing disappointment of my entire day effectively pushed my heart back down into place. Or lower. My dark mood was also probably the reason I was thinking silly thoughts about a complete stranger.

I felt him approaching, his presence tangible. My breath grew shallow when I looked up again to find him right beside my booth. His gaze wandered over me, touching on my eyes behind my glasses, up to the dark blue streak in my blonde hair, then back over my face to my mouth.

God, he was such a man. Big and rough-hewn, but with thick-lashed eyes and black eyebrows that softened the planes of his face and made him downright handsome. I could feel the power radiating from him, could sense a purely male appraisal of me raking through his mind. My skin tingled. I saw what he saw—a professional woman in a tailored, gray business suit and silk blouse, drinking alone in a corner booth, as if she were just waiting for him to approach.

Maybe I had been. Though I had avoided men like him for years, at the moment he was a welcome distraction from the series of recent failures that had put my hard-won research project on the skids.

Frustration clawed at me again. I stifled it and tried to match his assessment of me by deliberately sweeping my eyes over his torso. I imagined the rigid muscles and planes of his abdomen beneath his T-shirt. I looked at the corded length of his forearms, the tattoos gliding over the biceps of his right arm—intricate feathers, like a bird's wing—then back up to his face.

He watched me, a faint smile curving his well-shaped mouth, his gaze a force that I, Kelsey March who knew all about the physics of geomagnetic storms, couldn't resist any more than I could resist the pull of gravity.

He dug a hand into his pocket and pulled out the coin. When he spoke, his voice was a smooth, deep rumble that settled in my core like a drumbeat.

"Heads… I leave," he said. "Tails… I stay."

I swallowed to ease the dryness in my throat. "Do you always let fate make decisions for you?"

"Fate makes better decisions than I do."

I looked at the coin nestled in his broad hand. My pulse quickened. He balanced the coin on his index finger and flipped it with his thumb. We both watched the coin spin upward.

Tails. Tails. Tails.

Before I could think, I reached out and grabbed the coin out of the air. I closed my fist around it, the edges pressing against my palm. It felt larger than a quarter and heavier, like a silver dollar.

The stranger and I looked at each other. The air between us vibrated with something hot and anticipatory, a ripening awareness of which decision we both wanted fate to make.

Tails… I stay.

I tightened my grip on the coin. My heart hammered. I felt as if I were on the cusp of a free-falling drop, like the steep incline of a roller-coaster that would sweep me off on an exhilarating, wild ride. I met the man's gaze again.

"You decide," I said.

He didn't move. I waited. The noise of the bar receded, leaving us alone together. Then he stepped forward and slid into the booth beside me.

My breath escaped in one, long rush. An undeniable sense of relief went through me, which was as unnerving as the fact that I'd wanted him to stay. I edged away only far enough to let him sit.

His hip brushed against mine. An electric spark shot over my skin. He rested his arms on the table, and like a magnet my eyes were drawn to his hard forearms, dusted with dark hair, and the elaborate bird's wing that ended at the crook of his elbow.

I still held the coin, my hand curled into a fist. A faint dizziness filled my head. It wasn't the alcohol. I'd been nursing my first drink for the past forty-five minutes, and the glass was still half-full. I'd also been watching him since he walked into the bar thirty minutes ago, which accounted for my lack of interest in the scotch. Just looking at him gave me a buzz.

"What are you doing here alone?" he asked.

"Seething," I said.

"You don't look like you're seething."

I knew I didn't. The blue streak in my hair was the only thing that made people wonder—otherwise, they only saw a cool, professional woman. Even now, after five hours in a stuffy boardroom fielding questions and accusations from six male executives, I looked composed and unruffled. No one would ever know that an hour ago, I'd been locked in a stall in the ladies' room, slamming my hand against the door and fighting waves of anger.

"What *do* I look like I'm doing?" I asked.

"You look like you're checking me out."

My heart jolted with a combination of embarrassment and pleasure. It was the truth. I'd been checking him out since he walked in the door. I'd watched him toss his leather jacket onto a coat rack before crossing to the bar. His stride had been long and certain, his movements decisive as he dug in his back pocket for his wallet and took a seat at the bar.

I liked the way he moved. I liked the way he handed the money directly to the bartender instead of putting it on the counter. I liked the way he nodded his thanks and took a drink, the way he rested one booted foot on the bar railing.

Hell. I liked everything about him. That was why I hadn't stopped staring at him.

He moved closer to me now. I felt the length of his thigh next to mine. I wanted to press up against it, to feel his body heat and the solid bulk of his muscles. The dizziness wound through me again along with a sense of unreality, as if I were no longer smart, sharp Professor March, but a mysterious, sexy woman who picked up men in bars with uninhibited ease.

Men like *him*.

"What are you doing here alone?" I asked.

"Brooding," he said.

I smiled. "You don't look like you're brooding."

"I stopped when I saw you."

Oh.

I hadn't stopped seething when I saw him. My anger had just shifted into a slow, pleasurable burn that uncoiled in my blood like a plant stretching toward the sun.

He reached out to curl a few locks of my blue hair around his fingers. He studied the strands intently, as if he were making sure they really were blue and not just a trick of the light.

When he smoothed them back into place, his fingers brushed across my forehead.

"Pretty," he murmured.

A flush rose to my cheeks. Despite my knowledge that flirting was second nature to a man like him, I let myself be softened by his admiration. So much better than feeling as if I were clawing my way up a brick wall and falling back on my ass every time I made any progress.

"So what… or *who*… made you seethe?" he asked.

"A group of SciTech executives."

"What's SciTech?"

"A scientific research agency. They took away funding for a project I've been working on for three years."

"Why did they do that?"

"They said my data was inconclusive."

"Was it?"

"Yes," I admitted. "But I'm far from finished with it. I needed the funding renewal to conduct more investigations and move into phase two. But they shut down the whole project."

Frustration churned inside me again, my brain crowding with raised voices, arguments, and my explosive anger that not one of the executives had understood or wanted to support what I was trying to do.

I reached for my scotch and took a swallow, letting the alcohol burn through my chest.

I felt him watching me again, this time with both curiosity and guardedness. As if he were trying to make sense of the woman with the dark blue hair and business suit who was fighting to fund her scientific research.

"What's the project about?" he asked.

I shook my head. I didn't want to talk about it, didn't want to relive the lengthy, combative meeting that had led to me sitting in a bar, badly needing a drink.

My stomach knotted. I didn't want to be Professor March right now. Professor March was angry, frustrated, and exhausted. Tomorrow she'd have to face her colleagues and admit that SciTech pulled funding for the Spiral Project. She'd also have to contend with the fact that most of the other professors would be secretly pleased by her failure.

Then she'd have to talk to her grad students, deal with their disappointment, and start the proposal process all over again. After that she'd have to find out how this debacle affected her chances for tenure and a permanent, full professor position at King's University.

Fuck.

I'd be Professor March again later. Not now. Not with this incredibly sexy man sitting so close to me, everything about him awakening desires that I'd suppressed for years. Desire for the forbidden, for bad boys who radiated danger, for risk-taking and spontaneity and the freedom to do whatever the hell I wanted.

I turned to face him at the same instant I shifted closer, pressing my thigh against his. Heat flowed through me.

"What were you brooding about?" I asked, skimming my gaze from his mouth up to his eyes.

"The fact that fate makes better decisions than I do."

"But you decided to come over here," I remarked.

You decided to stay.

He studied me. He had beautiful eyes. Framed by thick

eyelashes, his eyes were dark as the earth, as midnight, and flecked with silver, like stars in an endless universe.

"Best decision I've made in a long time," he said.

Pleasure unfurled in my veins. I was still holding the coin clenched in my left fist.

Emboldened by his words, I reached out and settled my other hand on his forearm. Awareness shivered through my blood at the sensation of his hair-roughened skin, the hard muscles taut with restrained energy. I ran my hand tentatively up to where the bird's wing hugged his upper arm before disappearing beneath the sleeve of his T-shirt. I wondered how far it went, if tattoos also decorated the slopes of his shoulder and chest.

I loved that he wore a bird's wing, that he'd made freedom a permanent part of him. I traced the feathers with the tip of my finger. A flame licked at me, flaring upward from my core and into my blood. I wanted to slide my hand beneath his sleeve and over his smooth, muscled shoulder.

I didn't have the courage to do that. Once upon a time, I had. Not anymore. Instead I swept my hand back down to his forearm. Before I reached his wrist, he put his hand over mine. It was a quick, decisive movement, like a hawk landing on its perch. My pulse stuttered, a combination of heat and shock rolling through me as I realized he was about to make another decision.

And I would agree with whatever it was.

He slid his fingers against my hand, gently caressing the spaces between my fingers. Live electrical wires sparked through me. I'd never before known how tender those little hollows were.

He traced the backs of my fingers. His hands were callused.

I could feel the hard ridges on his forefinger and thumb. A burn spread low in my belly. I gripped the coin tighter in my other fist. He leaned in, closer, and when his lips brushed mine, fireworks exploded in my blood in complete disproportion to the gentle pressure of his kiss.

My whole body sighed with pleasure. His lips were warm, slightly chapped, and he tasted like salt and maleness. Oh, how long had it been since I'd kissed a man like him—a man who reminded me of the excitement of risks and the reckless, heady feeling of plunging headlong into the unknown.

He put his hand against my cheek, his fingers sliding into my hair. I parted my lips to taste the heat of him. Our tongues touched. A bolt of lust shot to my center. My lower body tightened. I pressed my thighs together.

Oh, god.

So good. Hot and gentle at the same time. He shifted his lips to my cheek, his stubble abrading my skin. Beneath the table, he settled his other hand on my thigh. The warmth of his palm burned through the material of my trousers.

I shifted closer, letting my body lean into his as he stroked his hand upward, his fingers dipping between my thighs and higher… higher…

I groaned, aching to part my legs and let him touch me. I had a sudden, blatantly explicit image of him sliding his hand into my pants and finding the satin thong I wore under my business suit. Then twisting his fingers around the thin strap and down into my—

I broke away from him with a gasp, my chest burning. I stared into his darkened eyes as our breath filled the space between us. My lips felt reddened, my cheek scraped from his whiskers.

I tore my gaze from his and grabbed my drink. My mind spun. Desire and caution rocketed through me like crazed fireflies.

I could leave with him. I could leave with him right this second, and let him take me somewhere, anywhere. I could let him strip off my clothes, touch and kiss me all over, make me writhe against his hard, powerful body...

I downed a swallow of scotch, but the alcohol did nothing to quench my raging fire. His hand, warm and possessive, settled on the back of my neck. He brushed his lips against my ear.

Behind him, the bar patrons moved almost in slow-motion, their images blurred. A group of men pushed through the front door, letting in a sudden burst of chatter that sliced through my haze of lust.

I went still. My vision sharpened and focused. A chill crept into my blood. Five men in their mid-thirties, wearing khakis and ties, one with a rumpled suit jacket and glasses...

They crowded up to the bar and called out their orders. I stared at them, my heart plummeting. They weren't SciTech executives, but they might as well have been.

The man beside me had stilled too. I felt him watching me, as if he sensed the frost that had descended over my desire. The reminder of who I was pushed back into my head.

I'd once been a girl who took risks and met challenges without fear, but that girl had been gone for more years than I cared to remember.

I was Professor March. Even when I didn't want to be, I still *was*.

I swallowed hard. My fingernails dug into my palm. The coin was still clenched in my damp fist.

I held out my hand. My breathing grew shallow. Slowly I uncurled my fingers. We both looked at the coin, the silver flashing in the overhead light.

Heads.

Disappointment stabbed me. I dropped the coin into his hand. It was a facsimile coin, vaguely medieval-looking. When I lifted my gaze to his face again, he was watching me with a shuttered expression, as if he knew that this time, fate had made the decision.

He shoved the coin into his pocket and stood. For an instant, he seemed to hesitate. My heart stirred again. Then he turned and walked away.

The noise of the bar filled my ears. Frustration rose in my chest. A blinking neon light flashed garishly through the window. As the world crashed back in, my regret became so bitter I could taste it.

Several people sat at the computers in the cramped synoptic lab of the Meteorology department at King's University. The smell of bad coffee and the sound of fingers clicking on keyboards filled the air.

I rubbed the back of my neck, twisting to ease the tension in my shoulders. My muscles were still tight, both with lingering anger over yesterday's meeting with SciTech and—I could now admit in the harsh light of day—sexual frustration at having thwarted that hot encounter with a stranger.

Intellectually, I knew I'd done the right thing by putting a stop to it. But my body didn't give a shit about intellect. It was just remembering how damn *good* that kiss had felt. Sparks and electricity. The smoldering burn of lust. The world slipping away, everything fading into the pressure of his mouth and the touch of his hand on my—

"This is pathetic." My grad student Derek made a noise of irritation.

I forced myself back to the present and focused on the NEXRAD screen. Derek hit the refresh button on the radial velocity loop for the third time. His face darkened with a frown.

"This department really needs upgraded equipment," he muttered.

"We're working on it," I said. "The board of trustees has yet to approve our budget proposal."

I leaned over to start up the mesonet page as we watched the storm encroaching on northeast Oklahoma. Three of my other grad students had left two nights ago to chase developing storms, which had the potential to grow into tornadic supercells. When they returned, I would tell all my students together about the disaster of the Spiral Project funding.

The phone beside the computer rang. I pressed the talk button to connect it to the speaker. "Colton?"

"Yeah." His voice crackled over the line. "We're on I-540 heading toward Fayetteville. Whaddya got?"

"We're looking at the mesonet observations," I said. "There's a convergence in Muskogee, moving east at five knots."

"Initiation?"

"At 19Z."

"Based on the shear profile, the storm splitting should happen half an hour later," Derek told him. "Right-mover dominant not long after that."

"Okay. Hold on." There was a pause. "We're switching directions now. Be in touch."

I disconnected the line and sat next to Derek. We spent the next hour watching the evolution of the storm on the OKC NEXRAD. Colton and the team got in front of the developing supercell and called again to report a massive wall cloud.

A few seconds later, my cell phone buzzed with a text from Colton. Below the words *holy shit* was a picture of a huge black-and-gray mass extending from the base of the cumulonimbus cloud.

I nudged Derek and showed him the picture. He breathed out a curse. I knew how he felt because I felt it too—envy, excitement, and fear that my students were possibly in the path of a forming tornado.

I tried to ignore the *envy* part. Envy meant wanting something you didn't have, and I'd long ago stopped wanting to be in a storm.

Never mind that one had brewed inside me just last night as I sat beside a man who made my skin tingle with his touch. A man with corded forearms and long, powerful legs, sandpaper stubble that branded my skin like—

Stop. Thinking. About. Him.

I shook my head to dislodge the memories. I was Professor Kelsey March again, which meant I had no business wondering where that sizzling, anonymous encounter would have gone if I hadn't come to my senses.

Trying to refocus, I watched the radar and mesonet. Colton

called again after another half hour to report that the storm had weakened and dissipated.

"You all okay?" I asked.

"Yeah. We got some hail damage, but the equipment is fine. We're heading back to Tulsa now. I'll send you the reports soon."

"You're staying overnight, right?"

"Luke wants to drive back after we get something to eat."

"No. You find a motel, okay? Drive back tomorrow morning after you've all slept. Use my credit card. Tell Luke that's an order."

"Can we use your credit card for a steak dinner?"

"Go ahead. Just don't get hammered."

"No, ma'am. See you in a day or two."

"Be careful."

After Derek and I speculated about the reasons for the storm's dissipation, I grabbed my blazer and turned to leave the lab. I almost bumped into a tall, broad-shouldered man who was standing right behind us.

"Shouldn't your grad students be here working?" Stan Baxter asked.

"I told them they could go."

"You shouldn't be using departmental resources to chase tornados," he said. "We're overextended with our equipment as it is."

"Derek and I were just helping them track it. We're done now."

Stan glanced behind me to the radar screen. He was an older guy, hefty and gray-haired, who'd been a full professor in the Meteorology department for the past thirty years and had been appointed the departmental chairperson last September. He'd always been respectful toward me, but lately he'd been on my case over my failure with the Spiral Project and my conduct as a professor up for tenure.

"How is your tenure review package coming along?" Stan asked me.

Irritation pricked my spine. He knew I was behind schedule in compiling a binder of my academic distinctions to present to the university board. And now I had to admit to the board that SciTech had pulled my Spiral Project funding.

I pushed past Stan and walked out of the lab, not wanting to have this conversation in front of a graduate student. Stan fell into step beside me in the corridor.

"You know, Kelsey, I'd suggest you write up a statement of commitment to present to the review board and chancellor," he said.

"What do you mean, statement of commitment?"

"Commitment to teaching a full course load," Stan said. "I was looking at your teaching schedule for the past few years, and you've managed to avoid teaching classes in favor of your personal research projects. That's not a fulfillment of the workload clause in your contract."

"I haven't avoided anything," I said, trying not to sound defensive. "I've been working on the Spiral Project for three years. The scope of the project required a massive amount of data collection that—"

"Look." Stan held up his hands to stop me. "I get that the Spiral Project was your baby. But you're up for *tenure*, Kelsey. If I were you, I'd consider it a blessing in disguise that SciTech killed your funding. Now you can focus on fulfilling your contractual duties and proving your commitment to this university."

My shoulders tensed. I didn't like his implication that I was slacking. But he knew I couldn't cause any waves or risk tenure. Hell, he was one of the professors who had to approve my application.

All of my colleagues in the Meteorology department had to agree that I deserved tenure before the university board and the chancellor made the final decision. If my colleagues or the chancellor voted no, my career at King's was over.

"*Now* you suddenly think I'm not committed to King's?" I asked. "After seven years?"

"You haven't even taught your intro courses for two years," Stan pointed out. "You've been too busy with the Spiral Project. Now that it's clear you haven't been able to *prove* you can better predict tornados, you need to kill your project and focus on King's agenda rather than your own."

"I'm not giving up on the Spiral Project, Stan." *No fucking way.*

He frowned. "Not even if it puts your tenure at risk?"

"I wasn't aware I had to choose between tenure and the project."

"You need to decide if you want to remain a strong asset to this department," Stan said, "or if you want to run around chasing tornados."

Maybe I should flip a coin and let fate decide.

Heat rose up my neck. Memories of my stranger filled me—how he'd tasted like salt, the pressure of his hand, the way his thigh pressed against mine...

I shook off the thoughts and straightened my shoulders.

"That sounds like a threat," I told Stan.

"It's a warning. For the past six months, the university review board has approved every stage of your application for tenure. The final decision is in four weeks. If it goes your way, you'll be guaranteed a permanent position at King's. If it doesn't..."

His voice trailed off.

You're fired.

And I had no hope of getting the Spiral Project off the ground again if I were fired from King's University and lost all association to an institution.

Shit. I had to play by the rules, much as I hated them.

"Okay," I finally agreed. "I'll write a statement of commitment."

"Good." Stan nodded with satisfaction. "The Spiral Project can't be your focus, Kelsey. In fact, I'd suggest you find another project that actually has some conclusive data to support it. You don't want to get a reputation as a fraud. No agency will want to fund your proposals then, tenure or not."

I forced myself to walk away before I said something that would come back to bite me on the ass.

CHAPTER TWO

ARCHER

THE CLOSER I GOT TO MIRROR LAKE NEAR THE MINNESOTA BORDER, the worse I felt. My hands sweated inside my leather gloves. My stomach was a ball of nerves. My brain fought a constant battle with my urge to turn the Harley around and fly in the opposite direction.

Back to a bar where I'd found a cool, blonde woman with hot blue eyes. A woman who'd made me forget the dry, empty desert, the smell of gasoline and asphalt, the sun burning a hole in the sky. A woman who had made me forget that my entire life could fit into a beat-up cardboard box.

I clenched my hands on the grips and kept going. She'd made me forget… until this morning when it had all crashed back in. Four days ago, I'd packed my stuff and left the garage and gas station where I'd worked for the past few months. My parents, recently divorced after thirty years of marriage, had sold the California house where I grew up and moved away.

Though my family had always been fractured, now it was broken for good. The only piece still intact was my brother Dean, his wife, and their baby Nicholas.

I'd never met Nicholas. Hadn't seen Dean or Liv in over a year. I didn't think they'd even want to see me. And yet here I was, driving over fifteen hundred miles north to Mirror Lake.

I didn't really want to visit my brother. What for? To dredge up all the crap between us? To prove everything he thought of me was true? But turning tail now like a coward would be worse than enduring this sick feeling.

At least, that was what I'd been telling myself. Time to man up, do the right thing, mend fences. Ignore the realization that I really just had nowhere else to go.

I turned off the interstate. My brother aside, I did want to see Liv again. I'd been an ass to her once, but I'd always known she was decent. Nice. Smart. And she'd pulled herself out of what had seemed like a crappy life before she met Dean.

Liv was the kind of woman Sarah might have been, if Sarah's life had taken a different path. Maybe even if Sarah hadn't met me.

A knot pulled at my chest. I drove away from the off-ramp and went left toward the sign pointing me to downtown Mirror Lake.

The lake itself stretched beneath a circle of mountains,

the water reflecting the surrounding trees and the clouds overhead. The main street wove along the lake path and was lined with little shops, boutiques, and restaurants that looked like a movie set for a romantic comedy.

After asking for directions at a gas station, I drove through a couple of residential neighborhoods to the hallowed halls of King's University. I parked in a lot and walked across the quad. I stopped again to ask directions to the history department and was pointed toward an impressive, columned brick building.

My heart pounded harder as I climbed the worn stone steps inside to the fifth floor. Too late, I thought I should've checked into the hostel to take a shower and change clothes. But if I left the university now, I'd never come back.

Voices rose in the hushed air. I caught snippets of conversation about course schedules, requirements, a paper about colonization, and a discussion about a war I'd never heard of.

I scanned the nameplates outside the office doors. Dr. Frances Hunter, Professor, American Studies. Dr. Michael London, Assistant Professor, European History. Dr. Amy Delafield, Associate Professor, Ancient Greek and Roman History.

Dr. Dean West, Professor, Medieval Studies.

I stopped. The door was half open. A young man inside was talking about… what else… homework.

"I've got the bibliography done, so I'll send that to you this afternoon," he said, amidst the sound of rustling papers. "And the archive department has a digitized copy of the codex."

"Good." Dean's voice. "Let me know when you want to discuss it."

I moved aside when the door opened farther. Slinging

his backpack over one shoulder, the student left. There was another rustle of paper, then the sound of Dean coming toward the door.

He glanced into the hall as if looking to see if any other students were waiting. His gaze stopped on me. Silence fell between us like a weight.

I cleared my throat. "Hey."

"Archer." Disbelief clouded his expression. "What are you doing here?"

My jaw tightened. "Hello to you, too."

"Sorry." Dean shook his head. "I wasn't expecting you."

"I should've checked your office hours." I jerked my chin toward the door. "Can I come in?"

"Yeah. Sure." Dean stepped back, allowing me to enter his office.

I shifted, too hot inside my leather jacket. Books lined the room, which had a window with a view of the tree-studded quad. Dean's big desk, covered with books, papers, and a computer, sat in front of the window.

The door clicked shut. A trickle of sweat ran down my back.

"Where did you come in from?" Dean asked.

"Nevada." I shrugged out of my jacket and tossed it on a chair. "Mom called a few days ago. She's going to live with Paige. I guess the house sale closed. Your stuff is in storage."

Dean nodded. "You hear from Dad?"

"No, but Mom said he's in San Francisco. He's going up to his cabin in Tahoe sometime."

"That's what he told me. I talked to him after the divorce was finalized."

We were both quiet, thinking of our father, former justice on the California Supreme Court, living out his retirement alone.

"Well." Dean sighed, dragging a hand through his hair. "Too bad."

"When were you last out there?"

"We brought Nicholas to see Mom over the holidays," Dean said. "Dad had moved out by then, but they were fine."

"Mom told me you have a kid now. Congratulations."

"Thanks."

Another silence fell. The medieval coin felt like it was burning a hole in my front pocket. It was one of two things I'd salvaged from the box of stuff my mother had sent me a week ago.

While packing up to sell the California house, she'd found a few of my old belongings and sent them to the garage where I was working. The box had included a few old dirt bike magazines, comic books, a lumpy, painted clay pot, a "participation ribbon" for a science fair, and a notebook half-filled with comics I'd drawn.

The facsimile coin had been at the bottom of the box. The size of a silver dollar, it was engraved with Latin phrases and a picture of King Arthur. When we were kids, Dean had liked the King Arthur legends, and our father had helped me find the coin to give my brother as a twelfth birthday present.

I had no idea how the coin ended up in a box of my stuff. I'd thrown most of the contents away, but kept the coin with the vague intention of returning it to Dean.

I shoved my hand into my pocket and closed my fingers around it. I felt Dean studying me, could sense all the assessments shifting through my brother's brain. I couldn't bring myself to give him the coin now, suddenly feeling stupid for being nostalgic about anything.

Dean's cell phone rang. He went around to pick it up from his desk, glancing at the screen before lifting the phone to his ear.

"Hi, Liv." His voice got all warm and gentle.

I slumped into a chair and watched my brother. Dean looked the same as he had a year and a half ago. Even five years ago. He looked okay for a guy pushing forty. Of course, he was a total starched shirt in his suit and perfectly knotted tie, neat haircut, shiny shoes. Like a kid dressed up for Sunday school.

That was Dean, all right. Responsible, smart, dedicated, play-by-the-rules. Mr. Do The Right Thing. If anyone was destined to be a successful historian, a wealthy investor, and a family man, it was Dean West.

I guessed I should have appreciated the fact that some people never changed. Dean never changed.

Maybe I didn't either.

That thought was less comforting.

I shifted. My boots scraped against the floor. It took me a minute to realize that Dean had ended the call and was looking at me.

"So when did you get in?" he asked.

"Just now. Stopped to ask where the university was."

"Did you come to tell me about the house?"

I knew what he was thinking and, truth be told, I didn't blame him. But I could preempt him.

I forced myself to sit up straighter. To look my brother in the eye. To shove aside the feeling that I was at the principal's office.

"No," I said. "I want to talk to you about my inheritance."

He didn't look surprised. No wonder. How many times had I demanded the money? How many times had Dean said no?

Dean folded his arms across his chest. Now he wasn't a principal, but a judge. *Like father, like son.*

"I still can't just hand it over," he said. "Not unless you've met all the conditions our grandfather set down—you needed to have a job, finish school, prove you were responsible."

I didn't like how he was speaking in past tense, as if it were already too late for me to prove anything. I pushed to my feet just to try and put us on equal ground.

"Look," I said. "I know you won't believe this, but I didn't come here to ask for the money again."

Dean didn't respond. I hated this. I had always hated being dependent on my brother for anything, especially my inheritance. And I still hated the idea that I had to prove myself. That only Dean—goddamned Dean—could declare me *worthy*.

Fuck.

I took a breath, curling my fingers into my palms. "I don't want the money. That's not why I'm here."

I'd also given up on the money a long time ago. And I sure as hell didn't want to earn it, especially not for Dean's approval.

"I was just in the area." I backed up a few steps. "Thought I'd stop in."

"How long are you staying?" Dean asked.

"Couple of days, I guess."

"Well, I'd like you to meet Nicholas."

"Okay." I took another step away. "Just let me know when's a good time."

I turned to the door. I was reaching to open it when the door flew open, smacking me in the forehead. Pain lanced through my skull. I stumbled back.

"Dean, you were supposed to… oh, shit." A female voice sharpened. "Are you okay?"

I nodded and blinked, my vision coming slowly into focus. A streak of blue. Red lips. A stare that looked like it could penetrate to the core of the earth itself.

The pain faded. I blinked again and found myself looking at a woman.

A woman I'd kissed the night before in the corner booth of a dive bar. A woman who tasted like honey, scotch, and sex.

We stared at each other. Behind her glasses, her blue eyes were wide with shock.

"Archer, this is my friend Kelsey."

I heard Dean's voice as if he were speaking from far away.

Kelsey. I wanted to taste her name.

"Kelsey, my brother Archer," Dean continued. "He just got into town."

She closed her mouth, her throat rippling with a swallow. "Your brother?"

"Yeah." Dean shuffled through the papers on his desk. "I told you about him."

My insides clenched. Dean wouldn't have told her anything good about me.

Kelsey was still looking at me with disbelief. Because she couldn't believe I was Dean's brother or because she couldn't believe she'd kissed me?

I deliberately let my gaze rake over her, taking in her smooth, shoulder-length blonde hair with the streak of blue and her piercing eyes behind her rimless glasses. She wore a pinstriped suit that would have looked stupid on most other women, but on her looked sexy as hell.

Maybe it was the strapped heels peeking out from beneath the hem of her pants, displaying her painted toenails. Or the shirt unbuttoned one button too many under the tailored blazer, showing the edge of her lacy, purple bra. Or her lips that were parted slightly and red as cherries…

Jesus. I shook my head. Dean was talking again, but I couldn't make out his words. I didn't want to. I just wanted to stare at Kelsey again and wonder what she looked like wearing nothing but her glasses.

"So."

The sound knocked me out of my fantasy. A little. Because even now her voice was as sexy as the rest of her—rich and smooth, with a hint of a rasp that heated my blood.

"You're Archer," she said, as if she needed me to confirm that.

You're Archer. I wasn't imagining the disdain in her voice. In fact, I should have expected it.

My jaw clenched. I knew that look she was giving me. The one that dawned in the cold light of day when smoky bars and anonymous meetings were a distant memory. She'd made a mistake last night and now she had to face it. Literally.

"I'm Archer." I extended my hand, grimy and dirty from being encased in a sweaty leather glove all day.

Her gaze flicked to my hand.

"Go ahead," I invited. "I don't bite."

She closed her hand around mine in a firm, warm grip. She met my gaze. When she spoke, her voice was as cool as river water.

"Pity," she murmured.

Heat jolted through my chest. I tightened my grip on her. She tugged her hand from my grasp and stepped away. She turned her attention to Dean and held out a blue folder and a glasses case.

"Here's the admissions review paperwork you need to sign. And Liv left her sunglasses in my car yesterday."

"Thanks." Dean put the sunglasses in his briefcase and grabbed a pen to sign the papers. "I'll go drop these in the office."

He stacked the papers and went past us to the corridor.

We were alone. I stepped closer to Kelsey. She watched me warily, her expression devoid of the heat I'd seen last night.

"What are you doing here?" she asked.

"Visiting my brother."

"He never said you were coming."

"He didn't know. Are you a professor here?"

"Yes. I study tornados."

"Yeah? Why tornados?"

"So I can predict the unpredictable."

"Ambitious."

She nodded. Her gaze flickered over me. There it was. What I'd seen from plenty of women before. She was intrigued, but now she clearly saw that I was lower than her.

"Where did you get in from?" she asked.

"The desert."

"What do you do in the desert?"

"Get hot."

She blinked. Good. She needed to be thrown off.

"Ambitious," she murmured.

The air thickened. Got hot. I pulled my gaze from hers when Dean came back into the office.

"Grace is sending the paperwork back to the chancellor's office today," he told Kelsey. "She said they're finalizing the meeting schedule next week."

"You were also supposed to send me your recommendations for the honors committee," Kelsey said, putting her hands on her hips in a school-marm stance.

"I did." Dean frowned and punched a few buttons on his computer. "No, sorry, it's still in my drafts folder. Hold on. Okay, sent."

"Are we on for racquetball tomorrow?" Kelsey asked.

"No, I'm working up at the house. Max Lyons said he'd stop by."

Kelsey blinked. "Max is back in town?"

"Got back last week, I think," Dean replied.

I frowned, not liking Kelsey's reaction. Who the hell was Max Lyons and why did she care that he was back in town? Jealousy scraped my chest.

Kelsey met my glower. She arched an eyebrow, as if she were daring me to make something of the fact that she was talking about another guy.

"So you're a weather girl, Kelsey?" I asked, deliberately baiting her.

Her mouth compressed with annoyance. "I'm an assistant professor in the Meteorology department."

She was still standing with her hands on her hips, like she was about to scold me. I thought I might enjoy it if she did.

"Kelsey is up for tenure this year, which would make her a permanent, full professor," Dean told me. "She's the one who told me about the job opening in the history department a few years ago. We met in college."

That meant she'd gone to Yale or Harvard. I'd figured she was educated with her talk about a scientific research project, but now the room was thick with overachievement and brilliance.

I edged toward the door, jerking my thumb at the corridor. "I'm going to take off."

"Hold on." Dean grabbed a pen and scribbled something on a piece of paper. "That's my cell, home number, and address. Do you have a place to stay?"

I nodded. "Haven't checked in yet, though."

"Okay. Give me a call as soon as you're settled."

"Yeah."

I left the room and strode toward the stairs. I was halfway there when the sound of heels clicked behind me. I turned to see Kelsey approaching, the overhead fluorescent lights glowing on her blue-streaked hair.

I stopped. I'd heard a lot of come-ons from women who had followed me in bars, clubs, coffeehouses, even grocery stores. Sometimes they were direct—*Can I buy you a drink? Do you have a girlfriend?* Other times they tried to get at me another way—*Can I borrow your cell phone? Will you walk me to my car? Is this seat taken?*

I didn't care which approach a woman used, not if I found her attractive, which I often did. But last night Kelsey hadn't needed a hook. All I'd done was turn and see her watching me. I'd thought that if I didn't approach her, she'd disappear. Just vanish.

I watched her come toward me now. I liked the way she moved. She had a long stride, a go-to-hell walk softened by the sway of her hips. I wanted to watch her walk from behind.

Now that we'd gotten the preliminaries out of the way, she'd be direct in her approach, just a point-blank invitation or—

She walked past me in a rush of cool, good-smelling air.

The click of her heels stopped at the elevators. I turned to where she stood, arms folded, her gaze on the lighted row of numbers above the doors. Ignoring the hell out of me.

"Hey," I said.

She turned her head.

"What've you heard about me?" I asked.

Kelsey shrugged. "Not much."

"He hasn't told you anything?"

"Sure he has." She said it so matter-of-factly, as if Dean had told her I was an insurance salesman. "Every family's got one like you, right?"

The tone in her voice, like I was nothing special, grated my nerves.

"You mean a fuck-up?" I asked.

"I mean someone who gets off on being a fuck-up," Kelsey replied, turning on her heel to face me. "Who thinks it's his life's work to screw with people and act like the world owes him a favor instead of getting off his ass and doing something."

"That's what you think?"

"That's what I know."

"You didn't care last night."

"That," she replied coolly, "was last night."

The elevator pinged, the door slid open. She stepped toward it, her blonde hair swishing behind her.

I moved before I could think, launching myself into the elevator doorway. The three students inside stared at me. I turned to face Kelsey, slamming my hands against the doors to stop them from closing.

"You don't know jack about me, sweetheart," I said, lowering my head to look into her eyes, daring her to back away. "Whatever the good professor has told you is bullshit. I've seen him twice in five years. He doesn't know a goddamned thing about my life. And just because I got you hot last night, don't you think you know me either."

She didn't take her eyes from mine, but her face reddened. I could see the pulse beating at the hollow of her throat. The edge of her bra still showed between the unfastened top buttons of her shirt.

"I'm disappointed in you," I continued, tracking my gaze down to the V of her neck. "I thought you were the kind of woman who'd form your own opinions about things. But if we're doing this based on second impressions, and if I'm the fuck-up who screws with people, then you must be the controlling bitch who hasn't gotten laid in years."

A shocked giggle came from one of the students in the elevator. Kelsey's flush deepened. She lifted her chin, ice coating her eyes.

"You can move now," she said coldly.

I stared at her. Unlike last night, today she was wound so fucking tight. I wanted to unwind her, mess up her world, rip that sexy lingerie right off her. I wanted to make her lose control.

"Say please," I murmured.

Her mouth tightened. Her eyes flashed blue fire at me. For a second, I thought we'd end up in a deadlock.

"Please," she hissed.

I pushed away from the doors, keeping my hand on one to hold it open for her. She stepped past me into the elevator. The clean, sweet smell of her drifted to my nose again.

I wasn't done with her. Not by a long shot. In fact, I was just getting started. I looked at her blue eyes again.

"Nice bra," I said. "I like the lace."

I pushed away and let the doors slide shut.

CHAPTER THREE

KELSEY

HOLY MOTHER OF GOD.

I struggled to draw in a breath, aware of the three students looking at me with intense curiosity, their attempts not to giggle over everything about that little encounter. Thank heavens they were undergrads or history students who likely wouldn't recognize me. I hoped.

I pulled the lapels of my blazer together. Inside my bra, which was indeed lacy, my nipples were hard. My pulse was pounding. I was *hot*.

Archer West. Of course the universe would throw me right

back in front of the man who'd shown up naked and smoldering in my dreams last night. The man whose touch made me shiver like a snowflake. The man I'd stopped in mid-kiss before I melted on the floor, or pressed my breasts against his arm, or stroked my hand down his chest to…

For god's sake.

When the elevator reached the ground floor, I hurried out to the quad, inhaling a deep breath of spring air.

What the hell was wrong with me? Sure, I'd once had a thing for bad boys, the *wrong* boys, but I was a thirty-six-year-old woman, for crying out loud, who'd long outgrown her wild and wooly side. A woman who'd learned a long time ago that, at some point, you had to get your shit together.

And no matter how hurt poor Archer West might be by my quick-fire assessment of him, it was the plain truth. Despite my temporary weakness last night, I'd been with enough men like him to know exactly how he viewed the world.

He was a walking cliché with a chip on his shoulder the size of Gibraltar and an inferiority complex a mile wide. Women loved him, wanted to take care of him, cried when he left them. He charmed them with his wicked smile and that glint in his gorgeous brown eyes and the promises of his powerful body, not to mention the sexual prowess that radiated from him like a goddamned aura…

I groaned softly, shaking off the image as I walked. I'd felt him the second I'd stepped into Dean's office, sensing the presence of a sexy bad boy like a Doppler radar homing in on a thunderstorm.

Just like in the bar, his dark gaze had sizzled right through me, causing my blood to rush into my ears and my thighs to tighten. And then when he'd touched me… I'd stripped him naked in my imagination in two seconds flat.

Again.

And oh, how I liked what I saw. Those tattoos inking his taut skin, rippling pectoral muscles and a rigid abdomen with a tantalizing trail of hair leading right to—

Whoa. Down, girl.

So wrong in so many ways. But from what Dean had told me, Archer was a drifter—well, of course he was—so likely he wouldn't be in Mirror Lake for long. I wondered if he was here for another reason besides a family visit. Even though it was none of my business, I made a mental note to ask Dean soon.

No. No, I wouldn't. *Because* it was none of my business. And because I didn't want to know more about Archer West than I already did. Therein lay danger, and I'd do well to heed the warning that was as loud as a tornado siren.

Even though I'd already kissed him and flirted with him. Deliberately. And honestly, too. It would indeed be a pity if Archer West didn't bite.

"Kelsey!" a voice called from behind me.

Oh, shit. I walked faster.

"Kelsey!" Peter Danforth, a young reporter in his mid-twenties, loped up beside me, all curly brown hair and bright, eager eyes. As usual, he wore an ill-fitting suit with a pencil-thin tie. He'd taken a few of my classes as an undergrad before starting the journalism graduate program, and now he viewed me as his main source of weather-related news.

"Go away, Peter," I said.

"Aw, come on. Talk to me." He quickened his pace. "You

said you expected to hear something conclusive about the Spiral Project funding this semester."

"I lied."

"You wouldn't lie to me."

"You're right. I'm sorry."

"Really?"

I shot him a glance. "No."

"Come on, Kelsey. You did say you'd hear by now."

Irritation ripped through me. I had no intentions of telling him about my disastrous meeting with SciTech, especially when I hadn't yet told my grad students. "Yeah, well, I haven't."

"Can you give me an ETA on when you'll know?"

I stopped and turned to face him. He smiled, still all puppy-dog anxious for me to throw him a bone. I had to admire his determination—not so much his expectation of a reward.

"Peter." I reached out and straightened his askew tie. "Leave me the hell alone."

His smile didn't waver. "Sure, Kelsey. If you'd just tell me the status of the project and future funding, I will be more than happy to leave you alone."

"I'm not telling you anything because there's nothing to tell right now." I stepped back. "However, *if* you leave me alone, I'll give you an exclusive as soon as I have something to tell."

Without waiting for a response, I continued across the quad. He didn't follow.

I turned toward the Meteorology building, catching sight of Archer West. I stopped and watched him, reacquainting myself with everything I'd found so appealing about him last night.

He was tall, well over six feet, with a lean, muscled body

that made me shivery inside. He moved with an easy, masculine grace, his biker appearance a stark contrast to the students wandering around with their backpacks.

A stark, gorgeous contrast. His black hair was overlong, unruly, curling around his ears and the back of his neck. As he walked, he took his phone out of his back pocket. My eyes followed the movement, down to the jeans hugging his long legs, and I remembered the way his thigh had felt pressed against mine…

I was half aware that I was standing there just staring at him. A student swerved to avoid me on the path.

"Kelsey, just one more thing…"

Oh, the fuck no.

I ripped my gaze away from Archer West and glowered at Peter. He jerked his chin in Archer's direction. "Who's that guy?"

"I have no idea."

"Then why were you staring at him?"

"I was wondering if he's a hitman I could hire to take you out."

Peter laughed, all white teeth and twinkling eyes. If he weren't such a pain in my ass, he'd have been adorable.

"Look, I just want to know if you could tell me when you go out for more data collection," he said. "Because, you know, maybe I could go with you when you do."

"No."

His face fell. I ignored a mild twinge of guilt.

"But if I did, I'd be a shoo-in as an embed reporter for the Spiral Project," he said. "You know it would make my career to travel with the biggest mobile forecast unit in history."

I couldn't blame him. Not really. He was a kid eager to

get ahead, probably had his sights set on working for CNN or The Weather Channel, anxious to impress and show off with some big scoop.

Not that the Spiral Project qualified as a scoop *yet*, but it had the potential to be a major breakthrough in tornado forecasting… and Peter knew it. He was annoying, but not stupid.

"I don't even do fieldwork anymore," I reminded him.

"But—" He glanced over my left shoulder.

"Take a break, Peter," I suggested, walking backward away from him. "Stop worrying so much about your career. Find a girl and have some fun."

"Ouch." He clutched his heart. "How can I do that when I'm saving myself for you?"

"You should be so lucky."

"No, he damned well shouldn't be."

The low, male growl jolted right through me. I whirled around and found myself looking up into a pair of intense dark eyes that ratcheted my heartbeat up.

Archer's gaze slid from me to where Peter was still standing.

Before I could speak, Peter squeaked out a, "See ya," and hurried off.

"Who was that?" Archer asked.

"A kid who thinks you're a potential hitman."

"Huh." He lifted an eyebrow in vague amusement. "Why does he think that?"

"I might have told him."

"Ah."

That one sound, escaping on his breath, was like a kiss. Heat zinged through my blood. I lowered my gaze to his mouth, so beautifully shaped with that slight indentation in his top lip, and tried not to remember what it had felt like to press my lips against his. I tried not to think about the fact that before last night, I couldn't even remember the last time I'd kissed a man, let alone…

Stop. Don't go there. Not with him standing right in front of you, the epitome of everything you shouldn't want.

And remember, he thinks you're a controlling bitch who hasn't gotten laid in years. Try and ignore the fact that he's right.

I dragged my eyes back to his. My heart still thumped hard, making me intensely aware of my body's reaction to our closeness.

"What do you want?" I finally asked.

He didn't respond, but stroked his gaze over my body in a look that clearly said, *You.*

Me?

Oh, yeah.

Oh, no.

Out of sheer self-preservation, I retreated a few steps, even as I was unable to stop myself from admiring the way his T-shirt stretched over his chest beneath his jacket, the outline of his pecs against the thin cotton, the worn fabric of his jeans with one button of his fly tantalizingly unfastened….

Jesus. I was starting to throb. I took another step back, painfully aware of the pulsing between my legs.

"How…" My throat was dry. "How long are you staying?"

He shrugged. "Couple of days."

Something stirred in my chest. Disappointment? I backed up another step. It was strangely hard to move with him looking at me like that.

"Have a good visit, then," I said. "I'm sure I won't see you again."

"I'm sure you will."

I came to a halt. I had to put a stop to this right here. Right now. Even if Archer was leaving in a couple of days, I wasn't going to let him fuck with me.

I also wasn't going to think of the words *fuck* and *Archer* in the same sentence ever again.

"Look." I crossed my arms, tilting my head to look him in the eye. "I'm sorry if I insulted you. If you're some upstanding, do-gooder Boy Scout in disguise, then I stand corrected. But I'm not one for playing games. I shoot straight from the hip. And I don't have either the time or the inclination to do this… this kind of *thing* with you."

There. My heart was beating even faster after that little speech. He closed the distance between us, all potent masculinity, his dark gaze lighting with the barest glimmer of amusement.

"You started it," he said.

I laughed. "Go tattle on me, then."

"No way." He shook his head. The sun glinted off his dark hair, making the strands glow like little bands of light. "This is between you and me. Yeah, I'm a fuck-up. I've been one my whole life. I've screwed with people. Gotten in plenty of trouble. But if you think that's it, you're wrong. And if you want to know about me, you don't let anyone else tell you. You deal with me."

"I don't want to deal with you. I don't even like you much."

"Yeah, that's exactly the vibe I got when you kissed me last night."

I swallowed hard. "That wasn't me."

"It sure as hell felt like *you.*"

"It wasn't. I'm not the kind of woman who makes out with strangers in bars. I was upset and angry, and you were…"

"What?"

"A distraction," I admitted, aware of a rising shame.

Archer studied me, his expression shuttered.

"I don't need you to like me, Professor March," he said. "But I've gotten enough bullshit from women who assume I'm pond scum. Don't you be one of them."

I stared at him, stunned by the forcefulness in his words. Why did he even care what I thought of him? And why did it feel like this was suddenly and intensely personal?

I opened my mouth to make a sharp retort, but what came out was the truth. "I don't think you're pond scum. I do think you're the kind of man I need to stay far away from."

"What kind of man is that?"

"The dangerous kind."

His mouth twisted. "You want a nice, classy guy, huh?"

I *should* want a nice, classy guy, I thought.

"Yes." I gave Archer a short, firm nod. "And now that we've got that straightened out, I'll be going."

His hand shot out so fast it was like the strike of a snake. His fingers closed around my wrist and he drew me closer to him.

"I'm not nice," Archer said, his voice low. "I'm not classy either. But I'll be straight with you too."

Wariness shot through me. He had layers that he wore like leather. I didn't want to even think about peeling those layers away to find out what was beneath.

"Let go of me," I ordered. "And I'm not saying *please.*"

He didn't let go. His fingers found the pulse throbbing wildly at my wrist. Again I felt the rigid calluses on his hand. Shivers sparked up my arm.

Desperation rose. I really had to stop this. And even if Archer West didn't know it, he'd all but handed me the weapon I knew would hurt the most.

"I don't need you to be straight with me," I continued. "I don't need you to be anything. You were a distraction last night. But now? You're not worth my time."

His expression didn't change. The edges of my vision faded into black and white so that the burn of his eyes seemed to be the only color in the world. His grip tightened.

"I was right about you, storm girl," he murmured. "When was the last time you were fucked real good?"

Heat bolted through me so fast and hard that it caught me off balance.

Archer released me. I stepped back, curling my hand around my wrist, still warm from the pressure of his hand. My breathing was choppy and shallow. I tried to muster up some indignation, but I was too busy trying to calm the fire raging in my blood at the idea of him being the one to end my lengthy dry spell.

"Thought so," he said. "Let me know if you ever want to change that."

"Hah. Fat chance." That was the only retort I could manage with my imagination kicking into overdrive.

Archer West would be one hell of a man to tackle after so long. He wouldn't be like a gentle rain on the parched ground that was my sex life. No. He would be an overwhelming, drenching storm with lightning bolts and thunder and the insane, crazy exhilaration of knowing you're in the middle of something wild and uncontrollable.

I was getting wet just thinking about it. I couldn't even imagine what would happen if I actually *did* it. With him. This sexy, dangerous, mouthwatering specimen of a man who had already made his interest in me all too clear.

I pressed my thighs together, which only increased the aching throb. I wanted his hand there. Wanted his mouth there. Wanted *him* there.

Oh, god. I swore I could have had an orgasm that second if I squeezed my thighs together hard enough. No question that Archer West made me hot.

And then a tiny little devil in my head whispered, *He could make you hotter. He's only here for a few days. What if you—*

I cut that thought off before it went any further. I let out a long breath, forcing my thighs to relax. Last night aside, I didn't run my life like that. Didn't make reckless decisions and plunge headlong into situations I knew were dangerous. Archer was here because of Dean, and…

Shit. *Dean.*

The thought of him effectively killed my arousal. Archer was Dean's *brother*. And while I would never let Dean dictate what I did, we'd been tight for years. He'd saved my ass more than once. I knew exactly how protective he could get. And clearly he and Archer had issues.

I sure as hell didn't want to become one of them.

Disappointment almost caught me off guard. I should have been relieved by that realization, not disappointed.

"I'll make it worth your time," Archer said, his voice a hot purr of promise.

"I can't do this." My protest came out weak, which increased my irritation. I cleared my throat. "I won't."

"You started it," he repeated. "And I'm going to finish it."

"We're already finished."

Proud of my sharp retort, I turned and walked away before he could. It was damn hard, especially knowing he was watching me from behind, but I did it.

And I hoped to heaven I wouldn't see him again. I wasn't at all sure I'd be able to walk away a second time.

CHAPTER FOUR

ARCHER

Kelsey March was killing me with her ice and fire. I'd practically smelled her heat as we'd stood there in the quad yesterday. I'd felt her body vibrating with lust when I'd kissed her in that bar. So why the hell had it been so long for her?

She wasn't frigid. She liked being hot in her lacy lingerie and fuck-me shoes. And aside from that, she radiated a tough-girl, take-no-prisoners sexiness. Even though I hated the idea of her with another guy… if she didn't get laid soon, she'd implode.

Not that I should care. An anonymous bar hook-up was one thing, but I was done with uptight chicks like her, the kind who liked me in the dark but knew I wasn't good enough for them. I didn't like their attitudes, their sense of entitlement. And I sure as hell shouldn't want to take things up with Kelsey March.

Except that I was burning to see her lose control. And to finish what we'd started last night.

I rested one foot on the terrace railing and stared out at the blue expanse of the lake.

Different. That was just one of the reasons I couldn't get her out of my head. Aside from her simmering repression and insane sex appeal, she was different. Uptight, yeah, but also interesting. A straight shooter who didn't play games. All sharp edges and self-confident intelligence.

A breeze rippled the water's surface. Felt good, the cool air, even though I'd always liked the desert. I liked that the desert was empty, hot, dry, dusty. Sharp cacti, gnarled Joshua trees, snakes, and lizards baking in the sun. It was a wild place, dangerous. Sometimes even the dawn seemed scared to rise. Like it was afraid the desert would bite.

Mirror Lake didn't even have teeth. It had flowers blooming from window boxes, sailboats gliding over the lake like huge birds, people strolling and chatting.

It was all so goddamn *nice*. Perfect. I wasn't at all surprised Dean had ended up here.

I put the lid back on a cup of take-out coffee and pushed to my feet. It was midday, so I figured Dean would be at work. Good time to see if Liv was home and maybe meet Nicholas.

I dug the address out of my pocket, checked the numbers of a nearby coffeehouse, and walked east. I stopped across from a row of stores.

Between a craft store and an art gallery was a worn wooden door painted with Dean's address number. I shaded my eyes and looked at the second floor, which had large windows framed by blue curtains and a balcony filled with plants and flowers.

I didn't get it. If that was their apartment, what was Mr. Overachieving Professor doing living in a multi-use building on a downtown street? I turned and started in the opposite direction.

"Archer?"

I stopped and looked across the street. A dark-haired woman in her early thirties was holding the wooden door open, peering at me.

Liv.

"I thought that was you," she called, waving me toward her. "Come on in."

Even though Liv was part of the reason I'd come to Mirror Lake, I had a rush of old embarrassment. I crossed the street. Liv smiled at me as if I were a long-lost friend, which made me feel worse.

"Dean told me you were in town," she said, holding the door open. "It's good to see you, Archer. Come on in."

"Thanks."

I followed her up the interior stairs to their apartment. The minute I stepped inside, something loosened inside me. It was filled with bright, airy colors, nice paintings, striped upholstery, plants, and a good smell like chocolate and cinnamon. Now I understood why Dean lived here, though I sensed Liv could make any place feel like this.

Sarah would have loved it. She'd always liked those interior design websites and magazines. She'd been making decorating plans even before we had any hope of living in a house.

"Toss your jacket on the sofa and make yourself comfortable," Liv said as she went into the kitchen. "I was just trying out a new cookie recipe, so your timing is perfect."

I shed my jacket, suddenly wishing my T-shirt was cleaner. I wiped my palms on my jeans and went into the living room. A baby swing leaned against one wall, a few soft toys and blankets scattered around.

"Have a seat." Liv emerged from the kitchen with a plate of cookies, gesturing for me to sit on the sofa.

I did, making a mental note not to get crumbs on anything.

"Dean said you were in Nevada," Liv said, holding out the plate to me. "You were working there?"

"Yeah, at a garage." I took a cookie and thanked her. "Where... uh, where's Nicholas?"

"Napping." Liv glanced at the clock. "He could wake up in five minutes or two hours. He's not exactly on a regular nap schedule yet."

She smiled again. She was pretty. Always had been. She looked the same, too, wholesome and sweet, her dark, straight hair falling to her shoulders and pulled back with a blue headband. She wore a blue skirt and white shirt, with a medallion on a silver chain around her neck.

The only two times I'd seen her, both at the house where Dean and I had grown up, Liv had seemed kind of unsure of herself, like she didn't know if she fit in anywhere.

I knew what that was like. But now she looked comfortable in her skin, more confident. Like she'd found her place. Like she'd found *herself.*

A strange feeling of relief filled my chest. *Good for you, Liv.*

"My mother told me you own a café now," I said.

Liv nodded. "My friend Allie and I opened it about a year ago. It's called the Wonderland Café, and it's geared toward families and children. We have a *Wizard of Oz* and *Alice in Wonderland* theme, a kid-friendly menu, birthday party packages. It's been great. A lot of work and a lot of fun."

"You and Allie are the owners?"

"Yes, and our friend Kelsey is a partner too, but she's not involved in the day-to-day operations. She's more of a silent partner."

"Kelsey the weather girl?" I couldn't imagine that hot, blonde spitfire being silent anywhere, at any time.

A sudden image flashed in my brain of Kelsey being *not silent* in bed. I wanted to see that. Wanted to *hear* it.

"Don't call her a weather girl to her face unless you want to lose a body part," Liv said with amusement. "Oh, hold on a sec. The lion awakens."

A baby's muffled wail came from the other room. Liv went in and emerged a few minutes later with five-month-old Nicholas. He had a shock of dark hair, a cherubic face reddened from sleep, and dark eyes. He was wearing sweatpants and a T-shirt with a picture of a cartoon dragon.

"This is Nicholas." Liv picked up the baby's hand and waved it at me. "Nicholas, this is your Uncle Archer."

Uncle Archer. It took me a second to remember I was blood-related to this kid. I waved back at Nicholas. He blinked in response.

"He's cute," I offered.

"Thanks. He's good, too, except for when he's hungry or tired. Then he gets pretty cranky. Not unlike his father." Liv grinned. "Hey, if you don't mind waiting a few minutes, I need to get Nicholas changed, and then we're going to see Dean."

"On campus?"

"No, Dean doesn't have classes this afternoon, so he went up to do some electrical work at the Butterfly House."

"What's the Butterfly House?"

"We bought an old historic property when I was pregnant with Nicholas," Liv explained. "It seemed like a terribly romantic idea to buy this dilapidated house so that we could restore it together and live there eventually."

My jaw tightened involuntarily. Old, jagged darkness encroached. I'd once had a similar plan to fix up a house with the hope of living there.

"How much work have you done on it?" I asked.

"Most of the exterior work and interior restructuring," Liv said. "It took a long time to go through the purchasing process, then make the plans and get all the permits... so we're still working on stuff. We're getting down to the wire, though, because our apartment lease expires at the end of July."

"The house is here in town?" I asked.

"Yes, up near campus," Liv said. "It's part of a residential neighborhood, but the lot is pretty big and surrounded by trees, so it's nice and quiet. It's a great property."

Sure it was. Dean wouldn't buy anything less than great.

Liv shifted the baby to her other arm. "I told Dean that Nicholas and I would stop by around three today. Would you like to come with us?"

I didn't know if I would *like* to since Dean was there, but I nodded. "Sure."

"Good." Liv looked pleased. "Just give us a few minutes to get ready."

Twenty minutes later, we went down to Liv's car and drove

through town. Liv turned onto a gravel driveway toward a house that looked like it belonged in a fairy tale—multi-storied with a gabled front porch, bay windows, decorative awnings, and even a tower rising from one corner.

I lowered my head to peer through the windshield. "Wow."

"It was built in the late 1800s," Liv explained. "The man who built it was a naturalist with a specialization in butterflies. He did all kinds of traveling looking for new species, and apparently had a big collection of live butterflies he kept in a greenhouse."

"How big is the property?" I asked, getting out of the car. The house was perched on a hill, with a view of the lake and downtown spreading out in the distance.

"A few acres." Liv unbuckled Nicholas from his car seat. "Dean's going to fence off the boundaries just for safety reasons."

She glanced toward the house.

"Oh, hi." Her voice warmed suddenly.

I turned to see Dean approaching. Wearing an old T-shirt, jeans, and work boots, he looked like a regular guy today rather than a professor. He stopped beside Liv and brushed his lips across her cheek.

"Hey, beauty."

Liv smiled. Dean took the baby from her, and she went to get a stroller from the trunk.

I looked at my brother. I knew he was wary about the fact that I'd obviously been spending time with his wife and son. My defenses locked together.

"Liv saw me outside the apartment," I told him. "Invited me in."

"I know." He crouched to buckle Nicholas into the stroller. "She texted me. Come on, I'll show you the house."

After Nicholas was settled, Liv pushed the stroller around to the garden. I followed Dean into the house. I had a flashback of a beat-up, clapboard bungalow that could have fit in the Butterfly House's front room. The house I never got to start, let alone finish.

By contrast, the Butterfly House had multiple rooms, a big spiral staircase, and three stories including the tower, which Dean told me was going to be his home office. They had taken down walls to increase the size of a few rooms and put in picture windows facing the garden and lake.

After Dean gave me the full tour, we went back outside to the garden. Nicholas was sitting in his stroller, playing with a stuffed elephant. Dean bent to squeeze the elephant's nose. The toy let out a trumpeting noise. Nicholas gurgled.

"So what do you think?" Liv asked me.

"It's beautiful. I like that you're making modern renovations to make it a really livable family home, but you're keeping the integrity of the original house."

"I'm glad you like it," Liv said. "Did you see the blueprints for the kitchen? That's the next big project."

"I'll show them to you." Dean gestured for me to follow him to a trailer at the edge of the property.

It was a typical, basic trailer with a kitchenette, pullout bed, and a table littered with papers. Dean unrolled the blueprints and explained the plans for tearing down walls to create an open-plan kitchen and dining area. The whole house would be *Architectural Digest* quality when it was finished.

"It's really nice," I said, as Dean put the blueprints away. "The whole place."

"Thanks. We've been working hard on it."

"You sleep here sometimes?" I asked, indicating the trailer as we left.

"No. We just use it as an office, a place to keep food and drinks for the construction crew, when we have one." He glanced at me. "Where are you staying?"

"Room at a hostel."

I hoped he wouldn't offer to put me up in a hotel. He didn't.

We walked to the front of the house. They'd replaced all the siding and trim with solid redwood.

"So you don't have a crew?" I asked.

"Not really," Dean said. "I contracted out most of the exterior work, but that's done. A few guys from a local construction company have been helping me out, but they got busy with another job last week. I'm doing most of the work myself."

"Still a lot to do."

"Yeah. I need to get the electrical work done and floors laid before we can move in. The kitchen, too. I don't want Liv dealing with a bunch of construction work with the baby to take care of and her work at the café. I have a call in to a contractor since I don't have the time to do it myself before our apartment lease expires."

I looked at the house. No aluminum siding here. No linoleum or Formica or laminate floors.

"I can help out," I said. The offer came out before I could even think, as if someone else had just spoken.

Dean looked at me. "Help out?"

"Yeah."

I had nowhere I needed to be, not unless Mick wanted

more help at the garage. I sure as hell didn't want to go back to the desert anytime soon. There wasn't anything to go back *to*.

And, unexpectedly, I was starting to like frilly Mirror Lake with its window boxes and painted white shutters. I liked Liv with her home-baked cookies, and Nicholas with his dragon shirt. I liked sitting on the terrace by the lake, drinking coffee. And though I didn't like my brother much, I could deal with him.

Especially if staying here meant I could see Kelsey March again.

"I've done a lot of construction," I said. "Had jobs laying hardwood and tile. I've done electrical work. Drywall. Painting. There was a house I was supposed to restore near Vegas, but it didn't get finished. I've worked on a lot of other houses, though."

Dean scratched his head. "I thought you were leaving soon."

"I can stay for a couple of weeks." I shifted and shoved my hands into my pockets. "You, uh, you wouldn't have to pay me."

"I wouldn't feel right about not paying you."

"I'm not asking for paid work." I wasn't asking for anything. Except that I didn't want to go back yet. Back to the dry heat and nothing else. "Look, if you let me stay in the trailer, we'll call it even."

"The trailer?"

"Yeah. It's got everything I need, and it'd be much better than the hostel. Hell, it's a palace compared to some of the shitholes I've lived in."

Dean's expression darkened. My fists clenched. I went on the offense.

"I'm not using anymore," I said. "Been clean for almost three years."

Some of his tension seemed to ease.

"That's great, Archer. Good for you."

"I can work," I said.

"I know."

"So?"

I'd never been able to read my brother's thoughts. He had a good poker face when he used it. But he also had a tell. He always shrugged right before he agreed.

He did that now. "Okay. Thanks for offering. I could use the help, especially with summer coming up."

"When do you want me to start?"

"As soon as you can. Let me know when you want to stop by the apartment, and I'll give you the spare key to the trailer."

"Dean, we should get going." Liv approached from the garden, carrying Nicholas over the rocky path. "Nicholas is getting hungry, and I'm working the dinner shift at the café."

Dean tilted his head toward me. "Archer's going to stay in town for a couple of weeks and help with the house."

"Oh, that's wonderful." Liv looked as if she really meant it. "We could use your help with the time crunch and all. Thanks so much."

"Uh, sure."

Liv gave Dean's arm a quick squeeze. "I'm leaving Nicholas with Marianne for a couple of hours, so you can pick him up at her house. Call me if you need me."

Dean leaned closer to her and murmured a response too low for me to hear. I figured I wasn't supposed to hear it anyway.

Liv smiled at him and stood on tiptoe to kiss his cheek before she headed toward the car with the baby. I started to follow when Dean's voice stopped me.

"Archer."

I turned. He leveled his gaze on me with unmistakable warning.

"I appreciate your offer, but you watch yourself around my family," he said. "Because I'll be watching you, too."

I got it. I had a history of asshole behavior. I couldn't hold a job. Slept with a lot of women. Talked our mother into giving me cash. I'd gotten into countless fights, did drugs, spent time in prison for theft. Dean had once beaten the crap out of me after I'd insulted Liv. He had no reason to trust me. No one did.

But I was also fucking *here*.

I took a step away from him, my fists tightening again. "What the hell do you think I'd do, man?"

"I don't know. That's the problem."

I shook my head. I knew coming here was a stupid idea. Knew there would be hundreds of little cuts. Most of which I deserved.

But I'd be damned if I was going to run now.

"You watch me, then," I told Dean, backing away toward the car where his wife was waiting. "You just watch."

CHAPTER FIVE

KELSEY

THE WONDERLAND CAFÉ WAS HOUSED IN A VICTORIAN BUILDING at the corner of Poppy and Emerald Streets. A whimsical sign held by a sculpted white rabbit hung from the roof, and red rockers sat on the front porch. Inside, the first-floor rooms were decorated with murals of the Mad Hatter tea party and Munchkinland, with a painted, "yellow-brick road" staircase leading to the upstairs rooms.

Though I didn't have much to do with the café's daily operations, I dropped by every so often to see how things were going and to sample the newest chocolate confections or cookies. Plus, though I'd never admit it aloud, I liked the crazy bustle of the place, the noise of birthday parties, the lively chatter, and the way Liv and Allie were always sailing around like happy little boats.

Today, however, I had the added motivation of thinking it would be easier to ask Liv rather than Dean about Archer West.

When I went into the café, I found her talking to Max Lyons, Allie's father, whom I hadn't seen in months. A handsome, older man, Max smiled and stood as I approached the front counter.

"Max, Dean told me you were in town," I said, after we had exchanged a brief hug. "Welcome back."

"Thanks. It's good to see you again."

"And you're just in time," Liv added, setting a glass of water in front of me. "We took some ham-and-cheese croissants out of the oven five minutes ago. I'll bring you one."

She glanced from me to Max and hurried toward the kitchen, as if she couldn't wait to leave us alone together.

Max slid his gaze over me. "You look great, Kelsey."

"Thank you." I was suddenly self-conscious. Max and I had gone out a few times months ago before he got busy with a commercial office project in Cleveland that took him out of town frequently.

I remember not being as disappointed by the waning of our brief relationship as I probably should have been. A successful architect, Max was as gentlemanly and responsible as they came. On paper, he was everything I should want, and our dates had been pleasant.

But that was all. Pleasant.

We sat at the counter and talked for a few minutes about his work and mine. And though Max was polite, intelligent, and a good conversationalist, I didn't hear much of what he said because I was too busy wondering what Archer West was doing right that very second.

Archer had said he was staying for a couple of days, so he might already be gone. But he'd also said he was going to *finish it*. What the hell did that mean?

"There's a new place over on Dandelion I've been wanting to try," Max said.

"Excuse me?"

"Friday night," he said, a crease appearing between his eyebrows.

"Friday night?" I repeated.

"I just asked if you'd like to have dinner with me on Friday night," Max said with a resigned smile.

I groaned inwardly, feeling like a terrible person.

"Max, I'm sorry. It's been a rough week."

"I'll take that as a no," he said gently.

"No… I mean, I'd like to…" I sighed. Truth was, I didn't want to go out with Max again, especially not when I couldn't stop thinking about Archer. I wasn't sure I'd want to go out with him even if Archer hadn't shown up in Dean's office.

"It's just a bad time," I admitted. "I'm sorry."

Max stood, dropping a few bills onto the counter. "No problem. Sometimes the timing is off."

"It was good seeing you again," I said truthfully.

"You too." He touched my shoulder and brushed his lips across my cheek. "Take care, Kelsey."

Oh, lord, he was so nice. My mother would love him to pieces.

The thought of my mother intensified my guilt. She would love it even more if I finally settled down and married a man like Max Lyons.

I watched him leave the café. I'd dated a number of men like Max over the years. Kind, well-mannered. Men with good jobs who liked sports and nice dinners. Men whom I always broke up with after I realized I was bored out of my skull.

And that always happened long before I'd considered sleeping with any of them. Hence the reason that it had been three years since I'd been "fucked real good." Or fucked at all. I couldn't even remember the last time it had been "real good."

Oh, but it would be so much more than that with Archer West...

I grabbed my glass of iced water and took a few gulps in the hopes of cooling myself down.

"Here you go. I brought you a strawberry tart, too." Liv came in from the kitchen with two plates of food. "Where did Max go?"

"I don't know. Home, I guess."

"Oh." Liv put the plates in front of me. "He asked about you when he first came in. He seemed quite interested."

"He was. Unfortunately, I wasn't."

"You turned him down?" Her eyebrows rose with surprise.

"Never let it be said I can't make a decision."

"What happened?" Liv asked. "He's such a nice man."

"I know. He's perfect, actually. A perfect gentleman."

"So what happened?"

"Nothing," I said. "That's the problem."

"I don't get it."

No, she wouldn't. I sighed. My sweet, lovely Liv with her trusting nature and heart of a lion. Not for the first time, I wished I had her goodness, her love for stability. I wished I didn't have this dark, urgent pull toward recklessness and danger.

I shook my head. I didn't have that desire anymore. I couldn't. I'd spent so many years trying to eradicate it. I wouldn't let a few encounters with a wild boy unleash my suppressed urges.

Except I was scared shitless they already had.

Liv went to ring up a customer's bill before returning to where I sat. Though I knew she would figure out the reason for my question, I asked it anyway. "Hey, have you seen Dean's brother since he got into town?"

"Yes, he stopped by the apartment yesterday, and we went up to the Butterfly House," Liv said. "Dean told me he showed up in his office without warning. You met him, right?"

I nodded. "In Dean's office. I hit Archer in the head with a door."

Liv grinned. "Good thing he's hard-headed, then."

He was hard everywhere, I thought. A shiver of awareness traveled down my spine.

"So why are you asking about him?" Liv asked.

"No reason." I tried to make my voice light, though I was glad to finally get it out there that he was on my mind. "I mean, he's hot and all, right? But I'm not stupid."

"You're anything but stupid."

"And Archer is a total slacker."

"Huh," Liv mused. "Sounds like something Dean would say."

"It's true, isn't it?"

"I wouldn't make that assumption based on one meeting," Liv said.

I thought of that night in the bar. My blood warmed.

"It is true that Dean has plenty of reasons not to trust Archer," Liv continued. "But as far as I can tell, you don't."

"What does that mean?"

"Just what I said. You sound like you're trying to come up with reasons *not* to be interested in him, even though you obviously are."

"No, I'm not." I shook my head. "He's a disaster waiting to happen."

Liv didn't respond, only looked at me with her thoughtful brown eyes like she knew me better than I knew myself.

"What?" I said.

"That's your life's work, isn't it?" she asked. "It's what you love."

"What is?"

"Disasters waiting to happen."

Irritated, I pushed away from the counter. "My life's work is figuring out how to predict disasters. How to warn people that a tornado is about to hit so they can get out of the way. I've already predicted Archer West, and he's as destructive as they come."

"You'd better get out of the way, then," Liv suggested.

I'd had that chance already. Instead I was afraid I'd put myself right in the tornado's path.

"The van got stuck on a muddy road outside of Muskogee," Colton said. "I had the camcorder in my pocket, but it fell into a puddle when we were trying to push the van out. Ruined all the video. I did get some good stills, though."

He turned the laptop toward me. Luke, Derek, and the others passed around photos and the log they'd compiled.

My conviction about the Spiral Project was solidified every time my students went out into the field. I knew to the core of my being, both emotionally and intellectually, that sending out a fleet of scientists and specialized vehicles to collect data would give us unprecedented insight into how tornados and storms formed. Our findings would lead to ground-breaking forecast improvement and could also launch my scientific reputation to a whole new level.

I wouldn't give up on the project, no matter how tough things got. I couldn't.

After we finished talking about the chase, I opened one of my folders. I had been dreading this announcement for the past few days. My grad students had always been so supportive and excited about tornado research.

"I wish I had better news for you," I said, steeling myself for their disappointment, "but my meeting with SciTech the other day was a disaster. They didn't like my results from the first phase, so they pulled the funding for the Spiral Project."

My students stared at me.

"You mean for good?" Luke asked. "How can they do that?"

"They'd agreed to sustain funding if we had conclusive results from the first phase, which we didn't. So they took the money away."

A ripple of anger passed through the room. I held up my hand.

"That doesn't mean I'm giving up," I assured them. "I've already sent the proposal to five other scientific agencies, including NOAA."

"But if everyone knows that SciTech killed our initial funding, what are the chances of another agency giving us a shot?" Colton asked.

Not good, Colton. Our chances are not good at all.

"I'm going to keep the agencies apprised of new data we're assimilating," I said in a voice I hoped was reassuring. "And things are changing all the time, so I'll keep trying."

That seemed to mollify them somewhat. After we worked for another hour, I gathered my stuff and returned to my office. There was a voicemail from my mother on my cell, and I called her back. Some of my tension eased as we talked in Russian about her activities and her gift shop.

"You will come for a visit soon?" my mother asked.

"I don't think so." Regret twisted inside me. "Not until summer, at least. With the tenure decision coming up and classes, I have a full schedule."

"You work too hard."

"I'm fine, Mama."

She sighed. "You know I worry about you, *dochenka*."

I tightened my fingers on the phone. I suddenly couldn't wait to see my mother again. I'd visited her over the Christmas holiday, but that had been almost five months ago.

Now I had a sudden, sharp longing for my mother's down-to-earth dependability, the way she cupped my face in her hands the minute I walked in the door, studying me for signs of stress, fatigue, worry, whatever. I wanted to be in her little Russian gift shop surrounded by matryoshka dolls, painted lacquer boxes, icons, and embroidered shawls. I wanted her egg bread, blinchki, and borscht.

I wanted her strength. For most of my life, I hadn't known

or acknowledged my mother's strength. She had always been the peacekeeper between my stubborn, iron-willed father and me. But after my father died, and my mother was forced to pull me from the wreckage of self-destruction while also fighting her own battles, I realized she had always been stronger than me and my father combined.

"Kseniya?"

"I'm here." I straightened, clearing my throat. "I'll come and visit as soon as I can."

"The university had better give you a vacation after all this work you do," she said. "I will talk to the board of trustees myself if they do not."

That made me smile. I didn't doubt she would.

"It'll be over soon," I promised.

"Next time you come, you bring me more *pysanky*."

"I will. *Ya tebya lyublyu*."

"*Ya tebya lyublyu*, Kseniya."

I ended the call and logged in to my computer to check email. There was a message from Stan reminding me about the deadline for my tenure review file, and another from the NOAA grant department declining to fund the Spiral Project.

Bitter disappointment flooded me. With a groan, I pressed my palms against my eyes.

I wasn't soft. I'd always been able to deal with shit. I could handle my work, the tenure process, my students, the pressure from my colleagues. I could handle having my research proposals rejected.

But being forced to contend with everything at once, and even thinking about giving up the Spiral Project…

Fuck.

I grabbed my satchel and went outside into the afternoon sunshine. The air and coolness eased some of the prickliness in my nerves. Spring was in full force in Mirror Lake, flowers and trees blooming, and pedestrians strolling on Avalon Street.

I ordered an iced coffee from an outdoor stand and found an empty table on the terrace near the lake. I should have powered up my laptop, but instead I just sat there and looked at everything.

A kid at a nearby table was eating a double-decker ice-cream cone. A college couple was sharing a plate of fries. A guy was sitting by himself near the fence, one booted foot propped on the wrought-iron railing.

Oh.

Not a guy. A *man*. And not just any man. Archer West. A big, sexy Archer West man.

He looked out of place amidst the crowd of families and college students, but he didn't seem to notice or care. A spiral-bound notebook lay open on the table. His body was relaxed, one hand curled around a cardboard cup of coffee, his eyes concealed behind a pair of sunglasses. He wore faded jeans and a navy T-shirt, the sleeves tight around his very well-defined biceps. He lifted the coffee cup to his mouth and swallowed, the muscles of his throat rippling.

Oh times infinity.

I had a flashback to the night when I'd watched him at the bar. I felt that purely *girl* flutter of awareness again, a deep stirring of all my fantasies about sexy rebels who stormed through life on their own terms and made no apologies for it. He was exactly like that. I knew it.

I also knew he was no whitewashed hero. Sexy rebels

always had a dark side. Sometimes too dark. The warning bells rang loud and clear in my head.

Still I watched as he lowered his foot to the ground, the movement stretching his jeans at the thigh. I swore my mouth was watering.

When he stood, I forced my gaze back to my work. I busied myself getting my laptop out of the case, watching Archer's movements from the corner of my eye. He was getting closer… closer…

Oh, lord. My heart thumped harder with every step he took in my direction. I felt like I was in the school cafeteria with the object of my heartbreaking crush walking toward me. I even held my breath as I waited to see if he would notice me, and if he did, if he'd ignore me and keep walking or…

"Professor March."

Never in all my years of teaching had anyone—*anyone*—said my name and title like that. Like he wanted to eat it.

"Archer." I lifted my head, shading my eyes from the sun as I looked at him and putting on my professor voice out of both habit and a twinge of desperation. "I thought you'd be out of town by now."

"Not yet."

He moved to the right, in front of the sun, and I realized he was blocking the glare for me. I lowered my hand. He was in shadow now, a halo of light around him. Dark angel.

He took off his sunglasses, his gaze like a hot caress over my skin.

"Your shirt is unbuttoned again," he remarked.

Oh, crap. While I secretly appreciated that Archer liked my choice of lingerie, I didn't want to get a reputation around the university for showing off my cleavage. I glanced down to fasten the wayward buttons—which were firmly locked into the buttonholes.

"Made you look," Archer said.

I smiled, temporarily disarmed. I looked up again to find him watching me with amusement and a touch of heat. The combination had a devastating effect on my senses.

And even though my reason was still at war with my instinctive attraction to him, I pushed the opposite chair away from the table with my foot.

"Have a seat," I said.

He put the notebook and his coffee down before sinking into the chair.

"What's that?" I asked, nodding toward the five-subject notebook.

"My little black book."

He grinned when my mouth dropped open slightly. I flushed. Apparently I was gullible as all hell where he was concerned.

"What are you doing here?" he asked. "No classes today?"

"No, I just wanted to get some air. My office is pretty stuffy."

"What do you do in your office?"

"Research. Write proposals. Grade exams. Help my students."

"You like the work?"

I'd told him I was a straight shooter. I certainly couldn't lie now.

"I like the forecasting," I said. "I love it, actually. Tracking storms, finding new methods of prediction. I like working with my grad students. I don't like the bureaucracy or the headaches.

I don't like writing proposals or having to publish tons of research papers. I don't like being stuck in a classroom or that other people get to tell me what to do."

"So why did you take a professor job?"

I shrugged, reaching for my coffee. That wasn't a question I could easily answer.

"Stability," I finally said. "And if I get tenure, my position is permanent. I'm set for life."

He didn't respond. I sensed he didn't think being "set for life" was necessarily a good thing. There had once been a time when I didn't, either. When I'd wanted freedom and spontaneity.

"And if you don't get tenure?" Archer asked.

"Then I'm fired from King's."

And the Spiral Project is dead.

An ache prodded at me. I looked at my laptop. The sun made it hard to see the screen.

Then I felt his fingers on my knee. My heart leapt. I jerked my gaze to Archer, who smiled faintly as he reached to cup his hand around my ankle and lift my foot to rest on the chair beside him.

"What..." I swallowed hard. "What are you doing?"

"Touching your leg." He skimmed his fingers over the arch of my foot and a few inches up underneath the hem of my pants. His touch rocketed heat through my entire body, so powerful that I almost gasped.

But I didn't pull away.

"Um... why?" I stammered.

"Because I've wanted to touch you since I first turned around and saw you staring at me," he replied, stroking his hand farther up my pant leg. "Then again when you stormed into Dean's office and whacked me on the head. And because you wear some damn sexy shoes. And because I meant it when I said I was going to finish this."

"What does that mean, exactly?" I asked, trying to inject a sharp note in my voice. "What's your definition of *finish*?"

"It's the principal language of the Finns in Finland."

A laugh burst out of me. It felt good to laugh. I didn't laugh very often. Archer smiled, his eyes crinkling at the corners and giving him a boyish look at odds with his sexy, rough-guy appearance.

He stroked his fingers over the outer arch of my foot again, tracing my skin right beneath where the strap of my sandal crossed. I could feel the ridge of calluses on his fingers. My blood warmed.

"You…" I had to stop and draw in a breath. "You didn't answer my question."

"My definition of *finish*." He leaned forward, lowering his voice to a deep rumble that made me hot and prickly everywhere.

I wanted to arch against him like a cat begging to be scratched. He would scratch so good.

"I want to sleep with you, Kelsey March," he whispered. "After I kiss, bite, and lick you. After I fuck you deep. After I make you come so hard you scream my name. After I make you lose control. That's my definition of *finish*."

CHAPTER SIX

KELSEY

I STARED AT HIM. I COULDN'T THINK PAST THE HEAT FLOODING me, the pounding of my heart, the insanely hot images of my naked body entwined with Archer's… no, not entwined.

I wanted him on top of me, behind me, his big hands gripping my hips. I wanted our bodies to slam together, to writhe, crash, and collide, not *entwine*. I wanted it dirty and rough and so, so hard.

I couldn't speak. Anything that came out of my mouth would have been a moan of lust. I squirmed in my seat, trying to breathe evenly. My wispy panties were not made to withstand the intense, potent effect of Archer West.

He ran his hand up my leg again, his coarse palm eliciting shocks of pleasure with every caress. It took everything in me to pull my foot off the chair, away from his warm touch, away from him.

I lowered my head, focusing on closing my laptop. My hands shook as I shoved it into the case. It caught on the strap. I cursed and tried to untangle the strap, to undo the stuck zipper that refused to budge.

Archer reached across the table and took the laptop from me. With a few quick movements, he unzipped the case and pushed the computer in.

"Come on," he said.

"What?"

"Where's your car?"

"On… on the other side of the street."

He picked up his notebook and the laptop case. We walked back to the street. When I indicated which car was mine, he opened the door and put the case on the passenger seat.

"Go home," he said. "Change into jeans. Boots, if you have them, but real ones. No heels. And bring a jacket."

I could only stare at him. "What for? Where are we going?"

"Meet me back here in half an hour." He glanced at his watch. "Your time starts now."

I noticed he didn't ask if I actually wanted to go… wherever. But since my brain had apparently short-circuited and lost all capability for independent thought, I got into my car and drove home. I was still shaken both by Archer's effect on me and my lack of ability to resist him. Every time he touched me, every time he *looked* at me, I went all weak and soft.

I'd never been weak or soft. And it bothered the hell out of me that I was with him.

I put on jeans, boots, and a King's University fleece before I grabbed a jacket and went back out to my car.

Archer was waiting on a bench where I'd left him, his leg crossed over his thigh in a purely masculine position. As I approached, he stood and tucked his notebook beneath his arm.

"Where are we going?" I asked again.

"I'm taking you for a ride." He slipped his hand beneath my elbow.

I jerked away, irritated. "Look, I get it, okay? You want to get into my pants. And I know I went overboard in the bar, but I'm already tired of you assuming that I'm just going to fall into bed without even a—"

"I meant," Archer interrupted, a smile tugging at his mouth, "a motorcycle ride."

"Oh." I flushed and disliked myself for it. I shot him a glare. "Well, what was I supposed to think with all the foot touching, sexy talk, and everything?"

"Exactly what I hoped you'd think." He stopped beside a beat-up Harley that had dented metal saddlebags and a seat patched with duct tape. He unlatched a saddlebag to put his notebook inside.

"Archer, I—"

He turned to face me. The protest died in my throat. He put his hand beneath my chin and lifted my gaze to his. My heart hammered with a combination of anxiety and anticipation.

"Yeah, I want you," he said softly. "You know exactly what I'm about. And I know you'd never expect more from a guy like me. But I also know you're going to spontaneously combust if you don't *let go*."

"Oh, thank you." Somehow, by digging deep, I managed to sound sarcastic. "Thanks ever so much for looking out for my well-being. I really appreciate knowing you want me to be your charity fuck."

My irritation only made him smile.

"You'd be anything but a charity fuck," he said. "Think about it. You and me. No strings attached, no holds barred. No expectations. I'm leaving town soon, so there wouldn't be any shitty breakup. Just us having fun while I'm here."

"Sounds like a great arrangement for you," I remarked. *And for me, but damned if I'm going to admit it.* "How many times have you used that exact speech on a woman?"

"Never."

"Bullshit."

"I don't need speeches, storm girl." He grabbed a second helmet from a backpack. "I don't play games, either. What you see is what you get."

I already knew that. I'd known the minute I saw him walk into the bar. And oh, how I liked what I saw.

He came around the bike and settled the helmet on my head. A crease of concentration appeared between his eyebrows as he buckled and adjusted the strap beneath my chin. Then he glanced up and saw me watching him.

For a moment, we just looked at each other. I could see the tiny flecks of silver in his eyes, the darker ring of brown around the irises, his incredibly thick eyelashes.

He reached up and took off my glasses, leaning closer as if he wanted to study my eyes without the barrier of glass between us.

I suddenly felt exposed and vulnerable. I tried to grab my glasses back.

"Give those to me."

He looked through the lenses first before settling them back on my nose. "Why do you wear them?"

"So I can see, dumbass."

"The prescription doesn't seem very strong."

I was startled. In truth, my eyesight wasn't that bad. I needed glasses to drive and for seeing far away, but I rarely wore them at home or on weekends. I liked the way they were sort of a shield between me and other people, and they gave me a sharper look that served me well at work.

Apparently Archer West had figured that out.

I straightened the frames. "Well, I need them, okay?"

"Okay." He put on his helmet and nodded to the Harley. "You ever ridden before?"

"Once or twice, but it was long time ago."

"You lean with me and the bike. Keep your feet on the foot pegs. If you need me to stop for any reason, tap me on the thigh. There's a handrail for you, but it's not very reliable. I strongly advise you to hold on to me instead."

He looked at me gravely. Suppressing a smile, I shook my head at him. He responded with a wink and a grin.

Well, crap. There he went disarming me again. One minute, hot sexy promises and the next minute gentle flirting. He kept throwing me off balance, and I both liked and didn't like it.

He swung his leg over the bike and gestured for me to get on behind him. I climbed on, hesitating a second before sliding my arms around his waist.

Oh.

A bolt of desire shot through me. I adjusted my thighs around his hips. He shifted, reaching down to clasp my hands and pull them more securely around him. He interlaced my fingers so my palms were flat against his abdomen—his rock-hard abdomen with muscles so clearly defined under his T-shirt. I exhaled a slow breath, feeling the warmth of him spread up my arms.

"Yes, the… um, the handrail seems a little loose." I hadn't even bothered looking for the stupid handrail.

"Told you." He sounded like he was smiling. "Hold tight."

He revved up the bike and guided it out of the parking lot. He took the ride through downtown slowly. While I appreciated the chance to get used to the feel of the bike and the roar of the engine, I quickly realized that I was dependent on Archer. I had to trust that he knew what he was doing, that he would drive safely, that he wasn't whisking me off to some dark cave where he could have his way with me.

I shifted closer, tightening my arms around him. God, he felt good. Solid, warm, and so strong. He could lift me into his arms without any effort at all. And whisk me off to some dark cave where he could have his—

A laugh choked my throat. Despite the fact that I kept telling myself *I couldn't do this*, it seemed, in fact, that I was.

At a stoplight, he turned his head. "Okay?"

"Yes." More than okay.

He reached back and patted my thigh. Another rush of heat filled me. I leaned against him and forced myself not to think. Though the growl of the bike between my legs was exciting, it didn't compare to the feeling of pressing against Archer's back, the heat of his abdomen warming my palms, the subtle shifts of his muscular body against mine as he drove onto the highway.

I had no idea where he was going. I didn't care. He could have ridden to Canada and I'd have loved just sitting there with my arms around him, the bike roaring beneath us, and the wind whipping past.

I felt free. Open. Unlocked. *Just for now.*

Archer pulled off the highway past Forest Grove and took a two-lane side road through a heavily forested area. After parking in a lot near a ranger's cabin, we both climbed off the bike. The hum of the engine still throbbed in my blood as I pulled off the helmet.

"Where are we?" I asked.

"A state park that I heard about at a hostel." Archer took off his helmet and dragged a hand through his black hair.

He fastened the helmets to the bike, and we started off on one of the trails winding through the trees. It was lovely and quiet, with only the sounds of birds whistling and the faint rustle of the wind.

"What were you doing at a hostel?" I asked, shoving my hands into my jacket pockets as we walked.

"I'm staying in a room there."

"Oh."

I felt his glance. "That bother you?"

"No." I was surprised, though. I'd figured Archer didn't have much money, but surely Dean could…

Shit.

Why was I constantly… and conveniently… forgetting about Dean? That Archer was Dean's *brother*?

"Whoa." Archer stopped and faced me, holding his hands up. "You just went dark on me."

"I was thinking about Dean."

He frowned. "Not what any guy wants to hear when he's alone with a woman."

"I mean… you're Dean's brother."

"So?"

"So Dean and I are friends."

"You've known him how long?"

"Since college. He was a couple of years ahead of me."

"You ever date him?" Though his voice sounded casual, a note of jealousy underscored it.

"No," I said. "I never dated Dean. We're friends. He helped me through some shitty stuff years ago. He's always been a rock. I'd never want to screw things up with him and me."

Archer looked at me for a second. "Okay."

"Okay what?"

"I can't compete with him. Never could. If that's the problem, then I'm out."

I stared at him. "You're out? You mean you'll fold, just like that? Just because I brought up Dean?"

"You want an excuse to stop this whole thing, don't you?" In his eyes was an unmistakable guilt and pain whose source I didn't want to know. "You found the best one, sweetheart. If you're backing off because of Dean, then yeah, I fold."

I couldn't believe what I was hearing. And while part of me was very aware that he was saying exactly what I *should* want to hear, a wave of hurt crashed into me.

"What the hell?" I snapped. "What happened to *I'm going to finish this* and *I want to sleep with you*? You can't come on to me like a fucking hurricane and then fold just because I mention Dean."

"If you're thinking about my goddamned brother when

you're with me, then fuck it, Kelsey. I'm not competing with him. No way."

"I'm not asking you to!"

"Then why did you bring him up?"

"Archer, you *ass*, you didn't think Dean just might be an issue? You knew from the beginning that he and I are friends!"

His features tensed. "I didn't know from the beginning."

I fell silent. My breathing was fast. A sudden yearning hit me—the desire to rewind time and go back with Archer to the corner booth of a bar where we hadn't known anything about each other. Where I'd pressed my thigh against his, and had the courage to touch his tattoo. Where I hadn't been Professor March. Where the world had distilled to a single, hot kiss.

"You made up your mind about me at first," Archer said. "Then you find out I'm Dean's brother, and suddenly I'm nothing but a fuck-up who screws with people."

I swallowed my rising shame. "That's… that's not true."

"No? That's not what you still think?"

I stared at him, my heart racing. Of course it wasn't. In less than three days, Archer West had shaken everything I'd ever heard about him. He'd also tilted my world off its axis, and I wasn't at all certain I wanted it back in place.

"No," I said honestly. "That's not what I still think."

His shoulders relaxed a little. "Well, I still think you're a controlling bitch who hasn't gotten laid in years."

I laughed. "You're not far off the mark, then."

He grinned, his eyes creasing as he approached me. He reached up to take a few strands of my hair between his fingers.

"I also think you're smart, incredibly sexy, and that you

want this to happen as much as I do. We could have one hell of a good time together while I'm here."

My breath shortened. I stared at the pulse beating at the side of his neck and wondered what it would feel like to press my lips against the warm, taut skin there.

"But," Archer continued, "not if you're worried about Dean."

"Not if you give up without a fight, either," I reminded him.

We looked at each other. The sunlight fell through the leaves, casting Archer's strong features in both shadows and light.

"I'll get back in the ring," he said, "if you don't use my brother as an excuse to back off. You don't want to do this? You give me a reason that has to do with *you*. Not him."

At the moment, I couldn't think of any reason at all why it would be a bad idea to start up with Archer West, even if he was only here for a few days. *Especially* if he was only here for a few days.

I knew I *had* plenty of reasons to back off. But standing there with him in the middle of the forest with birds tweeting and the sun practically dancing around us like we were in a Disney movie… not a single reason came to mind.

Then he kissed me. A warm capture of my lips, just like that night in the bar. Except this time I didn't succumb to escape my problems. This time I wanted to be caught. By him. I wanted him to fight for me, pursue me, want me, and capture me.

I parted my lips and let him inside. Heat spread through me, and my head filled with the taste and scent of him. I put my hand against his chest. A shiver ran up my arm at the sensation of his muscles beneath his T-shirt. He was such a man, all hard edges and coiled strength. He cupped his hand against the back of my neck to hold me in place. I let him take the lead, already knowing he would take me somewhere thrilling.

He edged closer, crowding me up against a tree, enveloping me in a cocoon of heat. He moved his mouth with increasing pressure over mine. Lust swirled through me, pooling in my lower body as he nibbled at my lower lip and flicked his tongue out to lick the corner of my mouth. My nipples budded up against the slopes of his chest. A hot, heady pulse throbbed in my blood and centered in my clit. I wanted to strip down right then and there, spread my legs, and let him…

He moved his hands down my sides to grasp my hips. Slowly he pushed his thigh between my legs, rubbing it against my sex. A moan escaped me. I squeezed my legs around his thigh, unable to stop myself from pressing against him. A jolt of electricity sizzled in my veins.

"Come on, storm girl." His voice was husky as he slid his lips across my cheek to my ear, his breath a warm trail over my skin. "Let's finish what we started the other night."

Excitement and a touch of fear rose in me. Though I knew the isolated trail was deserted, I glanced around nervously. Archer took my earlobe between his teeth. My nerves tingled with pleasure. The world felt dizzying, a riot of colors centering on the sensation of Archer's hands on my hips and his body against mine. I drove my fingers into the thick strands of his hair, turning my face toward him.

"Kiss me again," I breathed.

His mouth covered mine. He tightened his grip on my hips and pushed me down on his thigh.

"Christ, I can feel your heat through your jeans," he murmured, his eyes burning as he lifted his head. "I can't wait to touch you. To watch you shatter beneath me."

A hard shiver rocked me. I couldn't even muster up any

indignation over his arrogant assumption that he *would* get into my pants one day.

"Do it," he ordered, shifting his thigh against me. "Make yourself come."

Heat flooded me. The seam of my jeans pressed against my clit. I squirmed, aching, writhing my hips up and down against Archer's thigh, then around in a slow circle. I wanted to prolong the delicious sensations building inside me, wanted to stay here forever, my body sealed to his, but my urgency spun like a vortex. Archer's voice was a deep rumble against my ear as I moved faster, faster…

I gasped. "Oh, I'm…"

His mouth crashed down on mine again, muffling my cry of pleasure as stars burst inside me, a wave of sensation. He held me against him, rubbing his thigh slowly against me while the wave receded. Breathless, I closed my eyes and let my forehead fall against his chest.

I could feel his heart pounding. Warmth rose from his skin. I wanted to slide my hand down to the hard bulge pressing against his jeans, but before I could move, he closed his hands around my shoulders.

"Just in case," he whispered, tugging me upright.

"But you…"

His chuckle brushed against my hair. "I'll survive. Maybe."

We separated reluctantly. I moved away from him, trying to calm the lingering pulses in my blood.

God in heaven. If he could make me so hot with one kiss and without either of us taking off our clothes, what would it be like when we were both naked?

If we were both naked. Not *when*.

"It's getting late," I said, disliking the regret I felt. Regret that had nothing to do with getting sexy with Archer and everything to do with cutting short this impulsive, dizzying time. "I should go home."

We walked slowly to the parking lot. As we got back on the Harley, my mind flickered with questions and rationalizations that I didn't know how to deal with.

Why shouldn't I have a fling with him? I was a grown woman. He'd laid it all out on the line. I knew what I'd be getting into. And I'd been so instantly attracted to him, that hot pull of lust like nothing I'd felt before. With all the crap going on at work, I deserved the mindless pleasure of a good time.

I just didn't know why I was so fucking scared.

CHAPTER SEVEN

ARCHER

AFTER A SATURDAY-AFTERNOON BIKE RIDE, I SHOWERED AND shaved before going to Dean and Liv's apartment before dinner. I half hoped Dean wasn't home. Liv was so much easier to deal with. But when I knocked, Dean called for me to come in. Smoke lingered in the kitchen along with the smell of something burned.

I went into the living room. Dean stood by the bedroom with the squirming baby in his arms. Nicholas was whining and crying.

"What's going on?" I asked. "What's burning?"

"Frozen pizza." Dean shook his head and shifted Nicholas

to his other arm. "Forgot it was in the oven when Nicholas woke up. I can't get him to stop crying. Usually bouncing calms him down."

He looked at the baby and jiggled him. Dean was dressed in torn jeans and a faded, stained T-shirt, and he also looked tired as hell. Not so much the perfect professor.

I approached and peered at Nicholas. The kid's face was red and damp. "Is he hungry?"

"I don't think so. I tried to feed him. Changed him twice."

"Did you burp him?"

Dean shot me a look. "How do you know about burping babies?"

"TV."

"Yeah, I burped him."

"Maybe he's tired."

"He just woke up. He screams louder every time I put him down."

"Could he be teething?" I asked, which I also knew from TV.

"I have no idea." Dean thrust the bundle of baby toward me. "Hold him for a sec, would you? I've needed to take a leak for the past fifteen minutes, but he won't let me put him down."

Hah. Professor West, at the mercy of a baby.

"Take him," Dean snapped at me.

I held up my hands in defense. "I've never held a baby."

"It's not rocket science." Dean grabbed my arms and put Nicholas into the crook of my elbow. Alarmed, I closed my arms around the baby.

"Bounce," Dean called as he headed for the bathroom.

"I don't bounce, man."

"So learn." The bathroom door slammed.

I looked down at the kid. He squirmed and squawked like an upset puppy. I tried to bounce him a little. He cried harder. He was loud for such a small creature.

"Where's Liv?" I asked when Dean returned to the living room.

"Working at the café. Allie's car broke down, so Liv went in to cover for her. I don't want to call her and bug her." Dean stopped, his hands on his hips, and stared down at his son. "You think he's getting sick?"

I had no idea why Dean would think I'd know if Nicholas was getting sick. I shrugged.

"Maybe he just has gas or something." I waited for Dean to take the baby again. He didn't, only continued looking at him with a frown.

"Maybe we should take his temperature," he suggested.

We?

"Uh…" I shifted Nicholas to my other arm and kept bouncing him. Even though it was having no effect, I didn't know what else to do. The baby cried louder.

I raised my voice above the noise. "You sure you don't want to call Liv?"

Dean scowled. "I can handle taking care of my son for a few hours."

"Yeah, you're doing a bang-up job."

His scowl deepened. I figured I couldn't do much worse calming Nicholas down, so I started walking around, still sort of bouncing him.

Dean went into the kitchen and returned with two bottles of beer. He put one on the coffee table and indicated it was mine before taking a swig from the other bottle.

A knock came at the door. Dean left to answer it. I opened the balcony door to let in some fresh air. Nicholas was sweating, and I unzipped his little hoodie so he could feel the breeze.

"What?" Dean groaned. "Oh, shit. I totally forgot."

"I can see that," replied a woman drily. "Unless your new aftershave is Eau de Baby Spit-Up."

A slightly husky voice that scraped my nerves. I'd have known it anywhere. I turned the second she walked into the room.

Jesus. She wore a black dress that hugged her curves in all the right places and fell just above her knees to show off her incredible legs. A strand of pearls draped to her breasts. Her blonde hair was loose around her shoulders with that blue streak like a lightning bolt down one side. She looked stunning. She *was* stunning.

Just the sight of her made me remember how hot and tense she'd felt writhing against my thigh. I tried to shove the memory aside before it overtook me.

Kelsey stopped, the faint surprise on her face quickly hidden by her cool fire. "What are you doing here?"

"Getting a key."

"What key?"

"The key to the trailer." Dean closed the front door and returned to the living room. "Archer's going to stay in the trailer while he's here."

"The trailer at the Butterfly House? Why?"

"I'm going to work on the house for a couple of weeks," I said.

Kelsey stared at me. I smiled at her. Her face reddened. I knew she wasn't the kind of woman who blushed easily. She sure did around me, though.

"A couple of weeks," she repeated.

"He's worked in construction," Dean explained. "He offered to help us get the place finished up."

"Oh." Regaining her composure, Kelsey turned to him. "Well, are you going to get ready or what?"

Dean sighed. "I can't go, Kels. Liv got called into the café, and Nicholas is… well, I don't know what's wrong with him, but…"

He stopped and looked at me. I looked at Nicholas, suddenly realizing he'd stopped crying. His face was still scrunched up, but he was staring outside at the plants on the balcony. Another breeze came into the room. He blinked.

I glanced up. Dean seemed surprised. So was I.

"Well, he was upset earlier," Dean told Kelsey. "I think he might be getting sick."

A crease of concern appeared between Kelsey's eyebrows. She came toward Nicholas and me, reaching out to touch the baby's forehead.

"He doesn't feel warm." She held out her arms.

I shifted Nicholas into them. I liked that she wanted to hold a drooling, damp baby even though she was all dressed up. The woman wasn't afraid to put herself in the line of fire.

She did some female cooing at Nicholas while rocking him. He gazed at her adoringly and gurgled.

"Kelsey, I really can't go," Dean repeated.

"I told you about this dinner four weeks ago," Kelsey said. I could see her feathers getting ruffled as she turned to face him. "It's to welcome the new head of the Physical Sciences College. I already signed up as bringing a date, and if I show up without you, they'll put me next to the chancellor but only because I'm a woman in a science department and not because—"

"I'll go with you," I interrupted.

Both Kelsey and Dean turned to look at me, as if I'd just offered to fly her to the moon.

Didn't think I could rescue a damsel in distress, huh?

"You?" Kelsey asked.

"Yeah, me." I narrowed my eyes at her. She'd kiss me and rub herself against me, but had issues with me going to her fancy university party?

"I can borrow Dean's clothes," I said, looking at my brother. "You've got a bunch of suits, right? One of them should fit me."

"Yeah, but…" Dean glanced at Kelsey. "I don't know if that's a good idea."

"I'm not going to eat with my hands and belch," I told him.

"He means that I drag him to these things because I need someone who's good with the faculty and administration," Kelsey explained. "Professor West can work a university crowd, you know?"

"What I *know*," I said, "is that you're desperate for a date and I'm the only other guy in the room. You want me in or out?"

Kelsey stared at me, her eyes darkening over the implications of that comment. I didn't take my gaze from hers. Her lips parted.

"In," she finally said. "I want you… in."

I wanted in, too. A thousand ways *in*.

"So, Dean, can he borrow a suit?" Kelsey asked.

Dean still didn't look as if he thought too much of this idea, but he couldn't stop me from going. He nodded and jerked his thumb at the bedroom.

"Take whatever clothes you need."

I went into the bedroom and opened the closet, unsurprised to see a bunch of tailored suits all lined up like soldiers. I took out a navy blue suit and white shirt. Glad I'd showered and shaved earlier, I stripped out of my jeans and dressed in the shirt and trousers. They fit okay. I found dark socks in one of the drawers and put on a pair of shoes from the closet. I returned to the living room.

Kelsey and Dean both looked at me. I stopped.

"What?" I asked. "You want me to go, you take what you get."

"No." Kelsey cleared her throat, her gaze sweeping over me. "You… you look great."

"You need a tie," Dean said.

Shit.

"I hate ties," I said.

He shrugged. "You need to wear one."

"You look great," Kelsey repeated, "but Dean's right. Ties are sort of expected at these things."

I returned to the bedroom and grabbed a striped tie from the closet. Embarrassment crept up my chest.

"Hey, Dean?"

"Yeah?"

"Come here a sec."

He came in, holding Nicholas. "What?"

"I… uh, I don't know how to tie a tie. Never had to wear one."

"Oh." He stopped and put Nicholas in a crib by the side of the bed.

He took the tie from me and put it around his neck. After

going to the mirror, he tied a loose knot with a few quick movements. Then he pulled the tie over his head and draped it over mine, fussing with it so that it was under my collar.

"You've worn a tie before," he said.

"When?"

"When Mom and Dad dragged us to the governor's mansion. Mom always made us wear suits and ties."

"Oh, yeah." A memory flickered. Dean and I had both hated those political events. We were expected to sit quietly and not touch anything in the governor's huge mansion. So we sat and fidgeted with our ties and tried to ease our misery by burping and making fart noises under our breath.

"Turn." Dean pushed me toward the mirror and got behind me, reaching around to adjust the tie into a perfect knot. When he was done, he nodded. "Good. Thanks for doing this."

Thanks was a damn sight better than a warning about treating Kelsey well. I'd half expected him to tell me to bring her home by curfew.

Kelsey looked me over again when we returned to the living room.

"Nice," she said. "You clean up well."

"I do other things well, too," I assured her in a low voice as we walked to the door.

"I know." She glanced at me, her cheeks getting pink.

It was fun to get her flustered. Anything unexpected threw off her balance, and I knew I was unexpected.

We went downstairs, and she took her keys from her purse. I extended my hand.

"What?" she asked.

"I'll drive."

"You will not drive. I'll drive."

"You want me to be your date, fine. But when I go out with a woman, I'm the one who drives. Car, bike, boat, whatever."

"Oh, for heaven's sake." Kelsey rolled her eyes, but dropped the keys into my hand.

"You don't like giving in, do you?" I asked. "Don't like giving up either, I'll bet."

"Do *you*?"

"Depends on what it is I'm giving up." I stopped to open the passenger-side door for her.

I caught a whiff of her scent, something clean and sweet that made heat pool in my groin. I deliberately didn't move away as she passed me to get into the car. I could've smelled her all night. Buried my face in her hair, pressed my nose against her neck, breathed her in.

I closed the door behind her and went around to the driver's seat.

"So where is this place?" I reached for the lever to push the seat back as she gave me directions.

We drove in silence for a few minutes. She was tense again. Arms folded, her gaze focused outside the side window.

"I'm not going to act like an ass," I assured her.

"I didn't think you would," she replied. "I would just like to establish that this isn't a *date*."

"The bike ride wasn't a date, either. Neither was the night at the bar." I shot her a smile. "But we had fun, right? I know I did."

"Why are you staying longer than a couple of days?"

Good question. I turned onto the road leading toward the

university. I wasn't about to give her all the answers. I didn't know them myself.

"Because I need to work," I finally said. "Because I don't have to be back in Nevada anytime soon. Because of you."

I sensed her turn to look at me, felt the rise in her tension.

"If that's supposed to be flattering, it's not," she said.

I shrugged. "Take it the way you want to. I told you I'd be straight with you."

"You've been more than straight with me," she muttered. "You've also been arrogant, overbearing, and downright rude. If I were a lady, I'd have slapped you ages ago."

I laughed. "You can slap me now, if you want. I might enjoy it."

A faint smile curved her mouth. "Don't tempt me."

"Are you sure?"

"No."

I pulled the car into a parking space in front of the red brick building of the university club. Neither of us got out right away. I turned to her.

In the dim light of the streetlamps, her features were shadowed, but her eyes burned bright blue. Her full lips, red as cherries, were parted slightly. I looked at her face, her thick eyelashes, the straight, narrow ridge of her nose, the slope of her high cheekbones and jaw. She had a regal look about her, like a princess.

I lowered my gaze to the white curve of her neck, the pearls draped over her breasts.

"Are you checking me out?" she asked.

"I've already checked you out. Completely." I reached out a finger and traced the pearls, skimming the curve of her breast. "Does it scare you?"

"What?"

"That I'm coming on strong."

She didn't respond. I looked at her again. Her features tensed.

"No." She shook her head. "I'm not scared of anything. Least of all you."

She grabbed her purse and got out of the car. I watched as she strode toward the building, all straight-backed determination and ice.

She wouldn't be icy for long. I was going to make her melt.

CHAPTER EIGHT

KELSEY

I COULDN'T STOP LOOKING AT HIM. ARCHER WEST, ALL DRESSED up in his brother's suit.

He looked incredible with his dark hair shining under the lights, and the collar of the white shirt emphasizing the masculine planes of his face. The suit sheathed his muscular body, just a little too tight around his chest.

Even in a suit and tie that he clearly didn't want to wear, he didn't appear subdued or even softened one bit. If anything, the suit underscored his hard edges, the sense of unpredictability and danger that was as much a part of him as his physical appeal. Like a beautiful, crouched tiger about to lunge for its prey.

He pressed a glass of wine into my hand. He dipped his head a little closer to the side of my neck and inhaled. My heart pounded.

"What is it?" His voice was a low, sexy rumble. I almost felt its vibrations against my skin.

"Um… what?"

"Not perfume. What kind of soap?"

"Almond milk and… and honey."

Heat radiated from his body, the leashed energy of his muscles. Even though the air in the hall was artificially cold, I was getting hot from the inside out.

"Hmm." Again that throaty growl that echoed in my blood. "No wonder I'm hungry."

I wanted to give him some smart-aleck retort, but couldn't think of anything. I wanted to move away, but couldn't. I wanted to give him a patented Kelsey March glare and push him away, but…

I moved closer to him. Inhaled. No scent of aftershave on him, just a purely clean, male smell of wind and leaves. A long-suppressed urge sparked to life inside me, the ache of longing for lightning bolts and black storm clouds, heavy rain, and thunderclouds.

Desire for everything that was Archer West.

Alarm bells went off in my head, faint but definitely there, everything Dean had ever told me about his brother combined with my own certain knowledge that Archer West was dangerous. I knew where men like him could take me, and exhilarating as the ride would be, the end was nowhere good.

I stepped away from him. Cold air filled the space between us. I shivered, tightening my fingers on the wineglass.

"So, you'd better come and meet my colleagues." I injected a cool note into my voice and turned to where a group of meteorology professors stood. "They're reviewing me for tenure in a few weeks, which will decide my professional fate. That means I have to be good."

"Pity." His murmur slid over my skin like a kiss.

Holy hell. I knew I was giving him openings, wanting to see where he'd go with them and liking wherever that might be. There was nothing safe about Archer West, and I had always been powerfully and instinctively drawn to the unsafe… until I discovered that it went hand in hand with a pain I didn't want to bear.

I started walking toward the professors, sharply aware of the pulsing between my legs, fighting images of myself tangled in rumpled sheets with Archer on top of me, his deep voice whispering all sorts of dirty things in my ear.

Oh, no. No.

I stopped and forced myself to smile at the professors, the sight of them effectively killing any hot fantasies still lingering in my mind.

"Archer." I grabbed Archer's sleeve and pulled him forward, feeling like I was bringing the sexiest bad boy in school to a math club meeting. "I'd like you to meet the other professors in the Meteorology department. Gentlemen, this is Archer West, Dean West's brother."

I made the introductions. Archer was polite, though I sensed his edginess, his feeling of being in the wrong place, a fish out of water. So different from Dean, who always navigated these events with easy self-assurance, making everyone feel like the center of his attention. That was why I usually brought him—he did the work so I didn't have to.

But Dean wasn't as captivating a date as Archer West. Not even close.

"What do you do?" James Margate asked Archer.

He hesitated for half a second, so brief I wondered if I was the only one who noticed.

"I repair bikes," he said.

"Where?" James asked. "My son just learned how to ride without training wheels."

"No, I mean motorcycles. I repair motorcycles."

"Oh." James looked a little embarrassed. "That's… uh, that's cool."

"Archer is visiting from Nevada," I interjected. "Weren't you in Vegas recently, James?"

"Yes, for the climate change conference." James launched into a recap of the conference.

A few minutes later, the dinner announcement saved us all from further conversation. Archer and I were seated at a table with Chancellor Radcliffe and his wife, plus most of the other meteorology professors.

Archer held my chair out for me before taking his own seat, which I found vaguely irritating. On top of being so sexy he had me wanting to rip off my panties right then and there, he also apparently had some gentlemanly instincts. That was a deadly combination. I'd need every defense in my arsenal to withstand it.

"Professor March, I understand the university board is reviewing your tenure application and file," Chancellor Radcliffe said, looking at me from across the table. A broad-shouldered, bearded man, he possessed a natural air of authority. "I hope to receive their recommendation soon."

I hoped he did, too. When he made the final decision, I would finally learn my fate at King's.

"I understand there was some concern about your teaching commitments," Radcliffe remarked, "and the fulfillment of your contract at King's, due to your preoccupation with a research project."

My stomach knotted. "I'm very committed to King's, sir. You'll find a statement to that effect in my file."

I straightened in preparation for more self-defense, but Radcliffe was distracted by the serving of the salad course. I turned to the woman beside me, Stan's wife, and asked about her nursing job so I wouldn't have to speak to the chancellor again.

I became acutely conscious of Archer's presence on my other side, his voice both deep and cordial as he talked to whoever was sitting beside him.

When the main course was served, I turned to the food. Archer picked up his fork and poked at the fish wrapped in parchment.

"Fish *en papillote*," I said.

"What?"

"That's what it's called. It's a cooking technique of wrapping the fish in parchment. It seals in the moisture."

His mouth tightened a little. "I knew that."

"Oh. Okay."

"You thought I didn't." It wasn't a question.

"No, I just..." I flushed when I realized that was exactly

what I'd thought, and I didn't like that he'd called me out. "You were looking at it like… well, never mind."

"Like I didn't know what it was or how to eat it."

His irritation fueled my own. My skin got hot.

"Well, it's not like you can get it at McDonald's," I replied tartly.

He laughed. His amusement didn't make me any less on edge. I felt him looking at me before he leaned closer, lowering his voice, his shoulder pressing against mine.

A wave of heat poured over me as I turned to look directly into his eyes. Thunderclouds. Lightning bolts.

"Do you ever let go, storm girl?" he murmured in a voice so low I had to ease even closer, determined not to be afraid of whatever he was going to say.

"Ever lose control?" he asked, his gaze tracking over my face. "Ever surrender?"

A thousand shivers fell through me even as I steeled my spine. I didn't take my eyes from his. I saw myself reflected in his dark pupils. I shook my head.

"Never," I whispered. "I never surrender."

A smile curved his beautiful mouth, a smile of both promise and warning. "You will."

I stared at him, shaken by the sense that he spoke the truth.

Muttering an excuse, I pushed my chair back and hurried to the ladies' room. After pressing a damp paper towel on my neck to cool my overheated skin, I gave myself a firm glare in the mirror.

"Get it together, Kelsey," I muttered. "He'll be gone soon. You don't have time for him. Even if you did, you know it would end badly."

Still, as I walked back to the main hall, a little devil inside me prodded hard, again pushing me for reasons to deny what I so obviously wanted.

Why not have fun with him while he's here?

Because I'm a professor up for tenure who doesn't have time to mess around.

He's only here for a couple of weeks. He admitted that he's staying for you. It's not like either of you would ever expect anything more.

I still don't have time. Or the inclination.

Not even if he makes you hotter than any man ever has?

Not even then.

Not even if you haven't had sex in so long you're about to explode with sheer frustration?

Not even then.

Not even if there are no strings attached, no holds barred, no stone left unturned?

Not even then.

Not even if you know it would be hot, sweaty, dirty, and sexy as all hell?

Oh, god. Not even then.

Not even if you're aching to touch him, to feel his hands on you, to spread your legs so he can—

No! Not even then!

You're a fucking idiot, Kelsey March.

After I regained my composure, I returned to the dinner and took my seat. I was grateful to discover that the conversation at the table had again turned to the Vegas climate change conference.

"The conference was sponsored by SciTech." Philip Harris glanced at me. "You didn't go, Kelsey?"

Irritation crawled up my neck. "You know I didn't."

"You should go to the next one," James advised. "Get yourself back into SciTech's good graces."

"I don't need SciTech."

Philip lifted an eyebrow. "You have other funding options for the Spiral Project?"

An unpleasant strain threaded the air. I felt Archer tense beside me. Though the condescending attitude from male scientists still rankled me, I'd become accustomed to it. Of course, not all of them were like that, but my colleagues had been competing with me for seven years, and they knew that most of the time, I got what I wanted.

Which was the reason they were enjoying my failure with the Spiral Project.

"I've sent out my proposal to several other agencies," I told Philip. "When the project is funded again, I'll be sure to let you know."

"What is the project?" Archer asked.

"It's a proposal to fund a fully mobile unit to track and study tornados," I explained. "I want to learn how tornados actually form so we can better predict them. That would have a huge impact on response times and potentially save lives and property."

"Ambitious," Archer remarked.

I almost smiled. "Yes."

"How many investigators have you included in the proposal?" James asked.

"At least fifty, including grad students."

"And you would all go on the road with the unit?" Archer asked.

"The others would do the fieldwork," I said. "I'd stay at King's to assimilate the data from a home base."

"The problem is she hasn't gotten anyone else on board yet, except for her students," Philip told Archer. "If she had some evidence that it could *work*, people would be interested, but so far it's a failure."

"Like the light bulb," Archer said.

Everyone looked at him with faint confusion.

"The light bulb?" Philip repeated.

"Yeah. Thomas Edison failed a thousand times before he invented the light bulb. He actually said he hadn't failed. He'd just found a thousand ways that didn't work before he found one that did. So if this is Professor March's first failure with the Spiral Project, it's only a matter of time before she succeeds."

A glow of appreciation sparked beneath my heart.

"I guarantee you, Mr. West, that no scientific funding agency will support her through a thousand failures," Philip said.

"I guarantee *you*, Dr. Harris, that Professor March won't fail a thousand times," Archer replied. "And if the agencies won't fund her project, she'll find another way."

The men all looked at him. No one else spoke. The glow intensified, surrounding my heart with a nimbus of light.

Another way.

"Professor March isn't afraid to fail," Archer continued. "That's an admirable quality in a scientist. In *anyone*. You could all learn a lesson from her." He pushed his chair back. "Now if you'll excuse us, we have another commitment."

We did?

I was so caught off guard that I didn't think to protest as

Archer went to retrieve our jackets. I managed to say a few quick goodbyes before we left.

I breathed in the evening air, grateful to be away from the noise of the gathering and the company of my colleagues. Archer and I walked toward the parking lot.

I wondered if he sensed that I'd always been on my own when it came to defending myself and my research. In fact, this was the first time I hadn't felt alone.

"Thank you," I said. "For what you did in there."

Archer shrugged. "I just told them the truth."

He wouldn't give anyone anything *but* the truth. I knew that with an instinct as old as time. It was only one of the reasons I was so attracted to him.

"She'll find another way," he'd said.

What if that was also the truth? What if there was another way to fund the Spiral Project? What if I *did* find it?

I brushed my hand against Archer's sleeve, right where the cuff exposed the skin of his wrist.

"I appreciate what you did," I said. "More than I can say."

There were a lot of things I felt around him that couldn't be expressed with words.

We crossed a patch of grass toward my car.

"So, I'll drop you off wherever you're staying." I dug into my purse for the keys. "Or you can drop yourself off, since you'll probably insist on driving again."

Archer extended his hand. I put the keys in his palm. I wondered why I wasn't fighting his overbearing attitude more strongly. Why it felt almost good to have him insist on taking the reins. I went around to the passenger side and waited for him to unlock the doors.

Stopping on the driver's side, he leaned his arms on the roof.

"You know of any clubs around here?" he asked.

"Clubs?"

"Someplace we could listen to some good music. Get a drink. Shake off the professors and small talk and whatever the fuck that fish was."

I smiled. The long-suppressed pleasure of spontaneity rose in me at the thought of heading out for a night on the town.

I tried to think. There were a bunch of clubs on the outskirts of downtown that students frequented, but I didn't want to go somewhere I might see one of them. Professor March didn't hang out at noisy clubs, drinking and dancing with hot, sexy biker guys.

She didn't frequent bars where she stripped such men with her eyes before blatantly stroking their tattoos and sinking into a kiss that—

Professor March didn't do that.

I took a breath. My heartbeat ratcheted up a notch.

"I should..." *I should go home.* That was what I meant to say. Instead, I said, "I should be able to find somewhere we can go."

"Good." He shot me a smile, so warm and striking that I could almost feel my defenses falling away. He'd shed his jacket and tie, and now wore just the trousers and white shirt, unbuttoned at the collar to reveal the strong, tanned column of his throat.

"Thanks for coming with me tonight," I said as we got in the car. "I know it's not your kind of gathering. Not really mine, either, truth be told."

"So why do you go?"

"I have to. Professional networking with the board of trustees and the chancellor. With the final tenure decision coming up, I need to prove I'm a team player."

"Are you?"

"No. But if you hum a few bars, I'll fake it."

He laughed. The warm, rich sound stirred through me, making me feel like I'd just sipped a hot café mocha on a snowy night.

"So where are we going?" he asked.

I pulled up the browser on my phone to find a place. After directing Archer onto the highway leading to Rainwood, he exited near the downtown area.

We parked and walked to the Queen of Hearts club. The sidewalks were crowded with people out on a Saturday night. Laughter and music filtered through the air. Archer rested his hand on the small of my back as we wove through the crowd.

I appreciated that he gave me some space. I'd never liked it when men tried to hold my hand as we walked or put their arm heavily around my shoulders, as if they had to prove they were manly and protective. Archer didn't have to prove anything. He just *was*.

He guided me into the club and paid the cover fee. Inside, colored lights lit the darkness, and couples gyrated on the dance floor. A reggae band was onstage, the rhythmic sounds of Caribbean music thumping.

After getting drinks, we found an empty table. Again, Archer sat close to me, but not too close. It was like he knew I still had boundaries and wouldn't cross them.

Unless I wanted him to.

Which I didn't.

Not even if he would make you ache and throb and probably scream—

Shut up.

I took a swallow of wine and turned my attention to the band. The reggae music was stimulating, the bass line thick and heavy. The beat of the snare drum began to echo inside me.

Archer leaned closer to my ear, raising his voice above the din. "Dance?"

I smiled and nodded. I hadn't danced in ages, but there had been a time when not a weekend passed that I wasn't out on the dance floor. Until I hit the straight and narrow with a precision that a laser would have envied. Anything *fun* got tossed to the wayside as I worked my way through grad school and post-doc positions.

I pushed the thought away and got to my feet. Archer closed his hand around mine, and we worked our way to the dance floor. It was easy to get into the rhythm of dancing with him. He didn't get all up into my space, but took the lead in a way that made it entirely natural to fall into the music.

My blood warmed, and my tension slipped away, all the stress about review boards, proposals, and tenure decisions melting into the primitive beat. The lights flashed in a kaleidoscope of colors. I spun and twisted and twirled. Energy filled me. I welcomed Archer's hands on my hips, his body brushing against mine.

My heart pulsed. Bodies gyrated around us. "Red Red Wine" pounded from the speakers, the heady beat pulling me closer to Archer. In the shifting light, his ruggedly handsome features looked sharper, harder, his eyes hot as coals as he raked his gaze over my body. My breath shortened. Our eyes clashed.

A current of electricity sizzled between us. He slid his hands down my sides, his touch burning a path clear through my dress. I drew in a breath, wanting him to pull me closer. I wanted to feel the length of his body against mine.

I closed the distance, unable to take my gaze from his, those midnight eyes in which I could see myself. My breasts brushed against his chest, a shock of arousal coursing from my hard nipples to my sex. He tightened his hands on my hips, the pressure evoking an unbearable craving to know what his touch would feel like on my bare skin. I wanted to put my arms around him. I wanted to press my cheek against his chest and let him take me to places that were dark, dangerous, and exhilarating.

The heat of his body enveloped me, drew me in. I moved where he moved, both of us swiveling our lower bodies, circling ever closer. My nerves burned. Then he was there, his hips pressed to my stomach, his chest against my breasts. We both slowed, still moving, the noise and dancing around us fading.

And then I felt the swell of his erection against me, a hard, unmistakable ridge pressing into my belly. Lust shot through me like a firebolt. He moved his hands slowly around to my ass and lowered his head, still guiding me to the rhythm of the music, his breath a warm trail over my cheek to my neck. I closed my eyes. My whole body went weak when he pressed his lips to my collarbone.

Oh, god. I was aching. I wanted him to slide his hands under my dress and caress my skin. I wanted him to push his knee between my legs and guide me to writhe against his strong thigh again. I wanted to feel his lips on my breasts, my belly, my—

A moan escaped me, barely audible under the noise of the music, the thumping bass line. I pressed my hand against Archer's chest, felt the warm, rigid slopes of the muscles beneath his shirt, and then without thinking, I slid my hand down to cup the hard bulge pushing against his trousers. His breath hissed out. I leaned my forehead on his chest and closed my eyes.

I couldn't do this. Shouldn't do this...

His hands tightened on me, and when he spoke his voice was a rough growl.

"Let's get out of here."

We couldn't move fast enough. He grabbed my hand and moved through the mass of people crowding the dance floor. I followed blindly, stunned by the intensity of my response to him, the hot fever coursing through my blood.

He got our jackets and hurried us out the front door, the rush of evening air a shock after the noise and heat of the nightclub. I shivered, struck by the sudden sense that I wasn't losing control of this situation. I'd already lost control.

Archer tossed my jacket around my shoulders and led me back to the car. Before I could get in, he pushed me up against the passenger door, his hips hard against mine, his body so big and muscular I knew there would be no escape, even if I'd wanted it.

I didn't. I wanted more. More of his body. More of his touch. More of him.

He stared at me, something feral lighting his dark eyes. He slipped his hand beneath my chin, tilting my face to his. My throat tightened with some indefinable emotion. I suddenly realized that the reason I couldn't remember how long it had been since I'd felt like this was because... I never had.

"You're beautiful," Archer murmured, his husky voice rolling over my skin. He reached up with his other hand to touch the blue streak in my hair. "You're like a creature from some exotic land that no one has discovered yet."

I managed to find my voice through a laugh. "That is the strangest, most amazing compliment I've ever received."

A responding smile tugged at his mouth before he lowered his head and captured my lips in a kiss of fierce possessiveness. I melted, falling against him, giving in to the urge to wind my arms around his neck and thread my fingers through his thick, dark hair. He shifted closer, his hands finding my hips again, sealing our bodies together. It was a kiss of command, of heat, of promise, of lust.

He urged my lips apart with the pressure of his, his tongue against mine bolting arousal to my core. A moan escaped me, sliding from my mouth to his. Our tongues danced as we kissed and licked and sucked. I pressed my hips against his and writhed, aching to feel the length of his hard cock, wishing desperately that I could see it, see him, touch all the planes of his body…

He lifted his head, breaking our kiss. His breathing was hard, rasping against my lips, tension coiling like wire through him. He leaned his forehead against mine and tightened his hands on my shoulders.

I couldn't speak past the heat still filling my throat. I closed my eyes, unable to stand looking into the burning darkness of his gaze.

"What?" I whispered.

"We keep going, I'm going to fuck you right here," he muttered, his voice rough with restraint. "You're so goddamn sexy, you make me forget I have any control."

"We could..." I swallowed hard and opened my eyes to stare at the unfastened buttons of his shirt, the V of tanned skin, the column of his throat where I knew his skin was warm and taut.

"We could go back to my place," I whispered.

Oh, no. No. I couldn't... I wouldn't... no...

"Where do you live?" He nuzzled his nose into my hair, his breath stirring the tendrils around my temple.

"Back... back in Mirror Lake. I—I can tell you how to get there." I knew I couldn't drive. I could barely walk.

Archer moved away from me, the sudden loss of his body heat causing a cold shiver to prickle my skin. He reached around me to unlock the passenger-side door.

"Professor March?"

For a second, the world turned hazy. I blinked. Tried to take in a breath.

"Thought that was you," said a young man's voice. "Whatcha doing out here?"

A blond guy stood nearby with a couple of other college kids, all urban chic in jeans and T-shirts. I forced myself to snap out of the sensual heat in which I'd just been immersed.

I recognized the blond guy as one of my undergrad students from the previous semester. Matt. I cleared my throat and straightened, pushing away from the car.

"Hi, guys. Just out for a night. Thought we'd get out of Mirror Lake." I sensed Archer behind me, but this time his presence wasn't comforting. "Where are you guys going?"

"Over to a bar on East Street," Matt said, his eyes flicking to Archer.

"Have a good time," I said, then because I knew I had to

sound like a professor rather than a horny woman who'd just been making out in a parking lot, I added, "Stay safe."

"We will. Good seeing you."

"You, too." The college kids headed away from us toward the noise and lights of downtown. I was still cold. Behind me, Archer was silent.

I turned to face him. I looked at his beautiful mouth, the angles of his cheekbones, his thick-lashed eyes and eyebrows that mitigated the hard planes of his face. His eyes were shuttered now, as if he knew something had drastically changed.

An ache split through my chest. I wanted to curse, even as the rational part of my brain knew this was a reprieve I would again be grateful for in the morning.

Or at some point. Like a year from now, maybe.

"I… I'm sorry," I stammered. "I should go home alone."

Archer tilted his head in the direction the guys had gone. "Because of a few college kids?"

"They probably saw us kissing."

"So?"

"They'll talk."

"So?" Irritation darkened his eyes. "Kissing won't get you in trouble."

"No, but… I don't need it getting around that Professor March was busy making out in a parking lot on Saturday night."

He pushed away from the car. "You don't need it getting around that you were making out with me."

"No!" A spark of anger flared. "This isn't about you, Archer, believe it or not. I'm a professor… a good one. No. A great one. My students respect me. I've worked hard for my reputation, and I don't want it getting around that I'm anything less than professional."

"Jesus, Kelsey. You need to be a professor even when you're off the clock?"

"I'm always on the clock."

Archer looked at me, his eyes filled with frustration. Then he yanked open the passenger-side door and indicated that I should get in. I did, my hands shaking as I pulled on the seatbelt and waited for him to start the car.

I didn't know how to explain it. I couldn't. It was more than just a few guys catching Archer and me in a parking lot. For all I knew, they'd forgotten about the incident already, and even if they didn't, they probably couldn't have cared less what I was doing or with whom.

No. It was slipping into the uncontrollable that scared the living shit out of me, the knowledge that I'd been about to take a wild, reckless plunge over the edge. And the unbearable, aching sense that I'd love every second of it, even knowing the fall would hurt like hell.

Because there was always a fall. Always a price to pay.

We drove out of Rainwood in silence. I spoke only to tell Archer how to get to my house on Mousehole Lane. When he pulled up to the driveway, I fumbled for my jacket and purse.

"I'm sorry," I repeated. "I know I was… I mean, I…"

Christ. I stammered more with this man than I ever had in my life. I couldn't form a sentence around him. I could hardly grab a coherent thought.

Get it together, Professor March.

"Archer, thank you for coming with me tonight," I said, forcing my voice to remain steady. "I apologize for leading you on again. I'm not… I'm not always myself when I'm with you."

"Yeah, you are. You just don't know it yet."

My stomach knotted. *A girl who took risks and faced challenges without fear…*

"Well, good night." I took hold of the door handle. "You can borrow my car to get wherever you need to go. You can either bring it back here tomorrow or leave it at Liv and Dean's."

I started to push the door open when his hand enclosed my wrist. I turned back to him. He was watching me, his face shadowed and his expression unreadable.

"Does the offer to come in still stand?" he asked.

"Archer, I said I—"

He held up his other hand in the gesture of a pledge. "I won't touch you. We haven't had a chance to talk all evening. Give me an hour alone with you with no one else around."

Something shifted inside me as I gazed at him, at his eyes that almost glittered in the night. I wanted to be alone with him, too. And while there was a whole hell of a lot I wanted to *do* with him, I was absolutely certain he wouldn't break his promise.

"Just to talk," I said, in case there was any misunderstanding.

"Just to talk. Though I won't turn down something to eat, if you were to offer it. That dinner wasn't enough to feed a cat."

"Okay." I let out a breath. "Eat and talk only."

"Okay. But I have to warn you that I'm still hard."

My heart jolted, my gaze snapping involuntarily to his lap. It was too dark to see anything. I forced my eyes back to his face.

Archer winked at me. "Made you look."

CHAPTER NINE

KELSEY

HE LOOKED GOOD IN MY HOUSE. I OWNED A CRAFTSMAN-STYLE bungalow that I'd fallen in love with because of the hardwood floors and built-in bookshelves, the bay windows, and decorative trim. A few men had been here over the years—though none in my bedroom.

And none of them had looked the way Archer did as he walked around, studying the architectural details, the paintings, the family pictures, the souvenirs I'd brought back from various trips.

He was wholly masculine, his hands in the pockets of

his trousers, his white shirt wrinkled now but still astonishingly sexy with the top buttons undone and the material tight enough to reveal the planes of his chest.

To avoid gawking at him, I disappeared into the bedroom to change. I stood staring at my closet, wondering what to wear. Should I go casual with jeans and a T-shirt or put on another dress or…

I shook my head at myself. It didn't matter. Well… it shouldn't matter. As if trying to drive that point home, I pulled on a pair of black yoga pants and a stretchy, dark blue shirt that had a rip near the hem. Exactly what I'd change into after a day of work when I didn't care what I looked like.

Except when I stepped back into the living room, Archer's gaze slipped appreciatively over me. Everything inside me responded to that look. I hurried to the kitchen and opened the refrigerator.

"How about eggs?" I called. "I can make an omelet."

"Sure." He appeared in the kitchen doorway, leaning his shoulder against the doorjamb. "This is a really nice place."

"Thanks. I bought it when I first moved here." I busied myself cracking eggs and getting out cheese and tomatoes.

"Anything I can do?" he asked.

I nodded toward a loaf of bakery bread. "You can slice that. Knives are in the drawer by the stove."

We worked in companionable silence for a few minutes. Though Archer was big, he fit well in my kitchen, moving with his easy masculine grace and making sure we didn't get in each other's space.

"So what made you become a meteorologist?" he asked.

I didn't answer right away. It was a personal question, and

I didn't get into personal stuff with just anyone. But Archer West wasn't *just anyone*.

"My parents were from Russia," I finally said, finding it easier to tell him more since we were both busy working. "We immigrated here when I was two. Neither of my parents knew much English, but they found an apartment that had cable included in the rent. My father discovered The Weather Channel. He loved it. Watched all the shows about weather phenomena and forecasting. That was how both he and my mother learned a lot of English. They'd even talk about the weather at the dinner table. So I grew up with it. Guess it was a natural fit."

"Your father must be really proud of you."

The comment caught me off guard. Secretly I'd always imagined that my father would be proud of what I'd accomplished, but to hear it from Archer felt like he'd looked right into my heart.

"My father died when I was a junior in college." I turned away so Archer couldn't see my face. "He had a heart attack."

"Oh. I'm sorry."

I shrugged. "My mother lives near Chicago. It's about a five-hour drive."

"You visit her a lot?"

"I try to. Hey, do you like bacon?"

"I love bacon. It gives me a lard-on."

I chuckled and took another pan from the cabinet. After we'd made a big, cheesy omelet, crispy bacon, and thick-cut toast, we filled our plates.

"Have a seat." I tilted my head toward the breakfast nook, a polished walnut table tucked beneath a half circle of windows.

Archer eased his tall frame onto one of the bench seats, putting my plate at the seat across from him.

"What do you want to drink?" I asked, peering into the refrigerator.

"Got any chocolate milk?"

"Chocolate milk?" I straightened and looked at him over the top of the refrigerator door. "What are you... ten years old?"

He gave me an engaging grin. God, he was cute. One minute he had me all hot, breathless, and writhing shamelessly against him, and the next minute he had me wanting to hold his hand and share an ice-cream sundae.

"I don't have any chocolate milk," I told him. "But wait a sec."

I rummaged in the cupboard and found an unopened container of hot cocoa mix. I made two mugs of cocoa in the microwave and joined him at the table.

"So where in Russia were your parents from?" he asked.

"Near St. Petersburg."

"You're an only child?"

I nodded. "My parents thought they couldn't have children, so after years of trying, I was quite a surprise. They immigrated because they wanted me to have a better life and a good education."

"Kelsey March doesn't sound like a Russian name."

"My father's last name was Markovich. Like many immigrants, he wanted to change it when he became a citizen. And because I was born in March, he changed it to March."

"And Kelsey?"

I picked at a crust of toast. "My real name is Kseniya. But I went to a school full of Emmas and Allisons, and... among other things, I didn't want my name to be so different. After I read a picture book about a girl named Kelsey, I told everyone to start calling me Kelsey."

"Including your parents?"

"They still called me Kseniya at home. But at school and in public, they called me Kelsey."

I felt him watching me, probing for all the things I wasn't saying.

"It sounds like your parents succeeded in giving you everything they'd wanted," he said.

I nodded. "When they moved to America, they couldn't afford a house in a good school district, but they were determined that I'd have the best education they could manage.

"So my father found a job as a janitor at a highly ranked school in an upper-class neighborhood outside Chicago. He was a strong-willed man, incredibly tenacious. He convinced the principal to sponsor him for residency and petitioned to let me attend the school, even though we didn't live in the district. A few months later, my mother began working at the school's lunch counter. And I started kindergarten there."

"That's when you wanted to change your name?" Archer asked.

I nodded, disliking the echo of old shame. "The other kids lived in big houses. Had parents who were doctors or corporate bigwigs. I was the girl who lived in a tiny apartment in a rough neighborhood. My parents had funny accents. My father was the school janitor and my mother was the lunch lady. I knew early on I'd be an easy target if I didn't do something first."

"So what did you do?"

"I became kind of a daredevil," I said. "Known for taking risks. I knew it'd be a way to get attention, even admiration. I was the kid who climbed the highest tree, walked on a roofline, jumped into a lake from the highest rock. And when I outgrew that, I became the rebel girl with a bad attitude.

"I was always a good student. Academics were easy for me, and I even skipped a grade. But I made everything else difficult. I got into fights. I made sure all the other kids were scared of me so they wouldn't give me crap. I started dying my hair in fifth grade. Wore ripped clothes, makeup, lots of black… so-called tough-chick stuff."

I looked out the window, seeing my face reflected against the dark glass. I remembered that girl, the one who wanted to be so adventurous, who didn't care what people thought of her, who wasn't scared of anything. Sometimes I even missed her.

"What did your parents think of all that?" Archer asked.

"It upset them," I admitted. "My father and I fought about it all the time. He wanted me to be a good, respectable girl. I knew my behavior pushed his buttons, which was probably part of the reason I acted out. My mother always tried to keep the peace between us. When I was offered several scholarships into college, my father eased up for a while."

"Until… ?" Archer asked.

I shook my head. I'd already told him far more than I'd ever intended.

I pushed my plate away. I wanted to ask Archer questions too, to find out more about him, to figure out why he was so different from Dean.

I shoved my curiosity back down. Knowledge created intimacy, and intimacy with a man like Archer West was dangerous.

I stood and picked up my plate. "Are you done?"

When he nodded, I brought our plates to the kitchen. We took our mugs into the living room and sat on the sofa. Archer stretched out opposite me, his long legs crossed at the ankle and his eyes closed.

Surely there was a way to know him without *knowing* him…

"What's your favorite band?" I asked impulsively.

"Stones. The Foo Fighters. You?"

"The Backstreet Boys."

He opened his eyes to look at me. I grinned. He shook his head.

"Liar," he murmured.

"I know you are, but what am I?"

We both laughed. A warm, rich pleasure filled me. I realized I'd laughed with him more in the past few days than I usually did in an entire week.

"Favorite food?" I asked.

"Pizza," he replied. "You?"

"Anything sweet."

"Really?"

"Yeah." I slanted him a glance. "Why are you surprised?"

"I thought you'd like something spicy like salsa or curry."

"Why?"

"Because you're incredibly hot." He slid his gaze down my body.

I tried to conceal my embarrassed pleasure with a slight cough. "So, um, favorite book?"

"*The Dark Knight Returns.*"

"Isn't that a movie?"

"It's one of the best vintage comics of the '80s. Frank Miller's finest. Batman comes out of retirement for one last vigilante crusade."

"You're a comic book aficionado?"

"Not so much." Archer shrugged. "I liked them when I was a kid. Dean and I used to draw our own comics sometimes." He took a swallow of hot cocoa. "What's your favorite movie?"

"Hmm. *Aliens*, probably."

"Not *Twister*?"

"*Twister*? No."

"Really?" Archer looked at me askance. "That movie is epic. Remember the flying cows? How can a tornado specialist not love *Twister*?"

"Because said tornado specialist is intelligent."

Archer groaned and thumped his chest. "You're killing me, Professor March. Flying *cows*."

"Udderly ridiculous."

He chuckled. I winked at him.

We talked for the next hour, exchanging favorite colors, TV shows, sports, cities, and seasons. Then we agreed to watch a movie, and though I was aware Archer had well exceeded his allotted "hour," I didn't want him to leave. We found a good car-racing action flick, both of us remaining firmly on either side of the sofa for the duration of the movie.

It was nice. Too nice. Tame and warm and... comfortable. I wasn't supposed to be comfortable with dangerous Archer West. Who, as it turned out, was proving to be *not dangerous* at all.

As if that weren't strange enough, the situation slipped into downright *cozy* when I woke up with my head pillowed against his strong thigh.

I blinked, trying to push aside the haze of sleep and focus.

His thigh was warm under my cheek, and there was a gentle weight on my hair that I slowly realized was Archer's hand.

Good. Everything about it felt good.

Morning sunlight glowed through the windows. An infomercial was on TV. Though I didn't want to move, I fumbled for the remote and turned off the TV. Archer shifted against me.

Embarrassment hit me. I sat up quickly, not looking at him as I shoved up from the sofa. I grabbed my glasses, which had somehow ended up on the coffee table, and put them on before turning to face him.

He was scrubbing his hands over his jaw, looking rumpled and mildly surprised. He rubbed his eyes before lowering his hands. Our gazes met.

"Hi," I said weakly.

"Hi." He pushed to the edge of the sofa. "I don't remember falling asleep."

"Neither do I." I gestured to the hall bathroom. "There should be an extra toothbrush in the drawer. I'm just going to go change."

I hurried into the other bathroom to brush my teeth and hair. I couldn't remember the last time I'd had to deal with a morning after, even though technically this didn't qualify.

Or did it? Deciding to try and act as normal as possible, I went to the kitchen to make a pot of coffee and clean up the dirty dishes from the previous night. Out of the corner of my eye, I saw Archer's broad frame fill the kitchen doorway.

"I'm making coffee," I said unnecessarily, gesturing to the full pot.

"Great." He leaned his shoulder against the doorjamb in that lazy way of his. His jaw was stubbly, his black hair ruffled and slightly damp, his shirt wrinkled. He looked edible, like a messy, decadent chocolate cake that I wanted to dive into headfirst.

"I guess we already had breakfast last night," I remarked.

"Yeah. And we slept together before we had sex. We even kissed before we knew each other's names. Seems we're doing everything backward."

Which was not the way I did things. Ever. Or at least… until Archer.

I poured a cup of coffee and handed it to him. I was pouring myself a cup when the doorbell rang. I went to answer it, easing past Archer in the doorway.

He moved only slightly, his gaze holding mine as our bodies brushed together. Heat zinged through my veins instantly at the light contact, the sensation of his muscular chest against my breasts.

"Tease," I whispered.

"Takes one to know one."

I shook my head at him, trying not to smile as I went to answer the door. I pulled the door open. Shock hit me at the sight of Dean standing on the front porch.

CHAPTER TEN

KELSEY

"HEY." DEAN WAS WEARING TRACK PANTS AND A RUNNING jacket, his hands shoved into the pockets. He glanced at my clothes. "I thought you were going running with me this morning."

"Oh." I could hardly form a thought, let alone a sentence. "Sorry, I… uh, I guess I forgot."

He glanced at his watch. "I'm early. I'll wait for you to change."

"No, I don't think I—"

Dean's gaze shifted past me. Warily, I turned. Archer still stood in the kitchen doorway, except now he was facing us.

Tension seized the air. My stomach knotted. I looked at Dean. I saw every single assessment clicking together in his brain. Archer was wearing his trousers and shirt from the previous night. He'd clearly just woken up. He was holding a cup of coffee. I was standing there looking like I'd just rolled out of bed…

I held up a hand. "Dean, I can explain."

"You're not the one who has to explain," he said.

Archer frowned, his expression darkening. "I don't have to explain anything to you, man."

I stepped closer to the middle of the doorway. "Dean, it's okay."

He shifted his gaze from Archer to me. More than anger, I saw the concern in his eyes. And I felt Archer's defenses locking into place like steel gates.

"I had her home by curfew, big brother," he said, lowering his head to swallow some coffee. "Next time, you want to give me a monitoring bracelet? I've worn one before."

Dean's mouth tightened. Hostility sparked between them. It was my worst fear coming to life, and Archer and I hadn't even done anything. Much.

I put my hand on Dean's chest and shoved. The push caught him off guard, forcing him back. I stepped onto the porch and slammed the door behind me.

"Don't," I said. "We're not in college anymore. I'm a grown woman. I know what I'm doing."

I didn't, actually, at least not where Archer was concerned. But I had to figure it out by myself. Not because Dean was launching into guardian angel mode.

"Archer's had a lot of trouble, Kelsey," he warned.

"I know."

"Doesn't that matter?" Dean paced to the porch railing, his shoulders tense. "Look, I take plenty of blame for his life getting messed up, but at some point, you have to man up and get your shit together. He never has. I doubt he ever will."

"Wow. Nice show of brotherly support."

Dean sighed, pulling a hand through his hair. "He's had chances. Plenty of them. He mooched money off our mother for years. Never had a steady job, as far as I can tell. He's here because he wants his inheritance money, but he has to actually work to earn it. He's never lifted a finger to try."

"It sounds like he is now, if he's working on the house with you."

Dean shook his head. "I know him, Kelsey. I know what he—"

"No," I interrupted, and suddenly I'd never felt so certain of anything since the second I'd encountered Archer West.

"You don't know him, Dean. You don't. What you've done is just assume he's been a fuck-up all these years. When was the last time you had a real conversation with him? When was the last time you gave him a chance?"

"I'm giving him one now."

"Not if you think he's incapable of change, you're not."

Silence fell. Dean crossed his arms, still frowning. I took a deep breath. The sky was starting to lighten to a pale gray. I backed toward the door.

"You don't know him, Dean, but you know me. You know I don't have any illusions or expectations. You know how strong my defenses are. And you know better than anyone how much I hate making mistakes."

He didn't respond.

"I'm not going to make one now." I put my hand on the doorknob. "And I can't change what you think about your brother. But I know you won't ruin fifteen years of friendship by not trusting me."

"It's not you I don't trust," he said. "Just be careful. And you come to me if anything happens, okay?"

"No, I won't. I'm an adult. I'm not that college girl who was so messed up she couldn't think straight. I've been thinking clearly for years now. Any decision I make is mine. Now go run it off. I'll call you later."

I wasn't at all sure he'd go, but he started down the front steps, his body still tense.

"Hey," I called.

He turned. For a second, I couldn't speak. I had to be straight with him. I approached him, mustering up the courage to tell him the truth even though I was having a hard time admitting it to myself.

"I've always been attracted to men like him," I said. "But I learned a long time ago how to protect myself. And I wouldn't start anything with him if I didn't *know* I could handle it."

Dean shook his head, slanting his gaze to the door again.

"It's not like you and Liv," I continued. "There's no hearts and flowers here. No happy ending."

"Then why, Kelsey?" Dean spread his hands out in frustration. "What's the point?"

To feel alive. Exhilarated. To stand in the middle of the storm, breathless, your heart beating hard and your blood streaming hot.

I knew Archer would understand that. I knew we both wanted it.

Dean and I looked at each other for a long minute before he appeared to realize I wasn't going to answer that question. I couldn't.

"I don't want you to get hurt," he finally said.

"I won't." I tapped my chest. "Armor of steel, right?"

A faint resignation appeared in his eyes that made my stomach twist. Dean was never resigned, and I didn't like that he was with me.

At the same time, I would hold my ground because everything I'd told him was the truth. And I would keep my promise to Archer by not using Dean as an excuse. This was about me, not him.

"You're my best friend, Dean," I said, disliking the anxiety constricting my chest. "You and Liv. If anything… I mean, if it would cause problems between us—"

"Kelsey." Some of the tension eased from his shoulders as he closed his hands around my upper arms. "Archer and I have been estranged for years. I've never known how to fix our relationship. But if you think for one second I would ever let him come between you and me, no matter what happens, then I'm telling the university to fire you because you're a complete bonehead."

I smiled. The tightness around my heart eased.

"Okay?" Dean said.

"Okay."

"I'm going to hug you now."

"Okay."

He enveloped me in a bear hug, then moved away and pointed to the door. "But you tell him if he hurts you, I'm going medieval on his ass."

"I don't think he needs me to tell him that."

Dean nodded then headed down the street. I went back into the house, my nerves tensing again. Archer no longer stood in the doorway.

I found him sitting at the breakfast nook, coffee mug in hand. He was looking out the window at the garden, but he turned when I entered. I saw his defenses locking into place. Mine were still up.

"How much of that did you hear?" I asked.

"None of it. I want to hear it from you, not him."

I let out my breath, rubbing my damp palms over my thighs. He eyed me warily. I joined him at the table, sliding into the seat across from him.

"So how is it your brother is Dudley Do-Right and you're Mad Max?" I asked.

He smiled faintly, but his expression darkened. I sensed it wasn't so much the question that caused his unease, but the answer.

"Dean never told you?" he asked.

"About what?"

"He and I have different biological fathers."

"Oh."

"My mother had an affair." He sighed, rubbing a hand down his face. "She got pregnant with me, but stayed married to Richard West. Dean and Paige's father. He was up for a seat on the California Supreme Court. They needed her family's money. Didn't need a bunch of gossip. My paternity was a big secret. I might never have found out the truth if Dean hadn't told me."

"Dean told you?"

He nodded. "When I was nine. He was thirteen. I broke his video game console on purpose. We got into a fight, and he told me our father wasn't *my* father."

I tried to get my brain around that revelation. I couldn't imagine Dean doing such a thing. "What happened then?"

"Everything got fucked up after that. But we kept the secret. No one knew."

"Did you ever find out about your biological father?" I asked.

"My mother told me about him when I was nineteen. He was an old high school boyfriend she hooked up with. The affair lasted six months. She never saw him again."

"Did you ever try and find him?"

"Once, when I was in my early twenties. He worked some office job in Sacramento. I never bothered contacting him. Didn't see the point. My mother always told me Richard West was the man who raised me, fed me, et cetera, which made him my father. I finally figured out she was right."

"But you weren't close to him."

"No. And when I figured out it was easier to be a troublemaker than to compete with Dean..." He shrugged.

I understood it, the pull toward rebellion. I'd rebelled for a whole host of very different reasons—to armor myself against other kids, to prove my independence from my parents, even sometimes just to clash with my father. And then I'd been hit hard by the realization of how badly such behavior could hurt other people.

I rubbed my finger over a crack in the table. I didn't want to push this, didn't want to ask, didn't want to know. But the question mushroomed in the back of my mind like a noxious cloud.

"Are you doing this to fuck with him?" I asked.

Archer lifted his head. "What?"

"Me." I couldn't look at him. "You know Dean and I are close. Are you..." *shit shit shit* "...pushing things with me because you want to get to him? Because you know it'll piss him off?"

If I'd expected an instant denial, I didn't get it. Instead Archer looked out the window again, almost as if he was actually wondering how to answer that. My chest constricted.

"I did that with Liv once," he finally said.

"What?"

"The first time I met her," he said. "Dean had brought her home for Thanksgiving one year. I knew they were getting serious. I figured out pretty fast I could get to him through her. So I did. I insulted her, and he beat the crap out of me."

I wasn't surprised. Not by Archer's hostility or Dean's rage. Archer would needle Dean every chance he got. And of course Dean would never let an insult go unpunished, especially one directed at Liv.

"He messed me up pretty bad," Archer continued. "Broke my nose. But it felt good to light his fuse. To make the perfect Dean West lose his shit. It wasn't the first time I'd done that."

Pain and sorrow stabbed through me. I hated knowing that Dean and Archer's troubles had lasted for so many years, breaking apart two brothers who might have otherwise been friends.

I studied Archer's face, seeing the slight bump on the bridge of his nose that was apparently evidence of this epic beating. The imperfection only added to his rugged beauty, and I found my gaze sliding down to the wide sensuality of his mouth, the prickle of whiskers darkening his jaw.

"That..." My ridiculously active heart had increased in pace again. "That still doesn't answer my question."

"No." He turned, a sudden and intense light in his eyes. "I'm not using you to get to Dean. Yeah, I've done stuff like that before. A lot. But I'm not doing it with you."

With everything I had, I wanted to believe him. And with everything I knew, I wasn't at all certain I could.

He knew it, too. I felt his gaze like the most potent of touches.

"Hey." His voice was soft.

I looked up at him. I wanted to drown in the midnight dark of his eyes.

"I'm not using you." He made an X over his heart. "Cross my heart and hope to die."

"You're still leaving in a couple of weeks, right?"

He nodded. "As soon as I'm done working on the house."

"Okay." I exhaled a slow breath. "I have rules."

"I figured you would."

"I don't want to get into any more personal stuff." I held his gaze, keeping my voice steady in spite of my wild, racing heart. "We only do it at my house and only at night. No motels or anything creepy like that. You can stay the night if you want to, but when I leave in the morning, you leave too. No calling me when I'm at work. If you want to reach me, use email. And I'm in charge of the remote."

For what seemed like a very long time, he didn't respond. He only looked at me with the morning sunlight sparking in his eyes and his arms folded loosely across his chest. When he finally spoke, his voice was smoke and honey sliding over my skin.

"No."

I blinked. "No?"

"You don't make the rules," he said.

"Of course I make the rules."

"No."

"Archer!" I put up my hands in frustration. "I am *this close* to caving and finally agreeing to sleep with you after a week of you sniffing around me like a dog digging for a bone, and now you're going to argue with me when I try to establish some boundaries?"

He nodded.

"Well." I slammed my palms on the table and pushed to my feet. "If that's the way you're going to be, then I—"

He was out of his seat in a flash, faster than I could even take my next breath, and then he was pressing me up against the counter, all heat and dark eyes and that insane, potent masculinity that ran through his veins. He cupped my hips in his hands, his breath warm against my forehead, and then he pushed our lower bodies together.

Oh, god. He was already hard. So hard. A thick, heavy ridge against my belly. I struggled for air, reaching behind me to grip the counter.

"You don't make the rules, storm girl," he repeated, lowering his head to trail his lips against my neck. "You don't do anything but what I tell you to."

My heart crashed against my ribs. "Um… what?"

"We're doing this my way," he said, shifting so that his cock rubbed against me. He nipped at my collarbone, his husky voice muffled, his whiskers scraping deliciously against my skin. "You're not allowed to tell me what to do. You don't say where it happens or when it happens. You don't even get to decide *what* happens. There's only one thing you get to do."

"What… what is that?" I could barely form the words past the heat filling my chest.

"Surrender." He moved his lips up my cheek before capturing my mouth with his.

Lightning streaked through my blood. A moan escaped me as his warm, delicious lips moved against mine, his hands curving around to my ass. I couldn't have resisted if I'd tried. I just melted, sliding my arms around his waist and falling into the kiss as if it were a place I'd already been and had deeply missed. My veins surged with desire, heat sparking as our mouths moved together with increasing urgency.

This… this was what I'd wanted since the moment I first saw him, the full press of his solid, muscular body against mine, the warmth of him engulfing me, the increasing pressure of his kiss as he parted my lips with his and drove his tongue in deep.

My heart hammered. I couldn't remember ever being kissed like this, with such all-consuming fervor, like he wanted to possess me. I closed my lips around his tongue and sucked. He groaned, tightening his hands on my ass. My tight nipples rubbed against his chest, and pure, white-hot desire flooded me to the core.

"Oh, god." I pulled my mouth from his with a groan. "All right, all right. I give in."

"Don't give in," he murmured, brushing his mouth against my lower lip. "Give *over*."

He lifted his head, his eyes smoky as he cupped my breast in his hand and pinched my nipple. An electric current rippled through me. I stared at him, flushed and so hot my entire body throbbed.

"You ready?" he whispered.

I couldn't speak. I could only nod. He grasped my hips and lifted me onto the counter, pushing my legs apart and moving between them. He eased his hand beneath the hem of my stretchy shirt.

The second his callused fingers made contact with my bare torso, I shuddered in response. I could hear my heartbeat pounding, could feel the rush of blood pooling in my lower body.

I didn't know what would happen next, if he'd slide his hand upward or… he went down, his fingers dipping below the waistband of my yoga pants. He smiled slightly, holding my gaze as he traced the lacy edge of my panties.

"You always wear sexy underwear?" he asked.

Jesus, his tickling touch was killing me. I squirmed, hooking my legs around his thighs and looking hungrily at the bulge in his trousers. "Most… most of the time."

He traced a line from my belly button down between my legs, where the satin of my panties was already wet. I flushed, a little embarrassed by my easy arousal, but Archer's quick intake of breath indicated his appreciation. He slid his finger down the crevice of my sex, once, twice, a slow easy rhythm that had me arching my hips toward him.

Tension coiled through me. I gripped the front of his shirt, wanting to unbutton it and finally, *finally*, touch his gorgeous chest, but I couldn't move. Couldn't do anything but hold on and let him take me places I'd never been.

He slipped his finger under the edge of my panties, and then he was touching me with no barrier. I moaned, pressing my hot forehead against his chest, writhing to try and tell him

I wanted his touch harder, faster. He dipped his head to the side of my neck again, capturing my earlobe between his lips.

"How often do you touch yourself?" he whispered.

I blushed. Blushed! Me, the hard-assed professor who took no prisoners. Archer West had reduced me to a quivering mass of arousal and blushing, and I'd fallen headfirst into the storm. I closed my eyes and pulled in a breath.

"How often?" he prodded, stroking his finger up to my throbbing clit.

"Often," I whispered.

"Every night?" He kissed the pulse pounding at the side of my neck.

"Yes."

"Do you use vibrators or your hand? Or both?"

My flush deepened, but the husky note of command in his voice indicated that not answering was not an option. He caressed me with slow strokes that made my nerves sizzle and ratcheted my urgency higher with every sweep.

"Usually just my hand," I murmured. Sweat broke out on my forehead. I breathed in the scent of him, clutched his wrinkled shirt in my fists.

"Yeah? Why?" He slid his finger back down to the opening of my body.

"It's… um, more efficient."

I felt his smile against my neck. "Do you finger-fuck yourself or rub your clit?"

Heat poured over me. "God, Archer."

"Both?" He started to press his finger into me.

"Both."

"One day you're going to show me." He slipped his finger

in farther, and I clenched around him involuntarily. He exhaled hard, his breath a hot puff against my shoulder, his voice hoarse with restraint.

"Damn, you're tight," he whispered. "I can't wait to sink my cock into you. Watch you take me in deep. So fucking deep."

I couldn't breathe. My head was spinning. My whole body quivered.

Then Archer flicked his thumb against my clit, and I came so fast, so hard, that a scream lodged in my throat. Vibrations quaked through me, my blood rushed hot, and my world distilled to the heat firing inside me, the slow massage of Archer's fingers, the rumble of his voice against my ear.

I drew in a gulp of air, my forehead still pressed to his chest. Another series of shudders filled me. I squeezed my thighs around his hand. The sound of our breathing rasped in the air.

When we separated, I was overcome by yet another foreign sensation of shyness. I couldn't look at him as I adjusted my clothes and scrambled off the counter. Then I realized that I hadn't returned the favor.

"Uh..." I pushed my hair away from my forehead, trying to regain my composure. "I'm sorry, I didn't... you're still..."

"Hard as a rock?" he supplied.

I smiled faintly, my tension easing. "Yes. I don't want to leave you like that again."

"Yeah, well." He put his warm hand beneath my chin, lifting my face to his. "We're not going any further until I give you the test results proving I'm clean. I don't want there to be a single doubt in your mind. And I know a scientist like you needs proof."

"But I—"

"It'll be your turn soon enough." He pressed his lips to mine. "I guarantee it."

My heart kicked into gear all over again at the thought of what, exactly, *my turn* would consist of.

The pressure of his mouth increased again, and for a moment our tongues danced and swirled in another heady rhythm. Then Archer lifted his head, stroking one hand down the side of my face before he backed toward the door.

"I'm going to go," he said. "For now."

I nodded. I didn't want him to go, but lord in heaven, did I need some time to myself. And he'd only be gone *for now.* I wondered what that meant.

And I realized, not without some consternation, that I hadn't objected to his dictate about the rules.

"About those rules…" I said, trying to get some starch back into my spine. "We're going to have to talk about that."

He shook his head slowly. "Deal's done, storm girl. You already surrendered."

"I did not."

"No?" He smiled, slow and easy, his eyes darkening. "Then I'll have to prove it to you again next time."

Next time. I was already throbbing with anticipation at the idea of *next time.*

"When is next time?" I whispered.

"When I say so."

He disappeared into the foyer. I went to the kitchen doorway and watched as he opened the front door. Before he stepped outside, he turned back to look at me.

"I do have one rule," he said.

"Just one?"

"Just one."

"What is it?" I asked.

He shot me a very wicked smile. "Your body belongs to me."

CHAPTER ELEVEN

ARCHER

KELSEY MARCH. SHE OF THE SHARP TONGUE AND INCREDIBLY hot, responsive body. A deadly combination. I couldn't get her out of my head. Didn't want her out. No, I wanted her *in.* In my head, in my blood. Making me jacked up and alive again. Driving everything else out with her *predict the unpredictable* and her cool, blue eyes and the blushing that pissed her off.

I was more turned on than I'd been in months. Aching. I cooled off a little during the long hike back to the hostel, but the second I walked into my room, I hit the shower and jerked off like a fifteen-year-old. Imagined pounding into Kelsey

March like a piston, her legs pushed up to her pretty tits, her body shaking with every thrust. She'd wanted to scream in the kitchen when she came. I'd practically felt her swallow that scream back down.

Next time, she wasn't going to hold back her scream. Not a single moan or whimper. I wouldn't let her.

Even after the shower, my head was still filled with thoughts of her. I got dressed and pulled my notebook out of my duffel.

An idea had kicked into gear last night as I sat on Kelsey's sofa. Characters and plots for a story. I drew a few sketches and wrote down some names. Though I hadn't written in years and didn't know if anything would come of this, it felt good to be inspired.

I worked for an hour before heading to Liv and Dean's to return my brother's clothes and pick up the trailer key, which I'd forgotten last night.

When I got to the apartment, a pleasant older woman opened the door and introduced herself as Marianne, the café hostess and part-time nanny to Nicholas. She stepped aside to let me in, bouncing Nicholas in one arm.

I took Nicholas's chubby hand between my fingers, giving it a little shake.

"Hey, buddy. You get some eggs and bacon for breakfast? A good cup of coffee?"

Nicholas scrunched up his face. Marianne laughed.

"Would you like to hold him?" she asked then plopped Nicholas into my arms before I had a chance to respond. "Liv said you needed the trailer key, so let me get that for you."

She disappeared into the kitchen. Nicholas and I looked at each other. He stuffed his fingers into his mouth and drooled.

"Don't do that, man," I told him. "Girls'll tell you it's not cool to drool."

He drooled harder. Since he'd liked the plants on the balcony the last time, I went over and let him look out the window. He was a good, solid size. I'd always thought newborns must be hard to hold since they were so small, but a five-month-old—or Nicholas, at least—was sturdy enough that it didn't feel like I could break him.

"Here we go." Marianne came out of the kitchen with a key attached to a plastic tag.

After thanking her and waving goodbye at Nicholas, I drove up to the Butterfly House and parked beside Dean's and Liv's cars.

I climbed off the bike as Dean approached from the house. Wariness flooded the air. We stopped a few feet from each other. My fists tightened. I was ready for a fight.

"You get the key?" he asked.

"Yeah."

"Okay. The wood was delivered a few days ago." Dean nodded to the house. "You can start on the first floor. We're doing the stairs, too. All the tools and equipment are in the front room. Let me know if you need anything. I'm working on rewiring the basement. Liv is painting one of the bedrooms."

He turned and walked away. My fists unclenched. I knew Dean wouldn't let me off the hook about Kelsey that easily, but I'd take the reprieve. And despite my spotty job history, I knew how to work. I could sure as hell work fixing up a house.

I dropped my stuff off in the trailer and went into the house. Felt good, the half-finished, empty rooms, the familiar smells of sawdust and drywall mud, the exposed subfloors. I found a tool belt in the front room and put it on, checked out all the equipment, and got to work.

I spent the next few hours putting down an underlayment and laying the first boards. Glad not to think too much except for measurements and planning. Too much thinking and my head would fill with the desert. Mick's garage, dirt biking, bars, nameless women. Dry heat, sharp cacti, and snakes.

I slammed a nail into a board. Too hard. The wood split. I cursed and grabbed a crowbar to yank it up. I tossed the broken board into the corner.

I stripped off my gloves and tool belt before going in search of something to drink. Liv and Dean stood together in the overgrown garden. Dean was gesturing toward the wooded area surrounding the property, like they were making plans about what to do with the yard.

I stopped at the side of the house. A stab of envy hit me. Hadn't felt anything like it in years, not since things broke between my brother and me. I went my way. Dean went his. Everything had always come easily to him, and I'd figured nothing would change.

But until now I hadn't had to actually confront it. Hadn't had to see his beautiful house, cute kid, successful career, and his generous, pretty wife.

Liv nodded in response to what Dean was saying and wrapped her arms around his waist. He kissed the top of her head, then slipped his hand under her chin and lifted her face so he could press his mouth against hers. She leaned right into him, like he was a magnetic pull she didn't want to resist.

Whatever they had together, it was good. Even I, a guy who didn't know much about *good*, could see that.

And it was easy, too. Like it always was for Dean.

They turned and started toward Liv's car. I walked around the other side of the house to the front porch. After the sound of the car engine faded, Dean approached the house, holding a six-pack of soda so cold the cans were sweating.

"From the cooler," he said. "Want one?"

I nodded. We sat on the porch steps. He handed me a soda and took one for himself. I popped the tab and took a gulp, wiping my mouth on my sleeve.

I was discovering that it was easiest to deal with my brother by preempting him. At least that way, I wasn't the one caught off guard.

"I'm not messing with Kelsey," I said. "Not in the way you think."

He didn't respond for a minute.

"She's a good friend," he finally said. "I don't want her to get hurt."

"You think I do?"

"I don't know what you want. I'm still trying to get used to the fact that you're even here." Dean glanced at me. "I've seen you… what, twice in five years?"

"Yeah."

"And for the last twenty years, I haven't even known what you were doing," Dean continued. "The only time I did was when Mom called to tell me you were in trouble or needed money."

Shame rose in my chest. Out of guilt, my mother had never turned me down when I'd asked for money or anything else. She'd spent years bailing one son out of trouble while idolizing the other for his successes. It would have been biblical, if it weren't so pathetic.

"If you want me to leave, I'll leave," I said.

"I didn't say I want you to leave."

You also didn't say you want me to stay.

Irritation scraped my chest. "So… what? You're going to spend the next couple of weeks snarling at me about Kelsey?"

"No." Dean shook his head. "You just watch yourself."

"'We're wanted men.'" I made my voice nasally and sharp. "'I have the death sentence on twelve systems.'"

Dean blinked.

"*Star Wars*," I supplied. "The Mos Eisley bar scene."

He still looked blank.

"Aw, come on, man," I said. "Don't tell me your head is so stuffed with medieval crap that you don't remember lines from a movie we saw a hundred times." I tilted my head back for another drink. "That would be a damn shame."

Dean pushed to his feet and started down the steps.

"'I'll be careful, then,'" I called after him.

"'You'll be dead,'" he replied, not turning around as he strode to his car.

I grinned. "Atta boy."

After working on the house all day Sunday, I called Kelsey the following morning. I had a limited time with her. I wasn't going to waste it by dragging things out. Especially now that I'd had a taste of her explosive heat. A taste of the fire that melted all her ice.

"Hello?" Her voice was scotch and honey.

"What are you wearing?" I asked.

"A frown."

"Mmm. Sexy."

"Archer, I'm at work," she said tartly.

"In a classroom?"

"No. I'm in my office."

"Alone?"

"Yes."

"So tell me what you're wearing."

There was a pause. Taut energy crackled over the line.

"Archer, I had *rules* because I have *boundaries*—"

"One rule," I told her. "No boundaries. Not with me."

"Or what?" she challenged.

"Or you don't get fucked."

She inhaled sharply. "You are so crude."

"Uh huh. And you like it. What are you wearing?"

"A suit." She sounded cross. "A tailored, gray wool suit."

"And underneath?"

"A blue, Brooks Brothers dress shirt."

"And under that?"

"I'm not going to tell you."

"I dare you to tell me," I said.

"I do not accept the dare."

"Then I double-dog dare you."

She gave a muffled laugh, like she was trying not to. "What are *you* wearing?"

"Jeans and a T-shirt. I'm all hot and sweaty from working."

"Really?" Now she sounded intrigued. "Are you wearing a tool belt?"

"I was."

"Hmm."

"Tell me about your sexy underwear," I said.

"No."

"You've got a bad attitude, lady. You need to be spanked as well as fucked."

She made a noise that sounded like a half groan, half laugh. "You do go all out, don't you?"

"You haven't seen anything yet. You ever been spanked?"

There was a second of silence, as if she was thinking.

"No." She almost sounded surprised. "I haven't."

"First time for everything. What color is your bra?"

A sigh came over the line. "Blue, okay? Dark blue satin with white trim."

"Matching panties?"

"Yes."

"Are they wet?"

"God, Archer. Yes."

I rubbed my erection through my jeans. "What about your shoes?"

"Gray pumps with three-inch heels."

"I'll be at your place at seven," I said. "I want you waiting in your heels and lingerie. Nothing else."

"And if I'm not?" she replied, putting some of that defiance back into her voice.

"You'll be in trouble."

"So if I am, I avoid… um, punishment?"

I laughed. "Nice try, storm girl. But you're getting spanked no matter what."

CHAPTER TWELVE

KELSEY

"HEY, KELSEY!"

I groaned, but stopped to watch Peter Danforth loping across the parking lot toward me. His mop of hair was rumpled, his suit wrinkled, and his pencil-thin tie was flapping over his shoulder. He stopped in front of me, breathless and grinning engagingly.

"I heard that the National Science Foundation is looking at the Spiral Project," he said. "Any word from them yet?"

I shook my head. I wasn't lying. I hadn't heard from the NSF yet, but The Weather Institute had also rejected my proposal in record time.

"A number of agencies are still looking at the proposal," I told Peter.

That, actually, *was* a lie. The NSF was the only agency left.

"When do you expect to hear something?" Peter asked.

"I don't know." I sighed and turned to face him. "Look, Peter, the Spiral Project's future looks dim, okay? It's a massive, ambitious, expensive project that, so far, is not backed by hard evidence. That's why SciTech cut off funding. And why it's an uphill battle to get anyone else interested."

Peter frowned. "I'd think King's would be all over such a ground-breaking project."

"They're not," I admitted. "If I did get reliable funding, I'd have to negotiate with the King's administration because I'd need to use university resources to assimilate all the data. And the meteorology lab is overextended as it is."

"You wouldn't go out into the field to collect data?"

"No. If the Spiral Project is ever funded again, my plan is to use King's as the home base and direct the unit from there."

"Seriously?" Peter asked. "You structured the project as a fully mobile, nomadic unit, and still you wouldn't even go out with your own team?"

"That's just it, Peter!" My frustration got the better of me suddenly. "Even if I wanted to, I couldn't, because King's would never let me abandon my commitments to run off chasing tornados. And I *wouldn't* want to because I don't storm chase anymore. But none of that matters anyway because the project is on life support, and King's has no intention of helping me revive it. *No one* does."

Peter blinked with surprise at that barrage of information.

Great. I'd just let off steam to an eager-beaver reporter.

All I needed was news of my irritation with the Meteorology department getting back to Stan and, god forbid, Chancellor Radcliffe.

I forced my tone to soften. "Look, Peter, if I find out anything new, I'll let you know. In the meantime, I'd appreciate it if we could keep this conversation off the record."

"What conversation?"

I smiled faintly. "Thanks."

"Okay, but I'm the first to know, right?"

"Second. I'm always first."

He gave me a salute and jogged off toward campus. I watched him go, trying to find my way back from renewed frustration and disappointment.

Last week when Archer had defended me in front of my colleagues, I'd felt something more than just appreciation. I'd felt a spark of new hope.

"She'll find another way."

Archer had sounded so convinced. But there were only so many scientific research agencies, only so much money, and word had already spread that SciTech killed the Spiral Project because of dubious evidence. No other agency wanted to jump on board a sinking ship.

If I could, I'd try to find funding through other channels. But who else would want to fund tornado research? And why? I had no other ideas. There didn't seem to be *another way.*

Peter disappeared around the side of a building. I got into my car, pushing all thoughts of him and the Spiral Project out of my mind.

Despite how all-consuming the project and my job had been in recent months, it wasn't at all difficult to stop thinking of them. In fact, it was a relief. Because the space they left in their wake was filled with a dominating male presence who both thrilled and unnerved me.

As I drove home, I thought about how Archer was also surprising me in all the right ways. Although I'd believed him when he'd told me he was clean, he'd forwarded me a copy of his most recent test results via email. I'd had a recent doctor's appointment since I was on the pill for endometriosis issues, and I'd also received a clean bill of health.

I hadn't even had to ask Archer for proof. He already knew how much I valued evidence, and I liked that he left me no room for doubt.

I parked in the driveway and went into my house. Usually my haven of peace and quiet, now even my house seemed filled with a tense, edgy air of impatience.

I was nervous. I normally didn't like being nervous, but I couldn't deny that this was sort of… fun. I didn't know what to expect. It was the thrill of the unknown, both exciting and scary. My nerves tingled with anticipation.

Plus… *Archer.*

Of course, I overthought everything. Should I follow his "order" or not? What would really happen if I did or didn't? If I did, what should I wear? If I didn't, what should I wear? Was he expecting dinner? Should I light candles? Why was I acting like such a ninny?

Maybe I should just cancel the whole thing. It really had been a long time. I wasn't even sure if I remembered what to do with a man, much less a man like Archer who was the crazy-hot walking definition of the word *virile.*

I paced the living room. I couldn't figure out if I felt like a total slut or a virgin on prom night, ready to lose it with the high-school bad boy. Somehow, it seemed possible to feel like both.

Finally, I took a shower, making certain to use the almond-milk-and-honey soap that he'd liked, then put on lotion and dried my hair. I studied my overflowing drawers of lingerie and chose a somewhat modest, navy blue chemise and a matching thong. After I wiggled into the lingerie, I pulled my Japanese silk robe on. I slipped my feet into a pair of blue, heeled sandals.

The doorbell rang.

My heart stopped. I clutched the bedpost. Was I trembling?

"Get a grip, Kelsey," I muttered.

I grabbed my glasses from the nightstand, putting them on as I strode to the door. I knew how to handle men. Whatever Archer West had in mind, I'd go *mano a mano* with him.

I opened the door and favored him with my sharpest look.

Oh, sigh.

He looked gorgeous, all rugged and sexy in black trousers and a dark green shirt unbuttoned at the collar, his thick hair brushed away from his forehead.

He smiled. My knees went weak. His gaze, hot and assessing, swept a path over me from head to toe.

"Nice robe," he remarked. "Take it off."

I held up a hand. Shit. I *was* trembling.

"Wait a minute." I tried to put some steel into my voice. "We need to establish some… oh!"

Before I knew it, he'd pushed his way in, kicked the door shut behind him, and was crowding me up against the wall so fast that all the breath escaped my lungs in one whoosh. Lust darkened his eyes the second before his mouth came down on mine in a kiss of crushing, aching possessiveness.

He shoved his knee between my thighs and thrust his tongue into my mouth. My head fell back, and my whole body swayed toward him, so flooded with desire that I swore his grip on my shoulders was the only thing keeping me upright.

"Say it," he whispered, his lips burning a trail to my ear, his breath warm on my neck.

"I…"

He nipped at my collarbone as his fingers found the opening of my robe. Then his hand was between my thighs, cupping my sex. The heat of his palm burned into my blood.

"Say it," he repeated, circling my clit with his thumb. He lifted his head to look at me, his eyes smoky but unwavering.

I swallowed hard. I was almost ready to come and he was barely touching me. He pressed harder. I gasped.

"I… I give up." I'd never said that before in my life. Never given up. Never given *over*.

"Not that," Archer whispered. "Say it."

I could hardly speak. "I… I can't."

"One day," he promised, "you will."

His mouth covered mine again. I parted my lips to let him in, sinking into the delicious sensation of his tongue sliding against mine. He moved his hand from between my legs and tugged at the belt of my robe. In seconds, he had it unfastened and pushed the robe from my shoulders. He took one step back to look at my lingerie-clad body.

"Beautiful," he murmured. "But I can't wait to get that off you."

His husky whisper bolstered my faltering confidence. My pulse streamed hot as he lowered his head to press his mouth against the swell of my breasts, cupping one in his hand. He pinched my nipple through the silk, and a thousand sparks shot right to my core.

I grabbed the edge of the foyer table to try and steady myself, watching as he tucked his fingers beneath the lace border and pulled the cups down to expose my breasts. I sucked in a breath, shocked by the sudden exposure, the rush of cooler air, the heat of his eyes.

And when he took my nipple into his mouth, I moaned, faintly aware I was reaching the point where I would do anything he asked me to. The point where I realized there really were no boundaries. Not with him.

"Archer, I'm—"

"Hold on tight."

I watched in disbelief as he went down on his knees in front of me and slipped his hands against my inner thighs.

"Spread them."

"I'm…"

"Do it." His voice was deep and hoarse with lust.

I did it. Trembling, I gripped the table with one hand and found the door frame with the other. I spread my legs, watching Archer as he tangled his fingers in the string of my thong and pulled it right off me.

Oh, god. I was exposed, wet, aching. And he was there, right there, his long fingers opening me to his questing penetration. A gasp choked my throat at the first touch of his tongue. And then he was licking me, slow and easy, up one side and down the other, drawing my clit gently between his lips. I trembled, panted, unclenched my fingers from the door frame and gripped a fistful of his hair.

"Archer…"

He made a muffled noise before pushing his tongue inside me. I couldn't stop a groan from breaking forth, and then again when he eased two fingers in and slid them back and forth, deep enough to reach the sweet spot that drove my urgency even higher.

He sat back, his chest heaving and his eyes black with lust. "Tell me."

I shook my head. I couldn't do it. And even through the drenching heat of need, I didn't get it. I didn't know why I was uncertain and *timid*, of all things. I didn't understand why I was like this with him. Only him.

He put his mouth back on me. So incredible. I closed my eyes and dragged a hot breath into my lungs. He worked me with his fingers and sucked my clit until I couldn't hold back any longer. I clenched my fist in his hair, pushing my hips forward as an orgasm ripped through my body and stole my breath.

I was shaking, gasping, sweating. I couldn't look at him, but he was still there, his mouth and fingers working the last sweet sensations from me, his breath caressing my sensitive flesh.

Then he rose, his sharp cheekbones crested with a flush, his eyes burning like coals. He planted his hands on the wall behind me and lowered his head for another long, deep kiss that tasted like both of us combined. I gripped the front of his shirt and tried to remain upright.

Archer slid his hands around my waist and lifted me. Just as I'd known, it took him no effort whatsoever. Like I was a feather, a leaf, a wisp of cotton. His body was hot and hard against mine. I wrapped my arms and legs around him, buried my face in his strong neck, and clung to him as he strode to the bedroom.

I was giving over. It scared the hell out of me, but I was doing it. He lowered me to the edge of the bed and stood in front of me. Heat radiated from him.

My chemise was half off, the straps falling down my shoulders, my breasts exposed with my nipples hard as pebbles. I fought the urge to cover myself, not wanting to give him the satisfaction of knowing I was so nervous.

Archer reached down to take my glasses off. Suddenly that was too much. I tried to grab them back.

"Give those to me."

He shook his head and put the glasses on the bedside table. I made another grab for them. He grasped my wrist, and his fingers circled it like a manacle.

"Archer!"

"Your hand belongs right here." He slowly but insistently brought my hand to the front of his trousers.

Blood rushed to my head. His grip tightened on my wrist. I spread my fingers out tentatively to cup the big, hard bulge pressing against his thigh.

Holy mother of god. A bolt of lust fired through me, centering in my core. My mouth went dry. I ran my hand over his length, wondering at the sheer size of it, trepidation already snaking through my belly.

He pushed his hips toward me. "Take it out."

Trembling, breathless, I unfastened his fly and tugged his trousers down his thighs. He wore boxer briefs that hugged his lean hips and did nothing to conceal the massive ridge of his erection. A thousand second, third, and fourth thoughts blistered through my mind. I sat back and just stared.

He started to unbutton his shirt. I felt the sheer burn of

his gaze on me. Unearthing some latent courage, I lifted my eyes. My heart crashed.

Beautiful. Oh, he was beautiful, his torso defined with muscles so sleek and rigid they looked as if a master artist had sculpted them. His shoulders were smooth and tense, his corded arms dusted with dark hair. Enhancing the beauty of his body were the elaborate tattoos inking his right shoulder, the design flowing up from the bird's wing coiled around his upper arm.

I was too enthralled by the utter perfection of him to study the tattoos I hadn't yet seen. Instead I let my gaze follow the slopes of his shoulders over his powerful chest, the ridges of his abdomen, down to where a line of hair disappeared beneath his boxer briefs.

I was shaking. Hard.

I tried to remember that I was a woman known for getting shit done. Taking a breath, I hooked my fingers into the waistband of his boxer briefs. My heart hammered as I pulled them down his legs.

I moaned. I actually moaned at the sight of it—his gorgeous, stiff cock projecting straight out. I wrapped my hand around the shaft, feeling the veins pulsing beneath his smooth, tight skin. Slowly I moved my hand up to the damp head, darkened to a deep red, and swept my thumb over the crevice at the tip. I squeezed my thighs together as I tried to imagine all that hot, hard flesh filling me.

"On your knees." His voice was dark and smoky.

Unthinking, I slid to the floor in front of him. His hand pressed against the back of my head. Gentle but insistent. Blood rushed into my ears.

"Open," he murmured.

I opened my mouth. He slowly pushed inside, past my lips, the taste of him flooding my tongue. He stilled, his breath rasping above me, his fingers stroking the back of my neck.

I could do this. I remembered how. By all accounts, I used to be pretty good at it, too. Except this was Archer West, a man who had crashed into my life like a lightning bolt and set it afire. I had the growing, unnerving sense that nothing would ever be the same again. Including me.

I closed my lips around his cock and sucked. His shaft throbbed, a beat that seemed to echo in my blood. I grasped the base and slid my lips as far as I could, stroking my tongue over the underside. His body tensed, and his fingers tightened on the back of my neck.

I moved one hand to cup the weight of his sac, tight and hard, before easing back and letting him slide out. I pressed a kiss to the smooth head and started to draw him in again. He clenched his fingers on my neck. I stopped.

"I'm going to fuck your mouth," he said.

My trepidation increased. But I relaxed my jaw, my throat, and took a breath before he thrust. I squirmed. Oh, it felt good. His thick cock pumping in and out of my mouth, his hand gripping my neck. Above me, his breath sawed through the air. The salty, male taste of him spread over my tongue.

"Pretty mouth," he whispered, brushing my hair away from my forehead, sliding his hand down my cheek. "You want more?"

I pulled back only long enough to nod. I wanted more than more. I wanted everything he could give me. I wanted to find out just how much I could take.

He buried his hands in my hair, his fingers digging into

my scalp as he pushed into my mouth again. I pressed my tongue against the vein throbbing on the underside of his cock. A groan rumbled his chest.

He moved back, letting me slide my lips up the shaft again, licking the tip before I looked up at him. From my position kneeling on the floor, he was bigger and more intimidating than ever, his eyes intense and his tattoos blazing.

"One day soon I'll come in your mouth," he said, grasping my arms to pull me to my feet. "But right now I'm going to fuck you until you scream."

A wave of heat poured through me. I backed up until my legs hit the bed, and then I fell backward, my arms spread out at my sides.

Archer's gaze raked over me. I was so aroused I couldn't even muster up any embarrassment over how I must look with my chemise half off, my lips swollen, and my legs already spread—a messy, disheveled slut aching to be fucked.

He undressed, pulling off his shoes and socks, pushing his trousers and briefs to the floor. Before kicking them aside, he reached into his pants pocket.

"It's okay." I struggled to push up to my elbows. "I'm… I'm protected, and I want… I want to feel you…"

He pushed his clothes aside and moved to the side of the bed. He grabbed my legs and tugged me toward him. Sweat glistened on his muscular chest. His eyes burned into mine.

"I won't be gentle," he warned.

Anxiety twisted in my belly. "I know."

He grabbed the top of my chemise, which had been pushed down to my midriff. With one tug, he ripped the thin material right off me. My heart slammed against my chest.

I was naked. Completely. He pressed his hands against my inner thighs and pushed them apart.

Oh, god. The preliminaries were over.

Archer took hold of his cock and pushed inside me, slipping past the entrance of my body. My breath stuck in my throat. I arched my back and spread my legs wider, opening for him. He hissed out a noise of pleasure and put his hands on my bent knees as he thrust hard.

"Oh!" The cry ripped from me as he surged, filling me, stretching me.

I squirmed backward instinctively, like I was trying to escape an invasion, drenched in sudden, overwhelming chaos. Archer clutched my waist and forced me down onto his cock. I shrieked. He thrust again. Our bodies slammed together.

I couldn't take it. It was too much, he was too big…

"Take it deep," he whispered harshly.

I twisted, unable to think past this onslaught of sensations, my hands fisting in the bedspread.

"I knew you'd like it rough," he continued, and his voice was like a hot, drenching rainstorm pouring over me. "Ah, you're tight… grip my cock hard… that's it… Christ, you're so fucking sexy all spread open and hot."

I tried to drag air into my tight lungs. He throbbed inside me. So hard. If he moved again… he pulled back and thrust, jarring me to the core. A whimper escaped me. Sweat ran down my neck, my breasts.

He climbed onto the bed, pushing between my legs and coming over me like a thundercloud. He grabbed my wrists, pinning my hands to the bed, his flat belly hitting mine, his hair-roughened legs abrading my thighs.

I couldn't move. Didn't want to. I only wanted to feel his weight, his incredible strength, his thrusts inside of me. So good. More than good. More than I'd ever imagined.

I strained against him, bucking my hips as if trying to dislodge him. He was locked tight against me, his powerful body pressing me into the mattress, trapping me. He shifted, thrusting again and again and again, the friction of his cock driving my tension to breaking point. My body writhed beneath his, my legs aching from the strain of being spread so wide apart.

His grip clenched on my wrists. My breasts rubbed against his chest with every surge. Electric currents streamed through my blood, lighting me on fire.

He increased the rhythm of his thrusts, pounding into me so hard that the headboard slammed against the wall and all I could do was concentrate on accepting his heavy thrusts. I tightened my legs around his hips, moaning every time he surged into me, my fists clenching and unclenching, my wrists still trapped in his grip.

"Come on, storm girl." His hot breath caressed my cheek, my neck, his chest a solid wall of sweat-slick muscles against my breasts. "Show me how hard you can come."

Oh, god. I barely felt that final tipping over the edge into bliss. I only knew that my world exploded with the sudden intensity of a supernova, and I couldn't stop it, couldn't do anything about it. I was helpless, capable only of taking this man's cock deep into my body, unable to silence the scream that tore from the very center of my being as I shattered beneath him.

All thought broke apart. His voice was a low rumble against my ear, but I couldn't make out his words past the dizziness in my head. He was still pumping into me, still rock-hard, and he was so big it was starting to hurt, but I wanted it to go on and on, never ending. My muscles ached. Everything inside me throbbed.

He released my wrists. I groaned as blood rushed back into my arms with tingles and prickles. Archer planted his hands on either side of my head and stared down at me, his face a hard mask of restrained, burning lust. His eyes were so black I couldn't see the brown of his pupils. I licked my dry lips. His mouth came down on mine, hot and possessive

"You want more?" he murmured, low and deep.

Heat flooded me anew. My throat constricted.

"I want more," I whispered against his mouth.

He lifted his head and got to his knees, putting his hands on my inner thighs as he plunged into me again, all hot, sweaty, demanding male. More than I could handle. More than I could take.

My face was wet. I pressed my hands to my eyes. I was fucking *crying.*

Archer put his hand on my damp torso and slid it down to my clit. I jerked in reaction when he splayed his fingers over the sensitive flesh. He murmured something and stroked, urging me higher.

This time, the wave trembled low in my belly before it spiraled outward in ripples of sensation. I gripped Archer's forearms, shuddering as I tightened my body around his cock.

"Inside me," I pleaded, digging my fingers into his arms, urging him to lie on top of me again, positive he was the only solid element left in the world. "I want… need you to come inside me. I want to feel it."

"You'll feel it," he growled, increasing the pace, his pelvis slamming against mine. "And you'll take it all, as deep as you can… squeeze your pussy tighter… you feel so damn good, baby… fucking incredible."

He plunged into me with a groan, his muscles tensing and contracting, and then his seed filled me. Shivers raced across my skin. Archer lowered himself on top of me, heavy and damp, his face against my shoulder, and his chest heaving.

I wiped my face with the back of my hand. Tears still stung my eyes. I blinked them back furiously, refusing to let them fall again.

Slowly Archer rolled off me and onto his back. He threw his arm over his face, still breathing hard. I moved away from him, realizing I didn't have anything within reach that I could put on. I started to ease off the bed when his arm clamped around my waist from behind.

"Archer, I—"

The words stopped in my throat as he dragged me back to him. With a low mutter, he pulled me hard against his side, burying his face in my hair. The bulk of his body blocked out everything but the heat of his skin and the smell of sex. He draped his arm around my shoulders and his leg across my hips. Trapping me.

Or… enveloping me. Before I could figure out which, his body shifted into the heavy rhythm of sleep.

And, before long, so did mine.

CHAPTER THIRTEEN

KELSEY

ARCHER WAS GONE WHEN I WOKE THE NEXT MORNING. HE hadn't left a note or even made a pot of coffee, a fact for which I was inordinately grateful. I didn't want any thoughtful little gestures. I just wanted some time to get my head together, and it was a relief to be left alone.

I was sore, of course, the pulsing between my legs reminding me of him with every step. I took a bath and scrubbed our mingled scents off my skin. Because I didn't have to be on campus until my late-afternoon office hours, I spent the morning lounging around in a dreamy sort of haze. I logged in to my computer and tried to get some work done, but my brain was so fuzzy that all my thoughts kept slipping away.

The only work I did was changing a light bulb on my computer desk. I went to the basement to retrieve a box of new bulbs, which were stamped with a corporate logo and the words *Edison Power Company.*

Something tickled the back of my mind. Edison. Archer had used Thomas Edison's invention of the light bulb to shut down my condescending colleagues.

Feeling a sudden kinship with old Mr. Edison and his string of failures, I changed the bulb and returned the box to the basement. I went online again and looked up Edison Power, curious about the structure and programs of the corporation.

Grant-Funding Opportunities.

I clicked the link on the menu bar and read about the grants and proposals Edison Power had recently funded. Nothing meteorological. I knew power companies were heavily invested in improved weather forecasting, as sudden storms, hurricanes, and tornados could damage electrical grids and impact power in urban areas.

Edison Power hadn't funded anything weather-related, though that didn't necessarily mean they *wouldn't.* Maybe.

Somewhat heartened, I got dressed and walked to the Wonderland Café. It was past two, so I'd missed the lunch crowd, and the place was relatively quiet.

I sat in an empty seat at the counter just as Liv came out of the kitchen with a tray of edible teacups and ice-cream sandwiches.

"Oh, hey, Kels," she said. "Hold on a sec. Let me drop these off." She hurried past to distribute the food, then returned to the counter and poured me a glass of water. "What's going on?"

"Just thought I'd drop by for lunch."

"Oh." She looked vaguely disappointed. "I thought you were here to meet Archer."

My heart did a ridiculous sort of twirl that irritated me. "Why would I come here to meet Archer?"

Liv blinked at my annoyed tone. "He's upstairs. Said he wanted lunch too, so I thought you were meeting him."

Heart twirl. *Again.*

"Archer is here?" I asked.

"Upstairs." Liv nodded to the stairs, eyeing me with speculation.

"Liv, we got the new birthday party brochures in." Allie Lyons came through the kitchen doors, her red hair swinging in a ponytail. "Hi, Kelsey."

"Hey, Allie."

"Check them out." She handed the brochures to me and Liv, then turned to the cash register.

I opened a brochure and pretended to study it. Liv glanced at me, leaning her elbows on the counter. I sensed what was coming.

"So if you're not here to meet him, tell me… how was the date?" she whispered, all brown-eyed curiosity.

"Date?" Allie turned from the register. "Kelsey went on a date? With who?"

"Whom," I corrected. I guessed Liv's question meant that Dean hadn't told her about finding Archer at my house.

"Archer West," Liv told Allie, ignoring my death glare. "That's *whom.*"

"Really?" Allie looked at me with awe. "You went out with Professor Hottie's brother?"

"And he wore a suit and tie," Liv added.

"Oh, wow." Allie shook her head, as if that image was too much to bear. "Where did you go? What did you do? Did he kiss you?"

"Answer that last one first," Liv suggested.

I took a sip of water and tried to keep glaring at both of them, which wasn't easy in the onslaught of their unbearably cute eagerness.

"He came with me to a university dinner because Dean couldn't go," I told Allie. "There was nothing romantic about it."

"Oh." She looked disappointed. "You know he's here, right? Archer, I mean. The girls almost got into a catfight over who'd get to serve him. What room is he in, Liv?"

"Castle Room." Liv was looking at me with way too much perceptiveness. "Hey, Allie, could you get Kelsey her usual?"

"Sure thing." Allie turned and went back into the kitchen.

Liv leaned closer to me. "What's going on with Archer?"

"Dean didn't tell you?"

"He said Archer was at your place the morning after your date."

It was just like Liv not to have called me immediately, demanding to know all the details. She knew some things were private.

"Dean wasn't all that happy about it," I admitted.

"He has reason not to be," Liv said. "But he also knows you, and he knows when to back off."

I rubbed my finger across a crack in the counter. Though I'd told myself a hundred times that I was making up my own mind about Archer West, I was still on very shaky ground after last night. And Liv was one of the few people I trusted most in the world.

"What do *you* think of Archer?" I asked.

She was quiet for a minute.

"I think he got a raw deal," she said. "That he was blamed for something that wasn't his fault and that he's probably made a lot of bad choices because of it. And I think he got stuck in a downward spiral he didn't know how to get out of. But I also think he's a good guy at heart. He's Dean's brother. I think he just got lost somewhere along the way."

I knew all about getting lost.

I stared at my glass. A drop of water ran down the side.

"So… um, if I were to start something with Archer… you know, theoretically…" My mind flashed with images of me spread out on the bed with him. I cleared my throat. "…you wouldn't tell me I was making a mistake?"

Amusement flashed in Liv's eyes. "I would never presume to tell Kelsey March she was making a mistake."

"But you'd never lie to me, either."

"True." She leaned her elbows on the counter, looking directly at me. "I love you, Kelsey. I don't know if Archer is worthy of you. I don't know what kind of future you could ever have with him, if you even wanted one. I don't want to see you get hurt. But God knows I've learned some lessons in life, and one of them is that nothing ever changes if you don't trust your instincts and take risks."

Not until that moment did I realize how badly I'd needed her reassurance. The band around my heart eased.

"Can we hug now?" Liv asked.

"Only if you don't tell anyone."

She grinned, and we exchanged a quick, tight hug. Then Liv nodded to the stairs again.

"Castle Room," she said. "I'll bring your lunch up if you want me to."

She picked up the birthday-party brochures and headed back to the kitchen.

Trying not to overthink it *again*, I slid off the stool and went upstairs. I was going to have to face Archer sooner or later, and the Wonderland Café with its tea parties and birthday balloons was about the safest place I could find. Not to mention I looked totally frumpy in old jeans and a T-shirt with minimal makeup on.

The Wicked Witch's Castle room was at the front of the second floor, with windows providing a view of the distant mountains. An ornate chandelier hung from the ceiling, a twilight-colored mural of the mountains and castle spanned one wall, and the black-draped tables were topped with crystal ball lamps.

All the tables were empty, except for one by the window where Archer sat alone, half slouched in the high-backed chair. His worn notebook was open on the table in front of him, and his head was bent as he wrote something on the pages.

I looked at his profile, the strength of his jaw dusted with whiskers, the ridge of his nose with the slight bump, the way his hair curled around his ears and the back of his neck.

I couldn't believe what I'd done last night. With *him*. For a second, it seemed hazy, distant, surreal.

Then he turned and looked at me, like a radar homing in on its target. All the breath escaped my lungs. I stopped, running my hands over my thighs.

"Hi," I finally said.

In response, he pushed the chair opposite him away from the table with his foot. I went to sit down.

He closed the notebook and looked at me, his expression shuttered but his eyes glittering in the light coming through the window.

"You okay?" he asked.

I nodded. "What are you doing here?"

"I hadn't seen the place yet, so I stopped by," he said. "It's nice. Liv offered to bring me lunch. I never turn down a free meal."

"Who said it's free?" Liv came into the room, bearing a tray with roast-beef-and-cheddar sandwiches and Scarecrow Straw fries.

"Oh, sorry—" Archer started.

"But you don't have to worry about it." Liv set one of the plates in front of Archer and winked at him. "I'll put it on Dean's credit card."

She and Archer exchanged a fist-bump.

Liv put the second plate in front of me. "Whoops, sorry. I forgot your drinks. Be right back."

She hurried back out. Archer watched her go.

"I don't know why, but she doesn't seem to hate me," he remarked.

"Liv sees the good in everyone," I said. "Unless you're a total shit. Then she gets her ninja on."

"Huh." He picked up his sandwich. "Guess I'd better stay on her good side, then."

"I'd recommend it." It occurred to me that even if Archer were using me to get to Dean, he wouldn't do anything to upset Liv. And he knew that using me would piss her off to no end. The thought eased my wariness.

Liv returned with a glass of lemonade for me and a glass of chocolate milk for Archer.

"Enjoy," she said, putting the glasses on the table. "Let me know if you need anything else."

She patted my shoulder and bustled out. I eyed Archer's drink.

"What's with the chocolate milk obsession?" I asked.

"When I was a kid I hated school," he said.

"Okay."

"Never could keep up," Archer continued. "Didn't like sitting at a desk. Acted out a lot. Teachers thought I had ADD or whatever. Elementary school was pretty bad. But every day we had what they called 'milk break' when you'd get a snack and some milk. For twenty minutes, you could do whatever you wanted. So I'd always get out a bin of Legos or whatever construction toys they had in the classroom. And I'd sit there drinking chocolate milk and building something. Best part of the day."

My heart tightened a little. I could picture it, clear as day. I could picture him, a rough-and-tumble boy with a mop of black hair and snapping dark eyes.

Archer closed his lips around the straw and took a drink, then offered me the straw.

"Want some?" he asked. "It's really good."

I shook my head. Sometimes he was so cute, I couldn't stand it.

Danger. Danger, Kelsey March.

I turned my attention to my food. "So you never learned to like school?"

"I always understood stuff when I was actually doing something," he said. "Like in art or wood shop. Auto repair. Even computers. But I couldn't get my brain around all the other stuff. I dropped out of high school my junior year."

I felt his glance, like he was gauging my reaction to that revelation. I tried not to have a reaction at all, but it was impossible not to. No wonder the guy had major issues with his brilliant and successful older brother.

And Archer and *me*… He was a high-school dropout who repaired motorcycles, and I was a university professor who'd graduated with honors. The chasm between us was huge.

Which I'd known from the beginning. Which was just one of the reasons this was a temporary, very hot fling.

I nodded toward his notebook. "So if you didn't like school, what's in that?"

"Poetry."

I caught my surprised *"Really?"* before it escaped my throat. Archer clearly sensed what I was about to say because he grinned.

"Liar, liar, pants on fire," I said instead.

"Oh, my pants are definitely on fire, baby."

I chuckled and let my gaze wander over him—the sunlight flickering on his strong features and glinting off his dark hair. His T-shirt was old, stretching over his chest and shoulders, a faded San Francisco Giants logo on the front. I wanted to slide my hands beneath the ragged hem and find the warm, hard muscles of his abdomen.

I hadn't touched him much last night. I'd been so overwhelmed, so *taken*, that I hadn't had a chance to take any initiative at all, to explore all the slopes and planes of his body…

I shivered. I felt him watching me.

"What?" I asked defensively, even as my brain suddenly flooded with worries that he was comparing the frumpy me of today with the… uh, fiery me of last night.

"You look good," he said.

"Liar."

"Not lying."

I shot him a glower. "I'm not even wearing sexy underwear."

"You are up here." He tapped his finger against his temple and smiled.

I might have melted. Just a little.

"So, Kelsey…" Archer lowered his voice to that deep purr that resounded in my blood. "When was the last time you were fucked real good?"

Heat bloomed through me. A noise came out of my mouth that I didn't recognize. Did I just *giggle*?

"Um…" I made a show of looking at my watch. "About nineteen hours ago."

"Hmm." He frowned with concern. "Long time."

"By some standards, I guess."

"Including yours?"

My heart thumped. I was already all in. I wasn't going to spend the next couple of weeks wondering what the hell I was doing. I was just going to… *do it.* I held Archer's gaze and nodded.

"It's been a very long time by my standards," I said, aware that my voice had gotten a little husky.

"We'll have to change that soon."

I could hardly wait.

"Hey, you guys okay?" Liv came into the room, a pitcher of water in one hand. "Need anything else?"

"No, we're done," I told her. "Thanks."

Archer stood, digging into his pocket for his wallet despite Liv's protests.

"Are you going up to the house?" she asked him. "I'm going to stop by before dinner to finish priming the bedroom. I'll drop off some drapery and tile samples later this week."

He nodded, and they had a short discussion of the week's plans. He handed her a few bills then turned to me.

"And I'll see you later, Kelsey," he said, his eyes dark with undeniable promise.

Heart twirl. Third time in the past hour. It was becoming a bad habit. I managed to nod and keep my voice casual.

"Sure. See you."

I watched him go, admiring the view from behind as he left the room.

"I think he likes you," Liv whispered.

I gave her a look of mock surprise. "You mean he *likes me* likes me?"

She grinned and nudged her elbow into my side. "Actually, it appears he more than *likes you* likes you."

I rolled my eyes. I couldn't get into this. Even so, my mind made an undeniable noise of excitement, kind of a happy cheer.

That, I thought, not without embarrassment, must be what my students referred to as a *squee*.

"Mr. Clement is expecting you, Dr. March." The receptionist at the satellite office of Edison Power rose from behind her desk.

I followed her down the carpeted hallway, my gaze scanning the historic photos on the walls that illustrated the history of Edison Power Company. We entered a corner office, and a bearded, gray-haired man with glasses and a tie patterned with light bulbs stepped forward.

"Professor March, I'm Harold Clement, Vice President of Energy Supply at Edison Power." He extended his hand, and I shook it.

"Pleasure to meet you," I replied. "I like your tie."

He grinned and adjusted the knot. "I have a Christmas tie that flashes with red and green lights when you press a button. It's the stupidest thing you've ever seen, but I wear it every year."

I smiled, liking him instinctively. "That's dedication."

"I'll say." He gestured to a small conference table by the windows. "Thanks for being available on such short notice. Our grant department forwarded me your email from the main office. I'm going out of town for a few days, but I didn't want to miss the chance to talk to you before I leave."

"I appreciate that."

Though that was true, I was still guarded. Just two days ago, I'd emailed a query to the Edison grant department, asking if they would consider funding a meteorological project.

This morning, the receptionist of the Forest Grove office called asking if I could meet with Harold Clement. I'd brought all the Spiral Project documentation just in case, but one meeting wasn't going to get me any funding.

"I brought you a copy of the full proposal." I passed the binder to him. "The intention is to learn more about tornado formation so that we can increase forecast accuracy at longer lead times."

I explained in detail about the project, admitting both the

inconclusive evidence of the first phase and SciTech's pulling of funds. Then I focused on the necessity of high-intensity data collection to revolutionize tornado forecasting.

"This is a project with measureable results," I said, easily launching into the presentation I'd given countless times before. "Results that will lead us to understand a great deal more about tornado formation and structure. Though that sounds like a simple question, the answer itself is incredibly complex. And that's where the Spiral Project comes in.

"If we can increase the lead time of tornado warnings, possibly even up to a full hour, first responders—including power companies—will be far better prepared to effectively carry out the phases of disaster management. And of course the economic, social, and governmental implications of disaster preparedness are immeasurable."

Harold Clement was an excellent audience. He listened attentively, looked at all the documentation, asked questions, and solicited my opinion about how the Spiral Project could fit with Edison Power's mission statement.

"It's fascinating, Professor March," he said, as we wrapped up the discussion. "I admit I'm concerned that SciTech killed their funding, but the concept of the study is remarkable."

"Do you think Edison would consider funding it?" I asked.

"I don't know," Harold admitted. "We've been looking for a program to increase our visibility in the community while also improving our business structure and practices. That's why your project caught my interest. At the same time, we've never funded a meteorology program before."

"I'd be happy to come to your corporate office for a presentation, if necessary."

"I'll have to take this up with the board and let you know." He stood, indicating our meeting was over. "I do personally find it very interesting, but I can't promise any of my colleagues will feel the same way. I'll be in touch."

I'd heard those words before. And even though I'd been ready for rejection again, I couldn't hold back my disappointment as I returned to King's University.

Archer might believe I'd find *another way* to fund the Spiral Project, but research grants were a two-way street. Agencies gave you money, and you proved your hypotheses had merit. I hadn't yet done that with the Spiral Project.

I went into my office and tried to forget about Edison Power as I worked on the coursework syllabi for my classes next year.

My cell phone rang a short time later. I looked at the caller ID. Anticipation flickered through me, banishing my earlier disappointment as I pressed the button to accept the call.

"What are you wearing?" I asked.

"A hard-on," Archer said.

I laughed. "I hope you're not in public."

"I'm at your house. You really shouldn't hide your spare key under a flowerpot on the front porch."

"Oh. Well, this is Mirror Lake, not Gotham City." I paused. "So, um, where are you in my house?"

"On your bed."

My heart gave a little leap at the thought of him stretched out on my bed with an erection pushing at the front of his jeans.

"What are you doing?" I asked.

"Well, I *was* looking through your underwear drawer," he said. "Thinking of you in all that flimsy silk and lace is what gave me this boner."

"You broke into my house and pawed through my underwear drawer?" I asked. "That is seriously creepy."

"I was picking out something for you to put on tonight before you suck my cock."

Heat jolted through me. I struggled for a breath.

"Um… wow?" I managed to say.

He chuckled. "When are you getting home?"

"Not for a few hours." I glanced at the clock with regret. "I have a couple of meetings and a seminar this afternoon."

He groaned. "Okay. I can wait."

"You could get yourself off in the meantime."

"Yes, I could," he agreed. "But I'm not into flying solo these days." His voice dropped an octave. "What are you wearing, Professor March?"

My skin tingled as his deep voice washed over me. Since this conversation was heading in a very welcome and specific direction, I found a thread of common sense and locked my office door.

"I'm wearing a gray linen skirt and white silk blouse," I told Archer as I returned to my desk. "White silk camisole underneath. Three-inch pumps."

"Nice. I like that you're wearing a skirt. Shows off your pretty legs."

"What are you wearing?" I asked again. "Besides the hard-on."

"I *was* wearing jeans. But I had to take my dick out."

I sank into my chair, my knees weakening at the thought of him lying on my bed with his cock sticking straight up like a sundial, indicating it was time for Kelsey March to have a meltdown orgasm.

"Are you *doing* anything with it?" I asked.

"Stroking it, yeah. Wishing I could plunge it into your sweet, warm pussy."

God in heaven. My heart was pounding. I pressed my thighs together.

"Does that make you wet?" he murmured.

"What do you think?" I retorted.

He laughed. "Are you in your office?"

"Yes."

"Pull your skirt up."

I squirmed. "Archer, I'm at *work.*"

"So pull your skirt up at *work.*"

With a groan, I edged the hem of my skirt up over my knees.

"All the way," he prodded.

I wiggled until my skirt was bunched up around my thighs.

"What've you got on under there?" he asked.

"Bikini panties. White silk."

"Touch them. Tell me how wet they are."

I eased my hand between my thighs and touched my damp panties.

"So wet," I breathed, slipping a finger beneath the material to my clit. "How the hell do you do this to me?"

"I know what you like, storm girl. Hold on a sec." The phone went silent for a second before he came back on the line.

"What are you doing?" I asked.

"Got some of your underwear. Pink satin. I haven't seen you in pink yet."

"What are you doing with my underwear?"

"Rubbing it all over my cock."

"Archer!" Shock flooded my chest.

"Mmm. Soft."

I choked out a laugh. "That is so perverted."

"Yeah? Why?"

"You're jerking off with my panties."

"Uh huh. Feels good too, but not nearly as good as your pussy."

"Oh my god, you are *killing* me."

"Take yours off." A husky note of command edged his voice. "Now."

Holy crap. I was totally going to do it. I didn't even have to think. I wedged my phone against my shoulder and stood to wiggle out of my panties. I kicked them to the side, shivering as a rush of cooler air tickled my sex.

"Are they off?" Archer asked.

"They're off," I said breathlessly.

"Pull your skirt all the way up to your waist."

I did it. "Okay."

"Now put one foot on your desk and touch yourself."

I sank into my office chair again and rested my foot on the edge of my desk. Before I could second-guess the utter inappropriateness of what I was doing, I spread my hand over my sex and rubbed. I knew what was coming. And I could hardly wait.

"Imagine I'm watching you," Archer murmured in my ear. "Spread open that pretty, pink slit and slide your finger inside. Feel how tight you are? You grip my cock like a fist. It's so fucking incredible when I thrust inside you. Put your other hand under your shirt and play with your tits. Your nipples are hard, aren't they? Is that why you like wearing sexy lingerie, so it rubs against your breasts and pussy?"

Heat filled my throat. My veins sizzled as Archer's deep

voice poured a ribbon of dirty talk into my ear. I closed my eyes and imagined his body lined with tension, his hand sliding over his thick erection—aided and abetted by a pair of my panties—the tautness of his muscles.

"I'm already about to come," I confessed, sliding my thumb over my slippery clit.

"Not yet. Tell me what you want."

I gripped the phone harder. I couldn't tell him *everything* I wanted. Too much of it had never been part of the deal.

"You," I whispered. *I want you. I want you with me, in my house, in my bed, in my body, in my life.*

My pulse pounded. I pressed the heel of my hand against my clit.

"I want you inside me," I said, pressure coiling through my lower body. "I want you pounding into me, hot and hard. I wish I was there right now, wish I could spread my legs for you… oh, I'm so ready…"

"Fuck yourself with your fingers," Archer ordered, his voice hoarse. "Like you do when you're alone at night."

I slipped two fingers into my opening and squeezed my muscles around them with a gasp.

"Feels good?" Archer asked.

"As a substitute, yes," I whispered, stroking my inner flesh. "But I want you."

"I want you too. Want to plunge into you balls-deep and hear you beg for more. Want to feel your sweet cunt tightening around my cock."

I worked my fingers faster, letting my legs open wider, picturing his hot gaze on the juncture of my thighs. Shivers rolled through me as the tension coiled harder.

"I need you to fuck me," I murmured.

"Soon," he promised, his voice a throaty growl. "Soon I will. Get yourself off now. I want to hear you come."

My breathing became faster, quick little pants in rhythm with the rush of my blood. A trickle of perspiration dripped between my breasts. I rubbed my clit harder, gasping as explosions burst through my veins. I closed my eyes and pictured Archer on my bed, his muscular body tensing as he worked toward his own release. And then his deep groan slid through the airwaves and into my heart.

Right where I was beginning to want him. And right where he scared me the most.

CHAPTER FOURTEEN

ARCHER

DEAN HAD HIRED A FEW CONSTRUCTION GUYS TO WORK TWO days a week at the Butterfly House, but the rest of the time I worked alone. I'd finished the hardwood in two of the downstairs rooms and had started work on the stairs. With the other guys also working, we'd be done with the floors by next week and could start on the kitchen.

I worked for a couple of hours cutting and fitting boards, thinking the whole time about Kelsey and what I wanted to do with her next. I should have been rattled by how I couldn't get her out of my head, but I wasn't. I liked her there. She was like a guard, blocking out everything else.

An incredibly hot, sexy guard with honey-blonde hair and lips like cherries and a sleek, gorgeous body that—

"Archer?"

I snapped my attention back into place. "Be right down."

I took a few breaths and went downstairs to where Liv was pushing through the door with Nicholas in one arm and a book of drapery swatches in the other. I hurried to take the book and hold the door open for her.

"Thanks," she said. "I've got some tile samples in the car, too."

"I'll get them."

I brought in the stuff from the trunk and joined her in the kitchen. Nicholas wore a little San Francisco Giants baseball jersey and shorts. He had his fingers stuffed in his mouth again. I picked up his unoccupied hand and gave him a fist-bump. He blew a spit bubble.

"The floors look beautiful, Archer," Liv said with admiration. "You really know what you're doing."

"Lots of practice, I guess. Is Dean coming up today?"

"No, he went to the library over in Forest Grove. He should be back soon, but we're going on a date tonight so I doubt he'll stop here to work."

"A date, huh?"

Her cheeks got a little pink, which was cute. "Marianne babysits Nicholas a couple times a month so Dean and I can go out."

"Where does he take you?" I asked.

"Medieval Times. We eat turkey legs, drink mead, and watch a joust."

"Really?"

Liv laughed. "No. Usually dinner, sometimes a movie or play. Probably sounds boring."

"No. It sounds nice."

"It is nice," she agreed. "Really nice. Hey, speaking of dinner, I wanted to ask if you could come over one night? I'll cook."

"Dean's okay with that?"

"Well, I haven't given him food poisoning yet."

I grinned. "I mean, with me coming over for dinner."

"He will be. It's about time you two sat down and broke bread together."

A ringtone chimed. Liv shifted Nicholas to her other arm and reached for her phone. "Hey, Allie… What happened?"

I stepped into the other room to give her some privacy, but her voice still echoed in the unfurnished rooms.

"I can't, Allie. I have Nicholas with me… Dean's not here, and Marianne is visiting her daughter this afternoon… wait, can you call Rachel?… oh. Okay, okay… I'll figure something out. I'll call you back."

"Problem?" I asked when she came into the sunroom.

"Oh, a scheduling snafu, plus one of the girls called in sick," she said. "Allie says they just got in a party of eight and she needs me to come in until the next shift." She punched a few buttons on her phone. "I'm going to call Kelsey and see if she can take care of Nicholas just for a couple of hours."

"I can take care of him," I offered without thinking.

Liv looked at me. "You?"

"Yeah." I shoved my hands into my pockets. "Uh, if you want me to, that is."

Of course she didn't want me to. I had no idea what made me offer.

"I mean, I guess Kelsey would be a better—" I started.

"That would be great, Archer. Thank you!" Liv plunked Nicholas into my arms without hesitation. "I promise, it won't be long at all. Let me grab his diaper bag."

She went out to the car. I looked at Nicholas. He blinked.

"Okay, here's all his stuff." Liv came back in and dropped a huge cloth bag on a worktable. "Toys, diapers, wipes, a bottle, change of clothes. You have my cell number and the café number, right?"

I nodded.

"Call if you have any questions." Liv dropped a kiss on Nicholas's cheek. "Two hours max. You're a lifesaver. Don't hesitate to call me if you need to, okay?"

"Sure. We'll be fine." I hoped.

Liv waved and hurried out the front door. With her departure, a hush fell over the house.

I was alone with a five-month-old kid. What the hell was I thinking?

At least Nicholas didn't seem to mind. He pulled his fingers from his mouth and grabbed my ear.

"Ow. Not cool, dude." I pulled my ear from his slippery grip. "Come on, let's go outside."

I took him out to the garden. The kid definitely liked trees and plants. He kept staring at the leaves and branches. I hoped Dean would build him a tree house one day. Nicholas seemed like he'd be a tree house kind of kid.

After a few trips around the garden, he started getting antsy. I went back inside and entertained him with some of the toys from the bag. Then he got a red, scrunched-up look on his face and farted.

"Oh, crap." I'd never changed a diaper before.

"First time for everything," I muttered, figuring I could call Liv for instructions if things got really complicated. I dug in the diaper bag with my free hand and found a soft, plastic mat, a diaper, and a baggie filled with wipes. "Okay, kid. Here we go."

I went into the living room and spread the mat on the hardwood floor before putting Nicholas on top of it. He whined and wiggled. No wonder. It had to be a bummer to have a loaded diaper.

I put my cell phone next to him in case I needed to make an emergency call to Liv. I figured out how to work the snaps on Nicholas's little shirt and shorts and examined the way his current diaper was configured. Then I steeled myself and unfastened the Velcro straps.

"Damn. Good one, man."

Working fast and holding my breath, I managed to take the diaper off him and clean him up before setting him on the new diaper. He squirmed, but overall was cooperative, like he knew I was doing him a favor. I threw the dirty stuff in the trash and washed my hands in the bathroom. I hoped babies didn't crap more than once in two hours.

When that task was done, I picked him up and got the bottle out of the bag. We went to the front porch and sat on one of the rocking chairs. Nicholas seemed content on my lap. I pushed my foot to rock the chair a little.

"Want to listen to some music?" I took out my phone and scrolled my playlist. "The first thing you need to learn is that the Rolling Stones created some of the most epic songs in music history. 'Gimme Shelter' is a case in point."

I pushed the play button and tapped my leg as the song started.

"Pink Floyd is a close second," I continued before playing "Another Brick in the Wall," then Dylan's "Like a Rolling Stone" and a few more.

"You should always have a top twenty list," I told Nicholas. "And be sure you have a couple of romantic type songs in there too, for when you want to create a playlist. Girls love that sh… stuff."

The sound of a car engine rumbled up the drive. I glanced at my watch. It hadn't been two hours yet, but maybe Liv had left the café early. I hefted Nicholas into my arms and walked down the porch steps.

A black sedan came to a stop on the gravel drive. Not Liv. Dean.

He got out, slamming the door behind him, and stopped when he saw me.

"Hey," he said. "Where's Liv?"

"At the café. There was some scheduling problem, so she had to go in."

He looked at Nicholas then back at me. The pieces clicked.

"You're here alone?" he asked.

"Yeah." A defensive note hardened my voice. "Liv was dropping some stuff off here when she got Allie's call. I told her I'd watch Nicholas for a couple of hours."

He didn't say anything. I couldn't read his expression. I went to hand Nicholas over to him.

"We just hung out," I said, backing away. "Listened to some music. He's fine."

"I didn't think he wouldn't be," Dean said.

"Yeah, you did."

Dean frowned. "I don't think you're incompetent, man."

"No, you just think I'm a slacker."

"You never gave me a reason to think differently."

"I'm trying to give you one now."

Shit. I didn't want to do this. Didn't want him to think I was after his approval. I didn't care if he approved of me or not. I also didn't like the idea of Nicholas one day thinking of me as his loser Uncle Archer.

"Liv left some tile samples," I said, heading toward my bike. "Soon as she decides, you can order the tile. I'll start laying it as soon as it comes in. It'll take a few days to set."

I put my helmet on and swung a leg over the seat.

"Archer," Dean called.

I looked up.

"Thanks," he said. "For helping out. You're really good with Nicholas."

A weird feeling of pleasure and embarrassment filled me. Not knowing how to respond, I nodded and started the engine.

Over the past week, Dean had complimented me often on the work I was doing in the house, but for some reason, this was different. As I drove away, I almost felt the way I had as a kid whenever I heard my brother's praise.

Just... good.

I parked on Avalon Street and grabbed my notebook from the saddlebag. I walked to a coffeehouse for a large take-out coffee, then went to the outdoor terrace overlooking the lake.

A streak of blue flashed across my vision as I scanned the crowded tables.

Kelsey sat with a younger woman at a table strewn with folders and papers. Since they looked busy, I started to turn away when Kelsey lifted her head. Her blue gaze arced right into me. Filled me with heat.

She gestured to the empty chair at the table. "Come sit down."

"You look busy."

"We're almost done. Archer, this is Tess, one of my grad students. Tess, this is my friend Archer."

"Hi." Tess extended a hand. "Good to meet you."

"You too." I pushed the chair away and sat, putting my notebook on the table. "You're also a storm researcher?"

Tess nodded. "Yes, I'm interested in storm genesis. We're going out next week to chase in northeast Texas."

"We?" I looked at Kelsey. "You're going too?"

She shook her head. Tess glanced at her.

"You should go," she said.

"I'm not going," Kelsey replied in a curt, "I'm your professor" tone of voice.

Tess appeared unfazed by it. "The last several runs of the global models look promising."

Kelsey started collecting the papers. "You go and send me the results. I'll be base support, as always."

"Why don't you want to go?" I asked Kelsey.

"I have work to do here," she replied. "Not that it's your business."

I frowned. What was with the attitude?

"Kelsey doesn't chase storms," Tess told me. "Though the guys and I are always trying to get her to come with us."

I suppressed a bolt of jealousy. “What guys?”

“My graduate students,” Kelsey said. “They go out all the time to collect field data.”

“And you don’t go with them?”

“I stopped chasing storms years ago.”

“Why?”

“It’s grad student work,” Kelsey said. “I assimilate the data and results in the lab and write up all the proposals and reports.”

“Why don’t you go into the field anymore?”

“It’s not my job.”

That didn’t sound right. I’d seen TV shows about storm chasing. Those guys were always meteorologists and professors.

“Could you go if you wanted to?” I asked.

“For a limited time, probably,” Kelsey admitted. “But my contract with King’s has clauses about outside work and teaching duties. And it wouldn’t be good for my reputation in the department or with the administration.”

Though that made more sense, something still sounded off about her excuse.

“What about the Spiral Project?” I asked. “Doesn’t that require fieldwork?”

When Kelsey didn’t respond, I glanced at Tess.

“It’s mostly about getting data on tornados from the field,” Tess said. “But Kelsey has structured the project around the concept of her directing it from a home base while others travel with the field unit.”

“Why do you want to work from a home base?” I asked Kelsey.

She shot me a frown that only made me want to dig deeper.

Apparently sensing the tension, Tess stood and shoved a few folders into her backpack.

"Kelsey, I'll take these back to the office, okay?" she said. "And I'll have the report to you tomorrow."

"Sure. Thanks, Tess."

After the girl had left, Kelsey glared at me. "What was that about?"

I had no idea. "Just doesn't make sense. You're in this because you love weather, right? So why aren't you out *in it*?"

"I'm a professor, for heaven's sake, Archer," she said. "Yes, atmospheric scientists need to do fieldwork all the time, but my grad students love doing it, and I don't have a problem letting them."

"Then why are they always asking you to go with them?"

"They're not. Tess was exaggerating." Kelsey shook her head. "Even if I wanted to go, I couldn't. I mean, every now and then I could, but I could never take off for months at a time to travel with the Spiral Project. Even if I did secure funding again."

"Does this have to do with tenure?"

"I need tenure to keep the Spiral Project alive," she admitted. "If I don't get it, I'm fired from King's and have to look for another job. And the Spiral Project would die."

"Why?"

"Because everyone will assume I was denied tenure because of the project," she replied. "And no other university or agency will want to touch it with a ten-foot pole."

She pushed some papers into a folder. "Anyway, I'll know soon enough."

"When?"

"A couple of weeks, I hope. The university board gave their recommendation to the chancellor, and now the final decision is up to him."

"Save a day to celebrate with me."

She arched an eyebrow. "And if there's nothing to celebrate?"

"We'll find something."

Kelsey nudged me with her foot. "What if you're gone by then?"

"I won't be." I grabbed her ankle under the table and ran my hand over the arch of her foot. "It'll take me at least that long to own your body."

Even though she rolled her eyes, a flush colored her cheeks.

"You do understand that I'm a well-regarded atmospheric scientist, right?' she asked. "Not just a floozy who stares at men in bars and whose body you profess to own."

"I understand, all right," I said. "That's exactly why I like you so much."

Kelsey shook her head at me, her eyes bright with suppressed amusement. "Why? Because I'm a scientist or a floozy? Wait, don't answer that."

"Both." I leaned closer to her. "And neither."

"Neither?"

"Mostly I like you because you're Kelsey."

Her flush deepened. She tore her gaze from mine and started putting her papers in her briefcase. She snapped it shut and pushed back her chair.

"Mostly I like you because you're Archer," she said. "But the fact that you're sexy as hell is a definite bonus."

She reached out to tweak my nose before she turned and walked away.

Text Message:

ARCHER:	What are you wearing?
KELSEY:	A scowl.
ARCHER:	You can't be at work. It's Sat afternoon.
KELSEY:	I'm at the grocery store.
ARCHER:	Why the scowl then?
KELSEY:	They're out of zucchini.
ARCHER:	So get broccoli.
KELSEY:	I wasn't planning to eat it.
ARCHER:	...
KELSEY:	Hah. I was going to pickle it.
ARCHER:	You pickle stuff?
KELSEY:	No. I'm just screwing with you.
ARCHER:	Soon you'll just be screwing me.
KELSEY:	Well, you are a tool.
ARCHER:	Spanking alert. What're you wearing?
KELSEY:	Raincoat and stilettos. Nothing else.
ARCHER:	Really?
KELSEY:	Hah again. Jeans and a tee. What's in the notebook?
ARCHER:	My diary.
KELSEY:	Diaries are for 12 year old girls, not dudes like you.
ARCHER:	It's a diary of my sex fantasies.

KELSEY: Like what?

ARCHER: Shocking, filthy, kinky fantasies.

KELSEY: Well, I would hope so.

ARCHER: Tell me one of yours.

KELSEY: No. I'm in the cereal aisle of the *grocery store.*

ARCHER: I'll frost your flakes good, baby.

KELSEY: Hmm. Sounds promising.

ARCHER: You fantasize about outdoor sex?

KELSEY: Done that.

ARCHER: Tied-up sex? Handcuffs?

KELSEY: I think I've done that.

ARCHER: You don't remember?

KELSEY: No. I guess it wasn't very memorable.

ARCHER: You never fantasize about it either?

KELSEY: Not really.

ARCHER: Ah.

KELSEY: Ah what?

ARCHER: No control. That'd freak you out.

KELSEY: Nothing freaks me out. Except earwigs. They're gross.

ARCHER: Focus. You ever think about sex with a woman?

KELSEY: Done that.

ARCHER: Yeah?

KELSEY: I liked girls for a couple of years in college.

ARCHER: I'm so fucking turned on right now.

KELSEY: Part of my wild past. But girls were complicated.

ARCHER: No kidding.

KELSEY: You ever been with two or more girls at once?

ARCHER: Yeah. It was hot.

KELSEY: I'll bet. Oh, the granola is on sale.

ARCHER: Way to kill the mood.

KELSEY: I don't like thinking about you with other women.

ARCHER: Good. I hate the idea of you with other men. Other women, though…

KELSEY: Don't get too excited. Those days are long gone.

ARCHER: Good. You're all mine anyway. Go home. Put on a raincoat and stilettos. Nothing else. Meet me at the Queen of Hearts at nine tonight.

KELSEY: No way.

ARCHER: Do it.

KELSEY: I can't.

ARCHER: You will.

KELSEY: If I don't?

ARCHER: No frosted flakes.

CHAPTER FIFTEEN

KELSEY

HE WASN'T SERIOUS. I WASN'T GOING TO DO IT. I COULDN'T. No way.

Except that I was in my bedroom, standing naked in front of the mirror in four-inch strapped black stilettos, holding a tan raincoat.

"You are so screwed, Kelsey March," I muttered to my reflection. "And I don't mean that in a good way."

My cell phone rang. My heart thumped.

"Hello?"

"You ready?" His voice was like dark, melted chocolate.

"No."

"Half an hour. Be there."

I tossed the phone on the bed. Last time I'd gone out with Archer to the Queen of Hearts, we'd run into one of my students. What if that happened again tonight? *While I was naked under a raincoat?*

What if I got stopped for speeding? What if the Queen of Hearts was having a "no coats allowed" night? What if I was in a fender bender and had to talk to another driver and a police officer? What if I saw someone get hurt and I had to whip off my raincoat to… I don't know, stop the bleeding?

I was beginning to think that maybe my *wild past* wasn't quite as wild as I'd always believed. Either that or I really had become an uptight stick-in-the-mud over the years.

That was a depressing thought.

With a sigh, I scrounged around in my closet and grabbed a stretchy blue dress that I hadn't worn in ages. I tugged it on. It was way too tight, clinging to my hips and waist, and very clearly demonstrating that I wasn't wearing a bra. I had to pull it down to make it reach mid-thigh.

Though my courage wavered again, I figured it was a decent compromise between Archer's order and the fact that I wasn't going to get out of the house unless I was somewhat clothed. I finished getting ready and put my glasses on.

My anxiety ratcheted up higher as I drove to Rainwood and parked in the same lot Archer had the previous week. I couldn't believe it had only been last week that we'd been here.

When I got out of the car, I felt a presence move from between two cars. Archer. He came toward me, breathtakingly handsome in jeans and a gray button-down shirt with the sleeves rolled up to expose his corded forearms. Shadows cut across his strong features, making him look faintly sinister.

"I thought we were meeting at the club," I said, attributing my shivers to the cool spring air.

"I'd never let you walk alone at night." His gaze raked over my buttoned, belted coat. "You follow orders?"

I figured he'd find out sooner or later, so I shook my head. "I have a dress on. But it's really tight and clingy," I added hopefully.

He frowned, crowding me up against the car. My breath caught. His gaze held mine as he untied the belt of my raincoat and worked the buttons. When the coat was open, he slipped his hands inside and ran them over my breasts and hips. The heat of his palms burned through the thin material.

Then… oh, god… he hooked his fingers under the hem and pulled it up far enough to touch my naked slit. A shudder racked me. He smiled, blocking me from view with his body as he ran his forefinger over my folds.

"It'll do," he murmured. "But you still disobeyed."

"I'm not a dog, you freak."

He chuckled. "No, you're a cat in heat. Hissing and scratching."

He slipped his finger into me. I gasped, curling my hands around his forearms. He lowered his head, and I caught a whiff of his delicious, clean male smell before he pressed his lips against mine. My body surged in anticipation of an open, possessive kiss, but this one was surprisingly gentle, almost chaste.

Which was a very odd contrast to the fact that he was still fingering my pussy.

"Let's go." Archer tugged his hand from between my legs and pulled the hem of my dress back over the tops of my thighs.

"We're… we're still going to the club?" I'd rather been hoping he'd whisk me off to a dark cave… or anywhere… and have his way with me. Like, right *now*.

"Sure, we're still going." He fastened my raincoat and tied the belt.

I bit back a protest. Archer put his hand on my lower back as we walked, our hips occasionally brushing against each other. I was already damp between my legs, and my lack of underwear heightened the friction.

When we entered the club, I realized I might have made a mistake. If I was naked under the coat, I could have left it on and remained fully covered. But with the dress…

Sure enough, Archer moved behind me to help me off with my coat. Now in a dress tight enough to be a second skin, I suddenly felt *more* than naked. Especially when the bouncer gave me the once-over.

Archer stepped in front of me, eyeing the guy with a caveman *back-off* look. The guy shrugged and pulled open the door.

Once we were inside, my tension eased a little. Lights flashed over the dance floor, but the tables were shadowed, and I thought I could lose myself in the noise and activity. A cover band was onstage, "We Are Young" thumping through the room. The lights spun over the couples gyrating on the dance floor.

Archer reached back to grab my hand as he navigated the crowd and tables. I saw nowhere to sit, but Archer scanned the crowd then spoke to the bartender. In a few minutes, a server gestured us toward an empty table at the edge of the dance floor.

I had to admit, as Archer guided me to the table, his ability to get what he wanted was pretty damn sexy. Maybe that was one of the reasons I was so willing to give him… *me.*

While he ordered drinks, I wiggled around in the chair, tugging my dress back over my thighs. Though I'd worn revealing clothes in the distant past, I'd always tended more toward the goth-chick look rather than outright sluttiness. And in the past ten years, I'd been all about tailored suits. Hiding the sexy underneath.

I shifted again, reaching for my drink. The lights were hot, the air compressed with the music and sounds of laughter and loud conversation. The bass line throbbed in my chest, my body humming with that urge to get up and move.

"Dance," Archer said.

With a smile, I nodded and pushed my chair back, discreetly tugging my dress down before going to the crowded floor. I turned to face Archer, only to find that he was still sitting at the table. I lifted my hands and gave him a "what the hell?" look.

A smile curved his mouth. He took a drink of scotch and made a circling gesture with his forefinger.

I just stood there. It took a second for his command to penetrate my hazy brain. He didn't want me to dance *with* him. He wanted me to dance *for* him.

Someone bumped into me from behind. I stared at Archer. Lights gleamed on his dark hair, over the hard lines of his face and his beautiful mouth that had done such hot things to my body. He was lounging back in the chair, his legs stretched out in front of him and crossed at the ankle, all taut, male confidence.

My heart pounded. I wanted to climb on top of him right there and straddle his lap, hike my dress over my hips and...

He lifted an eyebrow. Imagine Dragons' "Demons" came through the speakers. Blue-and-yellow lights drifted over the crowd. A couple passed in front of me, gripping hands as they came together, their lower bodies gyrating close.

A throb coursed into my blood. Archer and I locked gazes. An electric current sparked through the air. This was a direct challenge. I wasn't going to let him win.

I started to move. I let the music fire through me, felt the beat pulsating in my core. I twisted, turned, spun. My dress rode up my thighs as I swiveled my hips, turning to shake my ass at Archer… *hah, take that…* then around again to face him.

Without a bra, my breasts bounced beneath the stretchy fabric, my nipples pressing against the thin material. I slid my hands down my torso, the heat of my own skin burning through the dress, around to the slopes of my rear.

The crowd swelled around me like a wave. My hair clung to my neck, damp and hot, the music and noise filling my ears. His eyes burned through the dim light like twin candle flames. The dress inched up higher with every twist of my hips, and when I reached to pull it down again, Archer shook his head.

My breath stuttered. I fumbled, grasping the hem with both hands, my pulse throbbing. He shook his head again, his gaze steely.

We stared each other down like jungle animals. He won.

I released the hem of my dress and moved back, slowly swaying to the beat again. I was hot and slippery between my legs, and he knew it. My dress hiked up farther. I tried not to wince as a rush of air brushed against the lower curve of my ass. A couple more inches and…

Someone bumped into me. Startled, I jerked away and turned to face the stocky, handsome blond man who had come up behind me. He lifted his eyebrows in an unspoken question.

I started to shake my head at him, certain Archer would intervene. Then I glanced over my shoulder and found him still sitting at the table, unmoving, his hooded gaze fixed on me and the other man.

Hah.

I turned back to the guy. He smiled. We started to dance, his body moving in rhythm with mine, a space clearing around us like the expanding circles of a pebble tossed into a lake. I closed my eyes and let heat wash over me. Music and noise drove everything else out.

My dress rode higher, the pulse between my legs getting stronger with every circling of my hips. Arousal shot to my core each time my hard nipples chafed the material of my dress. A faint dizziness wound through my head. I felt the guy looking at my breasts, his eyes hot, and I knew he wanted to—

Two large, male hands grabbed my hips from behind, pulling me backward. I came up hard against Archer's body, my ass hitting his thighs as he slid his hands around to my front and flattened his palms against my torso in an unmistakable show of possession.

The other man didn't even try to protest. He took one look at Archer, held his hands up in defeat, and turned to disappear into the crowd.

All the breath escaped my lungs. Archer's hot, hard body pressed against my back. Arousal flooded me. For an instant, we just stood there, his grip holding me in place, my heart racing wildly. Then he moved and the ridge of his erection pressed against the upper curve of my ass.

I moaned. Aloud. I reached back, desperate for something, anything, to hold on to. I curled my fingers against his hips as he lowered his head to press his lips on the side of my neck. The room tilted off balance, the lights spinning. His thick hair brushed my damp skin.

He slid his hands down the front of my body, his fingers brushing the hem of my dress and the bare skin of my thighs. Shivers rained through me. He moved again, shifting his hips, guiding my body to the beat of the music. I felt him against my lower back, the top curve of my rear, his chest a solid wall of muscle. His breath was hot on my neck, his lips still against the pulse beating wildly under my skin.

I tightened my grip on his thighs and writhed my hips, rubbing my ass against him, aching to feel him pull my dress up and slip his hand between my legs. Dizziness washed over me.

I didn't care that we were standing in the middle of a crowded dance floor, didn't care who was watching, didn't care about anything except the sensation of Archer pressed against me, holding me to him, his lips on my neck, enveloping me with all his male possessiveness.

And then, oh god, my dress rode up even higher, and my bare ass was against his groin, his jeans abrading my skin, his cock so hard I could almost feel it throbbing through the denim. He pushed closer, sealing our bodies together so my nakedness was concealed from view. I squeezed my thighs. Sweat collected between my breasts. My clit throbbed.

I shifted, rubbing my ass against him. It was so good, the rough fabric against my naked skin, his hands cupping my thighs and holding my body against his, his lips sliding from my neck to my shoulder in a sweeping, unbroken line. Lust unfurled inside me like a ribbon.

A rough noise rumbled through Archer's chest. His hands

flexed on my thighs. He moved enough to edge his hand between us and tug my dress back over my rear, but not before running one finger swiftly down the crevice between my cheeks. Shock and heat bolted through me so violently that I stumbled.

He grabbed my waist to keep me upright. "Come on."

Blindly, I let him guide me forward, past the twisting and spinning bodies, off the dance floor to a corridor leading to the back alley. I fumbled for the door handle, gasping with relief when a rush of cool night air washed over me.

The door closed. Archer was still there, his breathing heavy, and when I turned to face him, his features were set hard, his eyes lit with a feral gleam.

Before I knew what I was doing, what was happening, we lunged toward each other like attacking animals. I flung myself at him, feeling his arms clamp around me as our mouths crashed together in a sudden, heated frenzy.

"Oh, god," I gasped, my mouth open over his as I latched my legs around his waist. "I'm going to come already… I'm so fucking turned on… I need you so much…"

"Yeah, you do," he growled, turning to push me up against the side of the building, already shoving my dress up to my waist. "Tell me what you want."

"You." I let my head fall back as his mouth sought mine again. "Your cock inside me… your fingers on my clit… oh, Archer, please."

He thrust his tongue into my mouth, holding me against the wall with the strength of his body, one arm beneath my thigh. He pushed his other hand between my legs. A thousand shudders rolled through me. He rubbed, squeezed, pressed two fingers into my opening, his thumb circling my clit. Need built inside me with unbearable force. I licked his lower lip, clutched at his shoulders, and drove my hand into his hair.

"Fuck me," I hissed.

"Say it."

My blood went into full boil. "Oh, you *bastard*..."

"Say it." He lifted his head, his eyes glittering.

"No."

He slipped another finger inside me. My thighs trembled. The world spun.

"Say it."

"No."

We stared at each other. The air crackled.

Archer leaned forward, his breath hot against my lips, working his fingers inside me. I shut my eyes, feeling myself tipping forward into the abyss.

"Say it," he whispered.

"I... I surrender."

"Good girl." His mouth crashed down on my mine again.

I surrendered. I was dimly aware of him pulling his hand away from me, the shifting as he worked the fly of his jeans, the strain of my thighs. But I couldn't even think past the lust clouding my mind and body, the beat of music pulsing in my blood. I could still hear it through the walls of the club, still felt the sweat trickling down my back.

"Hold on," Archer muttered, a second before thrusting into me with a grunt.

I gasped, gripping his shoulders, tightening my legs around him. His cock filled me, stretched me, his body slamming against mine as he clutched my thighs and thrust again and again. I let my head fall back, closing my eyes, the bricks behind me vibrating with the noise from inside.

"Archer…"

He plunged into me, thick and hot. A cry broke from my throat. The rough wall chafed against my ass and lower back. I squeezed my inner walls around his shaft. So big. He was so big I felt the blood pumping through his cock, the slap of his testicles against me.

"Oh, fuck…" He groaned, lowering his head to capture my lips again.

I opened, letting him drive his tongue into my mouth in the same rhythm as his thrusts. I was electrified. Consumed. His breath scorched my lips, his stubble-rough jaw abrading mine as he slid his mouth across my cheek to my ear.

"You are so fucking hot." His voice was as deep and dark as the ocean. "So tight… let me feel you come again… harder than you ever have… come on, baby."

He surged into me. I cried out and came violently, shuddering and quaking around him an instant before he gave a muffled shout and shot deep inside me. I clung to him, my blood pulsing. Heat drenched the air.

Before the quivers had eased from my body, he lifted me from against the wall, sliding his hands over my naked rear. I wrapped my arms and legs around him and buried my head in his shoulder. I was shaking hard.

The world steadied back into balance with the dizzying, windswept sensation of slowing after a wild roller-coaster ride. Again I had the sense that Archer was the only solid element in the entire world.

His breath rasped over my temple. Music still thumped

through the walls. I squeezed my eyes shut and felt his heart pounding against my breasts.

"I need to go home," I whispered.

Archer didn't release me right away. I think he might have even held me tighter. He was so strong. I had no fear of falling, not with him holding me, our bodies sealed together like the pages of a closed book.

He slowly lowered me to the ground, steadying me even as he gazed at my disheveled body. He tugged my dress down and smoothed his hands over my waist and hips. He straightened his clothes before we went back into the club. He retrieved our coats, draping mine around me.

As we approached the parking lot, I handed him my car keys without him needing to ask. Part of me was dimly aware how unlike me all this was, turning things over to anyone. Especially a man like him. But I was thrown totally off balance, not even sure if I knew who I was anymore.

And increasingly terrified that I only wanted to be *his.*

CHAPTER SIXTEEN

KELSEY

I WOKE NAKED IN MY BED. GRAY MORNING LIGHT STREAMED through the curtains. I blinked. A sheet draped over my body, but I had nothing else on. I shifted and rose to one elbow, shoving my hair out of my eyes. The scent of fresh coffee drifted to my nose.

Oh, no, he wasn't. Archer West was *not* in my kitchen right now making coffee. No way.

I stumbled out of bed and into the bathroom. I got in the shower, welcoming the spray of scorching-hot water, trying to wash away all the thoughts I didn't want to think, the feelings I didn't know what to do with.

I was surrendering. That meant I was giving up, relinquishing control, waving the white flag because I'd lost all hope of winning the battle. At the same time, I wasn't even certain what *winning* actually meant where Archer West was concerned.

I stepped out of the shower and pressed a towel to my wet face. I could hardly remember what had happened last night after we'd left the club. I'd closed my eyes in the car, but after that everything was a blank. I couldn't imagine that Archer and I had engaged in more hot sex and I'd forgotten about it.

I dried my hair and pulled on yoga pants and a T-shirt. I'd be damned if I was going to give up my weekend frumpiness for him. A girl had to hold on to something.

Even so, I quickly brushed my hair and powdered my nose. I found my glasses on the nightstand and put them on before I went in search of him. A delicious, intoxicating smell drifted through the house.

Bacon. The man was frying bacon. I had to get him out of here.

I stopped in the kitchen doorway. Bacon sizzled and popped in the frying pan, and a carton of eggs rested on the counter. Archer stood by the stove, dressed in the same jeans and wrinkled shirt from the previous night.

I leaned a shoulder on the doorjamb and tried to ignore the flutters of awareness tingling through me.

He turned. "Morning."

"What are you doing here? What happened last night?"

"You fell asleep in the car."

"I did?"

He nodded. "You crashed pretty hard. I carried you in and put you to bed."

"Did you, um…" A flush crept up my neck, which was silly considering how raw he and I had been together. "Undress me?"

"I did." Archer looked at me solemnly. "But I did not cop a feel."

I narrowed my eyes with suspicion. "You didn't?"

"Well." He held up his thumb and forefinger close together. "Maybe just a small one. I couldn't help myself. You have an incredible pair of breasts."

My flush deepened. He really couldn't do the cute Archer thing. Not now.

"Where did you sleep?" I asked.

"Next to you."

Next to me.

Archer glanced down at his wrinkled shirt. "Gonna have to bring a suitcase next time."

A suitcase. Something twisted inside me at the idea of him bringing his stuff over. *Staying* here. In my house.

"Hey." He turned from the stove, resting his hips against the counter. "You okay?"

I was not okay. I'd gone out last night dressed like a slut. I'd let him finger me in a parking lot. I'd rubbed my bare ass against his erection in the middle of a crowded dance floor. Then I'd let him… no, *begged him*… to fuck me against the side of the building in a goddamn garbage alley.

My throat constricted. What the *hell* was I doing?

I rubbed my hands over my thighs. "You need to go."

He lifted an eyebrow. I shook my head. I couldn't have him standing in my kitchen making coffee and frying bacon, like we were suddenly some warm and cozy domestic couple. Next thing I knew we'd be going to the hardware store and paying a visit to the fucking mall.

I cleared my throat. "You need to go now."

He reached back to turn off the stove burner. "You're going dark again."

"Damn right I am." I stalked across the kitchen and yanked open the refrigerator. "Because of you. Because I agreed to whatever the hell it is we're doing."

Archer frowned. "Why does it scare you so much?"

"What?"

"Giving up control."

"It doesn't scare me!"

Even as the denial burst out of me, I heard the quaver in my voice, the pathetic attempt to sound brave even while I was trembling.

But it wasn't just giving up control that scared me. It was Archer West. It was the way I felt about him, whether he was fucking me up against a wall or standing in my kitchen frying bacon.

I pressed a hand to my tight chest. My heart raced. He moved closer. I felt him with every step he took in my direction. Next thing I knew, he was crowding me up against the open refrigerator, his body a solid wall of muscle and heat. I tried not to go weak in the knees as he put his hands on my waist and turned me to face him.

He studied me for a second and reached up to run his finger across my lower lip. I looked at his beautiful eyes. I had fallen, spinning wildly, into their bright darkness.

"Don't be scared, storm girl," he said. "I'll protect you."

I knew he would. That was the problem. I had spent most of my life protecting myself. The instinctive pull toward danger might be part of me, but there was no way it would ever fit in my life for good. I knew that. It was the reason I had armor.

And yet with Archer, I could surrender to the wild, impulsive side of me that I'd buried for so long. Even though he was a force of nature I couldn't control, I wanted to live right in the center of him.

I groaned softly and leaned forward to press my forehead against his chest. I couldn't figure out if this thing with him was completely fucked-up or the most natural, normal relationship I'd ever experienced.

"God in heaven," I whispered, closing my eyes. "Last night was so hot I thought we'd set the whole world on fire."

His soft chuckle brushed against my hair. "One day, we will."

I didn't doubt it. His lightning-bolt intensity would ignite the first spark.

He slipped his hand under my chin and lifted my face for a kiss. Gentle and sweet, his lips brushing against mine. I spread my palms over his chest. The heat of him was a striking contrast to the open refrigerator behind me.

"My ass is getting cold," I murmured.

"Hmm." He reached around to squeeze my rear. "I can think of a few ways to warm it up."

I smiled, even as a hot shiver coursed through me. I hadn't forgotten his remark that I was "getting spanked." Clearly he hadn't, either.

He lowered his mouth to my ear. "Does that scare you?"

"No," I admitted, though it did make me a little nervous. "Not with you."

"Good." His breath heated my neck.

I was getting all melty and soft again. Hadn't I just ordered him to leave?

He didn't seem at all inclined to follow my order as he moved his lips back to mine. He put his hands on either side of my head, angling my mouth against his. I fell into the delicious sensations, letting him overtake me.

After a minute, he moved us both away from the refrigerator and closed the door. He grasped my waist and lifted me onto the counter.

I wrapped my legs around his hips, expecting him to get back to the serious business of kissing, but instead he rested his hands on my thighs and looked at me with that unnerving, penetrating gaze.

"What?" I said.

"Why did you quit storm chasing?" he asked.

Frustration stabbed through me. I looked at his throat so I wouldn't have to meet his eyes.

"I know you loved it," he continued. "You loved the danger and unpredictability, even though it scared you."

"I was not *scared.*"

"You sure?"

"Oh, for god's sake." I shoved his hands away from me and climbed off the counter. "I stopped because I got a job and started doing the work from a university computer lab. That's it. There's no big, dramatic reason. I chased storms a thousand years ago when I was young and liked the challenge. Then I grew up. End of story."

"Bullshit." Now he was frowning. "Tell me."

"No. And stop barking orders like a drill sergeant. I don't like it."

"Yeah, you do. Because I'm the only person who's ever ordered you to do anything. And even with all your tough-girl talk, you're attracted to anything or anyone stronger and more powerful than you. Things that challenge you. Things you can't control. That's exactly why you love storms."

All the air escaped my lungs. It was like he had just opened up a secret part of my heart that even I hadn't known existed. And I couldn't figure out if it was exhilarating or terrifying to discover that Archer West was the only person who had ever unlocked me.

"Come on, storm girl," he said. "Show me how *not scared* you really are."

I took a breath. My skin tingled.

"Is that a challenge?" I asked, injecting a note of disdain into my voice.

"No." Archer grinned. "It's a triple-dog dare."

Well, shit.

CHAPTER SEVENTEEN

KELSEY

"THANKS FOR COMING, MR. CLEMENT." I PUSHED AWAY FROM the computer in the lab and went to greet Harold Clement of Edison Power. "Sorry I didn't get your message sooner, or I'd have come to your office again."

"That's all right." He gave me a warm smile as we shook hands. "I wanted to see your department anyway. I've always been fascinated by atmospheric sciences."

"Hence the tie?" I asked, glancing at his necktie, which was patterned with lightning bolts.

"Better than a hula-dancer tie, right?"

I chuckled. "Much better. Classier, too."

"So this is the lab for the entire department?" He glanced around at the computers and equipment. "I'd expected King's would have bigger facilities."

"It's a thorn in our side," I admitted. "We need upgraded equipment, even another lab entirely, but the university doesn't have the money right now. We're submitting a new proposal for it, though. Can I show you around?"

"Another day," he said. "I know you need to leave soon, but I wanted to talk to you in person again."

I nodded, and we went to the conference room. I kept my outward composure, though I'd been nervous since he'd called yesterday, asking to meet with me early this morning.

He hadn't said why, so my mind had been spinning all night. Did he want to invite me to give my presentation to the head brass at Edison Power? Did he need more data? Did he have more questions? Did he want to return something I'd left in his office?

"I always think it's more respectful to talk to people face-to-face, if you get a chance," Harold said as we sat at the conference table.

"I agree."

"So rather than send you an email, I wanted to tell you personally," he continued, and the expression on his face indicated he wasn't about to deliver good news.

I steeled my spine.

"I'm afraid the Edison board of directors doesn't think the Spiral Project is the kind of program we're looking to support at this time," Harold said.

I absorbed the rush of disappointment, reminding myself I'd half expected a rejection.

"I'm sorry to hear that," I admitted, glad that my voice remained steady.

"I'm sorry to have to tell you," Harold replied, his forehead creasing with regret. "I think your project is extraordinary, but Edison wants a program the community can get better involved with and that will help the Edison brand. Tornado research is so specialized, not to mention the board thinks the Spiral Project is too expensive and risky…"

He went on, but I stopped listening. I'd heard similar things from other agencies. Different music, same lyrics.

"I'm genuinely sorry, Professor March," Harold continued as I walked with him to the elevators. "If it were up to me, Edison would throw a bunch of money at you. It's an ambitious project, and I'd love to see you succeed with it."

"You and me both."

"Do let me know if there's ever anything I can do to help you."

I shook his hand and thanked him for his time. After he was gone, I returned to my office, gathered all the project data, and stuffed it in the desk drawer.

I glanced at the clock. Colton had said he would be on campus around nine. I called him to see if he was waiting for me, then grabbed my satchel and went downstairs.

Though Edison's decision wasn't unexpected, the rejection still hurt. Every rejection hurt, especially one that might have been *another way*.

The Spiral proposal was still with the National Science Foundation, and while I had a hard time mustering any hope that they would approve funding, they hadn't yet said no. At least that was something.

I walked to the university parking lot, where Colton was taking some crates out of the back of his van.

"You're good to go." He slammed the van doors and handed me the keys. "I'll call if I see anything promising on the Doppler."

"Thanks. I'll be back by Tuesday at the latest. Tess is taking over my classes on Monday."

Colton nodded. "I'll give her a hand with grading. Good luck."

He waved as I got into the driver's seat. Even before I pulled out of the campus parking lot, my heart started to race. I gripped the steering wheel as I drove to the Butterfly House. I parked by the front porch and let myself inside.

A radio blared. I found Archer in the front room, sexy as heaven and hell in his faded jeans and dirty white T-shirt, his head bent in concentration as he measured a slat of hardwood.

I turned down the radio. He looked up.

"Hi," I said.

He straightened, his gaze sliding over me. "Hi, yourself."

"It looks good," I said, gesturing to the hardwood floor.

"Sure does." He kept his eyes on me.

I smiled. I was wearing a silk-lined navy suit, a silk blouse, and navy pumps, an ensemble I was accustomed to, and one that made me feel in command. Like I'd been the day I met Archer in Dean's office. I hadn't felt quite so *in command* since then, but I liked that he appreciated how I dressed and looked in real life.

Which meant this thing with him was… what? A fantasy life? That was the only way I could think of it, even though everything about Archer West was more real, raw, and earthy than anything or anyone I'd ever encountered before.

He watched me. Little pinpoints of light glowed in his dark eyes. I tried to muster up my courage, knowing that once the invitation was out there, I couldn't take it back. I wouldn't.

"The model forecast is showing some activity moving into western Kansas," I said, the words coming out fast. "Instability, lift, wind shear. I borrowed Colton's van. I have a travel bag, food, my cell, a camcorder, an emergency kit, laptop, weather radio and scanner, and a full tank of gas. I need to make one detour, but if we leave now and drive through the night, we could be in Kansas by tomorrow morning."

My heart pounded fast and frantically, like a moth fluttering wildly around a hot light bulb.

"Give me ten minutes," Archer said. "And we'll be on the road."

I swerved my gaze to him, my breath catching. The light in his eyes burned brighter. I felt it in him too, that rush in his blood at the thought of getting out there, navigating through the darkness with only a scant idea of where we were going or what we'd find once we got there. Pulled by a storm.

We went outside, and I stopped at the van to grab a change of clothes while Archer locked up the Butterfly House. On our way to the trailer, I told him about the meeting with Harold Clement.

"I'm sorry." Archer gave the back of my neck a gentle squeeze. "But maybe it'll be the next one."

"Yeah." I sighed. "I guess it's fall seven times, get up eight. That's what Liv and Allie always say."

Not all that easy to do, though, when your ass was bruised from hitting the ground so many times.

Archer stopped and wrapped me in his arms, hugging the

disappointment right out of me. I couldn't be disappointed when I was about to embark on a storm-chasing adventure with the man I… really, really liked. A lot.

In the trailer, Archer took a shower while I changed into jeans and a knit shirt. He threw his stuff into a duffel bag and picked up his worn notebook from the counter.

"Ready?" he asked.

"I'm ready," I said, pushing to my feet. "Let's do this."

We went back outside and headed toward the van.

Archer extended his hand. I tightened my fingers around the car keys. We stared each other down for a second before I held out the keys. I dangled them over his outstretched hand.

"For the record," I said firmly, "I'm ordering you to drive."

Amusement flashed in his eyes. "Message received."

"And I'm in charge of the playlist."

"I order you to be in charge of the playlist."

I dropped the keys into his hand. We got into the van and started out of Mirror Lake. It was close to ten as we entered the highway heading south. I plugged my phone into the stereo and turned it on.

"So what's the detour?" Archer asked.

I looked out the window. I was sort of knotted up inside about this, but again there was no turning back.

"I need to drop something off at my mother's near Chicago."

I felt his glance of surprise. "We're going to your mother's?"

"Just for a few hours. It's not on the way, but I mapped out a route." I forced myself to look at him and gauge his response.

He was silent for a minute, as if trying to unravel all the reasons why I'd even suggest that he visit my mother with me. I wasn't sure of them myself.

"Is that a problem?" I asked.

"Not for me," he said. "I assume she knows we're coming."

"Of course." It was only a half lie. She knew I was coming, but I hadn't yet told her about Archer in case he'd balked.

When we stopped for gas, I stepped around the side of the building to call my mother and tell her I wasn't coming alone. Thankfully she didn't interrogate me about Archer aside from asking how I knew him. When I told her he was Dean's brother, she made a noise of happy surprise that caused a rustle of unease in me. Soon she'd find out that Archer and Dean were nothing alike.

My stomach tensed the longer we drove. I busied myself with a forecasting model so I wouldn't have to think too much about the fact that Archer was the complete opposite of the type of man my mother always wanted me to be with.

Several hours later, Archer pulled the van into the driveway of a one-story ranch house in a tranquil, Highland Park neighborhood. My mother came out of the front door before Archer had even stopped the engine.

In a tailored, navy dress with her graying hair pulled back into an elegant chignon, she looked achingly familiar and reassuring. Just the sight of her flooded me with relief.

I hurried out of the van and went to hug her. "Hi, Mama."

"So happy to see you," she said, tightening her arms around me. "*Dochenka.*"

I breathed in her tea-rose scent, welcoming the hard embrace that put the world back into balance. No unpredictable storms here—only solid ground and stability.

My mother pulled back to look at me, giving me the once-over before taking my face in her hands.

"You look tired," she said. "Beautiful as always, but tired."

"It's just been such a busy semester." I eased away from her to turn toward Archer. "Mama, this is Archer West, the man I told you about."

I saw her gaze flicker over his faded jeans and leather jacket, but her smile didn't waver as she extended her hand to greet him.

"Come in, come in," she said, waving us toward the house. "I have tea and cookies. You must be tired after the drive."

Inside the house, my anxiety eased further. I'd bought the house for my mother a few years ago, and it contained all the things that I'd grown up with in our two-bedroom Chicago apartment and, later, the tiny house my parents had bought when I was a teenager. A few icons hung on the walls, embroidered shawls were tossed over the chairs, and well-worn books lined the shelves. Even though I'd never lived here, it still felt like home.

The scent of black tea and walnut cookies filled the air. If I'd been vaguely worried about any awkwardness, my concerns were allayed the moment we sat down.

Archer was easy company—polite, gracious, and entirely comfortable carrying on a conversation with my mother about her house, her shop, even her life in Russia and experiences immigrating to the US. He drank three cups of tea and ate about a dozen tea cookies, which pleased my mother to no end.

"I like a man who eats well," she remarked, patting him on the shoulder and pushing the plate of cookies toward him again. "My cooking I learned from my mother years and years ago. But Kseniya never had interest in cooking. She was more interested in watching The Weather Channel with her father."

"She told me." Archer glanced at me, his eyes warm.

My mother reached across the table to squeeze my hand. "He was a good man, Alexei. Strong-willed and stubborn, but good. So determined to learn English, be a worthy American. Such a hard worker."

I stood to gather the empty plates and cups. "I brought you a box of *pysanky* for the shop. I thought we could stop by before we leave."

"Of course." A faint worry darkened her eyes. "You be careful on this trip. It's been a long time since you've done such a thing."

Didn't I know it. "We'll be fine. Archer is a great driver."

My mother glanced at Archer. "What work do you do, Archer?"

"I repair motorcycles at a garage," he said. "Cars, too. Right now I'm helping my brother finish work on his house."

"You remember I told you about Liv and Dean's new place," I said to my mother. "Archer is installing the hardwood floor, among other things."

I sounded like I was trying to prove he did more than just repair bikes. Irritated with myself, I brought the dishes into the kitchen.

I heard my mother and Archer talking as they left through the back door. I went to the living-room windows that overlooked the garden. They walked along the flagstone paths, Archer matching his stride to my mother's slower one as she pointed out all the plants and flowers.

Something twisted in my chest. I returned to the kitchen to wash the dishes.

Maybe this hadn't been a good idea. I didn't want my

mother to think my relationship with Archer was actually… significant.

I groaned softly.

"That was not a good sound," my mother said from behind me.

I turned. "Where's Archer?"

"In the garden fixing a broken fence. I was showing him my roses, and he offered to do some repairs."

She joined me in putting the dishes away before she wrapped her arms around me. "What made you want to go after a storm again?"

"He did," I admitted.

She was quiet.

"He's nothing like Dean," I told her, knowing well how much she loved and admired Professor Dean West. "In fact, he's just the opposite."

I waited for her to ask me why I was with him. She didn't.

In truth, I'd almost stopped thinking of Archer as Dean's brother. Not only had I taken Dean out of the equation where my relationship with Archer was concerned, I just couldn't make any kind of a link between them.

Archer was so… *Archer*. Fire and bad jokes, danger and outright cuteness, scorching heat and scars.

He was who he was. Stood on his own. Blunt, honest. A straight shooter. Making no apologies. No wonder he'd escaped the Wests as soon as he could. He burned too brightly. He'd have suffocated there, in Dean's extensive shadow and the cold perfection of their parents' lives.

I knew how that felt, to be trapped by your surroundings. I'd secretly felt that way since starting work at King's, and I couldn't help envying Archer for his ability to live life on his own terms. Answering to no one.

"Aren't you going to interrogate me about him?" I asked my mother.

"Why should I?"

"Because you're always telling me how you want me to be with a nice man."

"He seems like a nice man."

"He is. But he's had a rough life. He didn't graduate from high school. He doesn't have a steady job. He's not *right* for me."

Still she didn't respond. Irritated, I pulled away from her. I'd been expecting a lecture about how my career was so impressive but that life wasn't complete without love and family. Then I could respond with the plain fact that Archer and I had no future together.

Because I couldn't possibly be imagining one, not even in the quietest, most secret place in my heart. Even if I were, reality would slap me upside the head sooner or later. I'd known from the beginning this wild ride would have to end.

Why wasn't my mother agreeing that Archer wasn't right for me?

"I need to get some stuff organized in the van," I said, going past her and through the living room.

I stopped at the fireplace mantel and looked at a picture of my parents and me. My father stood with one arm around my mother and the other arm around me. He wore a flannel shirt and jeans. His expression was serious behind his beard, his dark eyes glittering with strength and intelligence.

Just looking at the picture, I could hear the booming

sound of his voice. Smell the pipe tobacco that always clung to his clothes. Feel the weight of his arm on my shoulder.

My father and I had had a contentious relationship, with him always trying to rein in my rebellious tendencies—and me refusing to allow it—but never once had I doubted his love for me.

Maybe that was why I'd pursued being different and defiant. I'd always known that no matter what I did, no matter what boundaries I pushed, my father would always love me.

An ache filled my chest. I walked past the photograph and out the front door. I suddenly felt very alone.

After I checked the forecast models again to make sure we wouldn't leave too late, Archer and I drove to my mother's gift shop near downtown. She'd gone an hour earlier and was restocking the *pysanky* shelves when we arrived.

Her longtime friend and partner, Maria, a plump woman with twinkling eyes and a creased, apple-dumpling face, greeted Archer with a hug before grabbing his arm and taking him on a whirlwind tour of the shop.

I helped my mother with restocking, then we worked on some accounting and mail orders. It felt good to be back to another familiar routine.

"When Vera told me you were bringing a man home, I didn't expect him," Maria remarked in Russian as she approached the front counter.

I glanced to where Archer was busy taking apart a ten-piece matryoshka doll. The painted wooden figures looked even more delicate in his big hands.

"What did you expect?" I asked, also in Russian. I disliked the defensive note in my voice. "A lawyer? Another professor? An architect?"

"Yes," Maria said without apology. "You are an accomplished, professional woman, Kseniya. Exactly what your father wanted you to be."

A pang speared through my chest. My mother squeezed my arm.

"Kseniya doesn't make foolish choices," she said, giving Maria a pointed glance.

"I didn't say it was foolish," Maria replied. "Just unexpected."

Both she and my mother looked at Archer again.

"He is handsome," Maria remarked.

"Handsome?" My mother shook her head, her gaze still on Archer. "He's more than handsome, Maria. He's what young people would call a complete *hottie.*"

She said that last word in English, which sent both her and Maria into a fit of giggles. I tried to give them a stern look, even though a smile twitched the corners of my mouth. My mother, after all, did speak the truth.

"He is a hottie," I agreed in Russian. "In more ways than one."

Maria nudged me with her elbow. "He is good in bed, hmm?"

"Maria!" My face heated. "My mother is standing right here."

"Well, is he?" my mother asked.

"I am not talking to you two about this." I tried to concentrate on the invoices again.

Maria and my mother continued staring at Archer, who

was now putting the wooden doll back together and paying no attention to the gossipy Russian women at the counter.

"I can't imagine he wouldn't be amazing in bed," Maria murmured. "Look at the size of his—"

"Archer!" I called. "Time for us to go."

"Hands," Maria finished, giving my mother a wink.

While they both dissolved into laughter again, I grabbed my bag and stalked around to the other side of the counter.

Archer put the doll back on the shelf and approached us. If he wondered why Maria and my mother were red-faced and giggling like twelve-year-old girls, he gave no indication as he complimented them again on the shop and said goodbye.

When he started toward the door, I turned to Maria and my mother.

"Yes," I said in Russian, with as much haughtiness as I could muster. "He does have very big and… remarkable hands."

Another fit of laughter consumed them. I grinned and hurried to catch up with Archer, who waited at the door. He pulled it open for me, and I went ahead of him down the sidewalk. He fell into step beside me.

"Big hands, huh?" he asked.

Shock bolted through me. I stopped in my tracks. "Um… what?"

He held out his hands in front of him. "Apparently my hands are big and… what was that word? Wonderful?"

I stared at him. "You *understood* what we were saying?"

He flexed his hands and stretched out his fingers. "Some of it."

"You know *Russian*?" I felt like he'd just told me he was from Mars.

"A little." Archer was starting to look both smug and highly amused. "Mick, the guy who owns the garage where I worked, is Russian. Mikhail. He and his wife Svetlana are from Moscow. I picked up some Russian from them."

I couldn't believe what I was hearing. "Why didn't you tell me?"

"You never asked."

"Argh!" I planted my hands on his chest and gave him a shove. "You! That is so… so *devious*!"

"Hey, I didn't even know you spoke Russian to your mother until we got here," he said. His tone was defensive, but his eyes were bright with suppressed laughter. "And even if I didn't know some Russian, I totally would have understood *hottie*."

"Archer!" My face felt like it was on fire. "You are so… ugh!"

I couldn't even believe that I was at a loss for words. I shoved him again for good measure and spun on my heel to stalk down the street. I heard him laughing behind me, and loath though I was to admit it, the warm, rich sound of his laughter resounded right in the middle of my soul.

He hurried to catch up with me. "Aw, come on, don't be mad."

"I am *furious*."

He poked me in the shoulder. "You're pretty sexy when you're furious."

"I am not."

"You are, *kotyenok moy*."

I stopped. My heart did that crazy twirling thing again. "What did you call me?"

"*Kotyenok*." He smiled, his eyes creasing at the corners. "Little kitten, right?"

I nodded. Actually he'd said, "*my* little kitten." For whatever reason, the *my* seemed to make all the difference in the world.

I must have looked dumbfounded because Archer frowned.

"I didn't just insult you, did I?" he asked. "I thought it was an endearment."

"No." I paused to clear my throat. "I mean, yes. It is an endearment. A very… nice endearment."

"Good." He reached out to tweak my nose. "Are you still furious, *kotyenok moy*?"

I tried to glower at him, just to make a point, but of course it was impossible with the "my little kitten," the laughing, the nose tweaking, and Archer standing there with his boyish grin that was such an engaging contrast to the pure masculinity of the rest of him.

"If you think I'm sexy when I'm furious, I can still be furious," I told him.

He moved closer, sliding his hands around my waist and settling our lower bodies together. Warmth slipped through me.

"You're sexy all the time, *kotyenok moy*," he murmured, lowering his head to brush his lips across my cheek. "Every second of every minute of every day. I can't get enough of you."

"Oh, yeah," I grumbled. "Lay it on thick and see if that dilutes my raging fury."

"Okay," he agreed before settling his mouth over mine in a hot, deep kiss that made me tingle from head to toe.

"Did it work?" he asked when we came up for air.

"Um… I'm not sure yet. Try again."

He did. It worked.

"It was nice to have met you, Mrs. March." Archer kissed my mother on the cheek as we stood in front of her house later that afternoon. "Thanks for everything. *Spasibo.*"

She smiled. "I'm glad Kseniya brought you to see me. Take care of her, *da?*"

"Yes, ma'am."

She gave him several foil-wrapped packages of blinchki and tea cookies. Archer went to put them in the cooler stowed in the back of the van.

I hugged my mother. "Thank you. I'll come back soon."

"And you take care of yourself, *dochenka.*" She eased back to pat my cheek, and I saw the worry in her eyes. "Don't work so hard. Even with tenure, they should give you a break."

"I'll be fine."

"Be careful driving." She glanced past me to where Archer was organizing stuff in the back of the van. "I feel better knowing he's with you. Bring him back with you next time, too."

"He's… he's leaving soon, Mama. He won't be in Mirror Lake much longer."

My mother returned her gaze to me. "Where is he going?"

"Back to Nevada, I guess. It was… he's just visiting for a few weeks."

She frowned. "You knew this all along?"

I nodded. A hint of shame rose in me.

"He's not the right kind of man for me anyway," I said defensively. "I didn't think you'd even like him."

My mother looked at me with growing insight. My shame intensified. Her gaze pinned me to the spot. I should have known I could never hide from her.

"Kseniya," she said, her voice stern. "Did you *want* me not to like him?"

"No." I looked at the ground and shuffled my feet. "I mean, not like that. I just expected you to remind me that he's all wrong for me."

"Why would I remind you of that?"

"Because you're always going on about how you want me to find a nice, respectable man," I said, spreading my hands out in frustration. "He's not like the kind of man you've always wanted for me."

She crossed her arms, her frown deepening, her stare way too perceptive.

"He may not be what I've imagined for you, but that doesn't mean he's wrong for you," she said.

"Oh, don't start this, Mama. He's *leaving*. It'll be over soon. Besides, you know there's no future for us. Not with a man like him."

"What kind of man is that?" she asked. "One who is kind and polite?"

"I meant—"

"I know what you meant, Kseniya." She took my face in her hands and forced me to look at her. "And even if you thought I wouldn't like him, *dochenka*, I do. I like him a great deal. He is a good man. A survivor. Just like your father."

I shook my head, trying to deflect her words. My vision blurred.

"You think I want for you a certain kind of man," she

continued, her gaze unwavering. "But I know you better than that. What I want for you is a man who challenges you, who loves you fiercely, who accepts everything about you, even your worst flaws. You are not an easy woman, Kseniya, and you should not have an easy man. I want you to have a man whom *you* want. A man who makes you laugh and makes you angry. A man who chases you because he is not afraid of the storm inside you. Because he loves that part of you."

I swallowed past the lump in my throat. My heart felt like it was about to crack wide open.

"I can't do this, Mama," I whispered.

"You can do anything, Kseniya." She pressed her forehead to mine. "*Anything.* You are so strong. So smart. But you have such a wall around you. You are so afraid to be happy."

Was I? Or was it that I didn't think I deserved to be happy?

In either case, it didn't matter where Archer was concerned. I tried to ignore the fresh stab of regret at the reminder that this was temporary. That he was *my* storm, fierce and exhilarating, but soon to end.

"I love you." I eased away from my mother and pressed my lips to her soft cheek. "I'll call you along the way."

We exchanged a hug before I reluctantly detached myself from her and walked to where Archer was waiting.

"Travel safely," my mother called as we got into the van. "And be happy."

CHAPTER EIGHTEEN

KELSEY

WE STARTED SOUTHWEST THROUGH ILLINOIS TOWARD IOWA. Archer was a good travel companion. He asked about the details of the Spiral Project, how I'd forecast the potential storm, what my grad students were working on. I asked about his travels, his work on the Butterfly House, the other jobs he'd had. We fell into comfortable silences and commented on passing scenery or towns.

He was easy to be with. Even with our intense, crackling heat and my own tension about the physical part of our relationship, I liked just being with him.

A couple of hours in, I reached into the cooler on the floor of the backseat and dug around for a plastic bottle. I twisted the lid off and handed it to Archer.

"Chocolate milk, you fourth grader," I said.

"You remembered." He flashed me a smile. "I'm touched."

"Yeah, well..." I reached back and grabbed another bottle. I opened it and took a swig. The chocolate milk slid rich and creamy down my throat. "You might be on to something here."

As the night fell, fewer cars populated the roads. We took a break around midnight, stopping at an all-night diner. We mapped out the remaining route as we ate. I gave Archer a rudimentary course on storm chasing and etiquette in the likely event that we ran into other chasers along the way.

After paying the bill, we stepped outside with take-out cups of coffee. Along with an increasing, cold wind, rain had started to fall, even though we were nowhere near our destination yet.

"Hold on." Archer shrugged out of his jacket and draped it over my shoulders as we hurried to the van.

Once inside, I slipped my arms into the jacket sleeves, giving in to the urge to nestle into the enveloping warmth of leather and Archer. The lining was soft and worn, his clean male scent clinging to the fabric.

I checked the radar on my phone and told Archer the rain would pass in about fifteen minutes.

"Come on." I gestured for him to follow me into the back of the van, where the seats were stored into the floor.

"Really?" Archer shrugged. "Okay. I usually like to take my time, but I can get the job done in fifteen minutes, if that's what you want."

I threw him a look. "I meant that you should take a short nap before we get going again. It's past midnight and we have at least another six or seven hours to go. Not safe for you to drive if you're too tired. Unless you want me to drive."

"Silence, woman."

I reached out to bonk him on the head. He grabbed my wrist and planted a warm kiss on my palm. We clambered into the back of the van and settled down on a couple of sleeping bags. Rain splashed across the windows.

"So why did you agree to storm chase?" Archer asked.

"I never could resist a triple-dog dare." I nudged his hip with mine. "And I wanted to do it with you."

He watched me, curious. "And why are you with me?"

The question sounded like he was referring to more than just storm chasing. I looked at the sky, the clusters of clouds, the spilling rain.

"That's a multicell storm," I said, gesturing to the windows. "It's formed by bunch of different cells that contain an updraft and downdraft. It's the most common type of thunderstorm."

I took a swallow of coffee. "The rarest is called the supercell thunderstorm. It creates the most destructive tornados, winds, and hail. It's usually isolated from other thunderstorms, but it's the most powerful type of storm. The most beautiful and incredible, too."

I leaned forward, aware of Archer's gaze. The rain came harder, pattering onto the roof like little pebbles. His leather jacket wrapped around me like an embrace.

"I used to chase supercell storms," I said. "Used to wait for them, watch for them. When I was in college, I hooked up with a group of storm chasers and we'd take off at a moment's notice when we saw something forming. Always hoped we'd catch a tornado or get caught in the middle of severe weather. Sometimes we did. I loved the risk, the excitement, the unknown. There was something so adventurous about chasing something completely unpredictable. Something you couldn't control."

"Why did you give it up?"

I shrugged. "I grew up. I'd been a risk-taker as a kid, but after my father died I learned some tough lessons about being an adult."

"What happened?"

"He died of a heart attack when I was in my junior year," I said, my chest constricting. "After he died, I hit the self-destruct button hard. I drank too much, slept around, partied a lot. Quit school. Ended up in a couple of bad relationships."

I felt his tension and held up my hand to stop him from saying anything. I stared past him out the window.

"Dean knew I was crashing hard, but I wouldn't listen to him when he tried to help me. So finally he called my mother and told her I was in bad shape. She came to bring me back home so I could get myself together. When we returned to Chicago, I found out my father had left her in debt. The house they'd worked so hard to buy had been foreclosed, and she'd been forced to move. She hadn't told me so I wouldn't be upset.

"Despite everything, my mother was undeterred. She was working three jobs. She'd rented an apartment. She was saving up money to go into business with Maria. She was dealing with her fucked-up daughter. Not once did she give up. Hell, not once did she even complain. She just buckled down and got to work. That woman has a will of iron. And I didn't even know it until then."

"That's why you straightened up," Archer said.

"Damn right. I went back to school. Finished undergrad work with honors and got into several grad programs. I've been a success story ever since."

"And this?" Archer reached out to tug at the blue streak cutting through my hair. "A souvenir of your wild past?"

My throat constricted. He had souvenirs, too. Reminders. Scars.

"Something like that," I admitted.

Once again, I was breaking my own rules. *No personal stuff,* I'd told him. And yet I'd taken him to meet my mother and was telling him all my secrets.

"Okay, well." Unnerved suddenly, I shifted around, pretending to arrange the sleeping bag. "That was weird. Subject change, please."

He didn't respond. When I turned to look at him, he closed the distance between us and pressed his lips to mine in a warm, lovely kiss. My breath caught in my chest. Our lips sealed together, moving with ease and growing heat.

"You didn't answer my question." Archer lifted his head. He put his hand against my cheek. "Why are you with me?"

I stared at him, into his midnight eyes with their starlike points of light.

"You're the first real risk I've taken in a very long time," I whispered.

A smile tugged at his mouth. He shifted closer, but instead of kissing me again, he pulled me down so we were both lying on our backs. He tugged me against his side.

I wanted to stay there forever. Enveloped in his leather jacket with his body heat warming me, and the rain falling, I was suddenly and intensely glad that I'd *given over* to him, even for a short time. It was a thunderstorm with him, brief but intense. One I knew I would never forget.

We got back on the road after we'd slept a couple of hours and the rain had stopped. As we headed southwest through Illinois and Missouri, we played road-trip games, drank chocolate milk, and ate tea cookies.

I offered to drive again, but Archer had his hands glued to the wheel and acted like my offer was a personal insult. By navigating through country roads, we missed the interstate traffic as we approached the Kansas border.

"There's a line of storms forming to the southwest," I told Archer, after checking the radar. "Take County Road 7. If we need to divert north, we can take the back roads."

I scrambled into the back to get the camera equipment ready. Storm chasers always traveled in packs or at least pairs so that one person could drive while the other tracked the storm. I slipped my Nikon around my neck and returned to the front seat with my laptop.

"Your grad students do this a lot?" Archer asked, leaning forward to look at the darkening clouds.

"As often as they can, though tornado season is in the spring and summer."

"And what do you do if you see a tornado?"

"Most of the time the objective is to get the best video possible," I said. "Video can be a huge help in confirming model results. Of course, if we had a Doppler on Wheels or other high-tech equipment, we could do much more."

I checked the radar on my laptop again. "It's shifting north. You can take 56 toward Topeka, but don't get on the interstate. We need to avoid the traffic."

An ocean of fields stretched out on either side of the road as we drove. My stomach knotted up with both anxiety and excitement.

I got out the camcorder and filmed the towering cloud that stretched toward the stratosphere. The rain started coming down harder, pushed by the increasing wind. We passed a few cars and vans parked on the side of the road.

I looked at the sky. My instinct told me the wind shear and moisture would move farther north, and that we could catch the storm if we were patient.

I didn't usually like being patient, but it had been so long since I'd even tried to chase a storm that I decided to play it safe. Archer navigated the van north. We stopped once for gas.

As Archer filled the tank, I grabbed the video camera and went into the convenience store. I bought a few granola bars and some beef jerky to restock our supplies and chatted briefly with the clerk about the storm chasers who had come through already.

On my way back to the van, I stopped at the edge of a field that stretched alongside the station. The clouds were tilting downshear at an angle that seemed favorable for supercell formation.

I pulled out my camera and filmed the sky. My heart swelled in response to the sheer beauty of the sky and clouds, the mysteries they contained, and the certain fact that no matter how hard I tried, part of them would always remain unpredictable.

"Ready, storm girl?" Archer called.

I paused the camera and returned to the van, pushing my windblown hair out of my face. Archer reached out to take the camera from me. I pulled a rod of beef jerky out of my pocket and unwrapped it.

"I'm going to map out a different route to keep us away from the interstate," I said.

"What were you filming?" he asked.

I gestured to the clouds and took a bite of jerky. "Those are likely to become supercells. The ratio of instability to shear is perfect."

"Tell me more."

I glanced up, realizing Archer had the camera trained on me. I frowned.

"What are you doing?"

"Filming you. Tell me about the supercell."

Though I wasn't all that nuts about being on camera, I figured it wouldn't hurt to lay out the basics since I'd have to review the video later anyway.

"We're looking at a storm formed from a specific set of weather conditions," I said into the camera. "If the wind changes too rapidly with height, then the storm will be ripped apart. If the instability is too strong, then the storm will destroy itself with its own downdraft. But when the two are just right, the intensifying rotation creates a self-sustaining storm that lasts much longer than your garden-variety thunderstorm."

I gestured to the sky behind me. "Behold the supercell."

Archer lowered the camera, his gaze on me. "You're great on film."

I shook my head. "Flattery will get you… well, it will almost certainly get you laid later on, but right now we have a storm to follow."

He grinned and climbed into the driver's seat. I adjusted the GPS as we started out of the gas station.

"We're going to divert south a short way," I said. "I don't think the low level jet is going to be optimal, but we need to stay on the tip of the moisture tongue."

"Sounds promising. I'd like you on the tip of my moisture tongue."

I poked him in the arm. "The moisture tongue is a region of dewpoints and instability. It's where storms often form, but the strongest are at the tip of it. Take E550 south."

He followed orders. I liked that he was willing to cede power to me out here. He clearly recognized that I knew what I was doing, and even with all his dominance and control, he could let me take the lead in my own sphere.

We drove for another hour. I watched the sky. Lightning split through the clouds, followed by the rumble of thunder. I looked at the radar again and called Colton, who gave me details from the Rapid Refresh model.

"One more hour," I told Archer. "It's heading in this direction. Let's stop and get something to eat. If it's not here by nightfall, we'll be done for the day."

He pulled into a diner, where several trucks and vans were parked in the lot. We went inside, the noise of male voices filling the interior.

I scanned the crowd, picking out at least four tables of storm chasers. If I hadn't caught snippets of conversation about wind shear and instability, I'd have known them from their attire of jeans, T-shirts, and baseball caps, and the laptops and tablets sitting between their plates of steak and eggs.

"Kelsey?" A male voice, sounding surprised, made me turn. A beefy, bearded guy approached, looking me up and down. "I'll be damned."

I smiled. "You were damned a long time ago, Henry."

"True enough." A grin split through his beard as we exchanged a hug. "What're you doing here? I thought you were stuck in a classroom somewhere."

"I usually am," I admitted. "But I thought I'd come out for a while. Henry, this is my friend Archer. Archer, Henry and I were in grad school together."

They exchanged greetings, and Henry invited us to join his group for dinner. As we followed him to a crowded table, the guys shuffled around to make room for two more chairs. Henry introduced us to the meteorologists, grad students, lab workers, drivers, and photographers who'd all gone out together in a fleet.

We compared notes on the storm, talked about their plans and ours, and checked our data against each other's. Everyone hummed with excited energy, all of us knowing the chase wasn't over yet.

This was what the Spiral Project unit would be like, if I ever had a shot at getting it off the ground again. I tried not to think about the fact that even if I did, I wouldn't be one of the project's storm chasers. I'd be stuck in front of a computer screen at King's.

I shook my head, not letting that thought encroach on my enjoyment. And as we ate, talked, and laughed with the others, something rose inside me like a perfect, shiny balloon.

Happiness. I was happy sitting there with the people who shared my love of weather, all of us speaking the same language and eager to hunt the elusive storm.

I was happy sitting beside Archer, his warm thigh pressed to mine. He was at ease too, comfortable with these no-bullshit guys who pursued a risk with both dedication and hard work.

But when Henry asked if we wanted to join their caravan, I looked at Archer and shook my head.

"We're going solo on this one," I told Henry.

Archer smiled and winked at me. A lovely sense of *togetherness* passed between us, as if he and I had been a team from the beginning. When we hadn't let the flip of a coin decide our fate.

I reached into my pocket for my phone. "Henry, take my cell number and we can keep in touch."

We exchanged numbers before Archer and I headed out again. Yes, I was happy sitting with a noisy crowd of storm chasers, but I was even happier being alone with Archer. There was no one on earth I'd rather have been with right then, on the road chasing thunder and lightning.

I checked the radar again, studied the sky, and mapped out a route. Archer followed my directions. The rain had let up over the past couple of hours, but as we approached the convergence of activity, it started again. It was late afternoon now, and the descending sun was hidden behind a wall of dark clouds.

Adrenaline simmered inside me. If today were a bust, we'd have to start all over again tomorrow. And while that meant more time with Archer, I needed to be back in Mirror Lake by Tuesday. The longer it took, the less chance we'd see a tornado.

We diverged onto the backcountry roads again. A crack of lightning bolted through the sky, followed by the rumble of thunder. Archer peered through the windshield at the gray expanse of the horizon.

The sky darkened over the landscape. Clouds boiled up. The wind whipped over the stalks of wheat and crashed against the side of the van. I stared at the clouds.

"It's a supercell," I murmured, excitement flaring in my chest. "Look, there's rotation at the cloud base."

I adjusted my camera settings and snapped some pictures of the cloud formation. My heart pounded hard. I felt it, like a flame licking at my skin, the sense that something big was churning through the sky, past the clouds, a convergence of air and energy.

Then I saw it. The funnel cloud. It was nothing more than a slight downward extension of the cloud at first, and then it became more prominent. A cold, dry gust of wind rushed past us—the forward-flanking downdraft.

The funnel grew, visibly rotating, reaching toward the ground. Dirt, grass, and leaves stirred and began swirling northward ahead of the tornado. The vortex expanded.

I lifted my camera, exhilaration and fear firing through me. "Archer!"

He slammed on the brakes, jerking the van to a halt. "What the—"

I couldn't speak. I could hardly breathe. I slid the window down. The roar of the tornado was like a massive, grinding machine.

Archer grabbed my camcorder and trained it on the funnel cloud. I tried to steady my shaking hands as I pressed the shutter button and snapped a series of pictures.

"It's an extreme right-mover!" I shouted over the noise. "Moving south of due east!"

He dumped the camcorder in my lap and took hold of the wheel. My body lurched against the seatbelt. Archer spun the van in a three-point turn and floored it. We shot after the tornado like a horse breaking free at the starting line. The tornado raced across the field, throwing around a mass of debris.

Archer drove right down the middle of the road, so fast the van hydroplaned. My heart felt like it was going to claw out of my chest.

"What are you doing?" I yelled.

"Film it!" he yelled back.

The order snapped into my brain. I forced myself to train the camcorder on the tornado and hit the video record button.

Wind slammed against the van, skidding us half off the road. Archer righted the wheel and kept going. The tornado moved toward us, roaring like a colossal beast.

"Archer, it's coming in our direction!"

He gripped the wheel harder, his knuckles burning white. "Hold on."

Oh, Jesus. He wasn't going to stop. He was going to try and outrun it. Terror ripped through me. The tornado launched toward us, a massive, swirling, destructive force. Somehow, I managed to keep my camera focused and kept filming. Branches and leaves rained down, hitting the windshield. I put the side window halfway up, but kept the camcorder trained on the vortex.

I braced my feet on the floor, my blood alive with fear. The column of rotating wind drew closer. We'd be airborne in less than five seconds, sucked into the tornado and dropped God only knew where. Chewed up and spit out.

"Archer, stop! We need to get into the ditch!"

He didn't stop. The van jerked and skidded against the force of the wind. Archer pushed the gas pedal, forcing the van to go faster. Faster. The van started to shake. The tires skidded. No way could we go faster than a tornado. I stared as the vortex approached, bearing down on us.

"Archer..."

"Holy fucking shit," he muttered.

"Go!" I screamed. "Go!"

He leaned over the steering wheel, his jaw set. The windshield was a mass of swirling wind and debris. The van plowed forward.

We were no longer chasing a tornado but being chased by one. Not predator but prey. I gripped the door handle. Fear burned through me.

A crash of wind hit the side of the van again, pushing us into the shoulder. I heard Archer's shout over the noise of the storm. He swerved, jerking the van back onto the road.

The tornado spun to the north just as our van flew past it. Archer kept driving at full speed, racing through the chaos. My pulse hammered so hard and fast I almost didn't notice the decrease in noise.

I twisted in my seat and stared out the back window as the tornado moved over the road and rampaged through the field. I watched it go, shaking so hard my teeth rattled.

Archer hit the brakes and brought the van to a stop. A

crash of thunder echoed across the sky. I leapt out of the van and stood watching the tornado until it disappeared from sight. A wide swath of crushed wheat and uprooted trees lay in its wake as far as the eye could see. Evidence of a fierce, violent force of nature no one could control.

Archer rounded the front of the van. His forehead was damp with sweat and rain, his body taut with the same frenzied tension that filled mine.

"Kelsey, are you—"

I spun to face him, my breathing harsh. Energy and heat crackled between us. With a sudden shriek of pure glee, I flung myself at him, wrapping my arms around his shoulders and my legs around his waist.

He grabbed me, pressing our bodies together, laughter shaking his chest. Fireworks burst into my blood, and then I was laughing too, the wind still whipping around us.

"You're crazy!" I yelled, thumping my fists against his back. "Totally fucking crazy."

"Damn right." Still laughing, he swung me around in a circle. "Crazy about a storm girl."

I tightened my hold on him, dizzy with relief and elation, wanting to relive that insanity all over again.

When Archer stopped, he grasped the back of my neck. His eyes blazed the instant before he brought my lips to his. It was a hard, hot kiss filled with the rush of danger and exhilaration.

A tornado spun through both of us, crashing and spinning. I drove my hands into Archer's thick hair and opened my mouth over his, deepening the kiss until it felt like I was drowning in him. When I lifted my head, I ran my palm over the side of his face as he slid me down the length of his body.

His heart beat against mine, powerful enough to feel through our clothes.

For a minute, I could only stare at him. A flash of lightning illuminated his face. His jaw was locked, his breathing still rapid. He'd loved the thrilling power of the chase as much as I had. The tight way he held me, the rigid power of his stance, and the bright, intense gleam in his eyes told me in no uncertain terms he could push me to my limits and protect me the entire time. That he *would.*

Thunder cracked and resounded inside me. The reverberations echoed in my blood, breaking open a long-buried seed filled with my deepest desires. They flew upward—free, unfettered, limitless. Because of him.

Because of us.

CHAPTER NINETEEN

KELSEY

AFTER I TOOK SOME FOOTAGE OF THE TORNADO'S PATH, WE GOT back into the van and drove on. Darkness fell. Another line of storms encroached on the night sky. We checked in to a roadside motel, bringing the equipment into the room along with our travel bags. Energy still zinged through my blood like thousands of electric sparks.

My hands shook as I sat at the table to check my cameras and identify what we'd captured. I looked at shot after shot of the vortex, the rotating column, and the mesocyclone from which the massive tornado had formed. The video was amazing, the tornado's roar filling the audio and almost drowning out Archer's and my shouting.

"I need to send this to Colton and Tess," I said, hitting the rewind button. I glanced up at Archer, who was watching the footage over my shoulder.

"Can you believe we did that?" I asked.

"You and me? Sure I can." He pressed a kiss to the top of my head and went to unpack.

I replayed the video, hearing our excitement and crackling fear. I uploaded it as an email attachment, but stopped just before hitting the send button.

I wasn't quite ready to let my graduate students see the video. Right now, with the rain still pouring and my heart still pounding, it was too intense to share with anyone else. Too private. Too *ours*.

I pushed away from the table and stood. "That was the most incredible thing I've ever experienced."

Archer lifted an eyebrow. "*The* most incredible thing?"

"Well." My breath caught at the look of heat in his eyes. "*Second* most incredible."

I turned back to close my laptop just as Archer slid his arms around my waist from behind. Another bolt of lightning flashed through the window. Every part of me responded to the fire arcing through the sky and downward into us. His arms tightened around me with an edge of undeniable possession. His body was tense, almost pulsing with energy. The same energy that roared in my blood.

We were both so jacked up that urgency and heat fired between us immediately. His lips touched the back of my neck. A shiver ran clear down my spine. My nerves sizzled. Rain pounded on the window. Thunder rumbled.

Archer unfastened my jeans and pulled them down, then slipped his fingers between my thighs and rubbed me through my panties.

"Nice," he murmured, his voice vibrating against my neck as he moved his finger beneath the elastic to touch my bare flesh. "You get so hot so fast."

Lust uncoiled in my belly. I tried to turn and face him, wanting his mouth on mine, but he held me in place and continued his slow exploration. My legs weakened. His touch was teasing but possessive, as he trailed his finger up over my folds and into me.

I moaned, clenching around him. The sensation of his muscular body against my back and his breath on my skin sent me into a storm of sensations. He didn't stop his easy but relentless stroking, and before I could stop it, the pressure began to build.

"Archer."

"Come on, my little kitten," he murmured, his lips moving against the back of my neck. "It'll be the first of many tonight."

Holy mother of—

I came with a choked cry, fast and hard, my thighs clamping around Archer's hand. He worked his fingers against me until the shudders faded, then eased my jeans and panties off. In another five seconds, he had my shirt and bra off, and my naked ass pressed against his thighs.

He ran his hands all over me from behind, the scrape of his callused palms delicious against my skin, my whole body quivering. He moved his hands to my hips and guided me forward to the bed. I started to turn.

"No." He put his hand on my lower back and pressed me down. "Say it."

My breath stuck in my chest. I squeezed my eyes shut.

"I give up," I whispered.

"Not that. Say it."

"No."

"Get on your hands and knees."

"I…" The words refused to form.

He stroked his hand up and down my spine like he was soothing a restless cat. My heart pounded, blood rushed into my ears. I let him press me forward, fisting my hands in the bedspread, my knees sinking into the mattress. Cool air washed over me. I shivered.

I twisted again, trying to look at him over my shoulder. I heard the slap before I felt it, the strike of his broad palm against my ass.

"Archer!"

"Told you you were getting spanked." His voice was heavy with lust and a trace of amusement. "I'm a man of my word, you know."

"Well, I didn't think you'd… ow!"

He spanked me again, the sting of pain radiating over my entire cheek.

"Archer, I swear—"

"Good girls don't swear."

"I'm not a good girl."

"Yeah, you are. You just don't want to be." He stroked my ass again. "It's what I love about you."

Shock bolted through me. I froze, fully expecting him to freeze too when he realized what he'd just said.

He didn't. He kept rubbing my rear end in little circles that created a pattern of warmth over my skin. Something trembled low inside me, like an earthquake starting far beneath the surface. I shoved it back down, forced it to die. I wasn't going to take this places it was never meant to go. Not even inside my own head.

I was glad when he spanked me again. The sting distracted me, brought me back to the present. Away from the approaching earthquakes and storms. I tightened my fists on the bedspread.

"Spread your legs," he said.

I did. Another clap of thunder shook the walls. My breath burned my chest. I heard the rasp of his zipper. I wanted to turn and look, to drink in the sight of his thick erection, the brilliant blaze of tattoos over his muscled shoulder, the smoky look in his dark eyes.

His discarded sweatshirt lay crumpled on the bed. I grabbed it and lowered my face into it. The shirt smelled like Archer—sweat, sawdust, wind, and rain.

I closed my eyes. The bed dipped as he climbed onto the mattress behind me. I was open, unhidden.

He slid a finger into me. My whole body tingled in response.

"You want my cock here?" he asked, his voice husky.

Jesus. His voice alone could make me come. I nodded. Heat washed over me from the inside out. My heart throbbed. And as much as I wanted it, wanted him, I flinched when the hard knob of his cock pressed against my entrance. In this position, so exposed, all I could do was take him. Nothing else.

He stilled. His breath sawed through the air above me. I pictured him behind me, all hot skin and hard muscles, one hand curled around his shaft, the other hand gripping my ass.

"Take it," he murmured. "Then I'll come on your pretty ass."

Heat surged through me. I couldn't believe how his raw talk could ratchet my urgency so high, so fast. I pressed my face harder into the sweatshirt and reached between my spread legs.

Archer's hand clamped around my wrist. "No. Not yet."

With a moan of frustration, I pulled my hand away and grasped the bedspread. He eased his cock into me. Impossibly big. A cry stuck in my throat. He stopped again, rubbing his hands over my lower back, then around my torso and up to my breasts. My breath shortened as he rolled my nipples between his fingers. Sparks shot to my core.

"Take me," he said.

"Yes."

He pressed his hand between my shoulder blades, urging my upper body down, which pushed my rear up higher. Anxiety twisted through me when he started pushing into me again. I felt myself stretching to accommodate him, felt the heavy pulsing of his shaft, the slow glide of every thick inch.

I squirmed, twisting beneath him. He gripped my hips to still me and pushed in farther. My legs trembled.

I couldn't do it. Fear snaked through me. It wasn't that I'd never done it like this before. I had, many times. But never with him. Never with a man who could break me apart and put me back together in the same breath. Never with a man who had lightning in his eyes, a man who made earthquakes tremble in my blood.

He stopped again, half embedded inside me, his hair-roughened thighs against mine. I pressed his crumpled sweatshirt to my face.

"You want more?" His voice was hoarse.

I bit my lip. Tasted blood.

"I want more," I whispered.

"How?"

"Rough. I want more, and I want it rough."

"You're sure?"

"I'm sure."

"Say it."

"I surrender."

I had just enough time to close my fingers on the bedspread again, to brace myself, before he surged into me with one hard thrust.

He groaned. "Oh, sweet fuck."

The impact jarred me to the core, pushed me forward, closer to the edge of the endless abyss. He didn't stop, not this time, only pulled back and plunged in again, his hands gripping my ass, his hips slamming against mine.

My body burned. I put one hand on the wall in front of me, tried to match his movements but couldn't. All I could do was take him. Take his repeated hard thrusts, the dig of his fingers into my skin, the slap of his flesh against mine. He spanked me again, a sting that intensified the sensations swirling through me.

It lasted for hours. It lasted for minutes. I lost all track of time. I arched my body and fell into the storm only he could create. He clutched my waist, turned my sweat-slick body around. I spread my legs and hooked them around his hips, letting him surge into me again, raking my gaze over his damp chest. His tattoos shifted with every flex of his hard muscles, the pattern like a beautiful, living creature sliding across his skin.

He came over me, overcame me, his body hot and hard as he crushed his mouth to mine. I wound my arms around him, slid my hand over the glossy, shifting wing on his shoulder, dug my fingernails into his smooth back.

Tension unleashed inside me. I pushed upward to meet his heavy thrusts, needing him deeper, as deep as he could go. His teeth scraped my neck, my breasts. We rocked and collided and crashed, again and again.

I shattered what felt like a thousand times, shuddering and writhing beneath him, then on top of him when he rolled onto his back to let me ride him, then again with him plunging into me from behind. Still he demanded more, his voice a rough whisper pouring into my ear, lighting fires in my blood.

His rough hand scraped my back, fisted in my hair, and tugged. My body arched like a bow, tense and quivering. Endless moans broke from my throat with every surge of his cock into me. I ached all over by the time he spilled into me with a deep groan, his body collapsing on top of mine, his breath scorching my neck.

Gasping, I took the weight of him, absorbed the feeling of his sweaty, muscular chest heaving against my back. I took a few deep breaths and swallowed hard.

Archer rolled off me and onto his back. He flung his arm across his face. Rain splashed against the window. Lightning flashed.

I curled onto my side, still feeling as if he were throbbing inside me. My heart raced. He pressed his hand to my hair.

"Okay?" His voice was gravelly.

I nodded. Though I was spent, my veins hummed with energy, the last burst of exhilaration before the crash. The bed shifted as Archer moved, but aside from his hand on my hair, he didn't touch me.

Again, I was grateful. I needed some space. It was strange how he sensed exactly what I needed or didn't need. What I wanted or didn't want.

The pressure of his hand increased slightly. I closed my eyes as the crash pulled me under and thunder broke the sky.

He was still sleeping when I woke. Wet dawn light seeped through the curtained windows, the rain having slowed to a drizzle. I got up slowly and went into the bathroom to brush my teeth.

I was sore everywhere, but oh god, did it feel good. It was the sweet, aching relief of knowing I could still withstand being pushed to the edge. That I still loved it. That I wanted more.

I took a shower, pulled on a clean shirt and panties, and left the bathroom. There was a microwave in a little nook by the wall, and I scrounged around in my bag for packets of instant coffee. I stuck two cardboard cups of water in the microwave. As I waited for them to heat, I saw Archer's worn notebook sitting on the nightstand.

I eyed it warily, as if it were a time bomb. What the hell was he writing in there? It wasn't his black book or his *diary*, for lord's sake. It certainly wasn't a book of poetry. A guy who hadn't liked school wouldn't spend his time writing poetry or stories.

As tempted as I was to open the book, I turned when the microwave beeped. I made the coffee and returned to the bed, giving Archer a nudge with my knee.

"Wake up. I brought you coffee. Don't expect this to happen again."

He rolled over and yawned. "You mean the tornado or the incredibly hot fucking or you bringing me coffee?"

A tingle of heat washed through me, along with an undeniable pleasure that he'd found our fucking to be *incredibly hot.* Not that I'd had any doubts about that last night, especially with both of us so revved up.

"The coffee." I handed him a cup and climbed onto the bed.

As he lowered his head to take a sip, I took advantage of his distraction to let my gaze wander over his perfect, muscled body, the rumpled mess of his thick hair, the planes of his face, his jaw dusted with whiskers.

He glanced up and caught me staring. I cleared my throat and gestured to his cup.

"Instant coffee is all I have," I said. "Sorry. I know it tastes like dirt."

Archer shrugged. "Well, it *was* ground."

I laughed. A genuine amusement filled me, in marked contrast to the intensity of the previous night. He grinned and put his cup on the side table. He reached out to trail his fingers over my bare leg to the bottom of my foot.

"Know any bad jokes?" he asked.

"Probably. Some of my grad students are as juvenile as you are."

He grabbed my ankle to keep my foot still so he could tickle it. I yelped and poked him in the shoulder until he released me.

"What does a wicked chicken lay?" I asked as he resumed skimming his fingers over my bare leg.

"No idea."

"Deviled eggs."

"Pretty bad," he agreed. "What does Archer West lay?"

I rolled my eyes. "Kelsey March."

"Mmm-hmm." He pressed his lips to the top arch of my foot. "Hard and well."

My body surged at the memory. "Indeed."

He shot me a satisfied, very male smile.

Too much. Everything about him was *too much*. He was too big, too beautiful, too dangerous, too goddamned cute.

I hid my sudden disconcertion by pulling my leg away from him.

"Go dress," I said. "We need to get on the road again. There's a front moving north of here, which is good for us since we might catch another storm on the way back home."

My heart suddenly clenched a little. I didn't like the idea of going home after this insanely exhilarating time alone with Archer. I wanted to stay, to chase storms, and have wild, mind-blowing sex—with *spanking*, no less. I wanted to kiss him in thunderstorms and feel the heat in his eyes when he looked at me.

I didn't want to go back to classrooms and my cramped little office, to the pressure of my tenure review and departmental bureaucracy. The very things I'd worked so hard for.

"Damn, woman." Archer ran his fingers across my toes. "You have perfect feet. I need to study them more closely in those heels you wear."

"Oh, god. You have a foot fetish?"

"I do now." He stroked his forefinger over my instep, making me twitch in reaction.

Though I was thoroughly enjoying his attention and touch, I didn't want him to know how ticklish I was. I pulled my foot away from him and tucked it underneath me. I reached out to rub the shifting wing on his upper arm. His skin was so warm and taut.

"I haven't studied your tattoos closely either," I remarked. "They're beautiful."

They were, too. Intricate and incredibly detailed, the wing spread from his right shoulder down to wrap around his biceps, the multi-colored feathers thick, the vanes holding them together both strong and delicate. The top of the wing curved over his shoulder into a rich pattern of flowers and silhouettes of two birds in flight. A cursive script flowed beneath them.

I peered at the letters, tracing them with my finger. *Fear is the mind-killer.*

"Wow," I said. "What's that from?"

"Frank Herbert's *Dune*." He touched the tattoo. "I read the novel years ago. I remembered that line, especially when I was trying to get clean and stay out of trouble. I was scared all the time."

A shadow fell over me at the reminder of his past. I couldn't imagine him being scared of anything.

I glided my fingers over the pattern of flowers and two birds. His souvenirs of life.

"Is that when you got the tattoo?" I asked. "When you were in rehab?"

He nodded. "The quote, yeah. I had the wing done when

I was twenty. Can't remember why. Guess I just thought it was cool."

"No." I slid my forefinger over the feathers, almost feeling their combined strength and softness. "It was about freedom. Flying."

He shrugged, studying me. "Why don't you have any tattoos? Tough chick like you?"

"I don't know." I brought my knees to my chest and wrapped my arms around them. "I always wanted one, but I never knew what to get. Then when I started thinking about grad school, tattoos didn't seem to fit with academics. Plus, they're pretty permanent."

"Not like blue hair, right?"

I nudged him with my foot again. "Go get dressed, or I'm driving."

He shoved to his feet with a groan. "Can't have that, now."

After he went into the bathroom, I finished getting ready. I didn't want to like this intimacy and silly teasing, but I did. Even if I couldn't admit that I did, my heart was doing this crazy floating thing, which seemed to be lifting all the weight from me. I couldn't ignore or suppress the feeling. I didn't want to.

And of course that scared the crap out of me. I could take Archer's heat and intensity, the challenges he issued, the sheer male power of him.

It was the other stuff I didn't know what to do with. His laughter and warmth, the way he repaired a garden fence for my mother, his habit of opening doors for me, the fact that he'd cooked bacon after an insanely hot night. His almost casual use of the word *love* in reference to me.

Especially that.

And everything combined into one handsome, sexy man. It was far more than I'd bargained for. And I was beginning to think it was much more than I could take.

CHAPTER TWENTY

ARCHER

KELSEY WAS PRICKLY AND IRRITABLE MOST OF THE DRIVE BACK to Mirror Lake. She snapped at me for leaving candy wrappers on the floor of the van, grumbled about her lack of sleep, and bitched about the classes she had to teach tomorrow.

Because I knew exactly what her problem was, I let her complain. She'd been thrown off, catapulted outside the safe, little comfort zone she'd built for herself and tossed into the path of a tornado.

Now there was the adrenaline crash. And everything else. For one, she hadn't expected me to get along with her mother.

Hadn't expected her mother to like me—not a rough guy with a lousy past and no future to speak of. She hadn't expected to love the risks we'd taken, and she didn't know how to deal with it.

I didn't, either. I liked jumping dirt bikes, driving too fast, fighting. I'd spent most of my life doing risky, sometimes illegal things. But nothing compared to facing down a tornado with a storm girl and winning.

When we got back to Kelsey's house, I helped her unload her stuff and drove the van back to the university. She needed time alone to decompress. So did I.

I went to the Meteorology department to leave the van keys for Colton. As I approached the building, a young, skinny guy wearing a wrinkled suit came through the front door. He hurried down the steps, glanced at me distractedly, and stopped.

"Oh, hey," he said. "You're Kelsey's… uh, hitman."

"Hitman?" It took me a second to remember this kid had been there the day I saw Kelsey in the quad. She'd snapped at both of us.

"Right," I said. "Who are you?"

"Peter Danforth. I took some undergrad classes with Kelsey."

He stuck out his hand. I shook it and started toward the building again.

"Colton just told me Kelsey went out to chase a storm," Peter said, coming up beside me as if I wanted to have a conversation. "Did you go with her?"

"Yeah." I slanted him a glance. "Why?"

"It just surprised everyone, you know? She's always been so against going out on her own. She structured her role in the Spiral Project around the idea that she would do everything *but* work in the field. She'd just sit at a computer and assimilate the data."

An image of Kelsey in a cramped office rose in my head, alongside a memory of her burning with excitement and adrenaline during the chase.

My chest tightened.

"Whatever she does, she'll do it well," I told Peter.

"So did you guys see anything?" Peter asked. "Colton said you did."

"Yeah, she sent him the video. She got some great footage of a tornado."

"Really? Where?"

"A field in eastern Kansas." I pulled open the building door. "You can ask her about it."

"I will, thanks. Good seeing you again."

I nodded and went inside. I left Colton's keys in his departmental mailbox before returning to the Butterfly House. After unpacking and showering, I dug my notebook out of my duffel.

I leafed through the pages, then sat down and did some more drawings. Not until my mother had sent me all my stuff in a cardboard box did I remember I'd spent a lot of my school days drawing in the margins of notebooks. And everything else—math papers, spelling tests, and science reports. Drawing was always easy.

Around dinnertime, I texted Kelsey and told her I was coming over. When I arrived, she let me in without a word. Much as I loved the scotch-and-honey sound of her voice, I also liked the faintly annoyed look she gave me, her blue eyes sharp with that regal, take-no-prisoners expression. The one that had made me want to capture her.

"I'm working," she said, gesturing to the kitchen. "Go get something to eat or drink, if you want."

I tortured myself a little by watching her pick up a few folders from a chair. Her incredible breasts curved the front of her shirt, and jeans hugged her perfect ass. Long legs. Shiny hair. She was all woman. All mine.

Mine.

The word flared in my mind. I'd never had anything that was really mine. Even my family hadn't been mine. But Kelsey… I would never think of her any other way.

My fists clenched. But after I left town, she'd be a free agent again. And though I'd told her we could have a hell of a good time together while I was here—and we were, more than I'd ever imagined possible—the thought of her with another guy made me want to slam my fists against a brick wall. Repeatedly.

I forced my fingers to unclench and went into the kitchen. I rummaged in the fridge and saw a carton of chocolate milk on the lower shelf.

I knew Kelsey had bought it for me. And stupid as the feeling was, I couldn't help liking the idea that she'd been thinking about me while grocery shopping. God knew I couldn't get her out of my mind, no matter what I was doing.

I didn't have much time left. The Butterfly House was almost finished. I had maybe two weeks left of this candy-box town, pine trees, mountains, and crystal blue lake. Two weeks before I had to go back to the dry, desert heat and sand, the smell of gasoline, the fireball sun.

Two weeks left of Kelsey.

I opened the cabinet to find a glass, noticing the door was tilting off the hinges. I checked a few of the other cabinets for a toolbox but found none. I opened a door that I assumed led to the basement and went down the stairs. I fumbled for the light switch and turned it on.

I blinked at the sudden glare and stopped. The room looked like something out of a magazine. Pale blue walls lined with white shelves, a wide, marble-topped table sat in the center of the room, surrounded by high-backed, cushioned chairs. The shelves were stacked with folds of bright fabrics, rolls of satiny ribbons, baskets, and jars of beads and buttons.

"Archer?"

Kelsey's voice broke me from my surprise.

"In the basement," I called.

Her footsteps sounded on the stairs. "What are you doing down here?"

"Looking for a toolbox. One of your cabinet doors is off the hinges." I turned to face her. She was watching me, her expression wary behind her glasses.

"I didn't know you had a craft room," I said.

She flushed. "No one does."

"Why not?"

"Because it's a *craft room*."

A strange feeling uncurled in my chest. Something warm and sort of soft. I approached her and reached out to run a few strands of her blue hair through my fingers. Her face was still pink.

"I like your craft room, storm girl," I said. "I like you, too."

"You mean you *like me* like me?" she asked. For the first time all day, she looked amused.

"Uh huh." I lowered my head to brush my mouth against hers. "And I like that you make crafts. It must be the daredevil in you. Sharp scissors, hot glue guns, pins and needles. Dangerous stuff."

The wariness eased from her expression as she laughed. "Or it's the girl in me. I don't like many people to know she still exists."

"No way you can hide her from me." I didn't want her to. Didn't want her to hide any part of herself from me. Even knowing I had to give her something in return didn't change that desire one bit.

"What kind of stuff do you make?" I asked.

"Some jewelry and mixed-media collages. I have an online shop where I sell stuff. Mostly I make Ukrainian painted eggs, which my mother sells in her gift shop."

"You mean all the eggs in her shop were yours?"

She nodded. "She'll only stock eggs I paint. That's why I wanted to visit her. I had to drop off a box of *pysanky* to restock her supply."

"Can I see more of them?"

Kelsey hesitated before nodding. She took several baskets from under the table and handed me a bright, intricately decorated egg that felt light and fragile. It was painted a glossy black and wrapped with an incredible geometric pattern of red, gold, and green.

"Where did you learn to do this?" I asked, pulling the basket toward me so I could look at all the other eggs. In truth, I hadn't paid much attention to the eggs in her mother's shop. But now, knowing Kelsey had made them, I was kind of awed.

"My mother taught me when I was a kid," Kelsey said. "We always painted them around Easter, though we also did them throughout the year as gifts. Even in my wilder days, I always liked sitting down to paint eggs with her."

She picked up a blue-and-gold egg and studied the pattern. "She developed arthritis in her hands and couldn't do the work anymore, but even now she still gives me ideas and suggestions. Or direct orders."

I could well imagine her mother issuing orders. Nice as Mrs. March had been, I sensed the same core of steel in her that Kelsey had.

"How do you do it?" I asked, nodding to the egg.

"It's a special technique using wax and dye." She dug around in a box and produced a tool that had a wooden rod and a metal tip. "This is called a *kistka.* You use it to apply the wax pattern, and then dye the egg. The parts of the egg that aren't covered by wax end up colored."

"Show me."

"You'll find it pretty boring."

"Nothing you do is boring to me."

She glanced at me, one eyebrow lifting. "Not even if I start talking about data assimilation?"

"Not even then. Especially not if you do it while standing in front of me wearing a sexy suit and holding a pointer."

"Dream on, baby."

"I will."

Kelsey smiled and opened a box filled with dye-stained jars. "Okay, you asked for it. If I show you the technique, you have to paint one of the eggs, too."

I looked at my ugly, callused hands that I used to turn socket wrenches. "I'll break it in two seconds."

"Not if you're careful, you won't."

"I'm never careful."

Kelsey looked up. Something crossed her expression that I couldn't define.

"Archer," she said. "You're always careful with me."

A blade twisted inside me. I wasn't careful with her. I was too rough, too demanding, too greedy. I'd started this whole thing because I'd wanted to make her lose control, to admit she was wrong, even to break her a little. Being *careful* had never entered my mind.

And I'd known she'd respond with fire and lightning. I knew she could take it, that she wanted it, that she'd beg for more. I'd give her more too, as much as I could, push myself to the edge right along with her.

Hell, we'd challenged a tornado together. I was more alive now than I'd been in years.

Her blue eyes. I didn't want to drown in them. I wanted to live in them.

The blade twisted harder. I pulled my gaze from hers.

"Where do we start?" I asked.

She showed me how to get the supplies organized—making the dyes, cleaning the hollow duck eggs, sketching a pattern with a pencil. She lit a candle and demonstrated how to melt beeswax into the funnel of the *kistka* before using different styluses to trace the pattern with wax.

"Why the nice, cozy secret room?" I asked her as we sat at the table, each of us concentrating on drawing wax lines.

"It's comfortable." Kelsey shrugged, looking faintly embarrassed again. "I like to come down here, put on some music, maybe have a glass of wine. I wanted a place where I could shut everything else out and just be… I don't know. Quiet. Alone."

"You're not alone now."

Our gazes met across the table, a crackle of energy lighting the air. I wasn't alone, either. For the first time in a very long time. Maybe for the first time ever.

Kelsey picked up another stylus and drew it over the surface of the egg.

"I'll be alone when you leave," she said.

I was *this close* to telling her I didn't have to leave. But I did have to.

I was no fool. I'd wanted to make Kelsey admit she was wrong about me, but she was in a class of her own. One that was way above me. A place I'd never belong.

A drop of hot wax fell from the stylus onto my egg. The pattern smeared.

"I'm messing this up," I said.

Kelsey came around to my side of the table. "You might have overfilled the *kistka* with wax. You can get that off with some wax remover. Hold it in your palm for a sec."

She poured the remover onto a tissue and took my hand, pulling the egg closer to her. She dabbed at the wax and used a cotton swab to clean it off the pattern. She'd taken off her glasses to do the detail work, and I could see the individual strands of her thick eyelashes.

I watched her face, the crease of concentration between her eyebrows, the way the blue locks of her hair fell over her forehead, the fine-grained silk of her skin. She had a tiny beauty mark just under her left eye, small as the head of a pin. I inhaled her scent of almond milk and honey. Her lips were full, and without lipstick they were a pale pink like the inside of a seashell.

So goddamned beautiful. A fierce, sexy, brilliant woman who loved to chase storms and disappeared into her secret craft room to paint eggs when the world closed in on her.

She glanced up and caught me staring.

"What?" she asked defensively.

I slipped my other hand under her chin and lifted her face to mine. Her breath caught, and her lips parted. I couldn't remember if I'd ever kissed her gently. She sparked my lust so powerfully that most of the time I just wanted to grab her and crush my mouth against hers. To get inside her as fast and hard as I could.

This time, I forced myself to kiss her gently. Her lips softened against mine, a murmur of pleasure passing from her to me. Filling me with heat.

I put the egg down and wrapped my arms around her waist, tugging her into the V of my legs. She settled her hands on my thighs and leaned in to deepen the kiss. I liked the way she tucked her body against mine without hesitation, as if she knew that even if I couldn't be careful with her, I'd never hurt her.

I lifted my head. She was already flushed, her eyes darkening to navy. I tugged a few strands of her hair. I knew I had a better chance of getting answers from her when her defenses were lowered.

"Because it's the color of the sky, right?" I asked, twisting a strand of blue around my fingers.

Kelsey blinked, paling a little. I'd struck a nerve.

"It was..." She pulled away from me and went around to the other side of the table. "It was something my father used to say. A Russian proverb, I think. When he missed Russia or when I moved away, or when things got rough. He said the sky was still blue no matter where you were or what happened. Even if it was raining… behind the clouds, the sky was blue."

She ducked her head, her hair falling over her face as she picked up an egg.

"Tell me," I said.

"No."

"Why do you blame yourself?"

The egg cracked in her hand. In her fist. I saw her internal struggle. She lifted her head. Eyes like a glacier.

"I get it," I told her. "I blame myself for shitty things all the time. But that doesn't change the fact that they happened."

"I never expected anything to change," she muttered. "Dead is dead."

"Does blaming yourself make it easier or harder?"

Her jaw tightened. "I didn't know psychoanalysis was part of our deal. Or your *rules*."

I shook my head. Christ, she could still get wound so tight.

"You think your father would want you to blame yourself?" I asked.

"Goddammit, Archer."

"Tell me."

"He shouldn't have died, all right?" Kelsey snapped, her voice trembling beneath the surface. "We got into a fight… it sounds so stupid now. I was such a fucking loose cannon, especially when I went to college because I thought I could do whatever I wanted. My father and I still argued, but I felt like I didn't have to answer to his disapproval anymore."

She clenched her fist around the broken egg.

"In my junior year, I told my parents I was leaving college," she continued. "Quitting. I was going to travel to South

America with some guy, hitchhiking and living off the land or whatever. My father said no way in hell would he let me do that. We had a huge fight about it. I stormed off with the guy anyway, in a fit of fucking stupid rebellion.

"My mother tried to stop me. My father was furious. I didn't care. I thought I was so goddamn cool, so free and independent. I got as far as Ecuador when my mother called to tell me my father had had a heart attack. He died before I got home."

She opened her hand and threw the broken eggshell into the trash.

"Since you want so badly to know, that's why I blame myself," she said. "My father died because I was a selfish bitch who thought quitting school and running off to South America would be *fun*."

"And that's why you self-destructed," I said.

"Yeah." She gave a bitter laugh. "You'd think I'd have learned my lesson right away, but instead I kept the hurt going. I didn't even think what it would do to my mother if something happened to me. Thank god she showed me what real strength was. I'd spent too many years acting like a spoiled child, and it was finally time to grow up. To take care of my mother for a change. So I went to grad school and started my career. The rest is history."

"So all these years you've played it safe."

"I've been responsible." Her eyes hardened with irritation. "I've gotten stuff done. I've been an adult, Archer. You can't say the same, can you?"

Her turn to jab at me. She didn't like that I was pushing her to open up and now she wanted to retaliate. I could take her punches. Hell, I'd let my guard down if it would make her feel better.

"What have you done all these years?" she snapped. "You can't find a steady job, can you? You just spend your time taking odd jobs, hanging out at bars, and sleeping around, right?"

"Pretty much."

My response threw her. She rubbed her temple and averted her gaze. "So why did you come to Mirror Lake?"

I shrugged, embarrassed by the answer even though I knew I owed her the truth. "Nicholas, I guess. Thought I should meet him. Didn't expect to meet you."

Kelsey was silent, but some of the anger seemed to drain from her. I felt her watching me again.

My heart was beating too fast. I pushed away from the table and went around to where she stood. I took her by the shoulders and pulled her in for a kiss, needing her sweet heat to dissolve the tightness in my chest.

It did. *She* did.

She pulled her mouth from mine. Faint desperation flashed in her eyes. "I need structure, Archer. I need a routine and—"

"I know you do." It was the reason she escaped the world to paint. She needed quiet solitude as much as she needed excitement. She wasn't only a risk-taker or a scientist or a crafter. She was finding ways to be everything.

She made me think I could be everything, too.

I put my hands on either side of her face and kissed her again.

"You need peace," I murmured, "and you need storms."

Her resistance slipped away as the kiss deepened. She put her arms around my neck and leaned into me. I loved how responsive she was. How she just gave over.

She ran her fingers over the feathers on my tattoo.

"You're not scared of anything, are you?" she whispered.

"Yeah, I am."

"What?"

"Leaving."

She was quiet for a minute before she confessed, "I'm scared of that, too. Scared of how I'll feel when you go."

My insides twisted. I couldn't help wondering how she'd feel if I stayed.

I tightened my hands on her waist. "Do you trust me?"

"You know I do."

"How much?"

"Why?" She moved back to look at me, her eyes narrowing. "Is this about some freaky sex thing?"

"No, but now that you mention it…"

She poked me in the chest. "Haven't I already proven that I trust you?"

I patted her ass. "Not like this."

CHAPTER TWENTY-ONE

KELSEY

HE WASN'T SERIOUS. I WASN'T GOING TO DO IT. I COULDN'T. No way.

Except that I was sitting in a recliner chair under a hot floodlight, my shoulder bare and my stomach in knots.

"This is insane," I muttered to myself.

Ben, the guy with the needle, peered at me. "You okay?"

"Sure. Fine."

I'd signed the release form. I knew what I was doing.

Sort of.

Tattoos were no big deal. I'd often thought of getting one.

Except I'd always assumed that if I ever did, I would know exactly what design I was getting.

At the moment, I had no clue, and yet Ben was getting the stencil ready to apply.

"You want out?" Archer asked from my other side. He was holding my hand.

I shook my head. I'd never wanted *out* with him. I'd only ever wanted *in*.

"What does he have to do in return?" Ben asked, nodding his shaggy head in Archer's direction.

"I haven't decided yet," I admitted. I'd barely come to terms with what I was doing, though I liked the idea that Archer would owe me something in return. That eased my anxiety somewhat. I'd have one helluva card to play.

I felt Ben applying the stencil. I tried to follow the movement of the pencil, as if that would help me figure out the design, but as far as I could tell it was just a bunch of curves and lines. The only thing they'd told me was that the tattoo would be colored and about an inch and a half across, which was the size I'd have chosen.

As Ben started drawing the tattoo, I had a million second thoughts. I was going to come out of this with a horrible tattoo of a silly cartoon animal or cute angel. I hoped Archer had picked something innocuous like a flower or butterfly, but he and Ben had consulted over the design for an hour, which led me to believe it was a custom drawing. God forbid I'd end up with Archer's name permanently tattooed on my arm.

No. He wasn't that arrogant.

Was he?

I closed my eyes and tried to keep my breath even. I heard

Archer and Ben talking above me, felt Archer's hand on mine, but I let myself drift.

It hadn't actually been a difficult decision to let him choose my tattoo design. I trusted Archer in more ways than I'd ever trusted anyone.

"All right, Kelsey." Ben wiped the tattoo with a soft cloth. "Ready to see it?"

My stomach knotted again as I sat up slowly. Though the tattoo was on my left upper arm where I could see it if I looked down, Ben gave me a handheld mirror.

"You can also check it out in the full-length over there," he said, nodding toward the mirror against the wall.

I held up the mirror. The tattoo was an intricate, shaded gray cloud with two golden bolts of lightning flashing from it amidst a shower of rain. Along the edge of one of the lightning bolts, in delicate flowing script, were the words *Storm Girl.*

"What do you think?" Archer sounded a little nervous.

I stared at the tattoo. It was small, colorful and...

"I love it," I said.

"You do?"

My heart twisted with ribbons of emotion—pleasure, gratitude, and relief that Archer knew me as well as I'd hoped he did. I looked at him and smiled.

"I absolutely love it," I said. "It's perfect."

And it would remind me of him every time I saw it. I should have been unnerved by that realization, but instead I liked the idea of having a reminder of Archer West, one that would go along with the collection of memories I had subconsciously been storing away. The memories I'd hold on to when we parted ways. The ones no one else would know about.

I looked at the tattoo again. My souvenir.

"Can this be our secret?" I asked Archer. "Just between us?"

"One of many." He extended his hand. "Pinkie swear."

I wrapped my pinkie finger around his. I wished neither of us had to let go.

"Because of the grant, they got fifteen new computers," Tess said. "And they integrated the synoptic lab into the rotating fluids dynamic lab. They even have access to the supercomputing lab's mainframes."

"Lucky bastards," I muttered.

"Yeah."

"Does Stan Baxter know yet?" I asked.

"I heard he's going to the board of trustees again to complain about the state of our equipment, so I think so," Tess said.

My envy over another university's state-of-the-art lab equipment was quickly surpassed by guilt. Though Stan Baxter had been on my case this year, I knew he was intensely committed to King's University and its students. That was just one of the reasons he was so insistent that I prove my own dedication.

Now Stan was going to fight for better computers and equipment in our synoptic lab. I made a mental note to ask him about it and find out what I could do to help. We'd all be at an increasing disadvantage if we had to continue working with outdated equipment, which in turn could hurt the reputation of the entire university.

The phone rang. I hit the speaker button, my gaze still on the radar. “Kelsey March.”

“Kelsey, it’s Peter Danforth.”

“Oh, Peter, I’ve been waiting for your call.”

“You have?”

“No.”

Tess laughed.

“Ha ha,” Peter said drily. “Is that Tess? Hi, Tess.”

“Hi, Peter. You’d better talk fast. Kelsey is scowling.”

“Okay, okay. Kelsey, rumor has it you got some phenomenal tornado footage on your recent chase.”

Shock bolted through me. Tess jerked around to stare at me. I grabbed the receiver and shut off the speaker phone.

“Where did you hear that rumor?” I asked Peter.

“From that guy who went with you. Who is he, anyway?”

“None of your business. What did he tell you about the video? *When* did he tell you?”

“I ran into him on campus, and he said you got footage. I tried to get the tape from Colton, but he played dumb, like he didn’t know what I was talking about.”

“Colton didn’t know,” I snapped, my anger rising hot. “I never sent him the video.”

“Why not?”

I turned away from Tess, not wanting to see the expression on her face. All of my students would be upset to know I hadn’t shared that incredible footage with them. And I could never explain why I still hadn’t. That video belonged to me and Archer alone.

Except that he'd told Peter about it.

"Peter, get your ass out of my business," I said. "The video wasn't that great, so forget about it."

"Yeah, right. You promised me that when you had a scoop, you'd give it to me first. I'd say close-up video of a tornado qualifies as a scoop."

"How did you know it was close-up?"

"You just told me."

"You little shit."

"Look, I've been waiting forever for you to give me something," Peter retorted. "I don't want to be a shit about this, and I sure as hell don't want to get on your bad side, but come *on*. You've been stringing me along for over a year, and I've still got nothing. Reporting on the Spiral Project would make my career. But you won't even give me lousy footage of a tornado, so why would I believe you when you tell me *again* that I'll be the first to know when something big happens?"

I tightened my hand on the receiver. Even through my anger, I registered the truth of his speech.

"Kelsey?"

"I'm here." I let out my breath slowly. It was a video, for heaven's sake. Yes, it was Archer's and my video, and yes, it was intensely personal, but it wasn't like I'd be sharing a declaration of our love.

A declaration of our love? What the—

"All right," I snapped irritably. "I'll send you the video."

"You will?" Peter sounded surprised.

"Yeah. You might have impressed me with that assertive speech."

"For real?"

"Well, not anymore since you just said *for real.*"

"Oh."

I shook my head and fought a reluctant smile. "Check your email."

"Wow, thanks, Kelsey. This is awesome."

I hung up and turned to face Tess. She was typing determinedly on the keyboard, as if she hadn't been listening to every word.

"Tess, I'm sorry I didn't tell you," I said. "I was going to send you the footage from the road, but…"

"Forget it, Kelsey. You don't owe us anything."

That wasn't true. I owed my grad students more than I could say. They were the only ones who had supported the Spiral Project from the start.

I accessed the video on my phone and sent it to Peter, then connected the phone to the computer. After fast-forwarding through images of the clouds, sky, and fields, the downdraft, and the interview Archer had taken of me, the tornado roared across the screen. My shouts mingled with Archer's yells, our excitement crackling and tangible.

"Archer!"

"Holy fucking shit."

"Film it!"

"Go! Go!"

"Kelsey, this is incredible." Tess turned to stare at me, her eyes wide. "I've never seen video shot so close."

I nodded. My heart was pounding again and my mind wanted to fast-forward to two hours later when Archer and I were in the motel room. I rubbed the Storm Girl tattoo through my sleeve, the spot still tender.

"I've already done a quick verification from the video." I forced myself to use my professor voice. "But I haven't done a rigorous validation yet."

"I can get that started, if you want," Tess offered.

"Sure. Thanks." I pushed away from the desk and grabbed my satchel.

I still heard the roar of the tornado in my head as I drove home. I needed some time alone before I talked to Archer about this. I didn't like the thought that our storm chase had meant more to me than it did to him.

I dropped my stuff on the kitchen counter and went down to my craft room. I spent the next hour painting a smooth, hollow egg with a star pattern of red, blue, and purple, letting the familiar design ease my tension.

"I'm not always myself when I'm with you," I'd once told Archer.

"Yeah, you are." His deep, warm voice echoed in my memory. *"You just don't know it yet."*

Kissing him in a corner booth of a dive bar. Giving over. Eating dinner in my dining nook. Stretched out on the sofa, my head pillowed against his thigh. Hot dancing in a nightclub. Mind-blowing sex. Outrunning a tornado. Painting eggs.

Archer was right. With him, I was everything I *was.* I knew that now.

But what would I be when he left?

CHAPTER TWENTY-TWO

ARCHER

ONCE I FINISHED THE TILE FLOORS IN THE KITCHEN, DEAN AND I started installing the new maple cabinets. We didn't talk much, but we worked well together and got most of the kitchen finished within a few days.

Liv came by often, sometimes with Nicholas and sometimes alone. She brought lunch, drinks, cookies, and samples of paint or wood trim. Whenever she came in, Dean always stopped whatever he was doing and went to join her.

I tried to leave them alone, after Liv insisted that I take a break and eat whatever she'd brought from the café, but sometimes I overheard them talking or saw them exchange a hug or kiss.

Dean called her "beauty." Sometimes she called him "professor," in a voice that was both teasing and full of admiration. He touched her hair a lot. She looked at him like he was a superhero. He looked at her like she was a miracle.

It should have been sappy, but it wasn't. I realized that Liv and Dean had the first good marriage I'd ever seen. And though I'd always envied how easily everything came to Dean, I knew he and Liv had had rough times. Seeing them now, I was glad their relationship had worked out so well.

I guessed that was because sometimes people just belonged together. And when they not only found each other, but fought for each other and won, even I knew the universe got it right.

After working for a few hours on the kitchen, I took a break and sat on the front porch steps. Kelsey's car came up the drive. Liv and Dean sat outside the trailer, drinking take-out coffees that she'd brought and looking through a catalog of door handles and hardware.

Kelsey got out of her car and came toward me with that long-legged, go-to-hell walk that I'd loved from the beginning. The blue streak in her hair glowed in the sunlight.

My risk-taking, brilliant scientist girl. She needed storms. She needed her mother and her secret craft room. She needed to chase tornados, to be pushed to her limits, to predict the unpredictable. And even if she didn't know it yet, she needed *me.*

She tossed her bag on the porch steps and put her hands on her hips.

I frowned. "What?"

"You told Peter Danforth about the tornado video."

"Peter… oh, that student of yours. Yeah, I saw him on campus."

"He's not my student anymore. He's a reporter with Channel Four news."

"Oh."

"You shouldn't have said anything to him about the video," Kelsey continued. She sounded defensive.

"I didn't know it was a secret. You sent it to your grad students, didn't you?"

"No, I didn't."

Now I was getting irritated. "You said you were going to at the motel."

"I changed my mind, all right?" Kelsey snapped. "I wanted to keep it private."

"Well, I didn't know that."

"I know you didn't." Her eyes flashed. "It just would have been nice if you'd *thought* before you spoke."

What the hell was this about?

I spread my hands in frustration.

"Why is this such a big deal?" I asked.

"Because it was special, okay?" Kelsey retorted. "The video. It's you, me, and a tornado. I've never experienced anything like that in my life. And I didn't want to share it with anyone else."

I stepped back, her confession hitting me right in the middle of my chest. A flush rose to Kelsey's cheeks, as if she'd just said something that embarrassed her. I reached out to touch the blue stripe in her hair.

"I've never experienced anyone like you in my life," I said.

She looked at my chest. "I didn't know if you felt the same way about it that I did."

"Hey." I put my hand under her chin and lifted her face. "I never wanted that tornado to stop. I wanted to stay on the road with you forever, chasing storms. And I'm sorry I screwed up by telling that kid about the video. I thought you'd already sent it out."

"I know. I was going to but…" She shrugged. "I would have had to eventually. The footage is too good not to share, and of course my students need to analyze it too."

"What happened when you talked to Peter?" I asked.

"He asked for the video, and I gave it to him. I had been promising him something for a while now."

"So that'll be good publicity for you, right? Spread the word about your tornado research and the Spiral Project." I put my arms around her waist and tugged her close. "We can make another *really* private video, if you want."

She made a harrumphing noise, even as she leaned closer and pressed her mouth to mine.

"What are you doing today?" I asked, brushing my lips across her cheek to nibble at her ear.

"Running errands." She shivered. "Stop that."

"You really want me to?"

"No. But I saw Liv and Dean over there, and I don't want to put on a display."

I lifted my head reluctantly. Kelsey gave me a quick kiss before moving past me toward the trailer.

I followed, watching her gorgeous ass as we walked. We sat in the empty lawn chairs across from Liv and Dean.

"Hi, Kels." Liv reached into the coffee holder for a cup

and handed it to Kelsey. "I brought extra in case you or one of the crew were here."

Kelsey took the cup, tilting her head toward me. "Did you bring chocolate milk for this one?"

"No," Liv said. "Should I have?"

Dean almost grinned. "You still drink chocolate milk?" he asked me.

"Every chance I get."

"Do you still like those ketchup-and-cheese sandwiches?"

"Nah. I prefer peanut butter these days. With strawberry jam."

Kelsey rolled her eyes. Liv smiled.

"When Archer and I were kids, we used to have this tree house in the backyard," Dean told them. "We'd pretend to be explorers, and we'd pack lunches in our backpacks before climbing up there. He always ate ketchup-and-cheese sandwiches on raisin bread and had chocolate milk. We'd spend all day in that tree house."

I was surprised he remembered the tree house at all, much less the details of what we'd done there.

"The Castle," I said.

"Oh, yeah." Recognition sparked in Dean's expression. "We called it The Castle. Sometimes we pretended to be knights defending our fortress."

"*You* pretended to be a knight?" Liv asked him in amusement. "Really?"

He reached over to squeeze her knee. "We also pretended to be pirates, superheroes in a hideout… what else?"

"Space explorers," I said. "Detectives. Bandits, cowboys, ship captains."

Dean shook his head. "I haven't thought about that in ages."

"We never took it down," I said. "The tree house. It might still be there."

"With the house sold, we'll never know."

"You should build one for Nicholas," I told Dean, gesturing to the wooded area around the property. "When he's older. He seems to really like being outside. Bet he'd love a tree house."

Dean nodded. "He would. We'll call it The Castle Two."

I almost offered to help build it, which was stupid since Nicholas was several years away from needing a tree house. But still, I liked the idea of drawing up blueprints, collecting material, building a tree house that was far more sturdy and elaborate than the one Dean and I had constructed. Nicholas's tree house could even have real windows and hinged doors. Maybe it could have two rooms or a balcony.

I took a swallow of coffee and pushed the thought aside. I was leaving soon. I was glad I'd come, but I'd never intended to stay. Even if I'd wanted to, I didn't belong in Mirror Lake. This was a place for people like Liv and Dean. For professors up for tenure like Kelsey. Not for guys like me.

I felt Kelsey looking at me. I had the sudden urge to touch her as easily as Dean touched Liv. Just to reach over and squeeze her knee, hold her hand. Anything to enforce the fact that she was mine.

"Archer, remember I told you about the Historical Society party tomorrow night?" Liv asked. "Would you like to come?"

I'd almost forgotten about the invitation. I glanced at Dean and waited for a look of caution or for him to suggest that maybe I had other things to do.

Instead he said, "You can borrow one of my suits again."

I shook my head. "No, thanks. I'm going to stay in tomorrow night."

"Too bad." Liv looked disappointed. "Let me know if you change your mind."

I could change my mind, I thought as I shoved to my feet. But my mind didn't want to change me.

The sound of another car engine came up the drive. A gray Lexus pulled up beside Kelsey's car, and a man wearing a suit and tie got out of the driver's side.

Tension gripped me. My fists tightened with an old defensive instinct, the sense that danger was near.

"Oh." Liv sounded disconcerted. "I didn't know Max was coming today."

"He said he'd stop by this week and see how things were going." Dean rose to his feet, apparently oblivious to the look Liv shot Kelsey.

Max Lyons approached. Tall, good-looking guy with graying hair. Looked like a businessman or a lawyer. Successful. Knew how to tie a tie.

Dean and Max shook hands, and Dean gestured to Kelsey. "You know Kelsey."

"Sure." Max smiled at her. "How have you been?"

"Fine, thank you," she replied. "It's nice to see you again."

"This is my brother Archer," Dean said. "Not sure if you've met. Max is Allie's father, and an architect who's given us some advice about the house."

Max held out his hand. "Good to meet you."

I nodded, shook his hand, and stepped back. I watched Kelsey. She was looking at Max. I hoped to hell it wasn't regret I saw in her blue eyes.

"Come on, I'll show you what we've done," Dean said.

Dean and Max started toward the house. I followed, but went into the kitchen to keep working on the cabinets. Their voices echoed through the house as Dean gave Max a tour, pointing out the reconstruction they'd done. He asked for Max's opinion on a bunch of things, and Max made suggestions in between telling Dean about a big office building project he'd recently finished.

My breath was choppy. I twisted a screw too hard and stripped the head. With a muttered curse, I yanked it out of the wall and threw it away.

"Hey." Kelsey came into the kitchen, her heels clicking on the new tile. "Can we have lunch later?"

I shook my head. "I'm going to work through lunch. The appliances are being delivered on Friday, and the cabinets need to be finished by then."

I felt her frowning at me.

"What's going on now?" she asked.

I turned to face her. "Your mother would like him."

She blinked. "What?"

I jerked my head toward the stairs. "Max Lyons. He's the kind of man your mother would like."

"So? What does that have to do with anything?"

I grabbed the screwdriver. "Why didn't you bring him to meet her?"

"What the hell are you talking about?"

"He's your type, isn't he? The kind of guy you should be with."

"But I'm not with him, am I?" Kelsey stepped closer, lowering her voice. "I went out with him a few times, Archer. That's it. He's a perfectly nice man, and yes, my mother would like him, but she also liked *you*. So stop acting like a jealous ass."

I shook my head. I couldn't fucking stand it. When I left town, Max Lyons would still be here. Plus other men like him. Men a hell of a lot better for Kelsey than I was.

Shit. Anger scorched my chest. I threw the screwdriver down and turned away from her.

"Don't you shut me out." Kelsey grabbed my arm, her eyes flashing.

I stared at her, into her blue eyes that sizzled into me like electrical currents. My head filled with her almond-and-honey scent. I grabbed the back of her neck and pulled her into me, crushing her soft mouth with mine. She resisted at first, pushing her hands against my chest, a noise escaping her throat.

I gripped her tighter. Slid my other arm around her waist and hauled her against me. Trapping her. I pushed my tongue into her mouth to taste her sweet heat. Shoved my hips against hers. Tightened my hand on her neck.

A fierce possessiveness flooded me. I wanted to mark her, claim her, own her.

She curled her fingers against my chest and forced her mouth from mine. Her breath caressed my jaw.

"I'm giving *over* to you," she whispered. "I chased a tornado with you. I got a tattoo for you. I told you about my father. I've never done that with anyone in my life. So don't fuck this up by being jealous. You're the one I want. You're the one I'm with. Since that night in the bar, I haven't been able to get you out of my head."

Just like I couldn't get her out of mine. Didn't want to. Ever.

I breathed her in. The tightness in my chest loosened. My

mind couldn't change me. But Kelsey March could. In fact, she already had.

The sound of a ringtone made us separate. She turned to dig into her bag for her phone and pressed the button.

"Kelsey March," she said.

Sudden tension radiated from her. She grabbed the edge of the counter. I crossed to her side.

"Maria?" she said into the phone. "What is it?"

Apprehension clawed at me. All the color drained from Kelsey's face.

"What?" Panic flashed in her eyes. "When?"

She listened, her knuckles white as she gripped the phone harder. She spoke some rapid-fire Russian and pressed a hand to her chest.

"Okay," she said. "Okay, I'll be there as soon as I can."

I grabbed her arm. "What happened?"

She lowered the phone slowly and stared at me.

"It's my mother." Her voice shook. "She had a stroke."

CHAPTER TWENTY-THREE

KELSEY

ARCHER BROKE EVERY SPEED LIMIT AND TRAFFIC LAW DRIVING me back to Highland Park. I kept calling Maria, asking for updates even though I couldn't do anything until we got there. And maybe not even then.

Liv and Dean both called only once, telling me they didn't want to tie up my phone, but that they'd told Archer to call them as soon as we got to the hospital.

It took forever, seconds stretching like hours. By the time Archer finally pulled up to the hospital entrance, my nerves were scraped raw with terror.

"Go," he said. "I'll park and be there in a sec."

I bolted out of the car and ran inside. I managed to ask at the front desk what floor to go to. Archer arrived as I was pacing in front of the elevators.

He put his hand on my lower back as we entered the car. When we exited on the fourth floor, I let him search for my mother's room. The hospital smell of disinfectant and stale air filled my nose. Nausea swirled in my gut.

"Here." Archer touched my arm and gestured to a half-open door.

I forced myself to move forward, knocking on the door once before pushing it open. I almost didn't recognize her.

My mother.

My *mother* was lying unconscious in a hospital bed, attached to tubes and machines, her head covered with a white bandage. Her skin looked paper-thin, cast with a gray pallor.

A nurse was adjusting one of the machines. "Are you family?" she asked.

I nodded. I was my mother's only family. Just as she was mine.

"I'm… I'm her daughter," I stammered. "Kelsey March."

"There's been little change in the past hour, Miss March. I'll see if the doctor is available to talk with you."

She fiddled with the tubes and left the room. Archer's hand touched my shoulder. He guided me to a chair beside the bed.

"I'll leave you alone for a few minutes," he said. "I'm just outside the door, okay?"

I didn't want him to leave, but couldn't find the words to ask him to stay. I pulled up closer to my mother and rested my head against her arm. The faint scent of tea-rose clung to her skin.

I couldn't find any words for her, either. And if I could, I didn't even know if she'd hear them.

I was frozen. Tears formed in my chest, but couldn't push past the knot in my throat.

"Miss March?"

I started at the sound of the doctor's voice. He looked at me with grave sympathy, which I tried to deflect.

If the doctor is already sympathetic...

"I'm Dr. Mills. I've been treating your mother. I wanted to let you know that she suffered a hemorrhagic stroke, which means there was bleeding in the brain. We were able to stop the bleeding, but can't assess the level of damage until she's stable. And with no changes in the past twelve hours, I'm afraid the prognosis doesn't look positive."

He didn't have to say any more. I sank back into the chair and realized I was about to start a vigil waiting for my mother to die. I looked at her face, her closed eyes, her pale, lovely skin.

A thousand memories assaulted me. My mother the peacekeeper, the artist, the lunch lady, the homemaker, the cook, the business owner. The woman whose strength and courage ran like a vein of gold deep inside her being.

"Kseniya."

I jolted awake from a doze, my heart hammering. For a hazy instant, I thought my mother had spoken my name. Then I blinked and saw Maria standing at the foot of the bed. Her eyes were red from crying.

I pushed to my feet and embraced her. She held me tightly.

"She was on the floor when I went into the shop this morning," she said, her voice choked. "I don't know how long she was there. I'm so sorry. I called 911 right away, but if I'd been there earlier—"

"No. Don't blame yourself. She wouldn't want that."

Though the ground itself was trembling beneath my feet, I was certain of that fact.

Hours passed. Maybe days. Doctors and nurses came in and out of the room. My mother didn't show any signs of recovery. I sat beside her bed, reading, sleeping, trying to work. I showered in the hospital bathroom. Archer brought in coffee and sandwiches. He tried to convince me to leave for a short time, to go for a walk or back to my mother's house, but I always refused.

What if... what if... what if... ?

I stayed. So did he. He answered calls from Liv and Dean, emails from my grad students, voicemails from Stan. I had the vague thought that someone else had to be teaching my classes.

My mother died at night, slipping from this world to the next with one breath. I held her hand and didn't cry. I heard her voice, the *dochenka*, "my daughter," a word that had been woven into the entire fabric of my life.

I'd never hear it again.

I didn't remember what we'd had to do after my father's death. I knew there was a lot of planning, arrangements to be made, papers to fill out and file.

This time, I welcomed the work because it kept the grief

at a distance. If I could focus on one task after another, I could avoid thinking about the fact that my mother was gone.

Liv and Dean drove down as soon as Archer called them. My mother's friends stopped by with food, to share in the sorrow, and tell stories. While it was comforting to have them all around, I had the same feeling I'd had when Archer and I were chasing the storm. Despite my appreciation for friends, I really just wanted to be alone. With him.

From the beginning, I'd thought of Archer as a storm. Wild, reckless, dangerous. He'd overpower me and then he'd move on, away from me. I'd be alone, but under clear skies again and back on the stable path I'd constructed for myself.

But in the confusing aftermath of my mother's death, I discovered that I'd been wrong. Archer was a storm, no doubt, one who electrified and consumed me, but he was also every part of the storm.

He was the calm right in the center of it. He was the blue sky behind the clouds. He was the sheltering place where I could crawl into safety.

In the days that followed, he was just *there*. I didn't ever have to look for him. I barely even had to need him. The instant a hollow feeling broke inside me, the longing for someone, something, he was there. His hand on my shoulder, his voice in my ear, his warm, gentle gaze.

He was the only solid element in my world. He helped me organize the funeral arrangements, the doctor bills, and the insurance papers. I should have felt alone after having lost my mother. But with Archer there, I didn't. Even though I had no other family, somehow, I'd become part of *we* again.

The day after the funeral, I got ready to return to Mirror

Lake. My mother had left her share of the gift shop and inventory to Maria, and I'd have to come back to meet with a lawyer and finalize the transfer. I'd also have to pack all my mother's belongings and find a real-estate agent to list her house for sale.

Suppressing a wave of sorrow, I zipped my travel bag and went into the living room. Liv and Dean had returned to Mirror Lake a few hours ago. A morning news program blared from the television.

I set my bag down and stared at the screen. A reporter and an actress were laughing over a comedy clip.

In a surreal way, I was shocked by the realization that the rest of the world was acting as if nothing had happened. It shouldn't have been that way, of course. Every person and every particle of the universe should have changed the instant Vera March died.

I rubbed a hand over my eyes. The house felt empty, bereft of my mother's warm presence.

Archer came in the front door from loading the trunk of my car. Now that we were alone, I wanted to throw myself into his arms, to press my face against his chest and absorb his strength.

He stopped and looked at me, his dark gaze searching my face. My throat constricted.

"You can cry," he said. His voice was unbearably gentle.

"What?"

"You've been holding yourself tight," he said. "It's okay to let it out."

Irritation rose up my spine. "Thanks for the advice, Dr. Feel-Good."

I folded my arms, slanting my gaze to the television so I wouldn't have to look at him.

"You've been like this for a long time," Archer continued. "So determined not to break. But sometimes you have to."

"Oh, for god's sake," I muttered. "I'm not keeping you around for your psychotherapy."

I stared unseeingly at a detergent commercial. I hated the regret filling my chest. Unwaveringly, Archer had stayed by my side this whole time, and now I was snapping insults at him.

I silently begged him to go away. I couldn't withstand his gentle persistence, his desire to weather the storm with me. I couldn't let myself fall sobbing into his arms. I couldn't become more attached to him than I already was.

He would steady the ground under my feet, help me navigate this new, changed world, but then I'd have to do the same thing all over again when he left. And I'd have to do it alone.

He moved closer and pressed his hand against the back of my neck, then up to cradle my head. Tears stung my eyes.

I swallowed hard and forced them back down. The weather forecast came on the news, a storm front moving north toward Chicago.

This was a storm too, but an intensely personal and private one. One that churned inside my heart and soul, destructive and painful.

I blinked. The weather forecast shifted to a special interest story about tornados.

Shock bolted through me suddenly. I grabbed the remote and turned up the volume. What the...

My own face appeared on the television screen above the words *Dr. Kelsey March, King's University*. Behind me, clouds boiled over the sky and threw shadows on the old gas station where I was standing. I was eating a piece of beef jerky while Archer's voice off-camera said, "Tell me about the supercell."

On-screen, the wind whipped my hair around my face. I looked into the camera and talked about the instability, wind shear, the growth of the storm. Then the shot cut to the massive roaring tornado and Archer's and my yells, peppered with *beeps* over our swearing.

"That was—" Archer began.

"Shitty." I hit the off button and threw the remote onto the sofa. "Sonuvabitch."

He frowned. "What's wrong?"

I grabbed my travel bag. "I never gave Peter permission to use that video of *me*."

"It's a great spot, Kelsey. You—"

"I don't want to be on TV," I interrupted. "I'm a scientist, not a weather girl."

"Plenty of scientists contribute to news and weather reports."

His rational tone irritated me further.

"I don't," I said curtly. "I get enough flack being a woman in the hard sciences without needing to add *glamour reporter* to my title. And my colleagues don't need another reason to snark at me about the Spiral Project."

"Kelsey, you're overreacting."

I stopped and turned to face him. My chest roiled with anger, fear, and a deep grief that felt like an endless pit, threatening to engulf me.

"I'm overreacting?" I repeated. "Really? Tell me, Archer, just what do you know about university politics and Meteorology departments? How much do you know about working your ass off for a PhD and post-docs? About writing textbooks and research papers and struggling to get your proposals funded? How much do you know about the process of tenure and the fucking fear that if you don't get it, you'll be fired from your job and have to start all over again?"

A hush fell in the air, broken only by the sound of my harsh breathing. Archer just looked at me.

"I don't know about any of that," he said. "But I do know about fighting to prove yourself. I know you've proven yourself countless times over. In fact, you're the only person who's ever made me believe *I* can prove myself one day too."

Shame scorched me.

"You don't need to prove yourself, Archer," I said, my voice ragged. "You just *are*."

Before I broke down completely, I turned and strode out the door.

I had to accept the stark knowledge that the day would come when he wouldn't be here anymore. I'd known that from the beginning, but now it was the one thing in the world I wanted to forget.

CHAPTER TWENTY-FOUR

KELSEY

"I'M SORRY ABOUT YOUR MOTHER, KELSEY." STAN BAXTER stood in my office doorway, his arms crossed in an authoritative stance. "But you should have cleared that interview with the administration. They'll view it as a conflict of commitment."

I had a hard time even caring anymore. I fiddled with a pen on my desk.

I wasn't going to get awarded tenure now. The university board had forwarded their recommendation to university chancellor, and the final decision rested with him.

Chancellor Radcliffe had already warned me about playing

by the rules. And now that I was the glamour-girl meteorologist who looked smokily into the camera while her hair whipped around her face… the chancellor had a perfect excuse to shut me down.

Hell. I was ready to shut myself down.

"The university has regulations about outside commitments and media," Stan continued. "And if you keep breaking them, you're going to end up hurting this department. We've been trying to get budget approval for new lab equipment, but the board won't look at us favorably if we have a professor who can't follow university policy."

"I know."

I thought about throwing Peter Danforth under the bus by telling Stan I hadn't signed a media release form. But the video was already out there, and getting Peter in trouble wouldn't change anything. Unfortunately.

"I'm sorry," I told Stan.

He was quiet for a minute. "Don't lose heart, Kelsey."

I couldn't look at him.

"Everyone, including the chancellor, knows you're an excellent scientist," Stan said. "Everyone knows what an asset you've been to this department. The problem is you've let the Spiral Project get in the way. You need to focus on your work at King's. And stop giving TV interviews," he added.

"It wasn't a… oh, never mind." Defeat was creeping up on me. It felt shitty.

"I know you're having a rough time," Stan said. "Let me know if you need more time off."

"No. I just need to work."

Stan nodded and left. I tried to focus on my computer

screen. Despite my assertion, the structure of work had begun to erode the numbness that had kept me together in the days following my mother's death. She had always been an intrinsic part of my routine, whether through a phone call or emails, planning a visit, even ordering *pysanky* supplies.

I could no longer slip into the fluency of Russian, which had always been like a private language between her and me. There was no longer anyone in the world who understood the guilt I carried over my father's death and yet didn't blame me for it. There was no longer anyone who loved me without condition, without reservation.

Liv and Dean had told me to call if I needed them, but truth be told, the only person I needed was Archer. And I'd been so horrible to him.

We hadn't even spoken on the phone since returning from Highland Park. I had no idea if he was trying to give me some space, or if he just didn't want to see me right now.

It shouldn't matter, I told myself as I left my office. Archer and I had agreed to have a good time while he was here. It shouldn't matter that I hadn't seen him in two days and missed him terribly.

I went into the conference room. I had a meeting scheduled with Colton, Tess, and Derek to review their work from the past week and a half. None of them had arrived yet.

I sat down and pulled out my cell, sending a quick text to Archer.

KELSEY: I'm sorry.
ARCHER: No reason to be. Where are you?
KELSEY: Work.

ARCHER: You okay?
KELSEY: I don't know yet.
ARCHER: Need me?

Oh, god. My breath stopped for an instant. I needed him so much. I needed him to touch me, fill me, want me, be with me. I needed him because he made me *not alone.*

And for that reason, I had to stay away from him for now. I'd been alone before I met him, and I'd be alone again when he left. I had to get my world back into balance, had to keep myself together even though I was on the verge of shattering.

My hands shook as I typed another text.

KELSEY: I'm okay. But I miss you.
ARCHER: I'm still here.
KELSEY: Couple more days, okay?
ARCHER: Okay.
KELSEY: I just need to be alone.
ARCHER: I know.

Of course he did. He knew me better than anyone.

Voices rose as my grad students came into the room. After I accepted their condolences about my mother, we sat down to review their work and the undergraduate papers they had assigned.

We talked for the next half hour when the phone on the conference table rang, the blinking light indicating it was my office line. I hit the speaker button.

"Kelsey March."

"Dr. March, my name is David Peterson." A deep male

voice crackled through the speaker. "I'm an executive producer over at the Explorer Channel."

Colton and Derek looked up. No wonder. The Explorer Channel was a major cable network focusing on documentary and science programs, as well as adventure-based reality shows. My students often talked about the various programs, debating both their scientific merit and entertainment value.

"Do you have a minute?" David Peterson asked me.

"Sure."

"We saw the tornado footage you provided to Channel Four," he said. "It was very impressive."

"Thanks."

"And we liked the interview of you, as well. You're professional, articulate, and you have a very strong, camera-friendly presence. You also have a sexy edginess that comes across well on television."

"Uh… thanks again?"

Tess and Derek glanced at me, their eyes bright with suppressed amusement.

"I'm calling because we'd like to set up a meeting to talk with you about a documentary program on storm chasing," David said.

Now all the grad students looked up with interest. I almost picked up the receiver to make the conversation private, but instead left it on speaker so they could hear. I might as well kill the glitzy lure of television for my students right off the bat.

"I'm sorry, Mr. Peterson," I said. "I'm not interested in consulting for a TV show."

"Oh, we don't want you exclusively as a consultant," David

Peterson said. "That's part of it, of course, but we'd also like to talk to you about being the star."

Colton's mouth dropped open. I glared at him.

"I'm not interested in starring in a TV show," I told the producer. "But thank you for your time."

"Wait," David said quickly. "I don't think you understand, Dr. March. We did some research on you and found out about the Spiral Project."

My heart stuttered. "What about it?"

"It sounds like quite an innovative and unique project," he said. "We'd like to have a copy of the full proposal, and we'd especially like for you to come and talk to our team about it."

I glanced at my students, who were all watching me and hanging on every word.

"Why do you want to know more about the Spiral Project?" I asked David.

"We want to understand how it will operate and function," he explained. "As well as what resources you'll need. Ultimately our goal is to determine if we can send a film crew along with your tornado research unit.

"If so, we can create a documentary program centered on the Spiral Project. We'd focus on why and how you study tornados, what technology you use, and the daily operations of storm chasing. Of course, we'd focus on a few main participants for a human-interest angle. You, of course, would be the headliner of the show, as well as the principal investigator."

My heart began doing some ridiculous flipping, which I tried to still with the cold light of reason.

"I could never leave King's to participate in a reality show," I said. "However, I do have a number of graduate students who—"

"We're happy to have additional cast members, Professor March," David interrupted. "But this offer is contingent upon your being the main participant."

I blinked, trying not to feel somewhat flattered. A major cable network seriously wouldn't do a show without me?

For an instant, I wondered what would happen if I agreed. Maybe I could demand my own luxury trailer. A daily supply of fresh cupcakes and French Roast coffee. Even a private Swedish masseur…

Kelsey!

I cleared my throat and refocused.

"I'm sorry, Mr. Peterson," I repeated. "Even if it were possible, we lost all funding for the Spiral Project."

"I know. That's part of the reason for my call. I need to know what other sources you have in the wings."

"Why?"

"The Explorer Channel could contribute to certain costs and, of course, compensation," David said, "but we would need to be assured that you have another reliable source of sustained funding in place."

"Well, I don't. I've just about exhausted all my sources."

"Then our hope is your attachment to a major cable channel will spark new interest in the project."

Apparently the man had an answer for everything.

"Mr. Peterson," I said firmly. "Even if I wanted to do this, I couldn't. I have commitments to this university. My role in the Spiral Project is to remain at King's to direct the fieldwork.

I can't leave for weeks at a time to storm chase with the unit. And I certainly can't star in a reality show."

I could only imagine the departmental reaction to such a venture.

"Mr. Peterson, I'm a scientist, not a TV star," I continued. "My answer is no."

I hung up the phone and turned my attention to my paperwork. The students were all silent.

"You should do it, Kelsey," Derek finally said.

"I can't. You know that. And if I need your advice, I'll ask for it."

Derek, somewhat unfortunately at the moment, had been my student long enough to know that my bark was worse than my bite.

"It could actually get the project off the ground again," he argued.

"The Explorer Channel isn't offering to fund it," I replied. "You heard Peterson. We'd still need another funding source. NOAA, Edison Power, and the NSF already rejected the proposal. There's no one left."

"Could you go back to them with the Explorer Channel's offer?" Colton asked. "TV does have a lot of pull."

I shook my head. "Even if I did, I could never participate in a reality show. King's wouldn't allow it. I have a contract that includes policies about outside compensation, media participation, conflict of commitment. I already got slapped on the wrist for that interview. The board would never let me run off to chase tornados."

I packed up my papers and went to the door. "Not to mention it's an insult to be wanted for my so-called camera presence."

I left the room and started toward my office. Halfway there, Tess fell into step beside me.

"You know—" she began.

I groaned. "*Et tu, Brute*? What happened to the sisterhood?"

"Look, I get that it would be irritating to have people interested in you for how you look on camera rather than your research," Tess said. "But that's not entirely what's happening here."

"No?" I kept walking. "How do you figure?"

"The Explorer Channel guys know you're a hardcore scientist," Tess said. "So does everyone else involved with the project. Hell, so does every meteorologist in the country. And maybe… just maybe… it would be good for people watching TV to see a smart, ambitious, innovative atmospheric scientist in charge of a ground-breaking forecast project… except *this* particular scientist just happens to be a woman."

I didn't respond.

"Have you ever seen a woman like you on TV before?" Tess asked. "Don't you think you would be an excellent contrast to the bachelorettes and trophy wives? And all those shows about extreme professions and storm chasing… have you ever seen one with not only a woman at the forefront, but a woman who is one of the top scientists in the country? Well? Have you?"

"No, but—"

"Women are… what, two percent of storm chasers?" Tess continued. "And you don't think you can use your status as Dr. Kelsey March to prove to the world, scientists and laypersons alike, that a woman can not only be the best, but successfully spearhead the biggest tornado prediction project *in history*?"

I stopped outside my office and looked at her. Her eyes were bright with conviction. For a moment, a rush of sheer gratitude filled me. I couldn't help wondering if she was right, if I could use my position in a new way.

I'd always believed in my work as a professor and a scientist, but aside from my students and the meteorology community, not many people knew about the importance of what I was trying to do.

And the idea of being a role model for girls and young women who might not otherwise think weather was interesting or exciting…

My parents would have liked that. Unexpectedly, so did I.

In theory.

"Tess, I get it." I tried to keep my voice gentle. "And you're right that it would be a good thing for a female scientist to get some airtime. But there is no way I can do this. The King's administration would never let me take so much time off to chase storms and be in a reality show. I mean, it just sounds *ridiculous.*"

"But—"

"Forget it, Tess. It's over."

I almost felt the frustration radiating from her. Before she could say anything else, I turned to go into my office. I shut the door and locked myself in.

CHAPTER TWENTY-FIVE

KELSEY

AN INTIMIDATING PORTRAIT OF VICTOR KING, THE FOUNDER OF King's University, glowered down at me from the wall of the chancellor's office reception area. Steel-haired and frowning, old Victor looked as if he'd never laughed once in his life.

I nudged Stan with my elbow and nodded toward the portrait.

"Think he's constipated?" I asked under my breath.

Stan chuckled. "He must be. He's been stuck on that wall since I started working at King's over thirty years ago."

I tried to imagine working at King's for thirty years.

"Why did you start studying meteorology?" I asked Stan, somewhat surprised I didn't already know.

"I loved the Ben Franklin story when I was a kid," he replied. "Thought it was so cool that electricity came from the sky. I always remembered that."

"It's funny that meteorologists love weather and nature, but so many of us end up in a classroom or sitting in front of a computer."

Stan looked at me. "You're still thinking about that reality show?"

"A little." I shrugged. I'd told him about the Explorer Channel's offer in case they contacted him at some point. I'd also told him that I'd turned the offer down.

"It's not really the show itself," I admitted. "I mean, sure it sounds fun, but can you imagine what that kind of exposure would do for tornado research? For the Spiral Project?"

Stan gave me a weary smile. "You know, when you applied for a position at King's, I was one of the professors who didn't want to hire you."

"Really? Why not?"

"I knew you'd rock the boat. Maybe even tip it over."

"I'm a meteorologist, right? I like waves."

Stan chuckled again. "More than any other meteorologist I've known."

"So are you so sorry I was hired, then?" I asked.

"No, because you're damn good. I wasn't wrong, though. You're a spitfire. Sorry if that sounds sexist, but I'm old school." He shook his head. "And I admit I've been impressed with how relentlessly you go after what you want."

"I don't always get what I want, though."

"But you take no prisoners in your attempt."

Unease pricked the back of my mind. "Stan, did you really mean it the other day when you said my conduct could hurt the Meteorology department's standing with the administration? Like with expanding the faculty or getting money for an upgraded lab?"

Stan shrugged. "You wouldn't be solely responsible, no. But everything we do reflects on our department. That's just the way it is."

He glanced at me again. "So why did you become a meteorologist instead of a fighter pilot?"

I smiled. "My father. He loved weather. So do I."

I looked at my watch. Ten more minutes before our meeting with Chancellor Radcliffe, when I would learn my fate at King's University. My cell buzzed with a text. I pulled up the screen.

The sky is blue, storm girl.

The tightness around my heart eased. I still hadn't seen Archer since we'd come back to Mirror Lake. Five days now. I'd promised to call him after our meeting. I slipped the phone back into my bag and exhaled slowly.

This day had been looming for a very long time, but I hadn't wanted to think about it. Because no matter what the outcome, the first person I'd have called would have been my mother.

"Professors March and Baxter, Chancellor Radcliffe is ready to see you," the receptionist said.

Tension knotted my stomach as we walked into the office. The chancellor greeted us, and we sat in the chairs in front of his massive, oak desk.

"Professor March, I've reviewed your tenure file and the board's recommendation," Radcliffe said, settling back in his leather chair. "You have an impressive CV and have been an excellent asset to this university for the past seven years."

"Thank you." I folded my hands to stop them from shaking.

"And I would like to reiterate the importance of tenure to this university," Radcliffe continued. "By giving you a permanent position here, we expect that you will conduct yourself according to the regulations and contractual duties we set forth."

I nodded. I understood that I was receiving a warning, and for a moment I faltered in my belief that Radcliffe had approved my tenure.

The thought didn't trouble me as much as it should have. Since receiving that call from the Explorer Channel, I hadn't been able to stop thinking about running off to chase tornados.

It was a stupid thought, of course. If I were fired from King's, I'd really lose all hope of future funding for the Spiral Project. And I'd told Tess the truth—I'd be devastated if I lost the support and help of my graduate students.

Even more, I'd miss them. They had always been the best part of my professorial career.

But that didn't stop a tiny part of me from wondering what it would be like to be on the road again, chasing storms. With Archer.

Which I couldn't do as a tenured professor.

I took a deep breath and focused on the chancellor, who was still rambling on about my duties. Finally he wound down the lecture and pushed to his feet.

"Congratulations, Professor March." Radcliffe extended his hand with a smile. "Based on the unanimous recommendation of your department and the board, I've approved your appointment for tenure."

All the breath escaped my lungs. Relief bloomed inside me, the unraveling of months of tension and pressure.

Kelsey March, tenured professor in the Meteorology department of King's University. Exactly what my parents wanted. Exactly what I'd worked so hard for over the last twelve years.

"Thank you, sir." I shook the chancellor's hand, and turned to accept Stan's congratulations.

I barely heard anything else as Radcliffe went on about the prestige of tenure before he walked us to the door. After we said goodbye, Stan and I walked out into the spring sunshine. My heart was racing, my stomach still tight with nerves.

"So, do you want to come back to the department?" Stan asked. For the first time since I'd known him, he looked faintly uncertain. "I know everyone will want to congratulate you."

"Thank you. If you could..." Something stuck in my throat. I started backing away from him. "Um, if you could just let people know I'm heading home for a while, I'd appreciate it."

"Okay. Congratulations, Kelsey. You really do deserve it."

"Thank you."

I turned and hurried toward the parking lot, digging into my bag for my keys. Without thinking too much or too hard, I drove to the Butterfly House. Archer's Harley was parked in the front, but there were no other cars, which meant he was alone.

As I walked to the house, the trailer door opened and Archer started down the steps. He caught sight of me and stopped. I fought the urge to run toward him.

"The meeting just ended." I started to shake in a delayed reaction as I approached. "Chancellor Radcliffe and everyone else approved my tenure."

"Of course they did." He extended his arms.

I walked right into them. Buried my face against his chest. Swallowed the lump in my throat. His T-shirt smelled like sawdust and sweat.

He pressed his lips against my hair. He didn't say anything else. Tenure was the brass ring every professor wanted. But Archer knew I'd grabbed it while falling, tipping forward into darkness.

"Come in," he said. "You deserve a toast."

I followed him into the trailer and sat at the table while he poured two glasses of chocolate milk. He clinked his glass against mine.

"Congratulations," he said. "Have you called Liv and Dean yet?"

I shook my head. "I just heard before coming here."

If he thought it was weird that I'd come to him first, he didn't show it. It certainly didn't feel weird—not to me, at least. It felt right.

We drank the milk in silence. I looked past him out the window to where the Butterfly House stood in its gorgeous splendor.

I couldn't find the courage to ask Archer when he would be leaving. Couldn't stand the thought of being here alone, locked into my permanent, tenured position, struggling to find enthusiasm for classroom teaching when my heart was out in the wildness of nature.

Oh, stop it.

I'd been granted tenure, for god's sake. I'd worked my ass off for it. I wasn't going to whine about achieving a distinction few people did. One that guaranteed I'd be set for life.

But oh my god, would I miss Archer. I'd miss his recklessness, his commands, his bad jokes, the heat that sizzled between us. I'd miss his unpredictability, his flashes of darkness. I'd miss the way he made me feel so alive. So wanted. So—

"Well." I stood to put my empty glass in the sink. "I just wanted to stop by and tell you the news."

"I'm glad you did. You deserve this."

I nodded. He was close to me. I gave over to the urge to lean against him one more time. Felt his arms enclose me, and the heat of his muscles through the cotton of his T-shirt. His warmth spread through me, melting the hard, icy ball that had been stuck in my chest ever since I got the phone call about my mother.

Holy hell. A month had passed since I'd walked into Dean's office and smacked Archer upside the head with a door. In that short time span, my life had both veered wildly off course and stayed unwaveringly on the same narrow path I'd constructed years ago.

A wave of dizziness washed over me. I slipped my hands under Archer's T-shirt to touch the planes of his abdomen. He flinched slightly at my touch.

"Sorry," I whispered against his chest. "My hands are cold."

I was cold. Everywhere. I needed him to warm me from the inside out.

No. I needed him to make me burn.

I lifted my head, saw the darkness of his eyes before he slowly lowered his head and captured my mouth in a kiss.

I sighed, sinking against him. I slipped my arms around his waist to touch his smooth, muscular back.

My tension shifted into urgency and the drive to obliterate everything else with pure, carnal pleasure. I opened my mouth to deepen the kiss, moving one hand around to trail along the front of his jeans.

"Kelsey…" Tension laced his arms.

I pressed the length of my body against his, squirming against the burgeoning hardness of his erection. My nipples budded against my bra.

I suddenly wanted us both naked, skin sliding against skin, my breasts bared to his touch, his muscles flexing beneath my hands. I wanted to hear his deep voice issuing orders. I wanted him to tell me what to do. I wanted him to control me. I wanted to be controlled.

I slid my tongue into Archer's mouth and fumbled for the buttons of his fly. My heart pounded with anticipation as I unfastened one button, longing for the sensation of his warm, hard shaft in my palm.

"Stop." His hoarse command broke through my fog of pleasure.

A hint of fear rose in me. I spread my hands over his chest.

"Come on, Archer," I whispered, pressing my mouth to his again. "I want you to fuck me."

A shudder coursed through him. I trailed my fingers over the line of hair leading to his fly. God, he felt so good. My nerves sizzled with anticipation.

"Kelsey, I…"

"I want you to fuck me hard and rough," I continued, nipping his lower lip between my teeth. "I want you to spank me. I want to spread my legs for you, and I want you to pound into me over and over, so hard that my whole body shakes. I want to tighten my pussy around you, cream all over your cock, and—"

"Kelsey, stop." Archer grabbed my wrists, halting my increasing exploration.

Shocked, I stumbled back and yanked my arms from his

grip. Our breathing rasped through the air. I shoved a swath of hair away from my face and stared at him.

"What?" I snapped.

"You don't want that. Not now."

"The hell I don't." A rising humiliation scorched my chest. "Are you going to fuck me or not?"

His mouth compressed with regret, but he looked me in the eye and shook his head. A column of heat rose up my spine. I bit out a curse and shoved him in the chest.

"Bastard."

I turned to stalk out the door. He grabbed me around the waist before I could escape, pulling me back against him, his arms wrapping around me in an unbreakable hold. Anger shot through me.

"Let go," I snapped.

"No." He locked his arms around mine, trapping them against my sides.

His chest was a solid wall against my back, and I knew even as I struggled that there was no escape. My throat constricted.

"To hell with you if you don't want me." I hated that my voice wavered.

"I want you," Archer said. "More than I've ever wanted anything or anyone. But I won't let you run. Not from me. Not from yourself."

An upwelling of emotion, hot and painful, boiled into my chest. Before I knew it, before I could stop it, tears flooded my eyes and spilled down my cheeks. My breath was choppy, too fast. The room tilted off balance. Archer tightened his grip. The only solid element in my world.

"Let me go," I hissed.

"No." He lowered his head to my ear. "I won't let you go, my *kotyenok*."

I think I broke. I felt a snap inside me, like the crack of a tree branch, something that could never be put back together in the same way again.

Sobs crowded my throat. I tried to swallow them back down, but with Archer holding me so tightly in his powerful arms, like he'd be there throughout the entire storm, no matter how long it took or how destructive it was, I surrendered and cried. Hot tears spilled down my cheeks, my whole body weakening under the force of the onslaught.

Archer sank into an easy chair, pulling me on top of him, his arms never loosening their grip on me.

I buried my face in my hands and let the tears fall, acute grief and pain whipping like wind through me. I cried until my throat was scraped raw, until the sobs left me shuddering and exhausted.

"I did everything right," I whispered, pressing my palms to my hot face, the confession tumbling out of me. "Everything."

"I know you did. So did she."

"Then why, Archer?" I was hollowed out. Aching. I pulled away from him and paced to kitchen, as if movement would ease the pain. "Why the hell did she die?"

"Kelsey, whether you did everything right or wrong makes no difference. There's only so much you can control."

Intellectually, of course, I knew that. But emotions were not ruled by intellect. My heart felt like it was being squeezed in a fist.

"I had a girlfriend," Archer said behind me. "She died, too."

My fingernails dug into my palms. "How?"

"Car accident. She was pregnant."

I turned to face him, my chest so tight it hurt. He unfolded himself from the chair and rose to his feet, his presence so potent that I took a step back.

"What happened?" I whispered.

"You called me a fuck-up when we met," he said, and I tried not to wince at the reminder.

"Archer—"

"You were right," he said. "I was much worse than you ever were or ever could have been. After I dropped out of high school and left the West family's perfect life, I did it all—drugs, fighting, stealing, jail time. Stayed away from my parents. Didn't want a goddamned thing to do with Dean. Especially didn't want to hear about all his achievements. Even as a kid, I knew he was destined for success. I was hell-bent to go in the opposite direction."

He shoved his hands into his pockets. "I was living with Sarah outside of Vegas. She'd also had a messed-up life, but she was trying to get her act together. Good person. Worked as a waitress. For some reason, she put up with me. We were living together for a couple of months when she got pregnant."

I sank onto the edge of the bed and buried my face in my hands. I didn't want to hear this, but I didn't want him to stop telling me. Didn't want him to stop giving me a piece of himself.

"After we found out, she convinced me to straighten up, get clean, try to do right by this kid we were going to have," he said. "I went into rehab, got my head together. We talked about getting married. A Social Services woman helped Sarah with prenatal stuff. I found a job with a construction company. The owner had a lead on a house that was going into foreclosure, and I asked him if I could help work on it. I had this..."

He paused and cleared his throat. "I had this idea that if I helped fix up the house, maybe I had a shot at getting some kind of mortgage so Sarah and I could live there one day. If nothing else, at least it would prove I could work. It was a little two-bedroom place."

He'd never had a chance to work on the house. I knew that already. My chest ached. I couldn't tell if my heart hurt so badly because it was so empty or because it was getting so full.

"Sarah was working at a restaurant," Archer said. "She was late coming home one night. The cops..." He paused again. "The cops said she'd gone off the road. The car hit a tree. They said she died on impact."

"Oh, Archer."

I couldn't stand it. My eyes filled with fresh tears. I felt his presence, felt him go down on his knees in front of me, pulling my hands away from my face.

I stared at him through blurred vision, seeing my own pain reflected in his dark eyes, the shared intensity of it seeming to steady the world again.

"Kelsey, I'm telling you because I did everything right." He tightened his hands on mine. "Sarah and I both did. Everything we were supposed to do, *we did*. And she still died. It's fate, you know? A lousy toss of the coin."

I buried my head in my arms again. Aching for what he'd gone through, for a girl's life lost too early, and a baby who'd never had a chance.

"I'm so sorry," I whispered.

He brushed his hand through my hair. "You take on too

much, storm girl. Pain happens. Sometimes like tornados out of nowhere."

Tornados that I still loved for all their fury and destruction.

After a few minutes of quiet, Archer lifted me into his arms and eased me onto the bed. He stretched out beside me, curving his body against mine.

A perfect fit. His chest pressed to my back, my rear against his groin, his knees tucked into the backs of mine. I buried my face in his pillow. He rested his hand on my hip. His breath stirred my hair. I fell asleep in the shelter of him.

I woke before Archer did and untangled myself from him to use the bathroom. I still wore my suit and trousers from yesterday, everything now completely wrinkled.

I borrowed Archer's toothbrush to brush my teeth, and his comb to pull the knots out of my hair. I looked tired, with dark circles under my eyes and my skin like parchment, but I was calmer. The worst of the storm had passed.

But I'd been an atmospheric scientist long enough to know that there was always another storm front on the horizon.

Always.

He was still sleeping when I came out of the bathroom. This time, I tucked my body against his from behind and slid my arms around his waist. I must have fallen asleep again because I woke when the bed dipped. Archer sat on the side of the bed, pulling his jeans off.

He looked over his shoulder at me when I stirred. He didn't ask me how I felt. He didn't mention the previous night. He just reached out to brush a lock of blue hair away from my face.

I pushed to one elbow and fumbled for my glasses, which I'd left on the bedside table. I closed my hand around the frames, then dropped them. Archer was still watching me.

Aside from his boxer briefs, he was naked. With his black hair rumpled, his sculpted torso bare, and that raven's wing tattoo skimming over his right arm, he looked like a magnificent, otherworldly creature about to take flight.

I leaned forward. He met me halfway, our lips colliding in a warm kiss that tasted of mint. He shifted, moving to brace his arms on either side of me, probing deeper but unhurried.

I let myself sink against the pillows, let him inside my mouth. I smoothed my hands over his arms and up to his strong shoulders.

He unfastened the buttons of my blouse, parting the folds to reveal my white lace bra. When he undid the front clasp and bared my breasts, I gave over. I knew I didn't have to do anything but fall into the cascade. I knew that wherever he took me, it would be a place of pure bliss. All I needed to do was surrender.

I watched him kiss his way down my body, rubbing the taut peaks of my nipples. He dipped his tongue into my belly button before pulling off my pants and the skimpy panties between my legs. His hot murmurs vibrated through my skin, creating a pool of warmth in my core.

I stretched and arched against him. We shed the rest of our clothes slowly, peeling them away like snakeskins. He moved over me, fitting his body against mine. He pushed. I yielded. He gave. I took. He captured. I surrendered.

The world rocked, like the rhythmic sway of a ship, the thunderclouds too far away now to be of concern. I shattered beneath him, a slow rise that unfurled in my veins before exploding into a thousand stars. As I was falling back down, I watched Archer above me, his chest muscles shifting, his face set and eyes dark with heat.

He lowered his mouth to mine again just as he plunged into me with his own release. I tightened my arms around him, wanting to feel every shudder coursing through his body, knowing he was feeling this bliss because of us.

When he rolled to the side, I sat up and did what I hadn't yet had a chance to in the weeks we'd been together. I explored all the slopes and planes of his body, tracing his pecs down to the ridges of his abdomen and the V of muscles leading to his groin.

I ran my hands over his thighs, his flat, hard belly, and the corded length of his forearms. I flexed my hands on his powerful arms, smoothed my palm over his raven's wing, the flowers spread across his shoulder.

The birds hovering over the flowers were both silhouettes with their wings outstretched. If you looked closely, you could see the threads of color woven through their wings—red, purple, blue, and gold.

"You're beautiful," I whispered, letting my fingers trace a flower petal. "So incredibly beautiful."

His jaw stiffened as he looked at my hand on his skin. For a moment I expected him to refute what was so obvious and true. But instead he grasped my wrists and tugged me so I was lying half on top of him. He closed his arms around me.

Moonlight shone through the uncurtained window. I could still see the outline of the Butterfly House.

"Are you finished with it?" I asked.

"Almost." He pressed a hand to my hair. "We're doing the final touch-ups on the floors and trim. Lots of little things left to do, but the major work is done."

Though I had known from the beginning he'd leave one day, pain stabbed through me at the realization that the day would soon be *here*.

"Oh," I managed to say. "So when are you leaving?"

Tension rolled through him. "As soon as it's done, I guess."

"Okay."

That was the biggest lie I'd ever told. It was not okay. Nothing was *okay* about Archer West swooping into my life like a beautiful, wild bird, sending my life into a tailspin, and then *leaving*.

Not just leaving. Leaving me. Leaving me alone.

"Okay," I repeated, only because he was looking at me with his dark, haunted gaze and all I wanted to do was throw myself at him and never let go. But I couldn't because he was leaving.

A knot formed in my throat. I could hardly remember my life before him. I didn't want to imagine my life after him.

"I don't want to go without you," he said.

"Then don't." Though I had never been one to ask for anything, the plea came out as easily as thread slipping from a needle. "Stay here."

His eyes darkened. I sensed the uncoiling of old pain in him, the regrets and sorrow we'd both felt for so long they had become part of us.

"Why not?" I whispered.

A faint smile tugged at his mouth. "Square peg. Round hole."

"That's not true. You... you fit here, Archer." *With me.*

Even as I stammered out the words, a black pit opened inside me because I'd come to know Archer as well as he knew me. He hadn't come to Mirror Lake to stay. He didn't fit here, not really, not with Liv and Dean's life and Avalon Street and my tenured professor career.

Still, I tried to picture it. I so wanted to believe it could happen—that I could convince him to stay in Mirror Lake and that we would both be happy. He could find a construction or motorcycle repair job. I'd teach classes and write papers and do all the professor things I was supposed to do. We would go grocery shopping together. Visit the mall. Take a trip every now and then. Share chocolate milk.

And beneath the surface would run a river of unease as I waited for the day when Archer realized he was bored out of his skull living such a contained life. The day when my guilt over forcing him onto my safe, narrow path became too much to bear.

I didn't think Archer would ever fit in anywhere. He couldn't. He was too bold, too fierce, too powerful. The world had to accommodate him, not the other way around.

A tight feeling gripped my chest. "I'm not... I don't mean that you should stay for good or anything. Maybe just a few weeks longer."

He turned away from me, his expression shuttered. He shook his head.

The black pit inside me opened wider. But I had known. I had known from the beginning.

I had no tears left to cry. The combined weight of our pasts and uncertain future seemed too heavy to escape.

I stroked Archer's tattoo down to the raven's wing curled over his arm. I traced the feathers and wished above all else that I could take flight with him.

CHAPTER TWENTY-SIX

ARCHER

STAY HERE.

Just a few weeks longer.

Though I'd never had illusions about anything, I couldn't get Kelsey's honeyed voice out of my mind. I wanted to stay. I wasn't ready to end things with her anytime soon. But the longer I stayed, the harder it would be to leave.

And I'd have to leave eventually. *I don't mean that you should stay for good.*

I'd never intended to. She'd never expected me to. Though we'd had an incredible time, though we cared about each other, the facts hadn't changed. I was a former addict with no job prospects, and she was Professor March. I'd been hit by reality enough times to know that some obstacles were permanent.

The Butterfly House was almost finished. Liv and Dean planned to move in their belongings the following week, and a furniture store truck was scheduled to deliver a bunch of new stuff.

It was raining the afternoon before the truck was supposed to arrive. A spring rain shower, heavy and warm but nothing like the supercell storm Kelsey and I had been in.

I walked through the house, checking the floors to make sure there was nothing I needed to touch up or fix. Everything was bright, shiny, new.

I went upstairs. Four bedrooms. Liv had told me Nicholas's room would be the one facing the back garden. There was an oak tree outside the window, and a view of the forested area beyond. I imagined The Castle Two in a big, solid tree somewhere out there. I'd subconsciously already mapped out a blueprint in my head.

The front door closed. I walked back downstairs, hoping it was Kelsey. Instead Dean was in the foyer, taking off his damp suit jacket. He held a large brown envelope under his arm.

"Just checking things out," I told him. "There are a few places that could use some putty. I'll do that before the furniture gets here."

"Good. Thanks." He tossed his jacket on the stair railing and tilted his head to the kitchen. "Got a second?"

"Sure." I followed him into the kitchen. There were a couple of stools beside the quartz-topped central island, and we sat down.

Dean opened the damp envelope and took out a stack of typed pages. It looked like one of his academic papers or something.

"I know you told me you didn't come here for this," he said. "And I believe you. But I also know you've straightened up over the past few years. You've helped me out a lot here, done excellent work, and you've earned this."

He pushed the papers across the island to me. *The Gerald A. Haverton Irrevocable Trust...*

A weird chill ran up my spine. "What... uh, what's this about?"

"Your inheritance," Dean said. "I talked to the lawyer last week, and he organized the paperwork to transfer the assets over to you. Most of the funds were invested in stocks and mutual funds that have done very well, so you can keep them there until you decide if you want to—"

"Wait a second." Now the chill was creeping into my veins. "You're giving me my inheritance?"

"I'm not giving it to you. You earned it."

I stared at the papers. Words jumped at me like insects. *Amendment, revocable, trustee, sum, condition precedent.*

I looked at Dean. He was watching me, like he was waiting for me to give a cheer of fucking joy.

I shoved the papers back in his direction. "I don't want it."

He blinked. "What?"

"This wasn't why I came here." My blood was getting hot, the cold evaporating. "Thanks for *believing* me, but I never wanted it. I sure as hell didn't come here to earn it."

"Archer, it's yours."

"No, it's not." I shoved away from the island and got to my

feet. "It's a goddamned shitload of money that our mother's father used to bribe me to go straight."

"Who cares if he wanted to bribe you?" Dean said. "It's still yours. You're right—it's a shitload of money that you can take with you."

When you leave.

Tension clawed at my neck. "What made you decide to give it to me?"

"I've *wanted* to give it to you for years, but I couldn't until you fulfilled the conditions our grandfather set."

"And now you've decided that I have."

"Yes." Dean started to look irritated. "What's your problem? You knew he listed me as the trustee and executor."

"Yeah, because *you* were always so fucking perfect." My chest tightened. "He knew you'd follow his rules to the letter."

"So what?" Dean frowned. "It's a legal document. Of course I had to follow the rules."

"You wouldn't even know *how* to break the rules." I pushed the papers at him again. A few fell to the floor. "My whole life, you've been the standard everyone else is measured against. Do you have any freaking idea how hard it is to measure up to perfection?"

Dean's frown deepened. "You never even tried to measure up to a damn thing."

"Because it was impossible."

"Bullshit," he said bluntly. He shoved off the stool, his expression darkening. "You didn't come from some destitute life. Mom and Dad would have helped you if you'd asked. And if you'd bothered trying, you wouldn't be a high-school dropout and a former user with a record. Don't blame me because it took you this long to get your shit together."

Anger and shame ripped through me.

"Easy for you to say, Boy Scout," I retorted. "You think Dad didn't hate me? I was a walking reminder of the fact that his wife fucked around on him. How would you feel if Liv did that to you?"

"Watch it." Dean stepped toward me, his eyes narrowing with a dangerous, hard glint. "You leave Liv out of this."

I knew I was pushing him. I wanted to. It was a horrible itch, like a thousand teeth gnawing at my skin.

"We may have lived in the same house," I said. "But we had totally different lives."

"What does any of this have to do with your inheritance?" Dean asked.

"That's not why I came here."

"I don't care. I know you could use it."

"Yeah, I could use it." I spun to face him. "But do you know why I didn't try to *earn* it and why I didn't come here for it? Because I've always hated the idea that you were the only one who could say I was worthy of it."

"It had nothing to do with *worth*, Archer. You just had to fulfill a set of conditions that—"

"That proved my fucking *worth*. Isn't that what you think I've done now? I've proven I can stay clean, hold a job, be responsible. I've proven I can work well. I've kept my word that I wouldn't treat Kelsey badly or—"

"Stop," Dean interrupted. "You leave Kelsey out of this, too."

How could I leave the woman I loved out of anything?

The question blasted into me like a hurricane.

"No." I pointed a finger at Dean, clenching my other fingers so my hand didn't shake. "You don't tell me what to do or not do about Kelsey. She's—"

Mine. Mine, goddammit. She's mine.

No way could I tell Dean that. I tightened my fists and let the anger rise.

"I've proven I can keep my word, right?" I snapped. "Now you're going to pat me on the head and tell me I'm a good boy, here's your money, thanks for the help, now goodbye?"

"Look, Archer, I don't know what the hell this is about." Dean yanked at the knot of his necktie, his face hardening with frustration. "I'm not the one who set the conditions, but you've known about them for the past seven years. You could have used the money to turn your life around, but you didn't even try."

"I couldn't!" I shouted. The anger boiled into rage, and suddenly I fucking hated my brother with his PhD and his big house and his perfect life. "Everything is so goddamned easy for you. Jesus Christ, Dean, I was an *addict*. I did drugs. I was in jail. I fucked around. I worked so I could get my next fix. Some days I woke up on the floor of a motel room without knowing how I got there or what I'd done. How the hell do you think I could have *turned my life around*?"

That shut him up for a second. Then he said, "Mom and Dad were—"

"Mom and Dad were glad to be rid of me, you shithead." I stalked to the other side of the room, my fists clenching and unclenching. "With me gone, they could spend all their time bragging about how successful you were with all your awards and trophies and scholarships. That's why our grandfather put you in charge of the inheritance, right? Because he knew you were so responsible."

"And you think that was *easy?*" Dean's mouth compressed. "I took care of the old man when he was sick with lung cancer. A fucking year. I went to live with him. He was a mean sonuvabitch, but I did it because no one else would. That's why he left me so much money and made me the trustee of your fund. But you'd better believe I never wanted to be in charge of your inheritance. I've hated the responsibility. You have no idea how many times I wanted to give it to you just to get rid of it."

"But you didn't because you had to follow the rules."

"It's a *legal document,*" Dean retorted. "And I tried to keep track of you, to find out if Mom had heard from you, to figure out what you were doing. Half the time I didn't even know how to reach you. Hell, I didn't know if you were alive or dead. What else was I supposed to do but follow the rules?"

"You could have talked to me yourself."

The words escaped me with a rush of pain. I turned away from him, embarrassment scorching my chest.

Dean was silent for a minute. Tension radiated from him.

"Archer, how was I supposed to talk to you? I couldn't even *find* you."

Did you try? I couldn't bring myself to ask the pathetic question.

"I never wanted to hold this over you," Dean said. "I know you got a shitty deal. You think I don't? But for Christ's sake, get over thinking it was so damned easy for me. I've worked my ass off. I've fought for everything I have, including my wife and son. The hell I'm going to let you say I have it all because of dumb luck."

My jaw clenched. I'd fought, too. But I'd lost.

A picture of Kelsey surfaced in my mind. Sharp, brilliant,

beautiful. Storms and laughter. Heat and softness. Chaos and peace. I'd never expected her when I came to Mirror Lake. Never imagined the thought of leaving her would break my chest wide open.

"Archer, our grandfather put this money aside for you," Dean said. "Take it and go do something good with it."

And get out of my life. He didn't say that, but he didn't have to. I'd always been the scar on the West family and there was no reason my status should change now. I was a fool to think maybe it could have.

Tension clawed at my neck. "I don't want it."

"Oh, for god's sake." Irritation cut through Dean's voice. "You want to carry a chip on your shoulder for the rest of your life? You're going to keep blaming me, blaming Mom and Dad when they did their best?"

"The hell they did."

"Mom and Dad gave you everything they gave me and Paige," Dean said.

"No, they fucking didn't."

"Oh, yeah?" He whirled around, his arms spread. "What, Archer? What the fuck did you not have that Paige and I did?"

"A family!" I shouted. "A goddamned family, okay?"

I saw his shocked expression the instant before my vision blurred. I bent to grab the papers off the floor. Tried to stop my hands from shaking as I pushed them back into the envelope.

"Forget it." I rolled up the envelope and shoved it in my jacket pocket. "I'm leaving."

"Archer—"

"I need to sign these papers to get the money, yeah?" I

held up my hands and backed away. My lungs were too tight. I couldn't pull in any air. "I'll figure it out when I'm back in Nevada. You're right. I'll turn my life around. Stop hanging out in bars and fucking whatever woman crosses my path."

"Archer, for god's sake—" Dean started toward me.

"Payment for services rendered, right?" I kept backing away. "I'm going to take off tonight. Say goodbye to Liv for me. And oh, hey, sorry for using your friend Kelsey, but I've done a few of those high-class women before. I knew she'd like slumming. And she was a great way to occupy my spare time while I was—"

"Don't." A woman's voice sliced through the thick air.

Shit. Fucking fucking shit.

Dean and I both turned. She stood in the kitchen doorway, her blue eyes blazing. Her name stuck in my throat.

"Go away, Dean," she said, her gaze on me.

"No."

Kelsey cut her eyes to him, her face flushing with anger. "Go *away*."

Dean's expression darkened. They stared each other down for a second before he backed off, pointing to the door. "I'm right outside."

"Stay there," Kelsey ordered.

When he was gone, she came toward me in three strides and slapped her hand across my face. Hard. Pain jolted through my jaw. I almost stumbled back.

"That wasn't for acting like an ass or because I think you really were just fucking with me," she said coldly. "That was for *saying* you were using me to get to your brother. It was for lowering yourself to that level *again*."

My chest constricted. "What the hell are you talking about?"

"I'm talking about the fact that it took my mother all of one afternoon to see in you what you haven't seen your entire life," Kelsey snapped. "You're a survivor, Archer. You've been to hell and back. You've fought battles and lost, but you've also fought them and *won*. You were dealt a shitty hand, but you played it the only way you knew how. You made mistakes and you tried to do things right. You know more about loss than most people learn in a lifetime. So don't you *dare* try and convince anyone, even your brother, that you've never been or ever will be anything but a user and a fuck-up."

I couldn't speak.

Kelsey backed away, her eyes still shooting blue sparks. "Do you think for one second I'd have started up with you if I thought that's all you were? That I'd have *surrendered*? You know me better than that, Archer. You're the only person in the whole fucking world who does."

She spun on her heel and stalked to the door. I stared after her, unable to move until I heard the door slam. Then I bolted toward the front porch.

The second I ran outside, Dean's hand shot out to close around my arm. Kelsey strode to her car through the rain, her spine stiff as metal.

"What did you say to her?" Dean asked.

I yanked my arm from his grip and ran after Kelsey just as she was getting in her car. "Kelsey!"

She slammed the car door. The engine roared to life, the tires skidding on the wet gravel as she backed up.

God*dammit.*

I got on my bike, shoving my helmet on. Curses split through my head. I hit the ignition and raced after her.

CHAPTER TWENTY-SEVEN

KELSEY

ANGER BURNED A HOLE INSIDE ME, HOT AND JAGGED. I GRIPPED the steering wheel, struggling to see through the rain splashing on the windshield.

Goddamned Archer West. Why couldn't he see what was so obvious? I pressed on the accelerator, the tires squealing as I hit the road. I didn't know where I was going. I didn't want to go home because Archer would find me there.

I drove through the residential neighborhood leading toward the university. Puddles of yellowish light shone on the wet pavement. I braked at a stop sign. A single headlight glowed through the darkness in my rearview mirror.

Tension gnawed at my chest. The windshield wipers whipped back and forth. I hit the accelerator again. The car leapt forward. I wound through the streets circling the university, knowing I could lose Archer in the tangle. I pulled away from the north side of campus and started on a narrow road twisting into the mountains.

My cell phone rang again and again. Archer, probably. Then Dean's ringtone. Liv's ringtone. I fumbled for the phone and turned it off, throwing it onto the passenger seat.

I've done a few of those high-class women… she'd like slumming… I'm going to take off…

Pressure flooded my veins. My own stupid voice echoed in my head.

Stay here.

He was still behind me. The single headlight burned through the wet night. I sped up and made a left turn. Pine and spruce trees grew in dense thickets on either side of the road. The only sound was the slap of the windshield wipers and tires.

He was getting closer. Fear lit inside me. Too close. I'd *let* him get too close. For all my tough-chick, I-can-handle-this crap, I'd broken the cardinal, unspoken rule and let emotions get tangled up with insanely hot sex. I'd asked too many questions, given up too much of myself, taken on too much of his pain, liked him too much.

I'd fucking *surrendered.*

My foot sank onto the accelerator. The car slipped on the slick road, veering toward the center yellow line glowing in the headlights. I yanked on the steering wheel to straighten it. The tires skidded again. Fear stabbed me. I hit the brake to slow down, as the headlights reached a dark curve in the road.

I swerved around it, trying to stay on track. My fear swelled into outright panic. The back tires skidded again. The front end of the car plunged off the right side of the road toward the guardrail. I gripped the wheel and just managed to bring the car to a screeching halt before the front end hit the rail.

My breath sawed through the air. I threw the car into reverse to get back on the road. The tires spun in the mud. With a curse, I pushed harder on the accelerator, but only drove the tires in deeper. The engine roared. The single headlight of Archer's motorcycle was rounding the turn.

"Shit."

Though I didn't know where the fuck I thought I was going, I hurried to get out of the car. I only knew I didn't want to see him, didn't want to face him. The rain hit me like pellets as I shoved out of the driver's seat.

"Goddammit." My heeled sandals sank into the thick mud. In seconds, my blue suit jacket and trousers were soaked.

Archer brought his motorcycle to a sharp stop on the side of the road. He was a menacing shadow in the dark. My panic surfaced fresh. I stumbled backward, needing to get away from him.

He yanked off his helmet. "Kelsey!"

His voice was like thunder. Oh, god. He leapt off his bike and started toward me. Suddenly aware that he was the predator and I was the prey, I yanked my shoes out of the mud and turned to run.

"Kelsey, stop!" Desperation ripped through the order.

Driven by fear—of him, of myself, of knowing I had already given him everything and had nothing left—I ran, stumbling blindly through the pouring rain, tripping over wet branches and mud-clotted grass.

I had no hope of outrunning him, but I tried. My lungs burned. I made it up the slope back to the road away from Archer. Just as I reached the pavement, he shouted my name again.

Adrenaline burst through me. I picked up speed, running down the road, away from my car, away from the university, away from town, away from him. His boots pounded on the road.

He grabbed me from behind, yanking me backward, his arms locking like steel bands around me. My ankle twisted with the impact. With a cry, I felt myself careening off balance. Archer didn't loosen his hold, keeping me upright.

"Don't run," he begged, his chest heaving against my back. "Please don't run. I'm sorry. Jesus, Kelsey, I'm so fucking sorry."

Pain lanced through me. I struggled for air. Before I could break away from him, he lifted me into his arms and carried me back to the car. He yanked open the door and put me on the backseat. Rain dripped down my face and hair. My ankle throbbed.

"Are you okay?" He crawled in after me, slamming the door to shut out the rain, his eyes bright and burning in the dark.

I scrambled backward, some part of me still needing to get away from him, overwhelmed by his presence in the confines of the car.

He reached up to flick on the light. Tension lined his features.

"Kelsey." He grabbed my arms, trying to pull me toward him. "Don't look so scared. You're shaking… come here. Please."

I knew if I got any closer to him, I'd be lost and never found again. As it was, tears flooded my eyes and ran down my already-wet cheeks.

I yanked my arm from Archer's grip and slapped his face again. A red imprint spread over his jaw. Grim satisfaction filled me.

"You want more?" Archer released me and yanked open his leather jacket to expose the damp white T-shirt underneath. "Go ahead. I'll take it."

"You sonuvabitch." I flew at him, hissing and scratching. My fists connected with his chest, his face, his abdomen. "How dare you? How fucking dare you come here and turn my world upside down and then *leave*? How dare you think I would fall in love with a man I thought was *less*? You've never been less, Archer! You've always been more… so much more… too goddamned *much…*"

The impact of my fists barely moved him, but I felt his unleashed pain. I could hardly see his expression past the blur of tears. I slapped him again. His hand closed around my wrist to stop another blow.

"Goddammit, Kelsey," he whispered. "I *surrender.*"

Oh, no. *No.* He couldn't. I'd never wanted to conquer him.

Fresh tears spilled down my cheeks. I grabbed the front of his shirt. Our breath rasped in the space between us. He closed the distance, crushing his mouth against mine. A moan escaped my throat, my hand fisting in his T-shirt. He put his hands on either side of my head, angling my mouth to his, deepening the kiss.

Desperation flooded us both. The air thickened, rain still streaming down the windows. I knew I could never stop it, this heat that even now burned so hot between us. Tension coiled through Archer's muscles as he moved closer, his knee pushing between mine. I shoved my hands under his shirt and dug my fingers into the ridges of his abdomen. He thrust his tongue into my mouth, licking, biting, sucking.

I gave up, gave in, gave over. With a sob, I let him push me back against the seat, his body edged with heat and urgency. He cupped my face in his rough palms, the gentle touch a striking contrast to the ferocity of his kiss. Lust sparked through my veins at the sensation of his chest pressing against my breasts, his erection throbbing against my thigh.

He ripped open my shirt and bra to expose my breasts. I gasped, curling my fingers into him as he drew the hard nipples into his mouth. Arousal flared through my lower body, driving my need higher.

I writhed beneath him, fumbling for the buttons of his jeans, my hands trembling. My need for him was drenching, all-consuming, like the fall of night studded by bright stars. He reached down to rip at the fastenings of my pants, lowering his head to slide his tongue over my neck. He closed his teeth around my collarbone.

"So fucking hot," he whispered, pushing his hand beneath my panties. "You *belong* to me."

Of course I did. I always had. Even before I knew who he was.

My face was damp. I struggled to pull air into my tight lungs as he pushed down my pants and underwear. His fingers moved with adept precision over my folds, sliding into me, his breath hot against my neck. I gripped his back as the pressure began to spiral through me.

"Archer." My voice was strained. I was burning.

He moved back only long enough to shove down his jeans, releasing his thick erection. Need enveloped us. Sweat trickled down his temple. I parted my legs, letting him in, my heart beating wildly as the hard knob pressed against my folds. I drove my hands into his hair, guiding his face back to mine.

"Kiss me," I whispered.

He pressed his mouth to mine the instant he pushed his cock into my body, filling me, claiming me hard and deep.

"Oh!" I arched upward, digging my fingers into his hips. I took the force of his thrusts, his tongue in my mouth, the scorching heat of him.

I needed him to drive away the darkness, to fill me with light and sparks and stars, even as I knew the clouds would fall again. I wrapped one leg around his thighs and braced the other on the floor. My head filled with the sound of moans and gasps, his flesh hitting mine, filling me.

I moved to grip his corded arms. Above me, his eyes burned through the shallow light. He lowered his head again, his lips on mine the instant the exquisite wave rolled through my body. I cried out against his mouth, shuddered around his cock, engulfed by his body. He didn't lift the pressure of his kiss as he plunged into me again and again, his muscles flexing as his release ripped through him. I drank the low groan that rumbled from his chest, both of us sliding back down together.

I wrapped my arms around him and closed my eyes. His breath rasped against my shoulder. When our breathing calmed and he pushed away from me, I felt like part of me had been severed.

I opened my eyes to look at him. Wariness fell between us.

"Jesus, Kelsey," he muttered, dragging his hands over his face. "When your car went off the road…" He shook his head. "Never been so fucking scared."

I fumbled to close my shirt and pull up my pants. My chest ached.

"You were going to do it," I whispered. "You were going to leave without telling me."

Self-disgust crossed his expression. "Because I'm a goddamn coward."

"No, you are not. Why… why can't you *see* that?"

He yanked up his jeans with an irritated movement. "I'm sorry. I never should have… I was… ah, fuck, Kelsey. I never thought it would come to this."

Of course he hadn't. He'd just wanted to have a good time. So had I. That had been the deal.

I sat up slowly, still feeling his scent on me, the trickle of his semen between my legs, the abrasions on my skin from his stubble, his teeth, and his desperate grip.

Too much. It was all too much. I had gone willingly into a storm that I'd known would leave me breathless and aching. I'd also been delusional enough to think I could protect myself, but even if my sharp, scientific brain hadn't see the truth, my heart now did.

I would never be able to protect myself from the storm. Because the storm was everything—love, desire, happiness, sorrow, pain. *Life.*

"You need to go," I whispered.

Archer turned to look at me, his eyes dark and shuttered. He knew as well as I did that a safe, happily-ever-after life could never work for us. Not for two people who had such a reckless, urgent pull toward danger and risk. We'd end up hurting each other and hating ourselves for it.

This time with Archer had shown me that with striking

clarity. I could manage to contain the storm inside me, but not the one in him too.

"I don't want to go without you," he said.

An ache split through my heart. "Please don't say that."

"It's the truth."

"Aside from the fact that there is no way I can go with you, it was never part of the *deal*, Archer."

Because I knew him so well, I saw the flash of regret in his dark eyes. I latched on to the fact that I'd found a sore spot.

"No holds barred, no strings attached, right?" I said. "Do you not remember saying that? Do you not remember me *agreeing*?"

Anger flared in his eyes. I recoiled. He gripped my shoulders and lowered his face closer to mine.

"I remember," he snapped. "But we both know everything has changed. I love you, dammit."

Painful sparks went off in my veins, creating a hollow longing for everything I wanted and yet couldn't have.

"You can't love me," I whispered. "You said from the beginning that we'd just have a good time *while you were here*."

"That doesn't mean I don't love you," he said, his voice tight. "And I was a fucking idiot not to realize from the start that it would be so damned easy to fall in love with you. You're mine, dammit. You're brilliant and good and beautiful. You're sexy as hell, you make me laugh and feel alive again... how could I not fall in love with you? How could I not have *known* that I would?"

My throat ached, even as his *I love you* and *you're mine* swirled through me with all the youthful hope I never knew I had. I'd spent so many years trying to be tough, putting up walls, that I'd ignored the romantic dreams flourishing like flowers in my heart. A sweet, secret garden.

I pressed my hands to my face. Rain pounded on the roof of the car. I suddenly realized my wet clothes were cold and clammy, sticking to my skin.

I couldn't ask him to stay again. Couldn't stand the idea of trapping a storm even if the storm asked to be trapped.

I wanted to, of course. I wanted to fall to my knees and beg him to stay with me, to live my life and never leave, but I knew well the price of selfishness. I would never pay it again.

"I'll call Dean to come and get me," I said.

Archer tensed at the sound of his brother's name, but he didn't move to open the car door.

"Ask me to stay," he said.

My heart broke right down the middle. "You can't stay. You left home at seventeen, Archer. You've been on the road almost your whole life. You need freedom."

"The hell I need freedom." He grabbed my wrists, pulling my hands away from my face. His features were rigid, his eyes burning.

"I need you," he snapped. "*You* are my freedom."

I couldn't speak. Love and despair battled inside me, hot and painful. I had never been needed by a man. Never needed one. Never *loved* one.

Archer released one of my wrists and reached into his pocket. He pulled out a quarter.

"Heads, I leave," he said, his voice rough. "Tails, I stay."

My heart crashed against my ribs. The edges of my vision darkened as he flipped the coin into the air. I grabbed it before it fell back into his palm.

Silence thickened the space between us. I heard the sound of his breath, sensed the desperation coiling through him.

Before I lost all courage, before the world could shatter me, I used the only weapon I had left. The one Archer had handed to me the day we met at the university.

"You need to go," I repeated. I forced my voice to harden. I couldn't look at him. "It was fun, but it's over. You'd never fit into my life, Archer. We're way too different. That's exactly why it was just a good time. And why it's time for you to leave."

My words rang hollow, much as I tried to sound convincing. I clenched my fists, ready to fight again if I had to, but then the car door clicked open. It sounded like a bullet firing. Archer slid his hand beneath my chin, forcing me to look at him.

I searched his unwavering gaze, the pinpoints of light that I swore no one except me had ever noticed.

"I don't for a second think you believe any of that," he said, his eyes glittering. "We're not so good together because we're different, storm girl. We're not night and day or sun and rain. We're so damn good together because we're the *same*. And you'll never belong to anyone else. Ever. Neither will I."

He released me and got out of the car. The door slammed shut.

I watched through the rain-splashed window as he walked back to his motorcycle. Then, like a cloud spinning into darkness, he was gone.

I looked at my fist and slowly uncurled my fingers. The quarter lay in my palm, flashing in the overhead light.

Tails.

CHAPTER TWENTY-EIGHT

ARCHER

"PEANUT BUTTER SANDWICHES WITH STRAWBERRY JAM." LIV extended two paper bags, shifting Nicholas to her other arm. "And some treats from the Wonderland Café."

"Thanks." I took the bags and put them in the saddlebag of my bike. "I have plenty of chocolate milk in a thermos, too."

Liv smiled, but the smile didn't reach her eyes like it always did. I couldn't tell if she was mad or sad or what, but then she reached out to hug me with her free arm.

"Have a safe trip," she said. "I'm really glad you came, Archer. I hope you'll visit us again soon."

"Thanks." I didn't know what else to say to her.

I took Nicholas's hand and gave it a little shake. He grabbed my forefinger. Tight, like he didn't want to let go. I pulled my hand away and rubbed his hair.

"Later, alligator," I said.

He blinked. Liv turned to where Dean stood slightly behind her. She touched his arm and started toward the Butterfly House with Nicholas. An awkward silence fell between Dean and me.

"Good luck, Archer," he finally said. "I'm sorry about everything."

"Yeah, me too." I searched in my saddlebag and brought out the medieval King Arthur coin I'd been carrying around for weeks. "I found this in the box of stuff Mom sent me. I don't know how it ended up there."

Dean took the coin. "You gave this to me as a birthday present one year."

"Yeah."

"I'd always wondered what happened to it. It was a great present."

I almost smiled. "For you, maybe. I'd have wanted Legos."

"I know." He looked at me. "Can I keep this?"

"I brought it for you."

"Thanks." Dean closed his fingers around the coin. "I'm sorry, Archer. I know I fucked things up by telling you. I wish to hell I'd never done that. It's the biggest regret of my life."

I shook my head, embarrassed by how things had gone down. "Forget it."

"No, I made a mistake. I didn't know how to fix it, either."

"It wasn't always your mistake to fix," I admitted.

"I could have tried harder." He stopped and cleared his

throat. "I've made a lot of mistakes, but by assuming you'd be happy to take the money after working here... I was thinking like Dad."

I didn't get it. "Like Dad?"

"Yeah." Dean shoved his hands into his pockets. "Whenever I earned something... a trophy or scholarship... he made such a big deal out of it. Bragged to all his friends. And when I wasn't at the top, like if I got a B instead of an A on a test, he thought I'd failed. It was shitty, being a disappointment to Justice West because he expected so damned much from me. I learned that anything less was the same as failure. It was a tough standard to uphold."

I guessed it was. I'd known early on that I'd never live up to the standard Dean had set. But I'd never thought he was struggling, too. That it wasn't easy for him.

"I do know that people can work and do good things because they want to," he continued. "Not because they expect a reward. And I'd never wanted to think like Dad or be like him."

"You're..." I swallowed. "You're nothing like him, Dean. Even I can see that."

"I've tried not to be."

"You succeeded. You've always succeeded." For the first time ever, the admission wasn't followed by the pain of jealousy because I knew my brother's success hadn't come without a price.

And he'd been right. I'd had chances to turn my life around. I just hadn't always taken them. I'd fixated on what I'd lost rather than what I'd been given.

Maybe, at the very least, it wasn't too late to change that.

"Thanks for everything," Dean said. "You did some impressive work, and you helped us out a lot. I really appreciate it."

I looked past him to the house. Even now, I was still glad I'd stayed for a while.

Dean hesitated. "And look, think about the money, okay?" he asked. "Even if you don't want it, our grandfather set it aside for you. And the reason he did was because you're family."

I nodded. I still had the lawyer's papers. I didn't want to be an ass about accepting a huge amount of money, but the truth was I'd lived my life the same way for twenty years. I didn't want or need a house or anything big like that. I no longer had Kelsey to spend the money on. At most, I'd buy a new motorcycle and stick the rest of the money in a bank account.

I scratched my head. "Look, if I take the money, could you tell me what to do with it? You know, invest it or give some of it to charity or whatever. Put it in a college fund for Nicholas. I don't know."

Dean's expression eased. "I'd be glad to help you. Thanks for asking."

I turned toward my bike, not wanting to ask my next question. I hadn't seen Kelsey in the two days since everything had gone to hell. "Do you know if Kelsey is still around?"

"She went to her mother's place to finish taking care of stuff. Left yesterday."

I reached back into my saddlebag for a thick, beige envelope. "Could you give this to her for me?"

Dean didn't ask what it was. He just took the envelope and nodded. "Sure."

"Okay. Well, see you." I straddled the bike.

"Hey," Dean said.

I looked back at him.

"You said you were bad off for a while," he said. "That you didn't know how to get help. So what made you go straight?"

"A girl." I pulled on my helmet and fastened the strap. "Sarah."

I expected him to ask more questions, but he didn't. Instead, he nodded, like he knew all about how a girl could change your life for the better and lead you places you never knew existed.

"Maybe you'll tell me about her one day," he said.

"Maybe."

I knew Liv and Dean had had their own struggles. Maybe one day he'd tell me about them, too.

But I didn't want to hear about them now. Dean had known from day one there would be a happy ending with Liv. Even I could see that.

Just as I had known from day one that a happy ending wasn't in the cards for Kelsey and me. For her, sure, with someone else. Someone nice and successful. For us, it was temporary. A hell of a good time *while I was here.*

My mistake for forgetting that.

"I have your number on my phone," Dean said. "If it changes, let me know, okay? I'd like to know where you are."

"Sure. Thanks. Take care of Nicholas. Don't forget about his tree house."

"I won't." He stepped forward. "Come back sometime, man. I know it's been tough, but maybe… well, it'd be good to see you again."

I didn't have a response to that. The idea of coming back and knowing that Kelsey—

Dean and I extended our hands at the same time and shook.

"Take care," I finally said.

"You, too. Stay on target."

"I copy, Gold Leader."

I caught his grin before flipping down the shield on my helmet. I revved the engine and went down the driveway, through Avalon Street, away from the Butterfly House, away from Mirror Lake, away from Kelsey.

CHAPTER TWENTY-NINE

KELSEY

I WALKED THROUGH MY MOTHER'S EMPTY HOUSE AND STOPPED at the windows overlooking the back garden. Weeds had begun to encroach on the flower beds. I ran my hand over the dusty windowsill. I'd given all the furniture to a charity organization, and offered most of my mother's belongings to her friends.

A single cardboard box sat by the front door, filled with the things I'd wanted to keep—family pictures, albums, an icon my mother had brought with her from Russia, my father's old pipe, a few shawls, lacquer boxes, and *pysanky* that my mother had painted.

I neither needed nor wanted anything else. I folded the flaps of the box and carried it out to my car. I left the house key in a lockbox for the real-estate agent and headed back to Mirror Lake.

Everything was finished now. All I had to do was put myself back onto the narrow path I'd created so long ago.

When I got home, I left the box in the living room and went to my basement craft room. I took a box of eggs from the shelf along with a container of dye and *pysanky* supplies. Nestled among the eggs were the two eggs Archer and I had worked on.

I picked up his egg and took off my glasses to study the design. He'd used dark red and black with a pattern of gold. I looked at the uneven colors, the rough lines, the smudged paint where the wax had smeared. The pattern was bold, brilliant, and imperfect. Like him.

My hand trembled. I closed my fingers tightly around the egg. The shell popped and cracked in my palm. My heart crashed. I tightened my fingers, crushing the delicate shell into a broken, irreparable mess. I opened my hand and let the shell fall into the trash can.

Then I grabbed the egg I'd painted and did the same thing. Crushed the shell in my palm, ground it to bits, and threw the detritus away. My pulse raced. A strange feeling of satisfaction and relief filled me—not unlike the wicked pleasure of getting away with something risky.

I put another egg on the table and slammed my fist against it. I swept the broken eggshell into the trash and picked up another one, breaking it in my palm before throwing it away. Bits of shell covered the table. Another one. Another. I would break them all.

"Kelsey?"

I stopped. Liv's voice penetrated my fogged mind. I grabbed my glasses and put them on as I climbed the stairs. Liv was in the entryway, holding a paper bag.

"Sorry for barging in, but I saw your car outside and your front door was unlocked," she said. "I got a little worried when you didn't answer your cell." She looked at me and frowned. "Are you okay?"

I nodded, pressing my hands to my flushed face. My heart was still hammering. I wanted to break something else.

"What are you doing here?" I asked.

She gestured to the bag. "I brought you dinner from the café. Ham and cheese quiche, salad, and cupcakes. I figured you'd be tired from your trip. Dean is on his way over from campus."

Shit. I didn't want Dean to notice how much I was hurting. How much I dreaded trying to put my life back together when my heart felt like a broken eggshell.

I took the bag from Liv and turned to go into the kitchen. I put the food in the refrigerator, hoping she wouldn't wait for me to ask the question.

She didn't.

"Archer left a couple of days ago," she said. "Have you heard from him?"

I shook my head. Liv watched me with perception.

"You fell in love with him, didn't you?" she asked.

I nodded, though the phrase *fell in love* sounded much too simplistic to describe everything I felt for Archer.

I hadn't just fallen in love with him. I'd fallen in need, in lust, in hope, in dream with him. I'd fallen crazily, headspinningly, recklessly *into* him.

I loved his determination, his energy, his humor, his scars, and his desire for control. I loved the way he'd known from the beginning exactly what I needed. I loved that he was the only person in the world who could give it to me.

Liv started to speak again when the doorbell rang. I went to answer it, my heart stuttering at the sight of a big, male silhouette behind the beveled glass even though I knew it was only Dean.

I pulled open the door.

"You okay?" He looked wary.

"Yes." I moved aside to let him in. "Don't worry. I'm not moping or crying or having a fit of the vapors."

"That wasn't what I was worried about," he said.

"I know."

I had a brief flashback of Dean and me fifteen years ago. I'd been a reckless girl hell-bent on punishing myself, and Dean had been… a younger version of the man he was now.

A smile tugged at my mouth. I gave his hand a quick squeeze. "Come in. Liv's in the kitchen."

Some of the tension eased as Liv and Dean had a brief discussion of the rest of the day's plans and the process of moving into the Butterfly House.

"What's that?" Liv indicated a package tucked under Dean's arm.

"I came to drop it off." He held a thick envelope out to me. "Archer asked me to give it to you."

The second my fingers closed around the envelope, I knew what was inside. My stomach twisted. I put the envelope on the counter.

"So, uh, how did everything end with you two?" I asked Dean.

"As well as it could," he said. "And none of it had anything to do with you. Archer and I have issues that go back thirty years. For now, we've figured them out the best way we can."

Beside him, Liv nodded at me. Relief eased some of my despair.

"Hey, you want to go for a run this afternoon?" Dean asked. "Maybe down by the lake. It's a nice day to be outside."

Good. Yes. Back to normal.

"Okay," I agreed.

Liv tugged at Dean's sleeve. "Let's go."

He didn't move for a second, his gaze on me.

"What?" I asked.

"I don't really get all this romantic stuff," he said.

I glanced at Liv. She rolled her eyes as if to say, *"Sure he doesn't."* I almost smiled.

"And I guess I never knew Archer that well," Dean continued. "But for what it's worth, he does really seem to care about you."

My heart clenched. "I know he does. It could just never work."

Dean scratched his head, as if my statement made no sense. Liv tugged on his sleeve again.

"Come on, professor. Kelsey needs to be alone."

"Okay." Dean looked at me again. "You know where we are."

"Yes. Thanks."

The pain in my heart eased a little as I watched them leave. I loved the crap out of those two.

After they were gone, I picked up the envelope and went to sit on the sofa. My hands trembled as I opened it and pulled out Archer's worn notebook. I turned to the first page.

In blue ink, he'd drawn a number of square panels containing intricate drawings and speech balloons. I leafed through the pages, all of which were full of the same thing.

A comic book. All this time, he'd been working on a comic book.

I looked at the title, the sharp-edged illustration of storm clouds and lightning bolts containing the word *Blue.*

In the center of a starburst was a woman clad in a skin-tight, blue uniform with a lightning bolt emblazoned across her chest. She had both hands extended, and two tornados twisted upward from her outstretched palms. Her shoulder-length blonde hair, embellished with a single streak of blue, was a windblown tousle around her head.

"Sonuvabitch," I whispered.

I curled up on the sofa and started to read the story of the superhero Blue, a woman who got her energy from the weather and used storms and tornados to protect the earth from a cadre of villains out to overtake and destroy it. Blue was strong, fierce, determined, and volatile. She could kick ass because of her martial arts training or with her use of weather.

She was also involved in a rather intense relationship with Stone Hunter, a Harley-riding inventor who wanted to harness her powers for energy use.

Blue, however, did not want to be harnessed. Except for when she did, a change of heart that often happened when Stone was involved.

He was hot, too, Stone Hunter. Big and muscular with dark hair and a devilish grin.

I'd half expected to be crying by the time I finished the book and read about Blue and Stone's victory over the evil Legion

League. But instead I was a weird combination of exhilarated and worn out, almost as if I'd fought the battle myself.

I pulled up the sleeve of my T-shirt and looked at the Storm Girl tattoo that was now a permanent part of me. I'd fought the battle, all right. With Archer, with the Meteorology department, with the Spiral Project, with myself.

Unlike Blue, however, I had lost.

You are so smart, Kseniya. So strong. But you are so afraid to be happy.

Nothing ever changes if you don't take risks.

I don't want you to get hurt.

You're the first real risk I've taken in a very long time.

You can do anything, Kseniya. Anything.

Come on, storm girl. Show me how not scared you really are.

I pushed to my feet. I wasn't a self-pitying, pathetic waif. I'd learned the hard way how to get shit done. And I'd been surrounded by heroes.

My parents had braved an uncertain new life as immigrants and shown me exactly what strength and tenacity were. My mother had been the epitome of *courage*. Liv had pulled herself out of a shitty childhood when she was thirteen years old. Archer had beaten drug addiction and the stigma of his paternity. He had survived his rough, heartbreaking past. Dean had fought for everything he wanted and everyone he loved.

And so, goddammit, would I.

Instead of destroying painted eggs in my basement, I was going to do what people around me had proven *could* be done.

I was going to change the direction of the storm.

I was so nervous I was shaking. Fortunately, I'd had years of practice looking cool and professional even if I felt like I was about to throw up. Or worse.

I finished passing thick binders around the boardroom table at the Edison Power corporate office. I took a drink of water and tried to steady my nerves. I couldn't help thinking of the night I'd first met Archer, when I hadn't wanted to be *Professor March.*

But he'd wanted me. As a mysterious stranger in a bar. As Kelsey. As Professor March. As a woman, a risk-taking girl, a storm chaser, a scientist, an artist, even a loner. He'd wanted me whether I was cranky, happy, riddled with grief, tired, sharp, frumpy, irritated, angry, sexy, or exhilarated. Archer had accepted and loved everything I was.

A man who chases you because he is not afraid of the storm inside you. Who loves that part of you.

The thought calmed me like nothing else could.

Conversation hummed through the room. Stan Baxter sat at the table along with three Edison Power executives, David Peterson of the Explorer Channel, Chancellor Radcliffe, and two members of the King's board of trustees.

Harold Clement of Edison Power was seated near the head of the table, wearing a tie patterned with electrical outlets and plugs. In an unspoken solidarity, I wore a pinstriped suit and a silk shirt embellished with embroidered lightning bolts.

"Nice tie," I told Harold as I sat beside him.

He smiled. "Nice shirt. Good luck."

I nodded. Though he was on my side, we both knew this was my show. All we needed to do was convince the King's board of trustees and the Edison Power board of directors that our plan was a good one. And ask them for their money and approval.

"Gentlemen, thank you for coming today." I stood up to address the meeting attendees. "I have a proposal for you. You all know about the Spiral Project. You all know about the Explorer Channel's interest in creating a documentary program. And you all know that I've struggled for three years with funding for the project."

My little speech was met with silence.

Don't be scared, storm girl.

Archer's deep voice echoed in my head. I took a breath and kept going.

"The Edison Power board of trustees has declined to fund the project on the grounds that it doesn't allow for enough community outreach," I said. "But Mr. Clement and I have been corresponding for the past week, and we've come up with a viable solution for all parties. First, I'd like to let Mr. Peterson tell you about the Explorer Channel's interest in the Spiral Project."

I stepped aside. David Peterson came forward to explain the Explorer Channel's plan to film several episodes of a documentary reality show. He then showed a five-minute video of a storm chase that we'd put together with my grad students. Tess had gotten video of a rotating wall cloud, and, for entertainment reasons, we'd included a few seconds of a van almost skidding off the road during a hailstorm.

"We believe Edison Power would be an excellent partner

for both the Explorer Channel and the Spiral Project," I said. "However, as I explained, my contractual duties to King's University and my recent tenureship make it almost impossible for me to direct the project from the field, much less participate in a television program."

"And that," Harold said, rising to stand beside me, "is where Edison Power comes in. If the Spiral Project and Professor March are the focus of an educational and entertaining program that would appeal to viewers of all ages, I would ask the Edison board to strongly consider funding such a venture."

"Why on earth would you do that?" Stan asked.

"By aligning ourselves with weather forecasting and entertainment, we can rebrand Edison Power as a company dedicated to the community. We can sponsor educational science programs related to the show, and help people understand the importance of early storm predictions and responses. Frankly, it would also just be good for our public image."

"With this proposal, Edison Power would be at the forefront of merging weather prediction and utilities management," I added. "King's University, the Explorer Channel, and Edison Power... all working together for a better tomorrow."

Harold coughed. A hum of conversation started.

"Too corny?" I asked Harold under my breath.

"Yeah, but it's okay. You can make power with corn. Alcohol, anyway."

I suppressed a laugh.

"Professor March, you're neglecting a major issue," Chancellor Radcliffe said, eyeing me narrowly. "You have contractual duties to King's. You really think the administration will let you run off to do a reality show?"

"I think King's University wants to remain one of the top-rated private universities in the country," I said, glad my voice was still steady despite my racing heart. "We all know the Meteorology department is easily among the best. However, in recent years due to budget cuts, our lab equipment has become significantly outdated, and our department has suffered. In order to stay on the cutting edge of meteorological research, we need the most advanced forecast and modeling technology available."

"That's where Edison Power comes in," Harold said. "Professor March and I have come to a compromise that will benefit us all."

I cleared my throat. *Here we go.*

"If Edison Power is willing to supply the funds to modernize the Meteorology department's synoptic lab, including the extra equipment needed for the Spiral Project's home base," I said, "then King's University will allow me to join the Spiral Project's field team for the five months of the tornado season. The Explorer Channel is welcome to join us to film. Of course, I will participate fully."

Dead silence fell over the room. The executives, professors, and trustees exchanged glances. Harold shuffled his feet. My heart felt like it was going to pound out of my chest.

"Supply the funds to modernize the synoptic lab," one of the Edison executives repeated slowly, as if he hadn't heard that correctly.

"Yes." I nodded, as if such a request were made every day. "Our department needs more terminals, high-resolution monitors and projectors, and two state-of-the-art supercomputers for our data assimilation studies. We also hope to have enough equipment to establish a second lab. All the details and projected costs are in the information binders."

The executives opened the binders. Frowns, mutters, and shuffling ensued. I couldn't look at Harold. My palms were sweating.

One of the Edison guys frowned at me. "This is a tall request, Professor March."

"I'm aware of that. However, if Edison Power agreed to initially fund only the second phase of the Spiral Project in addition to providing us with the upgraded lab, your financial commitment and risk would be lessened. And if the second phase is successful, which I have no reason to doubt that it will be, we can renegotiate the contract and hopefully extend it into phase three."

Silence again.

"That still doesn't solve the problem of your contractual duties to King's, Professor March," Chancellor Radcliffe said.

"I have no intention of reneging on any of my duties." I picked up another stack of papers and passed them around the table. "I've written a new proposal explaining the value of fieldwork and ways to incorporate teaching and investigations for the benefit of my students. I would just take my teaching out of the classroom for a few months a year, mostly during the summer.

"Students could apply for internships and grants, sponsored by Edison Power, to participate in the Spiral Project. I guarantee you, Chancellor Radcliffe, that we'll have a huge influx of application and students once word spreads about the program."

"And your contract?" Radcliffe asked.

"My hope is that the board of trustees will approve certain amendments to allow me to direct the Spiral Project from the field."

I looked at Stan, adding, "If they do and Edison Power agrees, the Meteorology department will have a much bigger and fully upgraded synoptic lab."

Conversation rose again, papers shuffling. I met Stan's gaze. His eyebrows rose, as if he were impressed. As well he should be, I thought. I'd be a hero in the Meteorology department, if I could pull this off.

"Edison funds the Spiral Project and the lab, and becomes the primary sponsor of the Explorer Channel program," I said. "And in return, King's agrees to let me direct from the field during tornado season and participate in the filming."

"It's an interesting proposition, Professor March," Chancellor Radcliffe admitted. "Unorthodox, but interesting."

"And both expensive and risky," added one of the Edison executives.

"No risk, no reward," Harold remarked.

"I'm sure you'd like to discuss this amongst yourselves," I said, gathering up my notes. "Thank you again for the opportunity to present the proposal to you."

I left the room and went toward the elevators.

"Now we wait." Harold Clement fell into step beside me, looking as relieved as I was to be out of that room. "It could take quite a—"

"Professor March?"

We turned to where Chancellor Radcliffe and Stan stood at the boardroom door. Radcliffe stepped aside and held the door open.

"Would you please come back in?" he asked. "We'd like to discuss this in more detail."

Harold and I exchanged glances. We returned to the boardroom. As I passed Stan, he reached out to stop me. He shook his head with both disbelief and admiration.

"Excellent work rocking the boat, Kelsey," he said. "I think you just got everything you wanted."

A wave of relief and exhilaration flooded me so fast that I grabbed the doorjamb to steady myself. I took a breath and closed my eyes.

Not everything I wanted, I thought. *Not yet.*

CHAPTER THIRTY

ARCHER

THE DESERT SUN BURNED A HOLE IN THE SKY. CACTI AND YUCCA plants peppered the sand dunes past the two-lane, black-ribbon highway stretching all the way to California. A mustard-yellow cloud streaked across the horizon.

I wiped my hands on a greasy rag, pushing away from the old sedan. I shoved the rag into my back pocket and grabbed a can of soda resting on the car roof. An eighteen-wheeler rumbled past on the highway.

I took a drink of soda, which had gotten warm and flat in the heat. I glanced at my watch. My shift was over.

The station owner, Mick, was letting me stay in the room over the garage, though I couldn't stand the thought of sitting there alone all evening. The other option, of course, was to hit the bars in town. Either option would lead to the same thing—a cold, tight feeling that not even the desert heat could melt.

"You done?" Mick called, his bulky frame filling the doorway of the store.

"Yeah. I can take the next shift, though, if you've got stuff to do."

"No, go on. I'll close up." He went back inside.

I tossed the can into the trash. The smell of gas and oil hung in the dry air. A car appeared through the sunbaked haze and pulled up to the pumps.

For lack of anything else to do, I approached the driver and offered to wash the windows while he filled the tank. A couple of college kids returning to LA after a weekend in Vegas.

After getting gas, they stocked up on junk food and hit the road again. I walked toward the store. The sound of another engine drew closer. Must be rush hour with all the traffic.

I turned. A heavy, dark blue VW XXL Amarok truck swerved into the lot, the tires kicking up clouds of dust and sand. The driver pulled into a space in front of the store and braked hard. Only when the door opened did I see the streak of bright blue that had wound around my heart like a ribbon.

For a second, I couldn't breathe.

Kelsey jumped out of the truck, one hand closed around a brown paper bag. She walked toward me, beautiful as all hell in cargo pants and a white T-shirt, her blonde hair shining. Her expression was guarded, but her blue eyes were unwavering behind her glasses.

She stopped in front of me, her hands on her hips, and tilted her head to look me in the eye. This close, I could see her uncertainty. I swallowed hard, fighting the urge to grab her and haul her against me, to kiss her senseless.

"Hi," I finally said.

"Hi, yourself."

I couldn't stop staring at her. "How… uh, how did you know where I was?"

"Dean told me."

I blinked. Though Dean and I had exchanged emails and a few phone calls over the past couple of weeks, he'd never said anything about Kelsey. I hadn't asked, either.

Kelsey extended the wrinkled bag. "He also asked me to give you this."

I opened the bag and took out a manufacturer's box. A Sega Genesis portable game player.

"I didn't know you were into video games," Kelsey said.

"I'm not." I slipped the game back into the bag and set it on the ground. "Well, except for this one."

"Oh." She looked confused.

I reached out with my thumb to smooth away the crease between her eyebrows. I wanted to explain it to her, and I couldn't help hoping that maybe later I'd have a chance to.

"You look great," I said. She looked more than great. She looked like heaven.

She smiled. My heart slammed against my chest.

"So do you," she said, her gaze sliding over my grease-streaked T-shirt and jeans. "I missed you."

Something flared to life in me, though I tried to ignore it. I'd gotten used to the cold. My defenses were all back in place.

I jerked my head toward the truck. "New wheels?"

"Just got it last week," she said. "I'm going to talk with some people at a weather research center in Texas. They're interested in sending along a Doppler on Wheels when the Spiral Project goes out into the field next season."

"You got funding for it?"

Kelsey nodded. "Edison Power Company is supporting the next phase."

I couldn't stop a smile from breaking over my face. Though I had no right to be proud of her, I was. This woman could move mountains. I knew it.

"En route to Houston, I'm meeting Colton and Tess in Amarillo," Kelsey continued. "There's a convergence of activity heading into northwest Texas that looks like it might become a supercell cluster."

She extended her fist toward me, her fingers wrapped around something. I held out my hand. She dropped a set of car keys into it.

The spark of hope grew stronger. I tightened my hand around the keys.

"I figured you would insist on driving," Kelsey said.

I looked at her. Though her gaze was steady, it still contained a hint of uncertainty. I opened my mouth to respond, but she held up her hand.

"Wait," she said. "I love you, Archer. Like… well, like crazy, okay? You're beautiful, intense, and so perfect for me, and only when you left did I realize how desperately I need you. I feel like… like I'd spent my whole life waiting for you and didn't even know it until you were actually *there*."

Her voice cracked. I grabbed her shoulders and crushed

her against me as the spark flared into a full, raging wildfire. Her gasp was lost against the pressure of my mouth.

I kissed her so hard. The almond-and-honey scent of her filled my head. I drove my tongue into her mouth, drinking in her sweet heat, wanting to possess her. She breathed my name, sliding her arms around my waist, her breasts pressing against my chest.

"Never again," I said, taking her face in my hands as I lifted my head. "I will never leave you again."

"Please don't." She rested her hand against my jaw, and her gaze searched mine. "Will you come with me? I… I need to stay in Mirror Lake and teach at King's during the fall and winter, but for the rest of the year, I'm going to travel with the Spiral Project.

"We'll have different units, at least fifty investigators and grad students involved, and we need someone to coordinate the equipment and vehicles, and work on repairs, not to mention all that driving…"

Worry darkened her blue eyes. "I know it might be tough for you to live in Mirror Lake, but it's only for part of the year and I was so hoping you—"

I stopped her words with the pressure of my mouth. She leaned right into me, like we were two magnets pulled together by an invisible force. She was mine.

"I love you, storm girl," I said. "I'd love to live in Mirror Lake with you. I'd love to work on the Spiral Project with you. I'd love to chase storms, outrun tornados, fix trucks, drive all over the country. Whatever you need me to do, I'll do it. As long as I'm with you."

Her smile made my heart stop and start all over again. She eased away to look at her watch.

"You have ten minutes to grab some clothes."

I did it in five. When I came down the stairs from the room above the garage, Mick stepped out of the store. He slanted his gaze to where Kelsey stood beside the truck. Then he looked back at me.

I shrugged. "She's my *kotyenok*."

Mick grinned. We shook hands. I went to toss my duffel in the truck.

I approached Kelsey and slid my hand to the back of her neck. I pulled her in for another kiss. I couldn't get enough of her. I never would.

"One rule," she whispered, her eyes darkening as she ran her hand down my chest.

"What's that?"

"Your body belongs to me," she said.

"Pinkie swear."

She smiled and hooked her pinkie finger around mine. I pulled open the passenger-side door for her and climbed into the driver's seat.

In seconds, I reversed out of the lot and turned on to the highway heading east. We drove toward the storm, toward thunder, lightning, rain and dark clouds boiling up over the horizon. And we drove with the unbreakable knowledge that under it all, the sky would always be blue.

EPILOGUE

KELSEY

MY MAN WAS SO DAMN SEXY. ESPECIALLY WHEN HE WAS IN THE pouring rain with his shirt plastered to his chest and his jeans streaked with mud as he shoved his muscular body against the back of a car to dislodge the vehicle from a swampy ditch.

Ah, yes. So sexy.

From my position in the passenger seat of the truck, I zoomed the camcorder in on him and kept filming. He was my own personal, insanely hot action flick.

He yelled something to Colton, who was in the driver's seat of the car. Colton accelerated as Archer pushed at the car's bumper again. His boots sank into the mud. The tires spun, splattering him with grime. He shoved harder, his jaw clenched.

With a jolt, the car lurched back onto the road. Colton gave a whoop of victory.

Archer climbed from the ditch, dragging his boots out of the heavy muck. His chest heaved with exertion, and water ran in rivulets over his hair and face. He went to talk to Colton, bracing one hand against the roof of the car.

I tracked the camera down his body, over his powerful chest to his legs encased in wet jeans. When he pushed away from the car, Colton sped off through the rain.

Archer turned, catching sight of me through the windshield of the truck. He frowned and stalked toward me.

A little shiver of apprehension went down my spine. I quickly hit the stop button on the camcorder and shoved it back into the bag.

"Nice work!" I called cheerfully through the open window. "Is he meeting us at the next pit stop?"

Archer didn't respond, his glower deepening. My apprehension grew stronger. He was soaked to the skin, filthy, and exhausted. With mud and rain streaking over his face and hair, he also looked more than a little menacing.

He stopped outside my window. "Were you *filming* me?"

"Um… maybe?"

"What the—"

"Not for commercial use," I assured him quickly. "Just for… er, well…"

A sudden blush fired over my skin.

Archer frowned. "For what?"

"For my own private use," I admitted. "You're just so sexy

with your muscles straining and your shirt plastered to your body like that, and you know how much I love it when you're dirty…"

The scowl between his eyebrows eased a little, but he still didn't look any too pleased. He shoved away from the window and strode around to the driver's seat. He climbed inside, slamming the door shut behind him.

Now in the confines of the truck, his irritation was tangible. I scooted away from him. He bent to unlace his mud-caked boots and yank them from his feet.

"Are you thirsty?" I asked, still trying to keep my voice bright. "I have chocolate milk in the… oh!"

Before I could finish, he'd grabbed me and hauled me against him. All the breath escaped my lungs as he brought his mouth down on mine in a hard, crushing kiss.

I fell against him, parting my lips under his to accept the sweep of his tongue. Sparks flared through me, but too soon he was lifting his head, his dark eyes hot. He jerked his thumb toward the back of the truck.

"Get back there," he ordered. "Now."

My heart pounded. I hurried to scramble over the front seat to the cab, where we kept a few boxes of equipment. Archer shoved some of it aside to make room before hauling me down on the seat and climbing on top of me.

The delicious shock of his weight combined with the rain still dripping off him fired me with lust. Cold water seeped through my shirt and pants. He took hold of my shirt and ripped it right off me, pulling my bra down to expose my breasts.

I gasped, squirming against him, already sizzling with heat and urgency. I wiggled out of my jeans, struggling to help him off with his, and then we were both half-naked and he was pushing into me with an intense, powerful surge.

I wrapped myself around him, gasps and moans streaming from my throat as he thrust again and again, his body still tense with strain and exertion, his breath hot on my neck. I came hard, arching up against him, thrilling in the force of our release, the sheer, uncontrollable power of him.

When he rolled off me with a groan, I nestled up against his side. I splayed myself half over his long, muscular body, resting my head on his chest. He stroked his hand through my hair.

"Next time, I get to film you being dirty," he said.

"Okay," I agreed.

He grinned. I spread my fingers over the tattoo on the left side of his chest—his own drawing of the superhero Blue with tornados spinning from her palms and her blue-streaked hair windblown by a storm.

He'd agreed to get the tattoo without knowing what it was—after I'd decided to play my trump card and choose the new design for him. Since the tattoo was on his chest, though, I'd insisted he wear a blindfold until the artist had finished.

"Exactly where my storm girl belongs," Archer had said after seeing the design. "Right over my heart."

Even the tattoo artist had smiled.

I eased closer to Archer, stroking my hand across his chest. A warm contentment filled me, along with the heady anticipation of not knowing what lay ahead for us.

In the two weeks we'd been storm chasing, we had already faced down another tornado, gotten lost on country back roads, driven through rain and hail, and had more explosive sex than I'd ever dreamed possible.

We were on our way back to Mirror Lake for the rest of the summer, where Archer had plans to look for construction or repair work over the winter as we prepared to launch the Spiral Project next spring.

Though Archer had wanted to give some of his inheritance money to the project, I'd refused to let him. Instead he was going to talk to Dean about investments, and he'd mentioned taking art classes at the local community college and possibly even earning his GED one day. I loved that his talents were so focused on fixing, repairing, restoring, and creating.

As we lay there in the back of the truck, the rain pounding on the roof and thunder rumbling in the distance, I felt it again, like a bright, shiny balloon lifting my heart. Happiness.

I was so happy with him, this man who had taken me once again into the beauty of storms. He was the man who loved all of me, even my worst flaws. He had proven that together we could challenge fear and win. He was my exhilaration and my peace.

And he had shown me that letting go and surrendering was a measure of strength. No longer alone, no longer afraid, we had both given over to loving each other forever.

Archer rubbed his hand across the front of my body, his touch warm and gentle. He lowered his mouth to mine. I sank into him, feeling the steady beat of his heart, the coiled strength of his body, the heat of his skin.

Pleasure unfurled inside me as he pressed his hand between my breasts. He shifted, deepening our kiss. My heart flipped like a coin, flashing silver against the palm of his hand. And then I was caught, swept up and spinning into my own perfect storm.

Thank you for reading Kelsey and Archer's story!

Reviews are always welcome! I'd so appreciate it if you would consider posting a review for *Break the Sky*.

I love hearing from readers and can be reached at nina@ninalane.com. Sign up for my newsletter for new releases and exclusives at www.ninalane.com, and join me on Facebook at www.facebook.com/NinaLaneAuthor or Twitter at www.twitter.com/NinaLaneAuthor

ACKNOWLEDGMENTS

I OWE MY DEEPEST GRATITUDE TO VICTORIA COLOTTA OF VMC Art & Design, who continues to elevate my books to a new level with her beautiful covers and interior design. Thank you, Victoria, for your endless patience, talent, understanding, and true friendship. You are a gem.

I am so grateful to Cathy Yardley, whose guidance and razor-sharp knowledge of story structure always improves both my books and my writing. Karen Dale Harris, thank you a million times over for your comprehensive and insightful critique, which shaped Archer and Kelsey's story in ways I never would have imagined. Lauren Blakely, thank you so much for your generosity, advice, and help in setting this book on the right path into the world.

Thank you, Marion Archer, for your most excellent suggestions and knowledge of pertinent details, not to mention making me laugh. Jessa Slade, thank you for your always perceptive evaluation, and to Deborah Nemeth for helping me look at the story from new angles. Thank you, Kelley Heckart, for your thorough copyediting, Jill Blake for verifying the Russian phrases, and Tiffani Drake for your eagle-eyed error catching.

Karen Seager-Everett, Michelle Eck, and Rosette Doyle of Literati Author Services, I am once again so grateful for your tenacity, professionalism, and endless support of both me and my books.

Thank you to my fellow word scribes at InkHeart Authors. I am so honored to have you as my friends and colleagues.

Jen Berg and Baba, your thoughts and opinions are gold, but your friendship is platinum. I am incredibly thankful to have found you. No holds barred.

Yesi Cavazos, Bridget Peoples, Patti, Debbie Kagan, Maria D., and Deidre, thank you so much for being my front-line soldiers. Your feedback never fails to improve both my books, and I so appreciate your time, honesty, and steadfast support. I still can't wait to hug you all in person one day.

A gigantic thank you to Nina's Ninjas, the best street team ever, including Jatana, Melanie, Kelly, Vanessa, Margie, Lena, Alexis, Kitty, Milasy, Rachel, MJ, Sally, Tracey, Stephanie H., Alicia, Vilma, Jaime, Jodie Rae, Camille, Renee, Connie, Tess, Melissa, Christina, and Stephanie L. You all inspire me, humble me, and overall just make me happy.

Bobbi Dumas, Rachel Berens-VanHeest, and Melody Marshall, thank you for coffee, critiquing, ideas, venting, brainstorming, laughing, and always being there.

And for the Weatherman, Lego Boy, and Cookie Girl—there really are no words.

ABOUT THE AUTHOR

NEW YORK TIMES AND *USA TODAY* BESTSELLING AUTHOR Nina Lane writes hot, sexy romances and spicy erotica. Originally from California, she holds a PhD in Art History and an MA in Library and Information Studies, which means she loves both research and organization. She also enjoys traveling and thinks St. Petersburg, Russia is a city everyone should visit at least once. Although Nina would go back to college for another degree because she's that much of a bookworm and a perpetual student, she now lives the happy life of a full-time writer.

Nina's Facebook: www.facebook.com/NinaLaneAuthor
Nina's Twitter: www.twitter.com/NinaLaneAuthor
Sign up for Nina's newsletter at www.ninalane.com

ALSO BY NINA LANE

THE SPIRAL OF BLISS SERIES

The intense erotic romance of Professor Dean West and his passionate beauty Olivia

"Come here, beauty," he says. "You need to be kissed."

Immersed in the pleasure of their blissful, lusty relationship, Olivia West and her husband Dean, a brilliant professor of medieval history, are unprepared when a crisis threatens everything they believe about each other.

THE EROTIC DARK SERIES

A dark, twisty tale of a woman enslaved…

Submission is her only escape… and punishment takes many forms. Seeking escape from her criminal past, a desperate woman enslaves herself to a dark trio of men who own an antiquated Louisiana plantation. Known only as Lydia, she becomes controlled by three very different men who introduce her to a world in which the lines between pleasure, pain, and shame are irrevocably blurred.

Made in the USA
San Bernardino, CA
05 December 2014